When all that remains is...

THE LAST DANCE YOU SAVED

WRITER'S DIGEST AWARD WINNING AUTHOR
LJ EVANS

When all that remains is…

The Last Dance You Saved

L J Evans

This book is a work of fiction. While reference might be made to actual historical events or existing people and locations, the events, names, characters, places, and incidents are either the product of the author's imagination or are used fictitiously, and any resemblance to actual persons, living or dead, business establishments, events, or locales is entirely coincidental.

THE LAST DANCE YOU SAVED © 2025 by LJ Evans

No part of this book may be reproduced, or stored, in any retrieval system, artificial intelligence gathering database, or transmitted in any form or by any means, electronic, mechanical, photocopying, recording, or otherwise without the prior written permission of the publisher of this book. If you find this book on a free book website or in artificial intelligence source not licensed by the author, it is stolen property and illegal to use or download.

No AI Training: without in any way limiting the author's exclusive rights under copyright, any use of this publication to "train" generative artificial intelligence (AI) technologies to generate text is expressly prohibited. The author reserves all rights to license uses of this work for generative AI training and development of machine language models.

LJ EVANS BOOKS

www.ljevansbooks.com

Cover Design: © Emily Wittig Designs

Cover Images: © iStock | Hiraman; Unsplash | Todd Kent

Chapter Title Images: iStock | Olesya Revenko and BarvArt

Developmental & Line Editing: Evans Editing and Michelle Fewer

Copy Editing & Proofing: Jenn Lockwood Editing, Karen Hrdlicka, and Stephanie Feissner

Library of Congress Cataloging in process.

https://spoti.fi/3YycRNl

THE LAST DANCE YOU SAVED

Chapter One - Wonder Woman by Miley Cyrus
Chapter Two - You, Me, And Whiskey by Justin Moore and Priscilla Block
Chapter Three - Heels In Hand by Priscilla Block
Chapter Four - Don't We All by Elle Langley
Chapter Five - Last Name by Carrie Underwood
Chapter Six - Devil You Know by Tyler Braden
Chapter Seven - Velvet Heartbreak by Carrie Underwood
Chapter Eight - A Lot More Free by Max McNown
Chapter Nine - Good Girl by Carrie Underwood
Chapter Ten - Damn by Jake Owen
Chapter Eleven - Cowboy Casanova by Carrie Underwood
Chapter Twelve - Under The Weight by Bobby Bazini
Chapter Thirteen - Dead Set by Max McNown
Chapter Fourteen - The Cowboy In Me by Tim McGraw
Chapter Fifteen - The Feels by Maren Morris
Chapter Sixteen - The Way I Wanna by Max McNown
Chapter Seventeen - Takes Two by Maren Morris
Chapter Eighteen - Ain't No Love In Oklahoma by Luke Combs
Chapter Nineteen - Cowboys Cry Too by Kelsea Ballerini with Noah Kahan
Chapter Twenty - Running On Empty by Max McNown
Chapter Twenty-one - Macbeth by Max McNown
Chapter Twenty-two - Two Is Better Than One by Boys Like Girls with Taylor Swift
Chapter Twenty-three - Losing Sleep by Chris Young
Chapter Twenty-four - Love Is A Cowboy by Kelsea Ballerini
Chapter Twenty-five - Trying by Jordan Davis
Chapter Twenty-six - Love I Got Left by Max McNown
Chapter Twenty-seven - Fix What You Didn't Break by Nate Smith
Chapter Twenty-eight - Good Woman by Maren Morris
Chapter Twenty-nine - Universe by Kelsea Ballerini
Chapter Thirty - I Found You by Nate Smith
Chapter Thirty-one - Say Don't Go by Taylor Swift
Chapter Thirty-two - Love Me Back by Max McNown
Chapter Thirty-three - He Called Me Baby by Lee Ann Womack
Chapter Thirty-four - Can't Hide Light by Max McNown
Chapter Thirty-five - The Man I Want To Be by Chris Young
Chapter Thirty-six - Laying Low by Danielle Bradbery
Chapter Thirty-seven - Under My Skin by Nate Smith
Chapter Thirty-eight - I'm Gonna Love You by Cody Johnson and Carrie Underwood

LJ EVANS

Dedication

To all the parents like me, who know we've made mistakes with our kiddos but are hopeful that the love we share and the determination to not repeat them will be enough. May you see forgiveness in their eyes and be able to watch them bloom.

To the one man who will forever be my one and only true love no matter which cards we draw. This, as always, is for you.

For every person who, with love at stake, takes the risk and bets it all.

Chapter One

Sadie

WONDER WOMAN
Performed by Miley Cyrus

As I stepped up to the line, carefully weighted dart in hand, a wild scream from the back of the bar had me glancing over my shoulder to the two burly men chanting my name. Naked from the waist up, they thrust their arms in the air, causing their overflowing bellies with *Tennessee Darlin'* written on them to jiggle. They had bandanas with the Tennessee flag on them tied around their heads, and their cheeks were ruddy from the alcohol they'd happily consumed.

I hid my disbelief by winking at them and then turned back to the dartboard exactly seven feet, nine and a quarter inches away. I hadn't expected anyone to know me, let alone call my name during this tournament. It'd been a few years since I'd been on the professional dart circuit. The piddly little competitions I'd entered in the last six months were nothing. Locals having a bit of fun. Teenagers trying to dip a foot into the scene. While I'd pulled together some wins in those smaller events, I was still a long way from the old Sadie who'd taken the circuit by storm.

The Marquis Vegas Open was the first time in three years I'd entered an event that might put me back on the Professional Dart Association of America's charts I'd first ranked on when I was sixteen. I'd moved up consistently while I'd been in college until I'd left the circuit due to the hell that had rained down on me. Hell I was still fighting through.

The Last Dance You Saved

The smug look on the face of the man standing off to the side, waiting for me to blow it, brought me back from panicked thoughts that might have derailed me. For two days, I'd bitten my tongue and dealt with his ego while I'd let his expression fuel me. It was just like my older brothers when they thought they had me beat. He'd learn, just like they had, that when it came to darts, out of practice or not, I hit the mark when it counted.

My mind narrowed on the distance to the board, focusing on my arm and the dart balanced in my fingers. I rotated my shoulder and my wrist and then let it fly.

I knew as soon as it left my hand where it was going to land. I was already smiling as it arrowed into the required double bed with a soft whoosh. I didn't need to hear the chalker's, "Game shot," to know I'd won, but relief flew through me when I did.

I hadn't embarrassed myself. I'd proven I could do it again. A lightning bolt of adrenaline raced through my veins, bringing the same wild joy that came from leaping over a stream bareback on a galloping horse. For a handful of seconds, I reveled in it.

Success. Accomplishment. A rub in the face of my smug competitor and all the others who'd whispered I couldn't come back.

But just as quickly as the lightning had appeared, it sped away, leaving nothing but the singe of ozone in the air and the loneliness of a gray sky. The triumph of the win that I used to live on for days, that wicked sense of glory, was missing.

Behind me, the naked-chested men broke into the lyrics to the Osborne Brothers' "Rocky Top"—one of Tennessee's many anthems—and I felt another quick flash of accomplishment. I dug out a piece of my old self enough to dance a little two-step in their direction, and it sent more cheers through the crowd. I curtseyed, and the two shirtless men hollered some more. It was an ego boost, for sure, but fleeting as their cheers came from seeing a shell perform rather than acknowledging the complicated mess that existed inside me.

My competitor stepped up, shook my hand, and said with a chagrinned look, "My manager said not to underestimate the *Tennessee Darlin'*. He said he'd watched tapes of you from back in twenty-three and was certain you were the real deal. I guess he was right."

"Could have gone either way with that last throw," I told him truthfully.

"You knew just what you were doing. You stayed cool and collected the entire time. Accept the win. You deserve it."

Another brief flicker of that old excitement tried to leap into existence but couldn't quite take hold. As the competitors grabbed their bags and left, I fought a strange urge to cry. Why had the win felt so empty when before it had fueled me for days?

From a hallway leading to the back of the club, a brown-haired man emerged, striding toward me with a confidence that had heads turning. In an expensive suit, fancy shoes polished to a shine, and a lavender dress shirt opened to reveal a hint of tan skin, he exuded a smooth charm. In Las Vegas, it could have come off as smarmy, but instead, he looked like a cover model. An actor. Someone famous who was blessing us with his presence.

Watching him stride toward me, my knees did something they'd never done, even after downing three shots with Willy at my bar back in Willow Creek—they wobbled. Maybe it was the way the man's focus was completely on me as he approached, or maybe it was simply the intensity of his warm chocolate gaze as he took me in. Either way, a buzz I was unaccustomed to ran down my spine as he stopped beside me.

His chiseled jawline was shadowed by a meticulously clipped beard, one layer past scruff, that emphasized the straight, strong lines of his face. The near perfection was marred only by a slight crook at the top of his nose where it must have been broken and never fixed, but that asymmetry only seemed to add to his sex appeal.

"Miss Hatley, congratulations," he said. Highly kissable lips curved into a small smile that didn't quite reach his eyes but showed off white teeth and a single dimple that made my heart stampede.

He extended a large hand, and as soon as I placed my fingers in his palm, a rush of lightning spun through me again—far stronger than the brief hit of adrenaline I'd felt from the win. This flash was so vivid, so real, I could almost hear thunder rolling and see the summer storm crashing over the hills behind the ranch.

His gaze jerked down to our joined hands as if he'd felt it too, but when he looked back up, his expression was almost blank, as if he'd drawn a curtain down over his emotions.

"Thanks, and you are?" I asked, happy to find my voice was steady even though I was shaking inside. The turbulent pull he caused settled low and warm in my stomach. When was the last time I'd felt this kind of instant attraction for someone? Had I ever felt it this strongly?

His smile turned into a slow, rumbling chuckle, emerging from his broad chest in a way that made the tempest inside me swell another notch. "Rafe Marquess. I sponsored the tournament."

Before I could respond, a blond woman in a red cocktail dress that clung to generous curves came hurrying over with a large trophy. She slid up next to Rafe, batted her eyes at him, and said, "Here's the award for the press photo."

"Thanks, Mindy."

He didn't even glance her way. Instead, his gaze remained locked on me, as if he was searching for the answer to a question he hadn't asked. He handed me the trophy and waved toward a handful of reporters who were waiting for this photo-op moment. Behind the press, the audience had dwindled, but the two men with my nickname on their bellies were still belting out the Osborne Brothers song on repeat.

As we faced the cameras, my shoulder brushed Rafe's, and tingles slid up my arm and down into my chest. When I was tempted to do something completely embarrassing, like touch him more to see if I could get that buzz to turn into a full-blown flame, I turned my focus to the trophy. It was shaped like the

Las Vegas sign and even had a neon strip lighting it up.

Once upon a time, trophies had meant something to me. Now, with the rush of the win having dissipated so quickly, I was left solely with the pleasure of knowing the twenty-five-thousand-dollar purse would be in my bank account by the end of the night.

I smiled as the cameras flashed and took a moment to answer a couple of questions sent my way. It took all of five minutes for the media to get what they wanted. As they finished up, my two fans made their way down to the last level of seats in the amphitheater-style bar. The two men waved me toward them with Sharpies and programs in hand.

When I looked up at Rafe, his lips were twisted upward again. Not quite a grin, but something close. "Your fans are waiting."

"Who knew a has-been like me could still draw them in."

Surprise drifted over his face before his hungry gaze traveled slowly over me once more, taking in the prim blue button-down top, dark dress pants, and black shoes I'd worn to meet competition regulations. Every place his eyes lingered, I felt as if he'd touched me, causing my body to all but vibrate with an unexpected need, and making me wonder what it would feel like if those eyes and hands were resting on my bare skin. I thought the fire might just burn me to ash.

Maybe that was exactly what I needed. To be burned down to nothing so I could reemerge like a phoenix. But then again, maybe I'd already had my chance to reemerge and missed it. Or maybe I was still ash waiting to be transformed.

Rafe's voice lowered an octave, a sensual rhythm to it as he said, "I'd have to disagree. It would be practically impossible for someone as stunning as you to be a has-been, Ms. Hatley."

When his stare locked with mine once again, I nearly drowned in those deep, chocolate pools. It took an enormous amount of effort to tease back. "Washed up at twenty-three."

The hunger in his look disappeared behind that blank curtain again. "Twenty-three." He shook his head as he said it, and I tried not to be annoyed that my age had somehow washed away his desire. His next words were cool and aloof. "Enjoy the fans. Try not to spend all your winnings at the casino's tables."

The words were spoken as if he was giving advice to a child. Embarrassment ran through me. It took far too long to come up with a response, so by the time I finally choked out, "Thanks for the advice, Dad," he was already gone, heading into the depths of the darkened club.

Pop music replaced the quiet. A crew worked to disband the dartboards and tear up the carpet and mats to reveal a shiny black dance floor, likely to be crowded with swaying bodies in a few hours. The sleek, modern club was a complete contrast to my bar back home. Here, rows of chrome tables and tufted, black-leather seats wound up to where pastel-neon strips turned the alcohol bottles into hidden gems behind the bar. One entire wall of the club was glass, displaying the sun as it set over the Las Vegas Strip. Bright lights flashed from every casino lining the street as the world-renowned fountains sprayed upward.

The Marquis Club was tucked into the top, right tower of the newest Las Vegas casino. In the two years since it had opened, it had drawn the young, rich, and famous to its doors like kittens to milk. A dart tournament didn't quite fit the vibe of the place, but the competition's sponsor certainly had.

No arguing with the fact that Rafe was as smooth, charming, and sexy as the bar. My hormones were still skittering around inside me with unfulfilled longing from merely being in his presence. But that longing was layered with irritation, knowing he'd walked away simply because of my age.

He wasn't the first person who couldn't see past the number on my driver's license. Hadn't I encountered it repeatedly since taking over Uncle Phil's place? The vendors who patted my arm. The fire marshal who explained things like I was two. Very few people could see past my exterior to what lay behind it. Even fewer knew that my near-death experience had left me feeling wrinkled and gray, even if the mirror didn't show it.

I shook myself out of my reverie and made my way over to the burly brothers who'd waited patiently. They congratulated me, had me sign their stomachs in blue ink, and offered to buy me a beer. I thanked them with a large smile and said I had plans but maybe next time.

When they disappeared with hang-dog expressions, I experienced a momentary wave of homesickness. It was ridiculous to miss Tennessee when I'd only been gone three days. In a week, I'd be back. And with the money tucked into my account from this win and the little discovery I'd made while going through Uncle Phil's things after he died, I might just be able to finagle the bank into giving me a loan for the project I'd been dreaming up.

I grabbed my bag from a nearby table before heading for the exit and the bank of elevators waiting just beyond. As the doors slid open and I stepped inside, I marveled at the antique birdcage-inspired design with the green screens behind the brass bars, displaying an exterior view of the hotel.

While The Fortress wasn't the largest hotel and casino on The Strip, it was the trendiest and, in my opinion, the most elegant. Built to resemble the tidal island of Mont Saint-Michel in France, it had a five-star hotel tucked into the spirals and towers of the island's abbey and a casino, stores, and restaurants hiding behind the façade of the village and seawalls.

As the door of my room slammed shut behind me, my phone buzzed, and when I swiped it open, I found a handful of messages in the group chat with my siblings. Over the last few years, the chat had grown to include not only my brothers and my sister but their spouses also. Ryder, Maddox, and Gemma had all found love at unexpected moments, and sometimes, their ludicrously happy faces made my heart ache for something I'd never anticipated wanting.

> *RY: Sassypants, do I have to catch a plane to Vegas in order to find out what happened? Or are you celebrating by losing yourself in a shirtless fan?*

I rolled my eyes at Ryder's dig. My fans had been fun and enthusiastic, but it wasn't their shirtless chests that immediately flashed in my mind at his words. No, it was the annoyingly attractive Rafe Marquess. Why was it the touch of a man who'd so easily dismissed me that my body craved?

> *GEM: How many times do I have to say this to you? I don't need to know about any of my siblings' sex lives.*

I smirked, tempted to torment Gemma just for the fun of it, but Maddox beat me to it.

> *MADS: I feel sorry for Rex, Gem-Mine. Does he even remember what sex IS after being tied to you for so long now?*

> *GEM: Rex is completely satisfied! And damnit, you used to be on my side, Woody.*

I snorted at Gemma tossing out the nickname Ryder had given our brother. Maddox hated it, even though, as both the sheriff of our small county and a life-long do-gooder, it fit.

> *RY: If Rex is truly satisfied, it should have removed that stick from your butt, Gem-Mine.*

> *GEM: Keep it up, Dipshit, and I'll make sure all the olallieberry pie is gone before you get here tomorrow morning.*

The fact that my sister and her A-list-actor husband were at the ranch for a few days was just another reason I was missing being home. When I'd entered the dart competition, I hadn't known they'd be stopping in Tennessee before heading home to LA after filming had wrapped on the movie Gemma had written.

But then again, it wouldn't have mattered if I had known. I still would have come to Vegas. I'd needed to be here for more than the dart competition. My family just didn't know it. I glanced over to my carry-on bag and the secrets it held. With the competition behind me, I could finally devote some more time to my research. I'd dot some more I's and cross some more T's, and then I'd tell them about the whole knotted mess.

> *GIA: Hey now, Gemma, that olallieberry pie was supposed to be for me and the baby.*

I smiled as I typed my response. I couldn't help taunting my sister-in-law after the way she'd abandoned me for just such a pie on our last girls' night.

> *ME: Are you going to eat it or use it for foreplay again?*
>
> *RY: Who says we can't do both?*
>
> *GEM: She's alive! Tell us how you did, Sadie, before I lose my dinner over sex talk!*
>
> *ME: I won!*
>
> *MADS: *** money falling from the sky GIF *** Okay, moneybags, what are you doing with all that cash?*

A sense of panic hit me at the question. I had so many secrets I was keeping from my family these days when normally I was an open book. I wasn't sure why I hadn't told them about the ideas I'd first doodled on napkins and then started to assemble into an actual business plan. Maybe because I wanted to prove I could do it on my own after being handed the bar. Maybe because, in going down this path, I was shutting doors on my past instead of reopening them like my family wished I would.

The emptiness that had quickly replaced the small sense of victory at my win returned.

With fingers that shook, I typed my response.

> *ME: I have some plans for the land around the*

bar.

> MCK: *** eye roll emoji *** Bar. Bar. Bar. That's all I hear from you these days. At least spend a little of that dough on yourself. You're in Vegas! Go shopping, buy yourself something nice, and see a show. Maybe do some of that dancing you love so much.

I hesitated. Maybe I should. Maybe it would kick the emptiness out of my soul for a few minutes before I turned to the more serious topics I planned to tackle this week.

> ME: Maybe.
>
> MCK: I saw a picture of the competition's sponsor on the website. He looks like he'd have some nice dance moves.

Rafe's dark-brown eyes flashed before me, sending a thrill down my spine once more.

> RY: Who the hell are you talking about?
>
> MADS: He looked like a slick asshole. This may be the one and only time I disagree with McK.

My smile grew at the protectiveness of my brothers. Even though Ryder had teased about sex at the beginning of the chat, it had only been to rile the others. He didn't want to think about me, the baby of the family, actually *having* sex any more than Mads did.

> ME: I need to change and get food before I pass out from starvation. Love you all.
>
> GEM: Stay safe, Sassypants. No drinking from anything but a bottle that you open.
>
> MADS: Maybe you shouldn't go out alone.

GIA: Sadie is perfectly capable of kicking ass and taking names.

Gia's faith in me swelled my heart. At my request, she'd graciously spent hours over the last year teaching me some of the offensive and defensive moves she'd learned as a former undercover agent for the NSA. Originally, it had simply been so I knew how to toss a rowdy customer from the bar without getting hurt, but it had ended up giving me back some of the confidence I'd lost.

Almost three years after being shot, I was still weak in places I despised. Still had curves and wobbles on my frame I'd never had before spending months in recovery. But I was tighter and firmer now than I'd been last year.

Tighter and firmer in more than just my body. I finally had a plan for my future sketched too. It sometimes felt as empty as the dart championship I'd won, but it was a goal. A direction to move in that would leave behind another Hatley legacy. That had to matter, didn't it?

As I ditched the straitlaced shirt and pants I'd needed for the competition, I stared in the closet at the other outfits I'd brought with me. They were all work clothes—jeans and T-shirts and worn cowboy boots. Not a single dress.

My phone pinged again, and I pulled it out to see a private message from my oldest brother.

> *RY: You know how I feel about you wasting your time and money on the bar. When are you going to figure out what you want, Sassypants? Go after your dreams instead of spending your life keeping a dying bar alive.*

It was an argument we'd had multiple times over the last year. When I didn't respond, he added on.

> *RY: You were right when you called me out on not living, Sads. I had closed myself off. Thanks to you, I not only have my daughter but Gia in my life and*

> *a new baby on the way. I have a family I never thought I'd have again because you knew when to push. Consider this me pushing. I want you to find your way back to your dreams too.*
>
> ME: *I'm here, aren't I? I threw again. Won again.*
>
> RY: *How'd it feel?*

If I told him the truth—that it felt hollow, like I'd stepped into a mirage from the past and not quite been able to pull the full joy of it around me—he'd never ease up.

> ME: *Amazing. I knew before the last dart landed that I'd won.*
>
> RY: *Go celebrate. But be safe. And regardless of how much we tease Gemma and Mads, I don't want to hear about it when you end up in bed with some one-night jerk-off.*

I smiled, suddenly resolved to do just what my family had suggested. I'd buy a dress, get a drink, find somewhere I could line dance, and enjoy the moment of being in the city that never slept. I doubted I'd bring someone back to my hotel room, but I'd let someone buy me a beer with a twist-off cap.

And maybe, somewhere along the way, I'd find the Sadie who'd once wanted to study international law, win the Triple Crown of Darts, and travel the world, righting wrongs. Maybe I'd turn back into that wild child who'd caused my siblings and parents to lose sleep rather than the one they counted on to help fill in for missing employees at the ranch and spent her nights pouring pints at a bar that had been in the family for over a century.

Maybe I'd figure out if the bar-owner, business-minded Sadie I'd become was really the new version of me, or if there was something else waiting around the corner I hadn't quite discovered yet.

Chapter Two

Rafe

YOU, ME, AND WHISKEY
Performed by Justine Moore and Priscilla Block

It was nearing eleven o'clock at night by the time I made my way to the piano bar tucked in the back corner of the hotel. It was always my final stop of the night after making the rounds. My routine started with The Marquis Club, with its loud music and packed dance floor, before moving on to the casino, with its jangling slots, spinning roulette wheels, shouts of customers, and clinking of glasses. I hit the registration desk and restaurants in varying order, based on the needs of the staff, but I always ended my workday in the quiet of the piano bar. I'd grab a single shot of bourbon, sip it while I reviewed the daily numbers, and then head to the penthouse suite I called home before starting it all over again the next day.

Of all the businesses I'd built from the ground up in the last twelve years, this one hit all the marks I'd wanted. I was prouder of it—prouder of calling it mine—than anything I'd accomplished yet. Watching The Fortress glow in the rising and setting sun almost gave me the same feeling of peace and satisfaction I'd once had staring at a rushing waterfall and acres of rolling hills.

For a fleeting few months, it had filled the hole that had taken over my life for nearly a decade and a half. But now, as the days grew long and routine grew cold, I felt the black hole creeping back over me, along with an antsy need to shovel it full of something new.

Maybe it wasn't the tedium wearing on me as much as it was my brother's death five months ago. Maybe being forced to step onto the hills of my childhood for his funeral had triggered this new wave of restlessness. Whichever was true, every time I watched the sun hit the spires of The Fortress now, it was the sun reflecting off the rivers on our family's land that haunted me.

My jaw clenched, and my shoulders tightened as I reminded myself the ranch would be gone for good by the end of the year. It would no longer have the power to attack my heart and tear through my soul. I'd have this instead—a hotel-casino brimming with life versus a ranch overflowing with nature's solitude.

A twinge of guilt hit me at the thought of selling the land. It wasn't at the idea of giving up a century-old legacy but because Fallon would hate me even more than she already did when it happened. My daughter would get over it though. Marquesses were resilient. We sucked it up and did what we had to do to survive. I'd learned that at the hand of my mother, who'd fought the devil called cancer twice before she'd succumbed to it when I was eight. Survival took many forms.

My daughter would learn it just as I had.

And Lauren? Did I care what happened to my brother's wife now that Spencer was gone?

I ignored the ache that tried to jump from behind the walls I'd built, quickening my stride along the mirrored hallway toward the back of the hotel, focusing on every minute detail to keep me present. The arrangements on gold-gilded side tables were wilting and needed to be replaced. It was the fourth time it had happened this month. Maybe the florist needed to be tossed out along with the dying blooms. Or maybe my operations manager should be exchanged for a new one if he couldn't keep tabs on something as basic as dead flowers.

As I neared the bar, instead of the soothing lull of piano keys I'd expected, a raucous and loud beat filled the air, causing my back to stiffen in disapproval.

Stepping inside, it wasn't the carefully crafted old-world

charm of the bar I saw. My vision funneled, the leather furniture, brass fixtures, and bar built into mahogany bookshelves all but disappearing as I focused on a singular moving object—a woman. She was twisting and twirling through a little two-step dance, accompanied on either side by two burly men.

Annoyance and attraction leaped through my veins in equal measure.

Someone had shoved aside the custom-made piano and replaced the soft sounds of its keys with country music that blared from hidden speakers. The trio on the stage stomped their cowboy boots on my smooth marble floors to a snappy rhythm full of banjo and twang.

The black-haired vixen at their center shot a lopsided smile at the man to her right, and I was overcome with the urge to toss him from the bar simply for having had the audacity to be on the receiving end of it. The little shimmy she did was almost the same one she'd performed after winning the dart tournament earlier. The movement sent the fringed layer of her sequined dress in a million different directions while the lavender silk underlayer hugged her frame. Full hips that begged to have fingers dig into them moved gracefully, while delightfully curved breasts bounced to the beat.

She was a vision. A tasty, tantalizing dream. But it wasn't her curves that had my breath evaporating. No, it was a pair of blue eyes the same color as the California bluebells that raced over the hills of the ranch in the spring. Those eyes had mesmerized me this afternoon as I'd watched Sadie Hatley toss darts with an ease that whispered of otherworldly powers.

My stomach and groin tightened uncomfortably, just as they had when I'd had her hand in mine. Walking away from her this afternoon had almost cost me a layer of skin and bone.

But she was only twenty-three. Practically an innocent babe.

You weren't at that age, the devil inside me taunted. And I hadn't been. I'd been a year away from opening my first club when I was twenty-three.

But I also wasn't the norm.

Maybe she isn't either.

Who knew? Not me. What I did know was Sadie was a distraction I couldn't afford and certainly didn't want.

If I wanted sex, I knew where to get it. All it took was a drink, a hotel room, and breakfast on the house that didn't include me remaining behind to share it. The woman in front of me may scream lust and desire, but it wasn't the kind I could slip in and out of. No, every shake of her body, every smile and laugh, screamed something more. She'd get her hooks into whoever took her to bed. They'd be unable to forget those mesmerizing eyes and the dare that seemed to reside permanently in them.

Sadie's hand landed on the arm of the man to her left, and I recognized him and his friend as the naked-chested fans who'd been shouting her nickname at the tournament. Something bitter filled my mouth at the idea of her dancing with them here. In my hotel. In my bar.

I told myself it was simply because it was in a space that was *not* intended for dancing, and my devil scoffed.

I finally freed my feet from where they'd taken root and stalked through the tables. I reached the threesome just as the song ended and laughter filled the air.

"What the hell is this?" I demanded in the silence that settled down.

From off to the side, I heard Mattie, the bar's manager, holler something I didn't quite register. Her voice simply faded away once Sadie turned eyes on me littered with pure mischief. Impish promises flew between us—ones I absolutely wouldn't be taking her up on.

"Line dance lessons," Sadie responded, and the lightness in her voice matched the curve of her lips. Upward. Joy-filled.

God, she was beautiful. And so damn alive at the moment that it burst through her like rays from the sun. What would it feel like to be that full of life for even a few seconds?

I was full of purpose and resolve, but she radiated with a

vibrancy that was all about eking out enjoyment from every second.

"This is a piano bar," I barked, feeling immediately like an idiot for stating the obvious. "This is not the time or place for any kind of dance lessons."

Her lips quirked higher. "Don't get your panties in a wad, Slick. We'll put everything back to rights."

My annoyance grew at the half-assed insult.

Mattie joined us. "They were just settling a quick bet, Rafe."

My gaze narrowed on the dark-haired enchantress in front of me, and I growled, "Take the betting to the casino. It's just out the doors."

Sadie laughed. "You want me to teach line dancing in the middle of the black jack tables?"

Her eyes actually twinkled. Who knew eyes could really do that? Her face was deliciously flushed, and the soft sweep of pink covering her high cheeks emphasized the sharp jut of her chin almost as much as the nearly black hair swirling around it did. I wanted to yank back those silky strands and expose the long column of her neck. I wanted to see if those vibrant blues would turn dark and mystical with the touch of my mouth and hands.

My annoyance at those provocative thoughts was displayed in every syllable as I said, "I don't want you teaching line dancing anywhere in the hotel or casino."

Her smile widened instead of lowering at my snarl. "I paid for twenty minutes, party pooper. In exchange for interrupting their quiet, I bought everyone here a round and promised to be done by the time they'd finished."

"Spending your prize money on alcohol isn't any better than spending it at the tables," I barked.

She laughed again, and the sound lodged itself deep inside me. I wanted to hear it again. I wanted to rip it away and make it permanently mine. The overwhelming strength of those notions and the unwanted feelings that came with them were what helped ease me back from the edge I felt myself slipping over. I despised all the strong emotions she'd yanked out of me today. I'd learned the hard way to keep them wrapped tight.

Sadie turned to the two men on either side of her. "Sorry, Leo and Deke. I guess our lessons are over. But I promise, if you go to any country bar and slide up on the dance floor with these moves, you'll have more dates than you can shake a stick at."

Both men leaned in at the same time, kissing her on opposite cheeks. She blushed, and I had to fist my hands to keep myself from ripping them away from her. From a woman I didn't know. Didn't want to know. A woman I needed to get out of my bar, my hotel, and my life before something terrible happened. Before I lost control completely. Lost everything all over again. And these days, I had way more to lose than I once had. I had billions spread across the globe rather than a few acres of hills and valleys.

The men thanked her, gave me another glance, and then scurried out of the bar.

Sadie shook her head and turned to Mattie. "Let me help you put things back."

My bar manager fought off a smirk as she said, "Dan and I got it. Go get that drink you paid for and never received."

Sadie seemed to hesitate for a brief second before she ran a hand down the beaded fringe of her sexy-as-sin dress and stepped away from the makeshift dance floor toward the bar.

I watched every step, noticing with surprise that Mattie's assistant bartender pushed a finger of amber liquid rather than a fruit-filled mixed drink her way. I liked the idea of her drinking my bourbon. Liked what those perky lips would taste like if I slid my tongue over them afterward.

I hated how much I wanted to do just that. How much I wanted her.

She slid onto the stool, and that delightfully flirty dress rode up just enough to give me a glimpse of a toned thigh. I turned away, gritted my teeth, and helped Mattie and Dan the Piano Man wheel the baby grand back into place.

Mattie whispered, "She paid for a round for the entire bar. It was a harmless diversion. A handful of songs at most."

"And a first-time customer who wandered in hoping for a quiet place to relax and heard that racket would have walked right back out and not returned."

Mattie didn't reply, but she did shoot me a remorseful glance before heading for the bar.

Knowing I'd made too much of the incident only irritated me more as I sank into the corner booth in the darkest part of the room with the permanent "reserved" sign resting on the table. It was my booth. My bar. My casino. My rules. I pulled my phone from my pocket, opened my management app, and attempted to scroll through the daily numbers. But I wasn't really seeing them.

My attention kept wandering to the bar, watching as Mattie said something to Sadie that made the vixen throw her head back and laugh. It was quiet enough I couldn't hear the sound of it across the room with the piano at work. My chest ached to hear the tinkling chimes, my body grew tight at the unfulfilled expectation, and my mind pushed it all away.

Sadie rose from the stool, turning so I could see she had two rocks glasses in her hands. My shoulders tensed even more, knowing before she'd even taken a step in my direction that she was coming to me, bringing me the one glass I allowed myself to savor each night.

She set the drinks on my table and slid into the booth without an invitation.

"Drink's on me," she said with a lopsided smile that caused my heart to backfire.

I scoffed. "It's all on me."

Her lips instantly flattened, the happy look replaced with an assessing one that I worried, for two beats, might actually see beyond my exterior walls. I instinctively reinforced them, tucking away every emotion. I'd be damned if she'd read any of it. Not the lust. Not the poetry that sprung to mind whenever those eyes met mine. Not even the irritation I felt for her ruining my peace.

"Mattie told me you own the place. Pretty young to have your own casino," she said. I wasn't sure if it was a taunt because of what I'd said earlier about her age, an attempt to wheedle her way into my life, or just conversation.

I didn't respond. I just met her stare with my own as I fought the desire to drag her around the booth and kiss her until those crystal-clear eyes turned cloudy, and the taste of bourbon on her lips was replaced with the taste of me.

She looked away first, fiddling with a strand of fringe on her dress before glancing back up. "I own a bar. My family owns a…hotel of sorts. It's a lot of work. You never really get a break. You're always on."

Every time I thought I had her sorted and pegged, she surprised me. "You own a bar?"

She huffed out another laugh, impish lips twisting upward again. "I inherited it from my uncle. It's been in the family for over a hundred years."

"What are you doing on the dart circuit then?" The question slipped out before I could stop it. I silently cursed myself. I needed her to go, not invite her to stay and spill her guts.

"I needed the money," she said with a careless shrug that had the dress's tiny strap slipping to the edge of her shoulder, tempting me to tug it down or rip it completely off. "What are you doing sponsoring a dart competition?"

I pulled my eyes up to her face. "My operations manager insisted the television coverage would be good advertisement. But I won't host it again."

It hadn't brought the type of crowd I wanted to The Fortress. It brought bare-chested mountain men who drank beer from ridiculous hats. It brought impish vixens who screamed temptation.

"Doesn't look like you need advertisement," she said, glancing around at the completely occupied booths.

Even without the dart competition, the hotel would have been fully occupied, just like every available seat at the casino tables was taken, and my restaurants had a waitlist. But I knew, more than anyone, how fast that could change. I had successful bars that had turned into duds and clubs that only pulled in profit when a steady stream of ad revenue was sent their way. Keeping everything in the black was a balancing act that took both hard reins and soft hands. It was a heady dance, different than the one I'd spent my formative years performing with the unbroken horses on the ranch, but still a dance.

Once again, she filled my nonresponse with another question. "Do you ever take a moment off? To breathe? To just relax?"

Ever since she'd walked into the club the day before with her dart case in hand, she'd worn a smile. Most of the time, it had been as light and alive as the one she'd had while dancing with the two fans moments ago, but once in a while, I'd seen the smile slip. Seen a glimpse of something deeper, darker that lingered for a moment before the smile returned. It made her all the more attractive.

Sadie ran a hand through thick strands, tucking them behind an ear, and then looked up at me with an expression brimming with hunger—that same longing that had been zinging through me since the moment she'd shown up in my club with a dart case in hand.

"I don't get to relax very often," she said. "My siblings told me to celebrate. Hence the dress." She waved down at the sparkling concoction dancing with a light that couldn't compete with her internal one. "And the drink." She picked up the glass, tossed back the remaining contents, and put it down before meeting my gaze head on again. "And you."

The desire smoldering in me burst into an inferno at those two simple words.

I'd had plenty of women come on to me over the years, but I'd never had this visceral of a reaction to one.

I wanted her. She wanted me. We were two consenting adults, years past the legal age, regardless of the gap between her twenty-three years and my thirty-five. Would tasting her douse the fire she'd flamed, or would it leave a burn I'd feel for days? Months? Years?

"They should call you the Tennessee Hurricane rather than Tennessee Darlin'," I grunted out, trying to reel myself back in. Reel us both in.

"Afraid of a little wild west blowing over you, Slick?" My body erupted all over again at the dare she accompanied by another mischievous smile.

In another lifetime, before I'd weighed and measured every single decision, every penny, every plan, every purchase, I'd been extremely good at accepting dares. *I dare you to jump off the cliff into the creek. I dare you to ride bareback on the unbroken stallion. I dare you to kiss me.* That last dare had changed my life. Cracked it apart. Shattered it until only one good thing emerged from the ashes.

This dare, issued from a sparkling, vibrant woman who lived thousands of miles away and would be gone on the next plane ride out of Vegas, was nothing compared to that one. And maybe it was all those reasons, the man I'd once been as much as who I was now, that had me accepting that dare, even knowing I wasn't seeing all the odds.

At the moment, all that mattered was the ache I had for her. The ache to hold on to someone who allowed life to pour over them. I wanted it to drown me for a few hours before I returned to the empty void my mistakes had carved into me.

I shoved my phone into my suit jacket and stood. I registered her disappointment, thinking I was leaving, just as I felt her body jolt when my palm slid along her nape. I lowered my mouth so it caressed the shell of her ear and said, "You should be more careful what you gamble with, Tennessee."

A shiver ran through her, but she twisted her face to mine, bringing our lips so close I could almost taste the liquor on them before she whispered, "I think I can beat the odds."

The fires that had been licking through me burned viciously. I let out a savage growl, low and dark, as I took her elbow and practically yanked her from the booth. She had the audacity to laugh. Light and elvish. Charming and sweet. But I ate sweet for breakfast and spit it out before lunch, and she'd find that out soon enough.

Chapter Three

Sadie

HEELS IN HAND
Performed by Priscilla Block

Rafe's hand on my elbow shot pure lust through my veins. While it had been a really long time since I'd tangled my body with a man's, I knew for a fact I'd never felt anything this strong before. This heady. This addicting.

I wanted to feel his touch on every inch of me.

That thought sobered me up slightly. Not that I was drunk—I'd only had that single glass of bourbon. No, the high I felt was all for Rafe and his dark, broody intensity. I wanted to see what the carefully leashed man in a pressed suit looked like when he let his feral growls have full rein. I wanted him to demand I forget everything but him and his caresses. But the realization that his hands would find the scars covering a portion of my body had me slowing as we headed down the corridor.

As if thinking of the wounds had brought them to life, the limp I still fought when exhausted found its way to the surface. I saw it reflected in the shiny brass elevator doors as we made our way toward them, and Rafe's all-seeing eyes caught it before I'd been able to rein it in.

"Are you hurt?" he asked. When I looked up, desire still burned, but his expression was twined with a concern I disliked. I didn't want concern tonight. Or gentleness. Or pity. God, pity would be the worst. I'd had enough of that after I'd been shot.

I raised a single brow, smiled my best smile, and let loose my full Southern accent as I said, "Nope. Not hurting. Just have an old gunshot wound that acts up now and again."

For a moment, several long heartbeats, he didn't seem to register what I'd said, and then something glorious happened. The scowl he'd been wearing ever since walking into the piano bar broke apart, and a smile emerged. Full and beautiful with that single-sided dimple that had set my pulse rate zooming earlier and increased it to full throttle once more.

"Trying to take back your ante, Tennessee?" Clearly, he thought I was joking. But he'd find out the truth soon enough, and he might be the one to withdraw. I hadn't risked showing them to anyone until now, but they still weren't pretty, even all these months later.

"You know us wild-west women, Slick. Gunshots don't slow us down."

And then something even more miraculous happened—he laughed. He'd done it earlier when we'd been in the upstairs bar, but that had been reserved and half-hearted. This felt real and full, and I swore the world stopped. Everything around us slipped out of focus as his rumble weaved through me. Deep. Enthralling. Full of hidden promises I wanted to explore.

The elevator doors opened, we stepped inside, and he waved his phone at the panel. The digital display requested a code, and he hesitated for a second before punching it in. The green screen behind the brass bars shifted, displaying the view of The Strip as we zipped upward.

My heart thudded against my chest as our eyes met. I swore I could see fire in his depths. I almost expected him to haul me to him and kiss me right then and there, but instead, he ran a single finger from my shoulder to my elbow and back. Just that simple action made my thighs quiver. I swallowed the nervousness that tried to flutter to life and stepped forward to eliminate the distance that remained between us, but his palm landed on my chest, halting me. He glanced up at the corner of the elevator.

"Not here. But once the door of my suite shuts, there won't

be a place on you I won't touch." The promise in his voice was a sensual purr.

The bell dinged, and the doors swooshed open. He held them for me, meeting my gaze with a heated one. "Last chance, Tennessee. Are you in, or are you out?"

I didn't even hesitate. I simply stepped out of the elevator, causing his jacket to brush against my bare arm as I went by, sending off another million sparks throughout my body.

"I'm not folding," I tossed back. "Are you?"

He didn't answer with words, but he stepped out beside me and tugged my hand into his, fingers twining with mine in a way that made me ache all over. Not just in my body, but in my heart and soul. And suddenly, at the very worst time, I realized I truly wanted what my siblings had found—a forever after. But that wasn't what this was tonight. This was simply a few hours of passion and sin and forgetfulness.

Only one door existed on this floor of the hotel, and when he unlocked it with a wave of his phone, it revealed a penthouse suite at the top of the hotel's spiral. The small entryway was layered with golden marble. An ornate mirror hung over a Baroque table dwarfed by a huge floral display in whites and golds. Short steps led down into a living area where two walls of glass revealed the night sky aglow with the neon lights of The Strip far below us. The stunning view of the Las Vegas streets gave way to a midnight shadow that hid the peaks of mountains in the distance.

The living room was decorated with the same mix of eighteenth-century Baroque and 1920s Art Deco as the rest of the hotel, except the luxury here was ratcheted up to a whole new level. A Monet I thought might be an original hung on the wall, Fabergé eggs encrusted with diamonds and rubies graced the side tables, and Tiffany lamps with vibrant geometric forms cast warm light over hand-woven rugs covering portions of the marble floors.

My cowboy boots clacked loudly in the quiet as I dropped my clutch on a side table and headed for the wall of glass. Not a single outside sound could be heard, and yet I still imagined them. The drunken laughter of the people carousing from casino to casino. The jangle of the slots spilling onto the streets. The music of the fountains.

"Nice view, Slick."

In the reflection of the glass, I saw Rafe take off his jacket and lay it neatly and precisely on the back of the couch. He stood for a moment, hands in his pockets, as if he was debating one last time whether he wanted to go through with this. I raised a brow, cocking my head sideways, and his eyes locked on mine in the window.

"I don't bring people here," he said, looking away for several long seconds before crossing the room in two purposeful strides. He came to a stop right behind me. Two warm hands found my arms, sliding slowly and tantalizingly upward, caressing my shoulders. "I certainly don't bring women into my space. But for some damn reason, I wanted to see you here, up against my glass. Bare."

I'd hardly had time to register the words, to have them land in my heart like an arrow, before his fingers slid under the thin straps of my dress and, with a smooth jerk, broke them both. The neckline sagged, and with a gasp, I caught it before it could reveal my chest.

His head dipped, and hungry lips found the curve of my neck where it met my shoulder. Warm. Wet. Strong. My legs wobbled, my core clenched, and his dark eyes held mine in the hazy reflection. *Holy hell, he's going to devour me in the best possible way*, I thought just as he yanked on the hem of my dress, pulling it from my hands and dropping it so it puddled around my cowboy boots.

When I tried to turn around, those strong hands captured my waist, keeping me facing the window. Every part of me was achy. Scorching. Yearning to touch as much as I was being touched. His mouth and fingers seared separate paths along every sensitive nerve.

A mewl escaped me. A sound I'd never made before and was almost embarrassed to have done until I saw, in the reflection, the way his lips curved upward. He tangled a hand in my hair, tugging my head backward, not quite cruelly but not gently either, so this time when our eyes met briefly, there was no glass between us. This time, it was all real connection. All fire and brimstone.

And then that delicious mouth found mine.

If I'd thought those lips were sensual and hot on my skin, the way they took command of my mouth was out of this world. Powerful. Hungry. Claiming ownership. God…he could easily ruin me. I panicked for a heartbeat, and then his tongue was demanding entrance, and I simply gave in to whatever was going to happen. My lashes fluttered shut as I accepted each stroke, each taunt, each delightful tease.

Time stood still as I lost myself to the single most beautiful, most potent, most incredible kiss of my life. One that would brand itself into my soul and stay there for an eternity.

When he drew back, I moaned my displeasure, lids fluttering open to meet dark and stormy depths. "I've wanted to do that since the moment you walked into the club yesterday," he growled, and then he was incinerating me again with demanding lips.

When I twisted again, to touch as much as I was being touched, he let me. The grip on my hair disappeared as his hands found my waist, fingertips digging into the skin, while his kiss led me on a decadent trip to sin and salvation. I blindly tugged at the buttons on his shirt, desperate to find skin.

My back hit the cool glass as his mouth dipped, trailing down my neck and chest. A flick of tongue and teeth had a tortured cry escaping me. He lifted me up, and my legs automatically surrounded his waist, my dress barely dangling from one boot. The thin lace scrap at my core pressed into his zipper sent another shockwave through me.

With his hands and arms so close to the scars on my right side, I hesitated again. As if sensing it, he drew back, eyeing me.

"What'll it be, Tennessee?"

The fact he was still giving me an out at every turn only made me want him more. My only response was a kiss fueled by need, daring him not to stop. Daring him to continue until we'd both gone over the wild edge I could already feel approaching.

With an ease that spoke to sculpted and carved muscles I'd been unable to glimpse in their full glory yet, he carried me away from the windows, down a hall, and through a darkened doorway. My legs flexed around him, and for the first time, I heard a grunt of pleasure escape him.

It filled me with power. Control. Desire.

I wanted to see him completely unleashed. I wanted to see him unraveled just like he was unraveling me.

He hit a switch with his elbow, and a room done in satiny blues and shiny golds came briefly into focus. He broke our embrace, setting me down on a mahogany dresser and putting a hint of distance between us. He pulled his shirt out of his pants, and I caught a glimpse of a flat, tanned stomach with muscled ridges and a delightful V pointing downward to where his pants tented, revealing his reaction to our heated embrace.

When I reached for the buttons on his shirt, craving more of the alluring visual, he pushed my hands away. His dark-chocolate gaze ate me up, dancing over my heaving chest, sliding over the curves of my stomach and hips I'd worked hard to return to their former shape over the last year.

I knew the moment he found the scars, because his breath caught. His hand landed on the largest one where the bullet had entered before stroking the crisscrossing white lines along my upper thigh. Because some of my nerve endings had never recovered, I couldn't feel everywhere he touched, but I could still see every brush of his fingers. It was almost more enticing this way, to feeling nothing in some places and then suddenly have other parts erupt in an explosion of lightning.

"What the hell is this, Tennessee?" Anger and concern dripped through every syllable. "You were serious? You were shot?"

His dark brows furrowed together. Just as I reached up to soothe them with my finger, just as I started to tell him it was nothing when we both knew it wasn't, the sound of the penthouse door slamming shut rattled through the space.

His head jerked toward the bedroom door as a female voice rang out. "Dad?"

Shock reverberated through me. He had a kid? Did that mean he had a wife too?

Panic spread over his face before it rippled with frustration and then closed off completely.

The next thing I knew, I'd been torn from the dresser, and my dress was shoved into my hands.

"Stay here. Get dressed. I'll come and tell you when it's safe to leave."

The door shut with a firm and yet quiet click behind him.

I stared at the back of it, lust turning to embarrassment that dissolved into fury.

What the actual fuck?

"What are you doing here, Fallon?" I heard him demand. His voice was dark and full of the same startled irritation I had swelling in me. I couldn't hear his daughter's response, but I heard his deep, furious exclamation. "You did what?"

Their argument drifted farther away. I looked down at the dress in my hands with its broken straps. Humiliation brought tears I blinked back. No way in hell was he going to find me crying. No. Way.

I slipped into the shimmering dress I'd been so happy to buy, allowing my anger to grow. I moved to the mirror over the dresser, found the broken straps, and tied them behind my neck in a way that would at least hold the top up until I got to my room. My cheeks were flaming. My hair was mussed. My mouth was bright red from the sensual kisses we'd shared.

I would have been happy to see this reflection if we'd finished what we'd started. I'd wanted one unforgettable night with a stunning man. If we'd been able to spend a few hours together, I would have left without ever knowing he had a kid…and maybe a wife. *Goddamnit.*

I'd lived nearly three years without sex. Lived three years growing the courage to let someone see my battered body, and this was what I got for it? Some asshole sleeping around on his wife? Some jerkwad who'd brought me back to his home and stripped me bare in his living room where his daughter could easily have caught us with my naked back up against the glass?

Asshole.

I had to squeeze my eyelids tight to keep the tears of anger and mortification from leaking out. I didn't want him to see them and think I was sad. Screw that. I was furious.

I was almost tempted to walk out the door, down the hall, and slam my way out of the penthouse, leaving him to explain to his daughter just who I was and what we'd been doing. It would serve him right.

But it wouldn't be fair to her.

And I needed my room key, which was in my clutch sitting on a table.

Would she notice? Would he remember to grab it?

I paced by the door, waiting in the quiet, and my temper grew the more minutes that passed.

Without my phone or any visible clock in the room, I could only guess how long I stood there before the doorknob turned.

He looked…stoic. The wall that had covered every emotion earlier this evening had returned in greater force. But his words were full of regret. "I'm sorry. You'll have to leave."

He had my clutch in his hands. I grabbed it and pushed past him. Even furious, with my body trembling now with anger instead of desire, the mere brush of his arm caused heat to sizzle through my veins. Those damn tears returned because what I'd experienced with him had been so beautiful. Stunning. Unimaginably powerful and real.

I stormed toward the door and felt him on my heels. I knew without looking that he was warily scoping the living room for sight of his daughter in order to slip me out like some dirty secret. What we'd been doing wasn't dirty. It was human and normal, and it might have been the best few hours of my life if we'd finished.

Was his daughter old enough to understand that? She'd

walked into the suite on her own, unless he had a wife who he'd also greeted, and I just hadn't heard.

That made my stomach turn.

I made it out the door, and I'd already reached the elevator and pushed the button before he caught me, tugging my elbow.

"I'm sorry, Sadie," he offered. It was emotionless. A half-offered apology.

My chin went up. "Do you have a wife to go along with the daughter?"

At least I got a true emotion this time. Shock and anger. "If I was married, you wouldn't have been in my home."

It felt like it was the truth, but what the hell did I know?

The elevator pinged, and the doors opened. I stepped inside and hit the button for my floor, but he held the doors.

"She wasn't supposed to be here," he said, voice low and dark and deliciously broody. "I wouldn't have invited you up if she was."

Somehow, that hurt even more. It shouldn't. I'd known what this was from the moment he'd stood up in the piano bar and answered my dare. One night. He wasn't bringing the woman he was dating home to meet his family. This was supposed to be two people sharing a few hours of pleasure and respite. And yet, the humiliating sting of being shuffled out the door like a bad seed burned through me.

"Don't sweat it, Slick. I'm sure I can find Leo or Deke or some other willing partner to finish what you couldn't." Something a lot like fury flashed over his face before the wall came down again. I had no intention of doing anything but running back to my room and washing away the embarrassment, but he didn't need to know that. He didn't need to know his kisses would be impossible to replace tonight. Maybe ever. Any others would seem like cheap knockoffs.

I raised a brow at his hand holding the door open.

His jaw clenched, and his Adam's apple bobbed as if he was going to say something, but instead, he let go and stepped back. His intense gaze remained locked on me while the doors closed.

I sagged back against the wall, deflating immediately.

Stupid. The entire night had been stupid. What had I been thinking? I hadn't come to Las Vegas to get laid. I hadn't even really come for the dart tournament. I'd come to get answers for my family. To find the truth about our past that we may not like and may be unable to set right.

I'd forget about tonight. I'd put it behind me and concentrate on finding out if our McFlannigan ancestors had really been the liars and thieves I'd started to fear they had been. The honor my sheriff brother served with, the noble way Ryder and Gia had taken down a cartel…it might all have been for nothing if, at our core, we were nothing more than the offspring of a mob family who'd ravaged the West.

Chapter Four

Rafe

DON'T WE ALL
Performed by Elle Langley

As the elevator doors shut, a battle waged in me stronger than I'd fought in a very long time. Maybe since I'd stood at the gate of the ranch all those years ago and debated leaving. Because the idea of Sadie looking at some other man with those blue eyes sizzling with lust, the idea of some other man setting his hands on that soft silky skin, made every single fiber of my being revolt.

She was supposed to be mine.

For tonight only, I reminded myself.

I wouldn't have kept her. I would have sent her on her way just as I'd sent every woman before her. Every woman since Lauren. So, it certainly wasn't my business if she hooked up with some other guy.

And yet, the thought of her giving those mewls and moans and sweet mouth to someone else made me want to pound my fist through the wall. It made me want to step inside the elevator and knock down the door of whatever room she was in. I could find out. I owned the damned place.

I could and would finish what I'd started.

Then, my gaze landed on the door to the penthouse where my daughter sat waiting. A daughter I didn't know how to connect with and who hated me as much as I'd once thought I'd hated her mother and my brother.

A teenager who'd done something unbelievably rash and a bit frightening.

Finishing what I'd started with Sadie was the last thing I had the ability to do at the moment.

I dragged my hand through my hair and tucked in my shirt before striding back into the penthouse and making my way to Fallon's room. The door was open, even though I'd shut it, and my stomach fell, hoping she hadn't seen me escorting Sadie out. I had no intention of explaining who Sadie was and why she'd been in our home. This was why I didn't bring women here. My teeth ground together in frustration—at myself as much as at my daughter.

I watched as she paced in front of her bed, chewing her cuticles.

"What the hell were you thinking, Fallon?"

She glanced up with wide and angry eyes. My eyes. She had Lauren's blond waves, but it was my brown irises and thick brows that stared back at me. For probably the millionth time since she'd been born, I thought it should be my brother's gray ones filling up her petite face. She should have been his. Instead, this fiery girl, simmering with fury, was mine. She'd been born into a contentious love triangle that had nothing to do with her and yet impacted her every day.

She placed her hands on her hips and glared at me. "You're the only one who can do something! And you won't! I had to come and try to change your mind."

"By flying a damn plane on your own?" When she'd told me she'd flown the ranch's Cessna from California to Vegas by herself, I'd thought I was going to have an actual heart attack. The muscles in my chest had felt like they'd atrophied. I silently cursed Spencer for having taught her to pilot it to begin with. One more thing to hold against my dead brother. "You don't even have your official license yet, and even if you did, no one should fly on their own, especially not a fourteen-year-old kid! What would you have done if something had gone wrong? What would I have done?"

She scoffed. "If something had gone wrong, then you'd

finally be free of me. You could have continued to screw around with whomever you wanted without worrying about some kid interrupting you."

Both statements hit like a dart to my chest and showcased just how shitty of a job I'd done as her father. Fallon's very existence was a reminder of all the things I'd done right and wrong in my life, but I wouldn't give her up just to undo those mistakes. She was the only person I allowed myself to truly love. Everything I'd done since Lauren got pregnant had been to ensure my daughter had the best life.

And to prove you were better than your brother, the devil taunted.

"It would have crushed me to lose you, Fallon," I said, hoping she could hear the absolute truth ringing through my voice. "And it would have absolutely destroyed your mother. She's just barely resurfacing after losing Spence. She would have drowned completely if she'd lost you too."

Fallon looked down and away, crossing her arms over her chest in a defensive move. She was tall for her age, taller than most of the boys she'd be starting high school with in September. And she had curves to her I didn't even want to consider. But her face…her eyes…still had the look of a child. Young and inexperienced and brimming with hurt.

Losing Spencer had been her first real loss. She'd loved him with the same absolute force she'd come to hate me. He'd been her true father, where I'd been a passing influence trying to give her a good life from a distance. Without my brother, she was floundering, and I didn't know how to fix the bleeding. It wasn't a dead floral arrangement I could simply toss out.

What was worse was the knowledge she didn't want me anywhere near her emotions.

She'd turned from a toddler, ecstatic to see the person who showered her with gifts and adventures, to a teen who saw only the way I'd been absent from her life. She didn't know it had nearly torn me apart every time I sent her back to the ranch, but I'd done it because I couldn't stay there, and it would have been selfish to drag her with me.

In Rivers, she'd grown up swimming in the clear blue of Castle Lake, riding her horses through fields littered with bluebells, and watching the sun set over the icy peaks of the mountains. It had been a much better life for a child than drifting from apartment to apartment in ever-changing cities around the globe where she would have only caught glimpses of the sky in crowded city parks while I built my kingdom.

But maybe leaving her to be raised by my brother and Lauren hadn't been my biggest mistake. Maybe it had been never setting foot on the ranch in the entire time she'd been alive and forcing Spence to bring her to me for our visits. Perhaps, instead of requiring her to leave the ranch she loved to spend a few weeks of her vacations in cold buildings where she could never run wild and free, I should have gone to her.

I certainly would have been more aware of the state of the ranch if I had. It wouldn't have caught me by surprise.

But then again, neither Spencer nor I would have wanted me to witness his failure.

Now, I refused to let my daughter take on the burden of a legacy that only promised to drag her under like quicksand. I wouldn't let her start her life with a dying albatross hanging around her neck just as she tried to spread her wings and soar. Any help, any money I might toss at the ranch, even if I wanted to, would only delay the inevitable.

"It doesn't matter what happens to me." Fallon's shoulders slumped. "Losing the ranch will kill her anyway."

She sat down on the edge of the bed, face in her hands. It wasn't until her shoulders started moving up and down that I realized she was crying.

A lump formed in my throat. I forced my feet forward and placed an unsteady hand on the top of her head. "You may not believe it now, Fallon, but I swear this is for the best."

She jerked away from me, full of fire and loathing. "Losing our family's heritage will *never* be what's best. Spence would be disgusted with you. *I'm* disgusted with you."

Even though I'd always known she didn't see me as the

hero of her story, those words still stabbed and sliced their way across my heart, carving at old wounds that had routinely been broken open and scabbed over. They'd heal again.

"I have business here tomorrow I can't get away from, but I'll fly you home on Monday. In my jet. We'll leave the Cessna in the hangar here until I can trust you not to take it out on your own again."

"Don't you even care that Spence was murdered?!"

That was what she'd come to tell me. Flew off on her own in a goddamn four-seater plane that was forty years old to tell me she thought my brother had been murdered by someone, maybe even her uncle—which was just as ridiculous as her flying by herself had been.

"The investigation ruled it an accident, Ducky."

"Don't call me that! I'm not some four-year-old who will think it's sweet. Spence would never have overturned the tractor, because he would never have taken it up on that crumbling hillside!"

"We all make mistakes. Even the best of us."

And Spencer had been the best of us, certainly the best of the adults in Fallon's life. Far better than me, who'd fallen for my brother's childhood sweetheart while he'd been away at college, and far better than her mother, who'd used my love as a way to get back at Spence for leaving her. Instead of holding any of it against the child we'd conceived in his absence, Spence had shown Fallon an unlimited supply of love.

I'd detested him for being able to do it. For simply being able to be at my daughter's side when I was forced to leave.

I was so tired of hate running our lives, but I didn't know how to fix it. Spence would have accepted me back into the fold if I'd asked, but there was no going back for me. I couldn't return to being the man who'd once dreamed of nothing more than spending his life breeding and training horses. That man had died at age twenty-one.

"Spence didn't make mistakes like that!" Fallon insisted. "And Uncle Adam—"

"Has been there for all of you."

Fallon shook her head, arms crossing over her chest again. "He's up to something."

I frowned, thinking of the calm and put-together Adam I'd seen in his expensive suit at Spence's funeral. He'd seemed a far cry from the whiny boy I'd grown up resenting for his freedom and who'd resented me back because of the name on my birth certificate.

I sat next to Fallon, and when she shifted to put space between us, I tried not to let it wound me all over.

"Tell me what's put this notion in your head about Adam," I said softly.

She wiped her face on her T-shirt sleeve. "They were fighting that night, and Uncle Adam has been acting weird. He's been going into the vault a lot and messing with the boxes stored there."

As far as I knew, nothing overly valuable had been kept in the safe for years. It had originally been built to house the diamonds as they were mined from the kimberlite pipes on the property before they could be shipped off. Now, it stored an antique weapons collection that might be worth a few thousand dollars and piles of old files dating back to the ranch's inception. Nothing worth killing over.

And as the manager of the ranch, there might be several reasons why Adam would need to look up an old legal document. But it was clear Fallon thought something underhanded was happening, and if I could ease her mind, if I could get her off this fixation of Spence's death having been murder rather than an accident, I could at least ask Adam about it.

I needed to go back to Rivers anyway. I needed to finalize some things with the realtor and ensure Lauren was actually prepared to pack the mansion and sell off the horses and cattle. What Lauren did from there, whether she chose to go live on the acre of Hurly land with Adam or come live with me, was still up in the air.

I'd prefer them near me, and I'd offered to buy them a

house here. I'd like to be able to visit my daughter whenever I wanted—every day if possible. I'd given up fourteen years. She'd had the best childhood I could offer her up until now, but I wouldn't let her sink with the failing ranch. So if she couldn't be in Rivers, she might as well be with me.

Dread filled me at the idea of going back to the ranch, even for a day, to see to all the things that had to be done. It was why I'd put it off for weeks. I was a coward, afraid to face the hurt that had sliced through me when I'd attended Spencer's funeral. Simply stepping on the property had torn open all those scabs and scars I'd thought permanently healed, proving they weren't. Proving some scars never healed.

Not like the pale ones that had been carved into Sadie's thigh and hip.

She was only twenty-three. How old had she been when she'd been shot? How had it happened? It made me want to hunt down whoever had done it. To destroy him financially, if not physically, for trying to squash her bright light.

It wasn't my place. Sadie certainly wasn't mine to protect. In fact, she might, this very moment, be with another man who was tracing his fingers over those scars and asking her about them. I didn't know why that thought made me so furious. Made me feel achy and out of control in a way no woman had made me feel in a very long time.

But control was what had made me the man I was.

So, I pushed aside every thought I had of the vixen.

One thing was sure, if I was thinking about hunting down and destroying people for some woman I didn't really know, then I could do more than that for the daughter I loved. I could help heal the wound my brother's death had left in her. And maybe, in doing this for Fallon, I could find a new place in her life. Maybe I could start a fledgling relationship we could grow into something more. Something that would leave me with one less regret when my life was over.

Maybe, if I worked hard enough at it, someday my daughter would forgive me for taking everything she knew and loved and replacing it with only a father she despised.

Chapter Five

Sadie

LAST NAME
Performed by Carrie Underwood

After getting back to my room last night, I'd tossed and turned, and it wasn't the bed's fault. No, my restlessness could be planted completely at Rafe's feet. My needy body hadn't been able to forget him, even after I'd attempted to finish what he'd started myself. It wasn't the same. It was as empty as my win earlier had been.

By the time I'd given up on getting any sleep and rose to get ready for my day, my eyes were bruised and my cheeks pale. I looked vaguely like I had in those first weeks after I'd been shot.

I packed my luggage and stowed it by the door, ready to leave Vegas behind after my breakfast meeting. Then, I double-checked I had the documentation and pictures I wanted in my bag and headed down to the café on the main floor of the hotel.

The glossy door of the elevator reflected back at me a completely different person than the one in the sparkly cocktail dress from the night before. I didn't even look like the uniformed dart-thrower I'd momentarily been for the competition. This image was the Sadie I knew best, wearing jeans and a plaid shirt with beat-up cowboy boots. My hat rested on my luggage upstairs, but even without it, I still screamed farm girl. I certainly wasn't any of the elegant supermodels and actresses who were normally seen at The Fortress.

The two in the opposite corner of the elevator fit into this place a thousand times better than I did. Just as they would have been a better match for Rafe Marquess last night than a twenty-three-year-old farm girl. But maybe that had been the kick for him. As if a hayseed from Tennessee could round out his portfolio of women.

I shook my head. He wasn't my concern. It didn't matter why he'd agreed to my dare or that he'd tossed me out. I wouldn't let it mess with my confidence. I was far from a hayseed. I was a business owner. A ranked dart champion. I threw back my shoulders as the doors opened, lifted my chin, and walked with purpose to the French café on the opposite end of the casino from the piano bar.

When I gave my name to the hostess, she informed me the other member of my party had already arrived, and for the first time since arranging this meeting, a hint of nerves ran through me. Gia would despise that I was meeting with Lorenzo Puzo by myself, but I was determined to follow through on our research while I was here. I was meeting with him in a public place. Nothing bad was going to happen.

Still, my palms turned sweaty as the hostess led me through the white wrought-iron tables and overstuffed benches to a table out on the veranda. The heat of the day smacked me in the face. Las Vegas in July was dry and hot, and the misters were already going in full force, causing a hazy rainbow to shimmer along the edges of the paisley-patterned umbrellas lining the patio.

A man in his forties was waiting at the table as we arrived, and he stood to greet me. He wore a custom-made suit that reminded me of Rafe and had a high forehead, strong Italian nose, and eyes almost the same color as his black hair. He was an inch or two below six feet and had an air about him that demanded attention. He wore a thick gold signet ring on his pinkie and a Patek Philippe watch on his wrist, screaming wealth and privilege.

He looked exactly like every television stereotype I could come up with for a mob boss, and I barely controlled a smirk at that thought.

"Ms. Hatley, it's a pleasure to finally put a face to the name," he said, sticking out a hand.

When I put mine in his, he turned it, kissing the knuckles suavely before releasing them. Not once did I feel even a hint of a spark, let alone the thundering blaze I'd felt with Rafe, and I was pretty sure it had nothing to do with the fact that Lorenzo and I might be related in some fourth-cousin kind of way. It was simply because the jerk last night had singed my nerve endings, and I hadn't been able to heal them yet.

"I feel the same way, Mr. Puzo. And please, call me Sadie."

"And you must call me Lorenzo," he said, holding my chair and tucking me in before returning to his seat.

A waiter was at my elbow before I could even pick my menu up, reciting the specials and asking if he could get a drink started for me. Once he'd darted away with our coffee order, I looked over at Lorenzo to find him slowly assessing me, and it sent a hint of trepidation through my veins.

He asked how I was enjoying Las Vegas, if it was my first time there, and what my plans were. Innocuous talk about nothing. Pleasantries that had me returning similarly mundane questions about his life in Vegas that he evaded answering as if I was asking top-secret information.

There was something smooth and not quite normal about the way he moved and talked. Every action he took seemed almost imperceptible, as if he was somehow doing it all without even flexing a nerve. I wasn't even sure he'd blinked the entire time we'd been sitting there, and I found my nerves jangling even more.

After our breakfast had been delivered, and I'd cut into the savory crepe, he said, "After you reached out to me, I dug into the old family albums to see what I could find, and then I discussed the situation with my great aunt."

"And what did you find?" I asked, excitement automatically seeping into my voice.

This entire adventure to the West Coast had been prompted by things I'd found while sorting through Uncle Phil's attic after he died. I'd carefully gone through over a century's worth of debris, researching and pricing each item so the family could decide what to do with them.

When I'd gotten to the trunks of old movie props our Great-grandma Carolyn and Great-grandpa Harry had brought back from their time working in a Hollywood studio, I'd almost just tossed it all into the donation pile. But something had stopped me. Maybe it was simply the idea of them giving up their dreams to return to Tennessee, raise a child, and work at the family bar that had hit too close to home. Regardless, it had me spending time on each of the items in the trunk.

When I'd found the velvet bag with the set of jewels my family had always considered well-designed pastes, I'd done the same thing I'd done with all the items. I started with a reverse-image search.

It was the tiara and not the layered necklaces, bracelets, or earrings that had gotten a hit. I hadn't been surprised to find it in an article entitled "The Most Fabulous Jewels of Iconic Movies" as Gemma had loaned the tiara to a movie crew when they'd been filming in Willow Creek. What *had* surprised me was finding the entire set had also been worn in a movie back in the 1940s. Below the image of the glamorous '40s film star draped in the diamonds was a footnote that listed the gems as rare California diamonds on loan from a private collection.

While the note about Gemma's tiara had the same note about a private collection, seeing it on a movie that might have had Great-grandma Carolyn working on it had made the hair on the back of my neck raise as if someone had walked over my grave. With a sinking feeling, I'd wondered if the jewels were actually something much more than we'd ever imagined. Something that should have been in a safe instead of a velvet bag tucked in an attic trunk.

I'd taken them to our local jeweler, and he'd practically twittered with excitement. He said the stones were priceless yellow and white diamonds from a rare California mine that was no longer in existence. In their platinum and gold Art Deco settings, the gems were worth hundreds of thousands of dollars.

After the shock had worn off, my mind had started reeling

with ideas for what we could do with the money if we sold them. Things we could do for our town and our community. Ways we could celebrate our heritage. Ways Great-grandma Carolyn and I might both get back a piece of our dreams we'd given up.

But my ideas had been followed by doubts. How had Great-grandma Carolyn afforded the jewelry? It wasn't like the McFlannigans were millionaires. And if she'd had something worth so much money, wouldn't she have sold them to help out in the lean times we'd experienced?

Those doubts had me digging through old family albums, Bibles, and documents, trying to find out more about her and Harry. I hadn't been able to find a single legal document on Great-grandma Carolyn. Not a birth certificate or driver's license. Not even her marriage certificate to Harry. It was pure chance that the back of one of the old photos of her had listed her maiden name as Puzo.

I'd reached a dead end on what I could do on my own, and still not wanting to take it to the entire family yet, I'd gotten Gia involved. My sister-in-law used her old resources from her NSA days to scour the internet. They'd helped us narrow down a list of Puzo families Great-grandma Carolyn might have been related to who'd also lived in and around California in the thirties and forties. Unfortunately, the bulk of those Puzos were in Las Vegas and were part of a mafia family who'd run the town from its inception.

With possible ties to such a notorious crime family, it had made Gia and I wonder if Carolyn had actually been a jewel thief. Someone who'd stolen incredibly priceless gems from a movie studio set while they'd been on loan.

That had turned any joy, any hope I'd had of selling the jewelry, into ash. We'd have to find who they really belonged to and return them. Except, I hadn't wanted to tell Mama her grandmother had been a thief tied to a mafia family—not without proof anyway.

So, I'd set out to find the truth, regardless of Gia's warnings.

I wasn't sure meeting with the current head of the Puzo

family was the way to get answers. But I had to try. And if Great-grandma Carolyn *had* been related to them, they might know who the jewels belonged to. They might even belong to them. Regardless, they might be able to tell me why she'd never even mentioned her family to anyone in Willow Creek.

Lorenzo scrutinized me the entire time I swung back and forth between excitement and dread, waiting for him to tell me what he'd found out about Carolyn.

Finally, he tossed me a bone, saying, "It seems we did have a great-aunt named Carolyn who disappeared in the early '40s."

Butterflies banged around in my chest. "We couldn't find a birth certificate for her in any of our belongings or on any of the government sites."

"Many women in those days gave birth at home. Immigrants, who weren't sure of their legal status, didn't always fill out the appropriate paperwork."

"Did you find out anything more about her?" I asked.

"My great-aunt told me she dreamed of working in the movie business and ran off to Hollywood."

My heart leaped. It had to be her. The coincidence of being in Hollywood was just too great. But why had she left California? Had Great-grandpa Harry missed his family and wanted to return to Tennessee, so she'd gone with him? Had they been as wildly in love as the stories I'd heard? And why had she never reached out to anyone in her family here in Las Vegas ever again? Were the jewels why? Had she really stolen them?

"And that's it? No one saw or talked to her again?" I asked.

"Something distasteful happened, it seems. Aunt Ada said her name wasn't to be mentioned. In those days, it typically meant a woman got knocked up outside of marriage or ran off with the wrong type."

I couldn't help bristling. "I don't think my great-grandfather was the wrong type."

His lips barely twitched. "Why is this important to your family now?"

Something about his tone set my nerves jangling once more. I'd originally intended to tell Lorenzo about the diamonds and ask if they'd belonged to Carolyn or her family. Instead, I bit my tongue. Gia's sources had said the Puzo family had cleaned up their act, but she couldn't be sure they just hadn't gotten really good at hiding their criminal enterprises.

I didn't want to offer up the jewels and possibly put a target on our backs if they rightfully belonged to Carolyn. If they were ours, I hoped to convince my family to use them to fund a special kind of Hatley and McFlannigan legacy in Willow Creek. A way I could leave a mark on this earth that might be different than the one I'd originally planned but would still be meaningful.

"Was the Puzo family wealthy back then?" I asked.

When his eyes narrowed at the question, I realized I'd messed up and he thought I was after their money. I attempted to soothe his concerns. "I don't care if they were. My family doesn't need money or anything. That isn't why I'm here. I just…there were some things I found while going through the attic of the house where she lived, and it made me curious. Why did she go to Hollywood? Why did she and Great-grandpa Harry leave California? Why was there no mention of her side of the family at all?" I was babbling. It was a habit I had when I was nervous. I took a deep breath, slowed down, and said, "I guess I just wanted to understand my roots."

He set his knife and fork down smoothly and slowly, in that same way that gave the impression he hadn't moved at all. "Roots are important. Traditions as well as the wishes of our ancestors. I'm afraid that's all I can tell you about her."

It was easy to tell that his "all I can tell you about her" wasn't all he *knew* about her. The congeniality he'd had during our entire conversation completely disappeared, leaving behind the tension of a coiled snake. Adrenaline pumped through me as I wondered just how much of a mistake I'd made in meeting with him.

Before I could respond, a shadow crossed over our table, and we both looked up to find Rafe glaring down at us. Not just glaring but shooting lightning bolts from those chocolate depths.

My heart stopped.

By the time he spoke, the simmering anger I'd glimpsed had disappeared back behind that emotionless wall he'd tossed at me last night. "How mad is your boss that you didn't get anything from me?"

Confusion spiraled as I realized the dry, scornful question was meant for me.

"Excuse me?" I asked, hating that I sounded breathless and unsure.

"Do you know each other?" Lorenzo asked, glancing between Rafe and me with a raised brow, interest sparking in his eyes.

"Not as well as she would have liked." Rafe's tone was as disparaging as it was icy.

I wasn't one to blush easily, but I felt my face heat as his words suddenly merged into a single, ugly thought. He was insinuating I'd tried to sleep with him for Lorenzo. For what reason? Blackmail? My embarrassment turned to disgust and then to fury.

"What the hell?" I hissed. "If anyone should be pissed about how things ended last night, it should be me!"

Lorenzo chuckled. It was dark and somehow incredibly satisfied and drew Rafe's gaze from me to him.

"You're not allowed on the premises, Puzo. Not on any of my properties."

Rafe's voice was calm but held a hint of threat that sent my flight instincts into overdrive. Lorenzo, however, seemed to get enjoyment out of it. He waved his hand at me and said, "But I was invited by the lovely lady."

Suddenly, that unease and trepidation that had been growing since I'd first sat down with Lorenzo morphed into something much larger. True fear. I'd stepped into the middle of something nasty between him and Rafe. Something that ended up putting the unsuspected heroine in the movies in danger. Or worse, got the unsuspected pawn killed off like a

Star Trek red shirt.

"The ruling the judge made was very clear after your attempt at corporate sabotage. Neither you nor your employees are allowed on Marquess Enterprises property," Rafe said. "But please, stay so I can call security and have Steele throw you out. He'd take great pleasure in it."

Lorenzo smiled and put his napkin down slowly and methodically before pushing back his chair. I rose at the same time, shaky and unsteady. Before I realized what he was doing, Lorenzo had leaned in and kissed my cheek. Way too personal. Way more than I'd expected. And entirely for Rafe's benefit. I stepped back automatically, nearly running into Rafe.

"It was a pleasure, Sadie. I'll be in touch soon." He sauntered slowly and carelessly away before I could even respond, his movements still a lesson in efficiency. Smooth and confident.

Rafe's hand closed around my bicep, and he jerked me closer to him. That flash of anger appeared again as our chests collided, and those damn sparks that had ignited yesterday flared right back to life at his touch. Even furious and glaring, he still caused delicious tension to sweep through my stomach.

By the time he spoke, he had himself in control again. The glacial edge was back as he said, "You tell Puzo he will never be able to blackmail me. And if he keeps sending his minions, I will file new charges."

I pushed against the solid wall of his chest, trying to put distance between us. "I don't know what the hell is going on between you two. This was the first time I've ever met Lorenzo. My business with him has nothing to do with you."

He didn't let me escape. If anything, the grip on my bicep increased as he scoured my face, weighing my truthfulness. "If that's true, I'd only advise you to stay away from him. Puzo will destroy you and everyone you care about and celebrate the fall. Go back to Tennessee, Sadie, and keep your nose out of my business."

He finally let me go, and I stumbled back, noticing for the first time people were trying not to stare at the scene we'd caused.

I rubbed my arm, and his gaze settled on it, a flicker of something that might have been remorse drifting over him before it settled back into his unreadable mask. Fear and regret and irritation all mixed inside me, but I refused to let him see it. I hid every emotion I could as I said calmly, "I was checking out today anyway. So, don't worry, you'll never see me again."

Then, I whirled around, weaved through the tables, and headed directly for the elevators. I felt him watching me the entire time. Felt the look burning through the back of my skull.

I was close to tears again, like I had been last night when I'd left the penthouse. And I hated that he was able to evoke these intense emotions in me. Hated him for interrupting my discussion with Lorenzo before I could set it to rights. Hated the cold disparagement he'd sent reeling in my direction when I'd seen the real him last night. That Rafe, the one nearly overcome with passion as we'd kissed, had been the true him. I'd almost bet my bar on it.

But I wouldn't. I didn't need to because I'd never see him again.

Thank God I hadn't slept with him.

Except, it wasn't relief that washed over me at that thought. Instead, it was an unspeakable sadness I didn't understand. As if I'd lost something that had never been mine.

Chapter Six

Rafe

DEVIL YOU KNOW
Performed by Tyler Braden

As I watched Sadie storm through the tables without once looking back, the betrayal I'd felt upon finding her dining with Lorenzo Puzo rose its furious head and beat against my rib cage.

When I'd first seen her on the patio, my heart had leaped with pleasure. Watching her in the warm sunlight, cast in the rainbow from the misters, I'd been overcome with a craving I'd thought long since buried. Ridiculous needs and wants flooding me and making me think of all the ways I could make it right between us after sending her from the penthouse the night before.

Those thoughts, those cravings, were confusing and unwanted, just like every emotion I'd experienced in her presence. Emotions I'd sworn I'd never have again for any woman. Only my child was going to stake a claim on my heart. And yet, Sadie had whispered things to my soul that had it dragging itself out of the locked box I'd exiled it to, clamoring to come alive.

I'd just taken an involuntary step toward her when I'd realized who was sitting across from her. Acid had burned through me, and any thought of finishing what we started had disappeared in a howling rage, screaming of her deception. I hadn't felt so double-crossed since I'd seen the ring on Lauren's finger that wasn't mine. Or maybe since I'd felt the slice of a knife in a dark alley.

The damned devil inside me laughed. He'd warned me, hadn't he? Or had he provoked me? Either way, it was clear what I'd thought she'd felt wasn't real. It was clear Puzo had put her up to it. I wasn't sure what he'd thought he'd get out of sending her into my bed, but he had something up his sleeve. Otherwise, he would never have met with her in my place, just like I'd never meet with someone in his.

When I'd confronted them, it had taken everything I had to throttle back my emotions and hide them behind the blank wall I was comfortable living behind. I refused to give them more than they'd already received from me. But my conscience had twisted at Sadie's shocked expression when I'd slammed my accusations at them. Doubts had wiggled in more when Puzo had looked entirely too pleased at the realization I knew Sadie, as if he'd received an unexpected benefit.

Unease settled in my chest as the hurt and anger on Sadie's face replayed in my mind. Had I overreacted? But what other business could she have had with them? How would a small-town bar owner who lived across the country even know Puzo? It could all have been some twisted coincidence, but I didn't believe in coincidences. Not like this.

What pissed me off almost more than seeing them together was the fact that, in giving him my anger and letting the doubts about her eat at me, I'd allowed him to step beyond my walls to mess with my head once more.

I pulled my phone from my pocket as I made my way through the restaurant, eyes lingering on Sadie waiting for the elevator. In jeans and a plaid shirt, she looked as equally enticing as she had in her sparkly dress. The curves of her body were still on display, this time in a way that made me want to toss her on a pile of hay instead of up against glass.

The head of my security, and my best friend, picked up on the first ring. "Steele."

"Puzo just left the café. I want you to trace every step he made inside my casino."

"We didn't get an alert," Steele said, irritation and concern laced through his words. Jim Steele had been at my side through the worst of my experiences with Puzo and understood just what it meant that he'd been in my place.

"I want to know why. Now." I hung up before he could respond.

Sadie got into the elevator with another couple, and my teeth ground together so hard pain shot up my jaw. The betrayal I felt should have left nothing but disgust in its wake, and instead, every damn nerve was still alive from when I'd yanked her to me on the veranda. My body yearned for the release I hadn't gotten the night before. Hungered for the sweet taste of her lips that had bled into me like an addiction. Honey and bourbon and fire. A flavor I'd never forget.

I tugged at the sleeves of my suit jacket before heading to the elevators, punching in the code that would take me to the executive suites and my office. I'd barely closed the office door behind me when my phone rang. *Lauren.* I debated sending it to voicemail for the third time that morning, but putting her off wasn't going to prevent us from having the conversation we needed to have.

My words were clipped as I answered, "I'm busy."

"Damn it, Rafe. At least tell me she's safe." Lauren's voice shook with fear and anger.

It took me too long to realize the truth—that Fallon hadn't called her mother. And more emotions I loathed bled in. Frustration. Remorse. "I didn't realize she hadn't called you last night."

"I didn't even know she was gone until this morning! And then she didn't pick up." Panic wafted through the ire. "I finally pinged her phone in Vegas. You should have called me as soon as she arrived!"

And maybe if I hadn't been so shocked to find out my fourteen-year-old daughter had flown herself to Vegas from California, if I hadn't been drowning in desire that I couldn't shake, I might have thought to do just that. More likely, I would have texted her, because hearing Lauren's voice was always a prick to my conscience. To my soul. Something I avoided at all costs. But now, the accusation in her tone just added to the rage I was still feeling over Puzo being in my hotel, over seeing Sadie seated next to him, chatting away with a damn smile that lifted higher on one side than the other.

"Why the hell didn't you know she'd left?" I demanded. "She took the goddamn plane, Lauren! Flew by herself, landed, and got a CarShare to the hotel like she'd done it a million times. Do you know what could have happened to her?!"

My fist hit the top of the black lacquered desk, leaving fingerprints on the shiny surface.

"Oh my God! She took the Cessna?" A sob broke over the line, and I immediately felt like an ass. Five months. Spence had only been gone five months, and Lauren was still drowning in grief. But we could have lost Fallon. We could have lost our little girl. My heart contracted at the mere thought.

My chest was a writhing viper's den of emotions I despised. Where had the control I prided myself on disappeared to in the last twenty-four hours?

Somehow, I'd lost it in a sea of Sadie and a tide of regret over Fallon.

"Where were you?" I snarled. "How did you not even know she left?"

"I took a s-sedative," Lauren choked on the words. "It's the only way I've been able to s-sleep without him." Another sob broke before she added on, "I won't take them again. I swear to God I won't."

I ran a hand through my hair and sank down in the oversized black leather chair that had been custom-designed to fit me ergonomically. Money I'd thrown around like it was water, simply because I had it to spend. Because I was still proving to myself and everyone in this business that I wasn't the farm boy from California who knew nothing except how to tame horses.

"I'm keeping the Cessna in my hangar in Vegas. She won't be able to do it again."

"I don't understand what she thought she could achieve by doing this." Lauren was slowly gaining control again, and I tried to do the same. We'd always been calm when discussing Fallon. Maybe because I'd never demanded more of my daughter's life than Lauren was willing to give. Or maybe because we'd wanted to make things easy for the child we'd recklessly created together. Somehow, without a single word, we'd agreed she wouldn't have to carry the burden of the love triangle that had torn the adults in her life apart.

And yet, she still had.

"She's got some strange idea that—" If I told Lauren that Fallon thought her brother was involved in Spence's death, it might send her over the edge again, and it was a ridiculous notion I was sure had no veracity. So instead, I told her the one truth we already knew. "She could change my mind about selling the ranch."

Lauren was quiet for way too long. "She needs this place, Rafe. We both do."

My voice was tight as I responded, "I survived without it. You will too."

"Spence would hate you for it."

"He already hated me."

"No. He really didn't. You were the only one who had hate in your veins." She sounded so tired she could barely say the words.

I felt equally exhausted, from the same old argument that neither of us would win. I'd destroyed our family because I'd taken what I wanted—what I'd known had belonged to Spence—and tried to make it mine. Then, when it all went to hell, I took the portion of my inheritance that was due to me and ripped it away from the estate so I could build my empire.

And the ranch had suffered because of it. It had staggered under the weight of the interest from the loan Spencer had taken out to give me my share. I hadn't known it was struggling, and in those early years, even if I had known how hard things were, I wouldn't have cared. Even now, there was a part of me raising my fist in the air and saying, "See! You'd needed me."

I turned to look out the windows at the Vegas Strip. At the town that had taken me in and given me refuge when my home had been off-limits. I'd been dazzled by the decadence. I'd thought I'd found something that could surpass what I'd lost. Something greater. But the constant restlessness that existed in my soul after the shine of each new achievement wore off was whispering to me lately that I'd been wrong.

The man-made mirage of Vegas could never match the beauty Mother Nature had crafted in my childhood home. The hills and valleys and waterfalls of the ranch were pure. In Vegas, manufactured splendor flickered in and out with the neon lights, disappearing with the dawn and leaving behind the sour taste of shame.

As much as I loathed to admit it, even the stunning architecture and elegant interiors of The Fortress were just more phony façades hiding the dirt and filth and crime that still existed below the surface. Filth like Lorenzo Puzo and his mob family, who'd shown me, firsthand, the evil that still existed in this city.

I turned away from the windows and looked down at the calendar opened on my laptop and the back-to-back meetings that filled my days. Irritation had me grinding my teeth. Not only at how my week had been blown apart, but at the desire stirring deep inside me to see the ranch again, to breathe fresh air, and take a long ride across flower-studded fields. My tone was sharp when I said, "I have meetings I can't move today, but I'll bring her home tomorrow."

"I understand why she did it, Rafe…but God…" She inhaled deeply. "I know she's hurting too, but we have to hold her accountable for this. There has to be consequences."

"I grounded her. Told her she couldn't leave the penthouse. I even took away her key card and said the cameras would alert me if she walked out of the suite."

"Will they?" Worry returned to her voice. No matter what had passed between Lauren and me, she'd been a good and loving mom. Just like Spence had been a good and loving father. A better dad than I ever would have been, even if I'd stayed in Rivers.

"Not right away, but she doesn't know that."

"She'll figure it out. She's smarter than even you," Lauren said, the backhanded compliment settling in my chest.

I didn't feel smart these days. I'd built an empire but had been unable to heal my family. I'd become one of the youngest billionaires in the bar business and still allowed a farm girl from Tennessee to just about undo me.

"We'll be back tomorrow sometime," I said brusquely to Lauren.

"Fine." She prickled at my terseness but softened, saying, "Thank you for keeping her safe."

But her words only served to raise my hackles more. "She's my daughter too."

"I know. I just…" She sniffled again. "I've been failing her since Spence died. I haven't… I don't know how to reach her…and I haven't really tried. I was—" She cut herself off, her breathing erratic, but her voice was strong and sturdy as she said, "It doesn't matter. I'll fix it. She's all that matters."

"You lost the love of your life," I said, forcing my voice to gentle. "Try not to beat yourself up too hard."

"And she lost her fath—"

Her unfinished sentence tore through me.

"I have to go."

"Rafe…"

"I'll see you tomorrow." I hung up before she could apologize for stating the simple truth, one I'd thought hundreds of times myself.

I sat down and pulled my laptop toward me. I needed to get ready for my meeting in thirty minutes. I had a list of things to review with the operations manager, including how every single floral arrangement in the hotel needed to be replaced. The ones in the café today had been in even worse shape than the ones by the piano bar last night.

But thoughts of the café only caused Puzo's pleased expression to come flooding back in and, along with it, Sadie's pissed-off shock. I closed the calendar app and found the app my assistant had used to handle the dart tournament entries. I pulled up Sadie's form and then clicked over to the employee background check software we used when hiring.

As soon as the data came tumbling back in, relief eased over my shoulders. She was exactly who she'd said she was—the youngest member of the Hatley family, with a bar in her name in some small town in the northeastern mountains of Tennessee.

The birthdate and the image on her driver's license proved just how young Sadie really was. Too damn young for me. Definitely too young for Puzo, who was another five years older than me. So, what had she wanted with him? How had they met? I couldn't see him wanting to invest in a tiny Tennessee bar that barely operated in the black. It wasn't his style at all.

Why the hell did I care?

Disgusted with myself, I closed the app and returned to my calendar. I'd handle the meeting with the operations manager about the florist, and then, I had a video call with my Far East operations manager to discuss the clubs in Japan and Singapore. It might be the middle of the night in Tokyo, but my business rarely slept, just like the city I'd made my home. Just like I rarely did. It suited me fine on most days. Kept me busy. Filled the void.

But I also had Fallon upstairs waiting, and when she was here, I always tried to finish early to give her as much of my time as possible. While this hadn't been a planned visit, I'd still do whatever I could to wrap things up so she wouldn't be alone with her thoughts and her worries and her grief.

♫ ♫ ♫

When I returned to the penthouse that afternoon, the place reeked of pizza, and it made my stomach turn. It was one of my least favorite foods, and Fallon knew it. It was her way of punishing me the same way I was punishing her by having locked her in the suite.

She was lying on the couch with the comforter from her bedroom covering her. The pizza box was on the glass coffee table, leaving grease and crumbs on the pristine surface. A soda can was leaving a ring, sitting next to two others that had already left their marks. My jaw ticked at the carelessness of it.

As I stepped into the living room, Fallon raised a brow uncannily like mine, picked up the soda, took a long drink, and then slammed it down on the table. She was daring me to say something, daring me to react to the mess she'd purposefully created, knowing I disliked it as much as I disliked pizza.

Instead, I took off my suit jacket and laid it carefully on the back of an armchair before joining her on the sofa. I had to shove the comforter aside to do so, but I wanted to be close to her. Hoping somehow to reach her. To somehow close the widening gap between us. I glanced up at the show she'd paused. Two teens kissing. Damn, did I dislike that.

"What are you watching?" I asked, keeping my tone as neutral as possible.

She huffed. "Are you going to tell me what I can and can't watch now too? You used to be the fun parent."

I had been, but it had only been out of desperation. I'd needed to build as many positive memories with her as I possibly could in the short amount of time we'd spent together each year.

"Can't I ask what you're watching without it being more than that?"

"*Buffy the Vampire Slayer*," she said reluctantly.

It was my turn to raise a brow. I knew the show but mostly by name. While it had a cult following, it had never been my thing, especially not when it had originally aired when I'd been a kid. Growing up on the ranch, there'd always been too much to do, too much I'd rather be doing than watch TV.

"What got you started on a show older than you?" I asked.

"She's badass." She looked at me as if I'd scold her for cussing, and when I didn't remark, she kept going. "Her dad isn't in the picture, and her mom is clueless, dealing with her own things, but Buffy doesn't let that stop her from killing vampires and defending the entire world."

I barely held back my snort at the obvious parallels she'd

made to her own life.

"Would have been nice to know you didn't talk to your mom last night," I said, changing the subject.

"Do you know how long it took her to realize I was even gone?" she asked bitterly.

Too long. "You can't possibly understand what she's going through. Maybe, someday, you'll love someone so much that you feel like they're the limb you never knew you were missing, and you'll start to appreciate it. But the only way you'd truly get it is if, God forbid, something happens to rip that person from you. Even then, you might not really get it because Spence and Lauren…" I swallowed hard. "They loved each other from the time they played tag in the barn as toddlers. They spent a lifetime loving each other."

She rolled her eyes. "Yeah, yeah. I've heard the story. But Mom obviously didn't love Spence too much. She had sex with *you*!" I didn't know which disgusted her more, the thought of us having sex or the perceived betrayal of Spence.

I didn't really want to be talking sex with my daughter at all. But she was watching it on television, probably reading about it, and for sure she'd had discussions in school about it. The messed-up triangle that was her parentage was likely to be even more confusing these days with all the information being tossed at her and the mixed signals her hormones were sparking.

"We all made mistakes," I said quietly. "But you were never one of them."

"Spence didn't," she said determinedly.

"Even Spencer," I said, trying to hold back the hurt that came from knowing just how much she'd idolized my brother.

She shook her head.

"He ended things with your mom and left her heartbroken. It wasn't until after he found out about us that he admitted it was a mistake and wished he could have taken it back."

Fallon looked away, picking at the comforter with fingernails painted bright teal. She was a girl. A teenage girl. And I didn't know what to do with her now. It had been easy when she'd been younger. I could buy her toys and ice cream and go to the movies or take her to a theme park or the beach. We'd made sandcastles and eaten junk food until our stomachs hurt when she was little and learned how to surf together when she was older.

Now, she wanted things I couldn't give her.

She wanted Spencer back. I gladly would have traded my life for his if I could.

And that thought nearly rendered me speechless. I'd spent so much time pushing thoughts of my brother away that it was hard to accept that simple truth. He should have been the one to survive. Not me.

"Of course you'd say that," Fallon said. "You'd love to lay the blame at his feet. You hated him."

"It's more complicated than that," I told her.

She ignored my response, saying, "Isn't that why you made me call him Spence instead of Dad? Because you hated that he was more of a father to me than you ever were?"

The dart she'd intended to land found home.

Had I done it on purpose? Had I used my daughter as a weapon against my brother and her mother? Maybe. I'd been screwed up for a long time. The truth was, I was still screwed up when it came to my family.

"Hating me isn't going to bring him back," I said as gently as possible. "But if that helps you, I'm happy to be your punching bag. I'm happy to be whatever you need."

Her mouth dropped open, and her eyes instantly welled. Her tears hurt me more than the dart she'd landed.

Her throat bobbed before she pulled herself together in a way that made me proud. Her voice was steady when she said, "I already told you what I need. I need to keep the ranch and to prove Spence was murdered."

My busy schedule had already been screwed up by having to take her home tomorrow. Staying at the ranch for the next week would mess with it more, but I'd do it. I'd do it and settle this for Fallon once and for all. "Fine."

"What?" she gasped.

"Let me qualify that. We're not keeping the ranch." I had to look away when her light dimmed. "But I'll stay for the week, and I'll investigate what happened. Me, Fallon. Not you. I'll share with you what I find out, and if it's nothing, you have to agree to let this go."

Her face turned stubborn—a look I knew well because I'd seen it in the mirror my entire life.

"But—"

"This isn't up for debate. Either we do this my way, and it's over when I say it's over, or we don't do it at all."

She met my gaze with a brave one. She was so damn strong it floored me. Her chin went up. "I agree. But only because I *know* what you'll find."

While she was talking, I reached over and grabbed the remote from her lap.

"Now, if I'm going to be forced to watch this crap, you better catch me up on what's happening and order me something besides crappy pizza."

She stared for a moment, and then a soft laugh escaped her, quiet and sweet and so like the laugh she'd had as a little girl that it almost brought tears to *my* eyes. It wasn't fair she'd been born into this screwed-up triangle. Wasn't fair that she'd lost the single best person in her life. And it wasn't fair I was going to sell the ranch out from under her. But I promised myself I'd find ways to fill the voids these losses had created. I'd turn her life around, even if I had to fight Lauren every inch of the way to make it happen.

Chapter Seven

Sadie

VELVET HEARTBREAK
Performed by Carrie Underwood

It took over half the drive from Las Vegas to Rivers in California for the steam to stop flowing from my ears at Rafe's high-handedness, his gross assumptions, and Lorenzo's cheek kiss that had purposefully fueled the misconception further. The high desert outside the windows of the subcompact rental, with its harder-than-a-rock seat, did nothing to distract me. Mile after mile of the same bland landscape made it feel as if I was going in circles instead of a straight line from one state into the next.

Once the scenery changed to fields of crops, I was finally able to lose some of the humiliation and anger I'd felt leaving The Fortress. The morning hadn't been an utter failure. I'd confirmed some of the things Gia and I had suspected about Great-grandma Carolyn.

I still had questions, maybe even more now, but whatever I needed to learn from the man who might be my long-lost cousin would only be done via messages and email from here on out. I wouldn't put myself in the same position of meeting with him alone again. I didn't need Rafe Marquess's scathing warning any more than I needed Gia's reports to know something wasn't right with Lorenzo. My instincts had screamed it.

For two seconds, I let myself wonder what had happened between the two of them that had caused such fury to appear in Rafe's chocolate eyes at the sight of Lorenzo sitting in his restaurant. It had felt like more than just a business rivalry. It had felt intensely personal. Had they fought over a woman? That pricked at something that felt, stupidly, like jealousy, but it would explain Rafe's accusations.

Even though it had nothing to do with me, I couldn't help being curious. It was my nature to pick at secrets and mysteries. It was what had led me on this wild goose chase to California after all, but I couldn't afford to try to unravel whatever existed between the two men.

This was one mystery I had to leave back in Vegas with Rafe Marquess—a man I never planned to see again. For the life of me, I couldn't figure out why that thought still stung so much, but it did.

Nearly five hours later, the farmland turned into hills that turned into mountains dotted with trees, and the view improved my mood further. A rushing river played peekaboo with the two-lane road, and I got a glimpse of a bright-blue lake that disappeared in the rearview mirror, replaced with craggy, white mountains and enormous sequoia trees.

I crested a hill and descended into the sweet little town of Rivers. The old buildings and wooden sidewalks reminded me so much of home that I felt another pang of homesickness. Willow Creek might not have the national parks on our doorstep to draw the tourists in like Rivers, but people still flocked to our charming restaurants and antique stores. And if I had my way, we'd have one more thing to draw them in.

I hadn't spoken my plans aloud to a single soul because I wasn't sure I could make them a reality. How could a twenty-three-year-old, with no college degree under her belt and minimal experience running a business, hope to launch a world-class performing arts center?

And yet, once I'd had the idea, I hadn't been able to shake it. It was a way we could use the jewels for something good. Not only to give something back to our community but to leave a mark that said Carolyn Puzo-McFlannigan hadn't given up her Hollywood dreams for nothing…that I hadn't given mine up for nothing either.

I just had to make sure the jewels were really ours to sell, which was why I'd made the five-and-a-half-hour trip from Vegas to the Harrington Ranch where the diamonds were originally mined. After some research, Gia and I suspected, if the jewels didn't belong to Carolyn or the Puzos, they might have belonged to the Harringtons themselves. So, I'd reached out to them via the ranch's website, asking about the diamonds and indicating I had some from the original mine I'd like to talk to them about.

The Harringtons' business manager had responded, and when I'd asked if he could meet with me in Vegas, he'd said it was impossible for him to get away at the moment. There'd been a death in the family, and things were a bit chaotic. I understood that all too well after making my way through all the paperwork and emotions Uncle Phil's death had left in its wake.

Several miles past Rivers, I finally reached the turn-off for the ranch tucked between mountains that rose up on either side. The dirt road wound through fields of bluebells and yarrow where cattle grazed lazily in the summer heat. Beef cattle were the ranch's primary income now, although it hadn't always been the case. The fate of the ranch had changed wildly in the last century when diamonds had suddenly been found in the hills, and then, just as quickly, the mines had dried up.

An enormous stone wall made of river rock came into view with a metal gate arching over the road that was open in welcoming. Passing through it felt like entering castle grounds, and the house that appeared beyond it only added to the mirage. Curls and flourishes littered the tall gables and towers that made up the golden Victorian manor. It would have shocked me to find the wannabe-English castle in the middle of the California foothills if I hadn't already seen the house on the ranch's website.

The circular drive was empty of vehicles, but I spotted a sign for guest parking and drove around back. A large gravel lot butted up against dozens of outbuildings, corrals, and a paddock filled with equipment for training trick horses. Beautifully crafted of river rock with vivid, green snow roofs, the barns would require a hefty sum to keep in such a pristine condition. It was an expense that could easily break a family. It had almost broken ours before Ryder had converted our ranch into a resort.

The Harringtons hadn't made a similar transition yet, but they'd recently started hosting weddings here. Large, elegant affairs that used the mountains, waterfalls, and flower-studded fields of the sprawling, five-thousand-acre estate as a gorgeous backdrop. As far as my family knew, that was the reason I was there. Not wanting to tell them about the diamonds yet, I'd said that I'd meet up with the Harringtons and see what they had done to draw such an exclusive, high-profile clientele to their ranch in such a short time, in hopes we could do something similar.

It wasn't a lie. The ranch's manager, Adam Hurly, had been as interested in swapping information about their wedding business for the details of how we'd transitioned our ranch into a resort as he had been about the diamonds.

Stepping out of the car, heat blasted me like opening the door of a steam furnace—hot but so dry it felt like it was sucking the moisture from my skin. It might be missing the heavy weight of the humidity we had in Tennessee, but it wasn't any less oppressive.

A gate slammed shut, and I turned to see a woman emerging from one of the paddocks. She was dressed in jeans and a T-shirt with work boots on her feet and a baseball hat on her head. A long, wavy, blond ponytail was pulled through the back. The brim of her hat shadowed her face, but when she finally closed the distance and lifted her chin, my breath caught at the raw sadness dripping from eyes a mixed color of hay and grass. She had high cheekbones, elegant brows two shades darker than her hair, and a dainty oval face. She was shorter than me, but not by much, and had the muscles that proved she worked the ranch as much as any of her employees.

On the website, there'd been a photo of her tucked up against a light-brown-haired man with their smiling, blond-haired daughter between them. They'd somehow looked both beachy Californian and down-home farmer at the same time, and love had practically wafted out of the picture.

"You must be Sadie," she said as she pulled off a work glove to extend a hand.

I took it. "And you must be Lauren."

She smiled, but it didn't once clear the shadows surrounding her. "Adam wanted to be here when you arrived, but he had some business to take care of in town that couldn't wait."

"He's been very patient with all my questions about your wedding business, and I'm very grateful he agreed to let me tag along this week. I promise I won't get in the way. In fact, I have two hands that are very used to being put to work."

"Your family runs a resort in Tennessee? A dude ranch, right?" she asked. When I nodded, she continued, "We'd been discussing converting our land for a while before Spence—" She bit back her words, swallowed hard, and looked away for a moment. When she turned back to me, that pain in her eyes seemed to have grown so large I could almost touch it. "None of us could agree on anything other than the fact that we needed to do something drastic—and soon. As Adam has been the biggest proponent of turning the place into a resort, he was pretty ecstatic when you reached out."

"It's a huge decision, but honestly, it saved us. It allowed us to keep all of our land when others around us were selling off pieces," I told her.

"But it's about more than just us, isn't it? What would it do to the hotels and businesses in town? The other bed-and-breakfasts in the area? For almost a century, the Harringtons have helped the community grow and businesses to flourish. Spence was adamant we not line our pockets at the expense of our neighbors. He'd still be against it." She wiped the back of her hand along her forehead and then gave me a tight smile. "And by Jesus, here I am, dropping half our problems at your feet the moment you step out of the car. I'm so sorry."

"Don't be, really. It's fine. I'm more than happy to talk with you about what we did and how we worked with the other businesses in town. It'll all be secondhand information, as my oldest brother was the driving force behind it, but he was happy to send me with his original business plans and the presentations he used to convince the banks it was a solid risk. Ryder said he was paying it forward after all the help he'd had. And if you have questions I can't answer, I can get them from him."

What neither Ryder nor I would share was how the person who'd assisted Ryder and my family in our plans to convert the ranch to a resort had ended up being evil. How he'd almost killed Gia and Ryder and tried to kidnap his little girl. Those things were behind us now. And they didn't change the fact that Jaime Laredo *had* helped us before it had all gone to hell.

"Why don't we get you settled," Lauren said with a wave toward the castle-like house. "And then we can take a ride over the grounds so I can show you the primary locations we use for the weddings—unless you're too tired after the drive?"

"Honestly, I'd love it. I feel like I've been cooped up for days." And I realized just how true it was. I'd spent the entirety of the days since leaving Tennessee inside, far away from the sun and the wind and the sounds of nature. I missed the early morning rides I squeezed in before heading to the bar almost as much as the physical work that kept me from obsessing over the past and the future.

Maybe that was really why I'd been so cranky on the first part of the drive. Maybe it had nothing to do with a brown-haired man who'd turned me on and pissed me off in equal measure.

I popped the trunk on the rental and grabbed my suitcase. Wheeling it over the gravel was awkward, and I realized how smart Ryder had been to pave the parking lot at our place, even though, at the time, it had seemed like a huge, unnecessary expense.

As we made our way toward the house, Lauren asked, "What airport did you fly into?"

"Vegas."

Her eyebrows lifted. "That's a long drive."

I laughed. "Longer than it looked online, but I was in Vegas for other reasons, so it made sense to drive over from there."

As she pushed the large carved doors on the front of the house open, the cool air drifted over me like a soft breeze, a welcome relief after the heat. The entryway was lined with dark wood paneling that led up to vaulted ceilings of embossed copper tiles where a chandelier dripped crystals. The staircase acted as the centerpiece with its oversized dark wood rails and red carpet lined in a classic, *Gone with the Wind* kind of way.

"No elevator," she said apologetically, heading directly for the polished stairs.

"I'm used to hauling kegs of beer at the bar and baling hay at the ranch. A suitcase isn't going to do me in," I promised.

She gave me her soft smile again. The one that still couldn't dislodge her misery. "Only another true rancher would know just how hard baling can be."

I smiled back, feeling her sadness eke over me. Adam had said there'd been a death in the family, and it had hit this woman hard. She'd cut herself off when talking about Spencer and then used his name in the past tense. My heart lurched, remembering the family photo on the website with Spencer Harrington's name below it. Loss was hard, no matter when and where it came from, but especially when it was the partner you'd chosen to be at your side. I might not know that from personal experience, but I'd watched my siblings go through it before they'd eventually found their happily ever afters.

Lauren led me up two flights of stairs to the third floor. The hall had the same dark wainscotting as the entry and was lined with thick, paneled doors. She opened one near the stairs to reveal a bright room full of antiques. The brass bed had a flowered comforter and was piled high with a rainbow of pillows. An antique armoire with scalloped edges stood against one wall, and a matching dresser with a beveled mirror was on another. Beyond it, white sheers were pulled aside to reveal the craggy mountains and winding river. A narrow door near the window was open to reveal white subway tile and a towel rack with pale-blue linens.

"We converted the closet into a small bath," she said,

waving toward the bathroom. "It limits the hanging space to the armoire, but it's nice for guests to have their own facilities."

"It's a lovely room. Do the wedding guests stay here?" I asked.

She nodded. "The bride stays in the main suite on the floor below us, and we have four other rooms we can use for the wedding party. Considering the size of the house, you'd expect us to have more space available, but we'd have to convert many of them and haven't had the money to invest. The original Harrington homestead and the old, ranch-hand bunkhouse were renovated before money grew really tight. We have twelve rooms between them, so the groom, his groomsmen, and the parents typically stay out there."

She retreated to the hallway. "Take as long as you like. When you're ready, I'll be in the sitting room. It's right off the main entrance. If you can't find it, just holler."

After she left, I took a minute to unpack. I hung some of my work clothes and the summer dress I'd also bought in Vegas in the armoire. I left the sparkly dress Rafe had broken the straps on at the bottom of the suitcase, but longing hit me in the stomach all over again thinking of the moment he'd snapped them. My body practically quivered at the memory. I'd wanted him so desperately. Desperately enough to almost beg for his touch.

Thank God we hadn't been able to finish. If remembering a heated make-out session could still cause my knees to wobble, what would the memory of having him inside me be like? It might have ruined sex for me for the rest of my life.

And why the hell was I wasting time thinking of him again?

I jerked myself out of the reverie and took my makeup bag into the small bath. With the stall shower, pedestal sink, and a toilet all but touching one another, you could tell it was a renovated closet, but it was still charming. The low ceiling made me feel like a giant when my five-foot-six-inch height was nothing more than average.

After splashing water on my face and pulling my long bob

that flirted just past my chin back into a clip, I headed for the door. Taking a ride over new terrain bursting with color and sounds and sunshine was just what I needed to forget everything that had happened in Vegas—or at least everything that had happened with a certain brown-haired, chocolate-eyed asshole. The twenty-five-thousand-dollar prize money I'd earned and a great-grandmother who might have been a jewel thief would require more thought.

Chapter Eight

Rafe

A LOT MORE FREE
Performed by Max McNown

It was later than I'd wanted to leave by the time Fallon and I headed out of the penthouse on Tuesday afternoon. I'd spent the morning firing both my hotel manager and the florist. After investigating the poorly maintained floral arrangements, I'd found out they'd lied to me about their personal relationship and were up-charging me for the flowers while pocketing the difference. This was what happened when I didn't have the time to keep a closer finger on all aspects of this business. I needed to hire a chief operating officer for Marquess Enterprises—someone I could trust. But wasn't that just the rub. Trust and me didn't come easily, and every time I took a gamble, something like this reminded me why I didn't.

Jim Steele's face appeared on my phone's screen. Thank God I had at least one person I could trust with both my life and my business.

"Have you left already?" Steele asked when I answered.

"Just heading to the elevators. What's up?"

"Can you stop by the control room on your way out?"

"I'll be right there." I hoped it didn't have anything to do with the manager and florist I'd had him walk out the door.

Fallon rolled her eyes at the detour but didn't comment.

Last night had been the first good evening we'd had together in more months than I could count. Even before Spence had died, things had grown strained between us. My daughter despised leaving the ranch every time she'd had to come see me and had started questioning all my reasons for not visiting her in Rivers.

But watching the ridiculous show, we'd been able to leave all that behind us. She'd laughed and screamed at the characters, and I'd teased and taunted her about the ridiculousness of the relationships and the impossibility of Buffy's powers. We'd followed dinner up with a fraisier cake I'd had sent up from my five-star restaurant simply because the strawberry sponge cake layered with pastry cream and topped with marzipan had always been one of Fallon's favorites.

Slowly, some of the tension had left her shoulders, and I'd marked it down as a win.

But when I'd walked back into the suite this afternoon after dealing with the hotel manager, she'd been pacing the living area with all the weight of the world having landed back on her. I wanted to tell her this was exactly the reason I was selling the ranch. She was too young to have it hanging on her already. I didn't want my daughter to limit herself, thinking she had to step into Spence's and Lauren's shoes to continue a heritage that was wrought with as much ugly as good. The estate had been founded in drama and turmoil from the moment our great-grandfather had won the ranch from Adam and Lauren's great-granddaddy in a poker match. Thousands of acres had become ours with the flip of a card.

And when the diamonds had been found and mined, turning our family into one of the wealthiest in California at the time, the Hurly family had all but declared war. They'd gone to court, fighting over whether the mineral rights had transferred along with the land in that godforsaken poker game. They'd lost that battle, and Tommy Hurly had shot himself, leaving his son to find him in the cabin he'd taken over after refusing to leave the property. In what I'm sure Great-grandpa Alasdair saw as a grand gesture, he'd carved out an acre right around the cabin, right in the middle of our property, to give to the widow and her children. Not enough to survive on. Not enough to find any of the diamonds studding the hills. But enough to call home without having to pay anything more than the property tax.

After that, Hurly's widow and their children had come to work on the ranch, and from that moment forward, there had always been a Harrington and a Hurly working on the land, side by side, twined in some sick, symbiotic relationship. One Spence and I had only added to by fighting over Lauren's hand.

Fallon would never see the truth, but selling the ranch might just rid us of the curses that had haunted our families from the very beginning. Maybe we could actually put it all behind us. Maybe we'd get a fresh start.

Maybe you just don't want to see the good that's still there, my devil taunted.

As the elevator doors opened in the basement of the hotel, I shoved that thought aside and strode down the hallway to the control room outfitted with top-of-the-line computers and equipment that allowed the security team to watch thousands of cameras around the casino. Whenever I was in Vegas, Steele made the control room his office, keeping an eye not only on the security here but the security of all my businesses around the world.

A decade older than me, Steele was a broad-shouldered, dark-haired former Navy SEAL with eyes the same color as his last name. He'd left the military due to a colossal fuckup by some bureaucrats that had cost him several members of his team and spent five years in private security before winding up running security for a casino near the alley where I'd been stabbed. He'd saved my life that night, running off the three individuals who'd attacked me.

I pointed Fallon to a chair near the front doors of the control room, far away from the cameras and activity. "Have a seat. I'll just be a minute."

She huffed but immediately took her phone out of her pocket and started scrolling. Maybe I should have confiscated it as part of her grounding, but I hadn't had the heart. She'd had enough loss this year. I couldn't take away the conversations she had with her friends on top of it.

I made my way through the desks to where Steele sat at a

long row of monitors hanging from the back wall. He was typing away at a keyboard, which seemed to be his favorite spot these days.

"Steele," I said.

He glanced up, pushed a few buttons, and the five monitors right above him flickered from their current views into Puzo's ugly mug. Between the different screens, they showed him strolling in through the side door of the casino and making his way calmly to the café. Steele let one of the videos play, and we saw the hostess lead him to the veranda where he waited for Sadie to join him.

Just the sight of her black hair swinging past her chin and those impish blue eyes dancing with life was enough to tighten every inch of my body in inappropriate ways. I could taste her all over again. I hated that I still hungered for what she'd offered before I'd had to send her away. Hated that I'd seen her with Puzo and yet still couldn't seem to get her out of my head.

Steele hit play on the video of her with Puzo, zipping through it at three-times speed until the moment I showed up at their table. Thankfully, the anger and betrayal I'd felt weren't evident on the screen. Still, Puzo had known I was upset, and my stomach rolled knowing I'd shown him those cards.

After he left, I had a firsthand look at the only real display of emotion I'd let out. Every ounce of frustration was clear in the way I'd hauled Sadie up against me and held on viciously to her arm. Regret swarmed through me.

"Care to tell me about the dame?" Steele asked.

"Is this what you brought me to see? She's no one," I said, careful to keep every emotion locked up and put away. When he raised his brow and flicked a different monitor to show Sadie and me on our way up to my penthouse Sunday night, my eye twitched with annoyance. "I'll repeat it so you hear it this time. She's no one."

"You don't take 'no one' to your suite, Marquess. You've never taken anyone but Fallon there. Hell, you don't even host parties in your home, and yet you took her. And the next day, she's all cozied up with Puzo? No wonder you were pissed."

"I've already done a background check on her."

"So have I. Sadie Hatley. Twenty-three. She won the grand prize in your dart competition. I can't find any links to her and Puzo online, but we both have eyes. We both see them sitting there having a snug little breakfast together."

It wasn't anything more than what I'd already thought, and yet every word knifed through me. "I won't ever see her again. She's probably already back in Tennessee."

"She left in a rental car just after the café incident, which is what caught my attention and why I asked you to come down."

I waited as he swiped a hand over the touch-screen monitor, bringing up another camera. This one was near the registration desk. Sadie appeared, stuffed her room key into the drop box, and headed for the revolving doors. She'd gotten all the way through it before a completely innocuous man in khakis and a green polo drifted out behind her. Another swipe of a screen brought up the parking garage. Sadie wheeled her suitcase to a blue sub-compact with a rental sticker in the rear window. She tossed the luggage in the back with ease before sliding into the driver's seat. She sat there for at least two minutes, and while we couldn't see what she was doing in the car, we could see the same man in the khakis and polo step into view. He got into a gray SUV parked across the aisle from her.

Eventually, Sadie backed out and headed down the ramp, and the man did the same.

Another touch of Steele's hand brought up the exit booth. Sadie put her ticket into the machine and the bar rose to let her out, where she was forced to stop at the red light just outside the entrance. The man in his SUV was parked on her bumper, and when the light turned green, he followed Sadie as she turned right.

Acid burned through my stomach.

It could mean nothing. Could just be a man leaving my casino at the same time as Sadie had, both of them heading down The Strip in the direction of the airport. But I knew it wasn't true. Steele wouldn't have shown it to me without a reason.

"Who is he?" I asked.

Steele tapped back to one of the screens showing Puzo sitting in the café before Sadie had arrived. It was then I realized the polo-shirted man was sitting at the table right behind him. They were back to back. It took Steele rewinding the film, enlarging it, and stopping several times before I saw it. They were talking. Puzo hid his words behind his napkin, but the man very clearly nodded in agreement, accepting orders.

"He works for Puzo?" That acid turned into a heaving, boiling pit.

"I'm still waiting on facial recognition. The man paid in cash at the café. I'm a day behind, so obviously the dishes had already been washed, so there's no chance of DNA. I double-checked the cameras, and I didn't see him touch a single thing anywhere else in the casino."

Puzo was following her, and I doubted she knew it. Debate waged war inside me. Should I tell her? It wasn't my business. If she'd gotten in bed with the devil, that was on her.

Or maybe on you, my demon cackled.

"Was the man here the night before? Did he see Sadie with me in the Marquis Club or the piano bar?"

Steele shook his head. "Not that I saw. I'll look through all the footage again, but as far as I can tell, yesterday morning was the first time he'd stepped inside The Fortress."

"Right now, we have nothing to tell her, and I have no desire to stick my nose in more Puzo business. She's not our responsibility." Even as I said it, something dark and feral and beastly inside me objected. The same animal who'd wanted to leap out of its cage when I'd first seen Sadie sitting with him. The same one who'd tried to claim her by biting her neck and baring her skin against the wall of windows in my suite.

I ignored the beast and headed for Fallon and the exit. I called back over my shoulder, "If you identify him, let me know. Otherwise, we move on."

"Marquess," Steele grunted, and I turned back. His brow

was furrowed. "She might need help."

"Not mine and not yours. She's not our business." The beast growled and banged on its cage, but I ignored it again.

Steele wasn't happy with my answer. But I'd had enough of the dark-haired vixen. I wasn't going to let her curse me more than I already was.

Fallon looked up as I passed by her. "Let's go, Ducky," I said.

She hefted her bag onto her shoulder and dragged her feet as she came to stand by me. "What did Steele want?"

"Nothing. Just a false alarm," I told her, holding the door open for her.

"Is Parker still at the Naval Academy?" Fallon asked as we stepped into the hall, and I raised my brows in surprise. I didn't know she'd kept tabs on Steele's son. My protective-dad warning bells went off in my head. Parker was a good-looking kid. Nineteen, muscled and strong. He'd entered the Naval Academy right out of high school with every intention of joining the SEALs just like his father and grandfather had. He was way too much for a hormone-driven teenage girl.

"As far as I know. Why do you care?" I asked as we made our way to the elevator.

Her cheeks turned every shade of red that was possible, and the beast I kept caged rattled against the bars for an entirely new reason. Steele was going to get a lecture from me, and Parker wouldn't be anywhere near my daughter in any near future.

"Don't make a big deal out of it, *Dad*," she said, sarcasm dripping. "He was just always nice to me when I was around."

Steele wasn't my bodyguard, but he went practically everywhere I did, especially when I was traveling out of the country. Steele's wife and son had traveled with us at times too. Parker and Fallon had been together in that way kids of friends often are, but I hadn't given it a moment's thought. The five years between them had seemed enough to keep me from thinking it could ever be something more.

But then, look at the twelve years that existed between Sadie and me. It felt like nothing. It *had* been nothing when I'd had my tongue in her mouth and my fingers digging into her hips.

"No boys, Fallon. You're too young."

"As if Parker would even look at me that way," she said with a heave of adolescent drama. "But that doesn't mean I can't date. Mom and Spence were dating when they were in high school."

The gleam in her eye just about killed me and had me growling, "Different times. Different situation."

She laughed and patted my arm. "Don't worry, Dad. I know every single boy at my school, and believe me, none of them are interesting enough to let them kiss me."

That wasn't any kind of reassurance.

I was suddenly very glad we were heading back to the ranch. I needed to talk to Lauren. Needed to get on the same page about this next stage of Fallon's life. Dating was out of the question, especially when I knew exactly what those senior boys at her high school would be thinking on the first day of the new school year. I'd heard the term *Fresh Meat* in the locker room way too many times growing up in our small town. The guys had thought the freshman girls were fair game now that they were in high school when, two years before, they wouldn't have been caught dead even talking to them. With just barely four hundred students in the school, the guys had wanted a new batch of girls to practice on.

No way would that be my daughter.

Selling the ranch and moving her the hell out of Rivers seemed to take on even more importance. I'd enroll her in an all-girls high school and keep her in the little bubble of safety for as long as possible. It would be one more reason she found me despicable, but I'd protect her any and every way I could.

♫ ♫ ♫

The sun was just starting to dip downward when we landed

at the private airport about thirty miles from the ranch. Stepping onto the tarmac outside the shared hangar where the Harrington Ranch Cessna had been kept, the heat hit me with a staggering force. People never understood that July in the foothills of California didn't mean seventy-degree beach weather. It was hot. Damn hot.

It was the kind of day growing up that would have ended with a trip to the falls to duck our heads under the winter run-off or sent us to the lake with inner tubes slung over our saddlebags. Anything to cool off, to shed the heat and dust of the ranch for crisp, clean waters.

My dark suit absorbed the sun like a sponge, and I shed the jacket as I made my way to the Jaguar F-Class that I'd left in the hangar after I'd driven to Rivers from Vegas for the funeral and then had to have my pilot pick me up so I could fly to Tokyo. The car now sat next to the empty slot where the Cessna had been parked, and my gut clenched all over again at the thought of Fallon piloting it alone. I cursed my brother again for teaching her to fly, even though I knew why he had.

Growing up, Dad had required Spence to learn how to use and repair every piece of equipment that was needed to run the ranch, and Spence had done the same with Fallon. The plane was just another tool, allowing them to assess the thousands of acres of land for issues and track the cattle with ease. Regardless of whether it was a necessary piece of equipment or not, it was going to be one of the first things I sold. If we needed a bird's-eye view, I'd have Steele hook us up with the latest drones to do the work.

I took my frustration at Spence out on the road, speeding along the mountain lanes with the Jaguar hugging the curves. I'd loved racing along these paths as a teen, taking them way too fast and feeling way too invincible. Both Spence and Lauren had given me a hard time about it. They'd always told me I was lucky not to have crashed, and in hindsight, they were right.

My jaw ticked.

This was why I hadn't wanted to come back to Rivers after Dad's funeral. Too many memories haunting me. Good ones that only bled into pained ones. Loss and humiliation and betrayal that clung to me. Mine and Spence's and Lauren's.

We were almost at the turn-off to the ranch when Fallon's voice, low and quiet, asked, "Did you always hate it here?"

I rubbed a hand over the short bristles of the beard I kept clipped tight as a thousand images filtered through me like a slideshow reel. Laughter. Horses. The joy of that moment when a wild mare finally submitted to the bridle. The smell of the flowers. The sound of the rushing rivers merging from different corners of the property only to spew out into the lake. The feathery touch of the first snowflakes falling and melting on your hand.

"No," I told her honestly. "When I was your age, I felt just like you—as if it was my entire world. As if it was the only place I'd ever want to be."

"But you hate it now?"

"No. I can just look at it without the haze of my childhood love covering up the truth. It will never be able to stand on its own. It's a losing bet, no matter how you play it. I don't want you to struggle to try to keep it alive when there's nothing you can do to keep it breathing in the long term. All you'd be doing is giving it life support. But once you pull the plug, it's still going to die."

The analogy was harsh, but I'd made it on purpose. She needed to hear it in those real, raw terms.

Her arms hugged her body tighter, and she turned her head to look out the window, chin raised. She was angry and frustrated, and I completely understood it. If someone had told me the same thing when I'd been her age, I would have taken a swing at them.

But the truth was still the truth.

We pulled through the gate, and the sight of the house kicked me in the gut, just as it had when I'd come back for the funeral. But just the money it took to maintain the buildings was enough to put the estate in the red. Fallon didn't have a clue how many dollars ran through the accounts each month.

I drove around the back of the house to the parking lot and pulled up next to a blue car I didn't know and yet still looked familiar. Fallon was out and running toward the front door before I could get another word in.

I grabbed my suitcase from the back and slammed the hatch. I'd just started to pass the blue subcompact when my feet stalled at seeing a rental car sticker in the back window.

The dark acid that had burned in my stomach in the control room returned.

What the fuck?

It couldn't be the same car.

I hadn't paid attention to the license plate while watching the video. I'd been much more interested in the man in the polo who'd pulled out after it. My head whipped around, eyeing the work trucks parked on the far side of the barns, looking for the man's SUV and not finding it.

The anger and frustration my daughter had been feeling decided to take its turn with me.

No way was this a coincidence.

No way Sadie Hatley ended up on the ranch without purposefully arranging it.

That same sense of betrayal and disappointment that had swarmed me yesterday morning returned, growing in leaps and bounds as that damn beast rattled around in its cage again. Was Sadie after something from me in particular? Or was she just after any rich man? Had she entered the dart tournament as a way of getting close to me, or was she really working for Puzo? His man following her made everything all the more uncertain.

But there was one thing I was sure of—I wasn't going to let her screw with me and my family. Whatever was going on, whatever excuse she'd used to get on the property, it didn't matter. I was going to kick her sweet little ass all the way back to Tennessee before she could do me or mine any harm.

Chapter Nine

Sadie

GOOD GIRL
Performed by Carrie Underwood

I'd spent a good portion of the last twenty-four hours on horseback, riding over countryside that almost put my home to shame. The craggy mountains were so much taller, rockier, and stoic than the hills of Tennessee. Flowers stuck out of white cliffs, and gorgeous waterfalls cascaded into clear pools where fish teemed. The Harrington Ranch was stunning.

Lauren knew every inch of it. She'd explained how she'd grown up there, sharing the story of how her family was twined with the Harringtons. A tale that felt like something you'd read about in a book or see in a show rather than having occurred in real life. A twist of fate that had turned with a flip of a card. Diamonds having been discovered on the property after the ranch had changed hands, made it all the more devastating. But she'd laughed it off as ancient history.

When I said it had righted itself now with her marrying into the family, it had caused clouds to cover her face that I'd kicked myself for. But she'd just shrugged and told me she hadn't inherited the land on her husband's death. The estate was in a trust managed on behalf of their daughter, Fallon.

It was a day into my visit, and I still hadn't met Adam, who was not only the ranch manager but Lauren's brother. He'd sent a text to Lauren this morning saying he was taking care of some things for his girlfriend, apologized for not being here to welcome me, and promised to sit down with me this evening.

While it was frustrating to not be able to talk about the jewels with him, it hadn't been a hardship to tag along with Lauren. I'd gotten a much-needed release of endorphins riding the same delightful mare as the day before, and it eased that homesick feeling enough to bring a smile to my face.

After helping Lauren feed the animals and muck stalls and pens, we'd saddled the horses and headed out. Our first stop had been down by the waterfall, where we'd weeded a clearing near a picturesque red bridge that crossed over the river as it merged from three into one. Lauren explained that an arch and chairs would be assembled in the clearing in the next day or so. They used a local florist and wildflowers from the ranch wherever possible and used antique linens that had been in the family for generations unless a guest required a specific color they didn't have in stock.

From the waterfalls, we'd returned closer to the main house where we'd mowed and smoothed out a large expanse of grass near the barns where the marquees for the guest tables and a dance floor would be set up. The guests would have the same majestic view of the mountains and rivers I had from my room.

After lunch, she took me out to the old homestead. It was a charming craftsman house that had been added onto over the years in a hodgepodge sort of way, decorated with a sweet, farmhouse chic. We cleaned rooms, changed sheets, and compiled a list of items that needed to be restocked in the kitchen and bar. Our final stop had been the bunkhouse done in a rustic cowhide and wagon wheel theme, where we repeated the process of freshening up the rooms and making a list of groceries.

Much of the work was familiar to me from helping on our own ranch. I'd worked the land and the resort from my earliest memories, sometimes loving it and sometimes hating it but always being proud of what we'd accomplished. I sensed that same pride in Lauren. That same sense of heritage and belonging, but her sadness seemed to hover around her like a bee, warning others away and ready to sting at any moment.

The one major difference between this ranch and ours was that Lauren worked mostly alone. Adam never showed up to schlepp the stalls or help with the animals, and her daughter wasn't around. There didn't even seem to be any other farmhands. When I asked about the lack of help, she said they'd had to cut most of the workers in the last year, but that her daughter was due back tonight.

I realized, with a twinge to my stomach, just how desperate things must be for them.

It was after five by the time we headed back to the main house. Once inside, Lauren told me to go on up and shower while she put the pasta dish she'd assembled before we'd left this morning in the oven. She said she'd join Adam and me in the office after she'd had a chance to clean up, and she pointed at the door as we went by it.

I showered quickly, dried my hair, and pulled on a clean pair of jeans and a loose floral tank before heading barefoot down the stairs in the direction Lauren had indicated. My leg was acting up after two long days of manual tasks and hard riding, and I had to grit my teeth and force myself not to limp as I approached the office. I knocked before opening the door and nearly stumbled across the threshold.

When she'd said office, my mind had flashed to the plain double desks crammed into a room off the barn Ryder and my dad used in managing our family's business. But this room was more library than office. Shelves lined the walls from floor to ceiling with a rolling ladder clipped to the ledge. The floral, embossed copper tiles from the entry's ceiling were repeated here, and another chandelier shed sparkles of light across the plush carpet. Warm woods, deep brocades, and a large fireplace made the room feel welcoming rather than intimidating.

Set before a large window seat was an oversized, formal desk where a man sat working on a laptop. He looked up as I entered, and the frown on his face turned to a smile. He shut the computer, dragged a pair of square-framed glasses from his face, and left them on the desk before striding over to me.

He wore black dress pants, a long-sleeve white button-down, and a blue patterned tie. Tall and lanky with the same wavy, blond hair as his sister, he greeted me with a smile that reached eyes several shades darker than hers. Eyes that were red in a way that matched the tip of his nose, as if he was battling a cold. Or maybe allergies. Maybe that was why he hadn't been out in the fields with us.

"Sadie, it's a pleasure. I'm sorry I haven't been around much since you got here. I had several things come up that needed to be handled immediately."

I shook the hand he extended. "I'm just glad to be here, and I thoroughly enjoyed spending the day with Lauren."

His smile disappeared, worry replacing it. "She's had a hard go of it since Spencer died."

"I'm so sorry for your family's loss."

He headed to a cabinet in the corner, opening the doors to reveal a shelf of crystal bottles. "Can I fix you a drink?"

"Honestly, just water if you have it. The heat wore me out today." I'd spent so many of my days at the bar in the last eighteen months that my body wasn't quite used to the long hours spent in the sun.

Adam poured water from a larger bottle, added a lemon slice, and fixed a shot of whiskey for himself before joining me where I stood staring up at a large painting hanging over the fireplace. The woman was dark-haired with chocolate-brown eyes and a smile that seemed all mischief. She wore an elegant evening gown, and a layered necklace sparkling with diamonds hung around her neck.

It wasn't exactly the necklace from Great-grandma's trunk, but it had the same yellow diamonds mixed in with the standard white. The gems were large and square cut, and the setting was a similar, almost gaudy, Art Deco style.

"Beatrice Harrington," he said with a wave. "She married the man who won the ranch from my idiotic great-grandfather. She was quite a bit younger than him, an up-and-coming actress who he snatched from Hollywood's grips and then wilted away here."

His voice held a calm that contrasted with his words. Unlike Lauren, who'd simply stated the facts of how their family had lost the land, Adam didn't seem to feel quite the same way. And yet, there wasn't bitterness in his tone as much as a sense of wonder at the stupidity of those who'd come before them.

"She's beautiful," I said. "The diamonds on the necklace are from here?"

He nodded, turning to assess me. "Lauren will be here any second, and I'd prefer not to talk about the jewelry with her. If it turns out the set you have is truly the jewelry stolen from the Harringtons in the forties, it could mean everything or nothing."

My heart skipped a beat, my stomach plummeted, and my palms instantly turned sweaty. "So there were some actually stolen?"

"Yes. A set had been loaned to a movie studio and then disappeared. That's all I know so far. I need to dig through more paperwork to see if I can figure it out in detail. The truth is, we could use the money if the jewels you've found belong to the family. They've already sold most of the last remaining diamonds—that necklace in the painting included—but the ranch is still struggling.

"I've been trying for a year to get Spence and Lauren to consider some drastic changes like the ones your family made in turning your farm into a resort. The wedding business, while nice, barely helps cover the maintenance of the equipment. In order to really be a successful resort, we'd need to renovate more of the buildings and hire back staff we've let go, and that all requires a cash flow we just don't have. The bank won't lend us more money as we're already struggling to meet the payments on a sizeable loan Spence took out a few years ago, so cashing in on the diamonds would likely save the ranch."

The sick feeling in my stomach grew, my plans whisking away like a dandelion blown in the wind. I wasn't sure who the jewels belonged to, but knowing the Harringtons needed the money made me want to hand them over now. Except, my family didn't even know they were real yet. I needed to discuss something this important with them, so we could all come to the same conclusion. It made me sadder than I'd imagined to know my great-grandma really was a thief. But then again, we didn't have the full story. I could hold out hope for a different answer until all the facts were in front of me.

"Did you bring them with you?" Adam asked. "I'd love to see them in person."

I shook my head and swallowed over the lump that had grown in my throat. "After I found out how much they were worth, I locked them up in the safe at my bar."

"After all Lauren has been through this year, I don't want to get her hopes up until I'm sure the jewelry is really ours." His tone was sad and hopeful all at the same time.

Did he realize, even if they were the ones taken from the family, they might not be able to keep them? "If the jewelry was stolen, an insurance company might have more right to them than either of our families. You'd need to find out if a claim was filed back then. If there was one, you'd have to buy them back if you wanted to keep them."

When Adam looked up at me, there was no longer any hope in his expression, and it made me feel horrible all over again. "We definitely couldn't afford to do that. I guess you can see why it's important to keep this between the two of us until we know all the details."

I absolutely understood. Seeing the raw pain surrounding Lauren all day had made me feel protective of her, and I wasn't even her family.

"Shall we have a seat, and you can tell me more about how you went about making the changes to your ranch and how long it took to be profitable again?" He waved toward the love seat and two armchairs in front of the fireplace. Made of worn leather and aged tapestry, the furniture appeared to have been on the estate for decades.

I'd just headed for a chair when a cold, dark voice halted my steps. "What in the hell do you think you're doing here?"

The sound of the gritty, sexy voice that had almost undone me this weekend caused me to nearly trip. It was only Adam's hand on my elbow that stopped me from falling face-first into a coffee table.

Panic filled me at the same time goosebumps littered my skin. My head swiveled to the door of the library and met eyes shooting lightning bolts at me just as they had yesterday morning. The electricity that zapped through the air was as much chemistry-riddled attraction as it was confusion. Mine and his. My mind whirled with the same exact question that had spun from his lips. *What the hell is Rafe doing here?*

As he stalked toward us, the simmering anger he'd briefly shown disappeared behind the stoic wall he was so good at assembling, and I couldn't help the instant craving for the Rafe who wasn't in control. The one who had shown his real emotions as he'd devoured me.

When he reached us, he leaned in, snarling, "It doesn't matter. Whatever excuse you used to get in these doors, you can take with you. I want you off my property. Now."

"Jesus, Rafe," Adam said, stepping in between us. "Stop threatening our guest."

"She's not a guest. She's a liar. Probably a blackmailer or maybe a simple thief. Have you checked the silverware?" His tone was as icy as it had been when he'd found me with Lorenzo, and it cut me just as sharply. I swallowed hard, guilt sifting through me because we'd just been talking about stolen jewels that were now, in all likelihood, in my possession.

Rafe saw my guilt and misread it, taking it as a sign I'd personally done something wrong. Before I could defend myself, he cut in, "I knew it." Disappointment bled through every syllable. "What exactly did he send you for? And what did he promise you for delivering it?"

"Dad?" A bewildered voice reached us from the doorway.

Rafe's daughter had been a bodyless voice the other night, but as I took her in, I could clearly see him in the shape of her eyes—a deep, warm chocolate set below dark brows that furrowed just like his. But it wasn't the way she looked like him that hit me with a sudden shock, but how much the teenager looked like Lauren. She was clearly the girl in the photograph with Lauren and Spencer from the Harrington Ranch website.

I'd thought the girl was Lauren and Spence's child. How could she be Rafe's? How did Rafe even belong here? He'd said *my property*, hadn't he?

My mind spun with so many questions I couldn't keep

track.

"Go to your room, Fallon," Rafe commanded. As a teenager, I never would have disobeyed an order said in such a steely tone from my father. Even when I'd rebelled and gotten into mischief, if Dad had spoken to me like that, I would have turned tail and run.

Not Fallon. She stepped into the library instead, scrutinizing the way Rafe and Adam were hovering around me like men fighting over a prize. "What's going on? Who is she?"

"No one," Rafe said just as Adam said, "A friend."

A scoff erupted from Rafe. "She is most definitely not a friend."

"I-I don't understand," I choked out, heart hammering inside my chest.

"Like hell you don't," Rafe said, and when he looked down at me, I was amazed by the hurt I saw. It was as if I'd stabbed him in the back. "How much did you think you could get? How much is he paying you?"

My cheeks flushed because it was the same insinuation he'd let drop the day before. My shock and confusion turned to anger. I stepped to the side, attempting to put distance between me and him and the wave of mixed emotions he was searing me with. "I'm not being paid by anyone. I'm only here to help."

He snorted in disbelief. "If you're here to help anyone, it's Puzo, and I'm not going to let you."

"Puzo?" Adam's voice was as confused as mine. "Lorenzo Puzo?"

Rafe's gaze settled on Adam with the same intense scrutiny he'd shot at me. Adam cleared his throat and also gave Rafe a wider berth. I took a tiny step toward the door, and Rafe's cold look landed on me again. "Care to come clean, Sadie? Care to tell us all the truth? Or do you just want to take it as a loss and run back to your employer?"

"What is going on here?" Lauren's voice was sharp and concerned as she entered the library and stood behind Fallon. "Are you okay?" The question was addressed to me, but it was her daughter who answered.

"I'm fine, Mom, thanks for asking." Fallon whirled around and flew out the door. Her booted feet were loud on the wood as she stomped down the hallway and up the stairs.

Lauren's eyes followed her daughter, more pain slashing through them before she turned them back to the three of us standing in a wide huddle. "Rafe? Adam? What's going on?"

"Why the hell is she here?" Rafe demanded, looking between the siblings.

Adam cleared his throat. "Not that it's really any of your business, but her family is part of the Eastern Dude Ranchers' Association. We're exchanging ideas. She's here to see our wedding business and give us ideas on how to convert the estate into a resort."

For two seconds, I thought Rafe might believe Adam, but then his expression darkened. "Even if that were true, it wouldn't matter. I've already told you we're not spending another dime on this godforsaken place."

Lauren came closer, saying, "We have options, Rafe. Just listen to Sadie. If we invest and do this right, we'd likely be profitable again in four years at most."

"Invest with what? No bank is going to lend you a penny. So I suppose you want me to use *my* money? You think I should steal from *my* business to try to save a dinosaur that should have gone extinct a decade ago? No. Absolutely not." He said it with a finality that brought tears to Lauren's eyes.

"Goddamn you. He'd never sell! He'd be looking for any way to save the ranch. Any. Way." She pushed the heels of her palms into her lids.

"And what makes you think I actually care what he'd want?" Rafe's voice was harder than I'd ever heard it, devoid of any emotion. Once again, I'd stepped into the middle of something ugly. This time, whatever was going on with these three people felt deeper, larger, and darker than whatever existed between Rafe and Lorenzo. Pain and betrayal practically flashed like a neon sign between them.

I was confused and intimidated and pissed all at the same

time. I took another step farther away from Rafe, darting a look toward the door and wondering how long it would take me to pack up and leave.

I could talk to Adam over email. I didn't need to be here to finish these discussions any more than I needed to be in Vegas for the ones with Lorenzo. I'd wanted to come and discover for myself the truth of what had happened. I'd hoped to clear my conscience enough to move forward with my plans for the jewels, but now, all I wanted was to escape the nastiness zipping between these people.

As I passed Lauren, she reached out and touched my shoulder. "Please. Please don't leave. Let me talk to Rafe and Adam. Give us a night. I'm sorry we put you in the middle of this. We don't normally behave like animals."

Rafe's grunt of disapproval contradicted her, and she glared at him.

"Please," she said, addressing it solely to me.

"She's not staying." Rafe's voice was glacial and so damn certain that it spiked the contrary, dig-my-heels-in-and-stay-the-course side of me. The one that had me walking without a cane even though the doctors hadn't been sure I would. It made me want to stay just to prove Rafe couldn't send me away like he'd tried to send his teenaged daughter. Prove that whatever he thought about me wasn't true. That the only truth that existed was the attraction zipping between us even with his cold disdain and my irritation shimmering between us.

Lauren raised her chin. "Regardless of what you think, Rafe, this is still Fallon's home. My home. You don't get to say who stays and leaves. It isn't yours! You exchanged it for a few million dollars that buried us in debt. You were the one who left and started us on this downward spiral. So the last thing you get to do is kick a guest out of this house."

I risked looking at Rafe and saw her words had struck some inner wound. Pain lanced through his expression before he covered it, the same raw pain I'd seen in Lauren all day, and my heart lurched at the sight of it. A stupid need to soothe them all filled me, to ease the pain, to smooth the angry waves that swam between them.

It wasn't my place, but my entire life I'd played that role. Teasing Ryder or Maddox or both when they were ready to punch each other into the ground. Laughing at Gemma's primness in order to smooth the sting of her tattling on them. At the bar, I was the one who stepped up to ease customer arguments before they turned into a brawl rather than Ted, the bartender.

But one look at the scowl on Rafe Marquess's face, and I couldn't imagine him ever wanting me to play that role for him. He didn't need anyone in that role because he made rash judgments and stuck to them like dung beetles to a cow patty, regardless if it made him into an ass.

An ass who still made my skin flicker with the heat of desire.

And maybe it was that as much as the desperation in Lauren's face that had me making a decision I knew I might regret.

Chapter Ten

Rafe

DAMN
Performed by Jake Owen

Irrational fury burned inside me. Some of it was directed at my body's reaction to Sadie Hatley and that damn lopsided grin she'd been giving Adam as I walked in, but the majority of the rage was directed at her, for weaseling her way into my family and their troubles. I couldn't imagine what Puzo would want with the ranch, but I knew it had something to do with me. And Sadie likely knew what it was. It was nearly impossible for it to be a simple coincidence that she'd been dining with him and then come here.

But then again, would she really have met with him at The Fortress if they were trying to pull a con here? It made no sense. I couldn't put the puzzle pieces together, no matter how hard I tried. And that had the anger and betrayal I felt slowly dissolving into a sea of doubts that was just as frustrating.

Was the guy Steele had caught following Sadie out of the hotel her muscle? Her backup? Was he tucked away somewhere nearby and would come running if she called? Or was Puzo trailing her for some other nefarious reason?

Was she in danger?

That thought made my lungs squeeze until I almost couldn't breathe.

Regardless of what was true, I still had the overwhelming urge to pick Sadie up, shove her in that piece-of-shit car she'd driven here, and send her on her way before she could do more damage. The guilt I'd seen slash through her eyes when I'd called her a thief meant she had something to hide. If she stayed, there was every likelihood my family, or her, would be harmed. The Puzo family used and abused and left a trail of dead in their wake.

I needed Sadie to leave so she couldn't wound us when that happened. So she wouldn't be another body Puzo left behind.

But the plea Lauren had issued had landed home with Sadie. I could see it in the way her face softened while her shoulders drew back, ready for a fight. She was going to stay, and I might dislike it with an intensity that was all-consuming, but Lauren was right in that I didn't have any say in who came and went from the ranch.

I had washed my hands of it. Or at least I thought I had until Spence had made the mistake of leaving me in charge of Fallon's trust. According to the lawyers, he'd made the change at the time she'd been born and never updated it since. Typical Spence. He'd detested dealing with legalese as much as he'd despised dealing with numbers and money. Still, I would never be sure if it had been an oversight on his part, or if he'd done it on purpose as a way of drawing me back to my roots. One last outstretched hand offering reconciliation or simply one last dare he'd issued from the grave.

Lauren glared at me before turning back to Sadie once again. "Please, stay. I promise in the morning things will have settled down."

Lauren couldn't promise that. I'd never settle if Sadie was nearby. My entire being was constantly in a state of alert, fighting the attraction and hunger I felt, while my brain was screaming *danger*.

Sadie tucked a strand of silky hair behind her ear before nodding. She cleared her throat and said, "I'll see you in the morning." Then, she whirled around on bare feet, walking out of the room with her scarred leg dragging slightly. All the crackling fire zipping through the air left with her, leaving awkwardness in her wake.

I stalked to the drink cabinet, poured myself a shot of bourbon, and downed it.

When I turned back, both Adam and Lauren were warily watching me, as if waiting for my next explosion. And that, more than anything, cooled me off because I loathed giving anyone my emotions, but especially not Lauren. She'd had enough of mine to last a lifetime.

"How do you even know Sadie?" Lauren asked.

"Funny, that's what I was going to ask you," I countered.

"Like Adam said, she's part of the Eastern Dude Ranchers' Association—or her family is," Lauren said. "Adam's been working on a plan to convert the ranch into a resort. Spence and I weren't sure about it because it felt like more work, requiring an outpouring of money we didn't have, but we already have the core facilities, and after the initial renovations, it wouldn't take much more than what we spend now to maintain them. We'd be able to keep the place full year-round with the snow junkies coming during the winter and the hiking and lake crowd in the summer. Even Fallon has been excited about the idea, offering to put on trick riding shows for the guests."

My teeth mashed together so tightly I thought the bone might crack. No wonder Fallon was so dead set on keeping the ranch. She lived to perform with her horses, and she was damn good at it. If Adam and Lauren had tied her love of trick riding to the success of the ranch, she'd do anything to make it happen.

"If you want me to be the bad guy, that's fine. I'll be the bad guy," I said. "You'd need a miracle to turn this place around at the rate it's losing money."

Lauren shot a look at Adam and then back to me. "Spence and I didn't understand how fast we were depleting our reserves. Adam tried to tell us, but…" Her throat bobbed, and she pushed the heels of her hands against her eyes again.

My nails bit into my palms. I didn't want any of this. I didn't want to feel bad for her and the choices she'd made. She'd loved Spence and the ranch more than she'd loved me. Stupidly, at twenty, I'd thought I could change that. I'd thought I could come first, until Spence had shown back up and proved me wrong.

"Even if you could find a way to turn this around, Lauren, I wouldn't trust anything Sadie said. She's tangled with Lorenzo Puzo somehow. I saw them together in Vegas."

Adam smirked. "Ah. The truth comes out. You wanted her, and she ditched you in favor of him? Jealousy was always your downfall."

I fought my immediate reaction to wipe the smirk off his face with my fists, instead demanding, "How the hell do you know Puzo?"

"He owns property in town and has been participating in the Better Business Bureau meetings."

The realization that he'd likely been in town for months, and I hadn't known, ate at me. "If he's taken an interest here, it's only as a way of getting to me. Trust me, a town as dinky as Rivers holds no long-term appeal for him."

Sarcasm littered Adam's response. "There's that Rafe ego we've all come to expect. Of course everything is about you. Well, I'll be damned if this is. He's stepped up and helped this community in a way the great Harringtons haven't been able to do since your dad died and you crippled the ranch. Lorenzo has saved several of the local bars and restaurants from going out of business. He's given them successful strategies to stay afloat during the challenges of the last few years."

At what cost? I wondered. An interest rate they couldn't afford, so they ended up defaulting, and he owned the property? I was under no misconception that what had drawn him to this town to begin with was my connection to it. He must have thought I cared more about where I'd grown up than I did. He'd be sorely disappointed when I rid myself of everything having to do with the ranch and Rivers, except my daughter.

But Fallon's concerns about Adam suddenly landed home with a force that almost sent me to my knees. Maybe he had been involved in what had happened to Spence. Or maybe it wasn't Adam but Puzo. Maybe I'd turned my back on my family and then drawn evil to it with my own actions. I'd sent his cousin to jail for life. Had he retaliated by sending my brother to the grave?

Acid burned its way up my esophagus.

Suddenly, I realized sending Sadie away was the wrong play. I could use the attraction that sizzled between us to find out the truth about what Puzo wanted with Rivers and the ranch. It would cost me layers of skin. I wouldn't be able to walk away unsinged, but I'd do anything to protect Fallon. And as much as I hated it, hated knowing he could still affect me, Spence would want me to make sure Lauren was okay as well.

My brother had contacted me the night he'd died. He'd left a message saying he needed to talk, that he'd discovered things about the ranch that had disturbed him. He needed a dispassionate observer to talk it over with. And just like every other time I'd heard my brother's voice over the last fourteen years, it had nipped at me. A bee sting that lasted for days and couldn't be ignored, even though I'd done my best to do just that. Whenever he called about Fallon, to make arrangements for dropping her off and picking her up, I returned the message instantly. But every other attempt of his over the years to narrow the gap between us, I'd ignored, since he and Lauren had eloped just days before our wedding. His last call had been no different. A message I'd deleted and tried to forget.

Would I find, in staying and investigating Fallon's worries, that I'd left my brother to die?

As much as I'd wanted nothing to do with him or Lauren or the ranch, I'd never wished death on either of them. I'd just wanted to prove to them that I didn't need them, didn't need anything from this family besides the cash that rightfully belonged to me. I may not have started my business with nothing. I may have used my inheritance to invest in my first club, but everything that had come after was due to my hard work. It was my time and energy and skill that had made Marquess Enterprises a global success story.

But had it cost my brother his life?

It would require more fortitude than either Adam or Lauren would ever know, but I'd stay. I'd stay and listen to everything Sadie and my family had to say so I could get to the bottom of all of it. But if it didn't pan out, or worse, if Puzo was trying to use them to get to me, then I had no qualms about putting an end to it.

"I've rearranged my schedule to be here this week. It was clear Fallon needed someone looking after her." Lauren visibly flinched at my words, but I wasn't going to sugarcoat things for her. "If, at the end of the week, I decide this long shot of a plan isn't going to work, I'll proceed with selling the ranch as intended."

Adam said nothing, quietly watching us. Lauren gave a curt nod. "Fine."

Then, she spun around and left.

I focused my attention on Adam, assessing him as I hadn't when I'd come back for Spencer's funeral. He'd been away at college the last few years I'd lived on the ranch and then gone to work for some high-flying financial firm in San Francisco. I'd barely seen him until he'd come home for a weekend trip after Lauren had told him she was pregnant, and we were engaged.

He'd been tall and lean in that way Lauren's entire family had been, and I'd been astonished by the strength he'd had when he'd planted a fist in my face and broken my nose. He'd always seemed soft as a kid, especially when compared to the steely muscle and weathered skin his dad and grandfather had carried from working the ranch. Maybe it had simply been the shock of witnessing the power he'd hidden that had allowed him to get the jump on me, had allowed him to back the single punch up with several others before I'd reacted. It wasn't until he'd gotten a rope around my neck that I'd ended the fight.

And just like when we'd battled at anything as kids—games, races, or arguments—he'd despised I'd come out ahead in that fight too. Most of the time growing up, Adam had kept his jealousy hidden, but the truth of it had always risen to the surface whenever Spence or I had beaten him at anything or any time we'd gotten something he'd wanted and didn't have because his family couldn't afford it. When that happened, he'd stomp and pout and go into hiding for days.

I wasn't exactly sure what had brought him back to the ranch after my father died, when he'd sworn he never would, but it was clear from the expensive suit he'd worn to Spence's funeral and the Cartier dangling from his wrist that he had money. It had to be from investments he'd made working for the financial company up north, because it certainly wasn't from the salary he was receiving as the ranch's business manager.

I hadn't cared. Hadn't given much thought to any of it—the reasons for him coming home or how he was getting his money—until now. Until the fact he knew Puzo had doubts coiling through me. Was he laundering Puzo's money? Was that what Spence had found out and called me about?

I narrowed my gaze on Adam. "Why are you even here, Adam? What exactly do you get out of any of this?"

His hand shook ever so slightly as he took a sip of the bourbon in my family's heirloom, crystal glass, but his voice was dry and calm when he responded. "Other than wanting to help my sister through the loss of Spencer? How about the satisfaction of seeing the ranch successful again after you stole from it and Spence ruined it? I like the idea of knowing it will be a Hurly who rights the ship after the great Harringtons ran it aground."

I bristled at his disparagement of my brother and the Harrington name. Maybe I hadn't chosen to keep it. Maybe, when I'd had the choice, I'd separated myself from it to spite my father and to honor my mother, but neither Dad nor Spence would ever have done anything to destroy this place. They lived and breathed it. It was as much a part of them as their skin and bones. To ruin it would have ruined them.

And maybe that, more than anything, was what had killed Spence. The failure. The loan he couldn't pay back. What I'd taken was far less than my half had actually been worth—a handful of old stocks that had been in the family kitty for decades and a couple of million when the ranch was worth nearly twenty, even failing as it was.

"I see. You were hoping to get a piece of the pie." It wasn't a question when I said it. "You wanted the Hurly name back on this land. How much were you hoping to get? A quarter? Half? All of it?"

He studied me, trying to read my emotions once again, but I'd finally tucked them all away after giving them away too freely. Finally, he said, "I hadn't really thought ahead that far."

Liar. Chess had always been Adam's game. He'd spent as much time studying it as I had training horses, so it had always made him angry when I'd won our matches anyway. Back then, I'd shot from the hip instead of playing by the rule books and still beaten him. It was the opposite of what I did now, carefully considering all my moves.

I didn't know which idea left me more disgusted. That I'd become him or that he might have come looking for a way to take back what he thought should have been his. He wanted to be the prince of the kingdom instead of the serf, and my father had definitely had a way of making everyone feel like servants. Even me. Spence had been the only real prince, whereas I'd been the spare who he'd seen as just another pair of hands.

As I watched Adam sip at the whiskey my brother had favored, the same brand my father had, my instincts screamed a warning I needed to heed. It was the same instinct that had saved my life in a dark alley. The same voice that taunted me when my demons struck.

Maybe Fallon was right. Maybe she had her own voice screaming at her. Perhaps Adam really had put something into play that had turned ugly. Whether that was with Puzo's help or on his own, I couldn't be certain, but I promised myself I'd find out. As much as I loathed the idea of owing my brother anything, I owed him this, and I owed Fallon answers so she could put the ranch behind her once and for all if we sold it.

Did I think Adam really killed Spence? It was hard to imagine, because if there was one person on this Earth Adam did love, it was his sister, and I couldn't see him putting Lauren through that sort of agonizing grief. But I could see Adam trying to win back the land in a way that would prove once and for all that poker was for idiots and chess was for winners.

So why had Spence trusted him? My brother didn't like

numbers or legalese, but he'd never been stupid. He had good intuition and natural common sense that should have seen through any sleight of hand Adam was trying to pull. But then again, maybe he'd been so entrenched in keeping the ranch afloat he hadn't had time to see the bigger picture.

"I want a full accounting of every dollar that's been earned and spent since I left," I told him. "Access to every account, every invoice, and every bill."

Something flickered through his expression I couldn't catch, but his shrug was casual. "I'll send you all of Spencer's logins and passwords."

The idea of following in my brother's footsteps caused my collar to grow tight, and I had a feeling Adam had done it on purpose to rattle me. And it had worked because suddenly the vaulted room with its floor-to-ceiling shelves felt too small, as if they were closing in. I needed air. I needed out. I needed to find some peace before I became so tight and brittle I broke in half at a mere touch.

Before I gave them more of my emotions than they'd ever earned.

I turned on a heel and headed for the back door.

The heat had faded with the sun, but it hadn't cooled enough to be chilly yet. The crickets were loud, frogs croaked down by the river, and an owl hooted somewhere in the dark. The path my feet found was worn smooth from years of shoes traveling along it rather than any formal attempt to carve one out. It wound through the fields dotted with bluebells and yarrow that waved in a small breeze, shifting the grass like a ghost running through it. The moon was bright and full, shining down and turning the meadow into waves of silver.

I wasn't dressed for hiking through the hills, and the dress shoes that had been perfect for my meetings in Vegas slid on the hard-packed dirt before I caught myself with a grunt of displeasure. This was a lawsuit waiting to happen if Lauren had her clients using this same path to travel back and forth from the falls in dress shoes and heels.

As I walked, I imagined Dad's reaction to the idea of

inviting people onto his land for weddings and even more if they turned the place into a resort. He would have cut off an arm rather than have allowed it. He'd kept the world at bay as much as he could, concentrating on the cattle and the hay the farm was known for once the granite and diamonds had turned to dust.

This close to the house, none of the sequoias grew. They were gathered at the back of the property, higher up where the hills turned into mountains, but brush and oaks and small firs took over as the ground began to slope upward. The air smelled of coniferous trees, the heady scent of sap and wood that smelled like the freedom I'd once found here.

Memories slammed into me that were almost as painful as the knife that had once sliced my chest open. This was why I'd never allowed myself to come back. To remember. To regret.

No. Not regret. Never that. I'd made the right choice for me and for my family.

The sound of the waterfall reached my ears, but it took several more minutes of walking before it came into view. In the moonlight, it glimmered like the diamonds that had once been found nearby. The river crashed from above onto large boulders, roaring into deep eddies. Mist rose from the dark pools before rushing downstream toward the lake just out of view.

My breath caught at the sight of the thundering display. My soul took flight, winging over the white foam, dancing in the moonlight, and soaring into a sky littered with so many stars it was as if a glitter bomb had gone off. It had been too long since I'd been here. Too long since I'd been reminded of the importance of keeping the property whole and free from developers who'd cut it up into pieces and stick tract homes along the shores of the lake and rivers.

The memory of the last time I'd been at the waterfall haunted me, flickering as if I was watching an old film reel in black and white. Lauren and I had argued. She'd said getting married just because she was pregnant wasn't the right thing to do, and it had torn through me with the ease of a scythe through hay.

We're getting married because we love each other and the baby, I'd said.

She'd looked down at her feet, and I'd known the truth. I'd finally let myself really understand it. She'd loved me…but not as much as she'd loved Spence. I liked to believe she hadn't realized it, that she hadn't used me as a placeholder, until he'd shown up at the ranch after hearing about the engagement and the baby. The hurt and confusion in his eyes had stabbed at me more than the punch he'd planted in my gut.

I hadn't swung back with my fists, but my words had been vicious. I'd reminded him he'd been the one to break up with Lauren, the one to shove his college girlfriend in her face by bringing her here the previous Christmas, and he'd blanched. I'd simply stepped up to fix what he'd broken.

You knew it was wrong, he'd told me, sounding very much like the devil who enjoyed laughing at me these days.

The worst of it was, I *had* known it was wrong.

But I'd also been raised to want what Spencer had. I'd been raised to compete with him for everything, and I'd swung in to take what I'd thought I deserved.

Movement down by the base of the falls drew my gaze, and a tiny hint of apprehension scattered over me. Bears and mountain lions were common here, especially at night. But as my eyesight adjusted, landing on a huge boulder near the water's edge, I realized it wasn't a predator—or at least not the wild-animal kind.

Sadie sat in the mist and the moonlight, looking every bit the siren I'd thought her from the beginning. An imp. A waif. A spellbinding witch. Her skin glowed in the moon rays the same color as the foam from the falls, and her black hair blended in with the shadows. Light and dark. Sweet and sin.

I'd seen many women here over the years. I'd been popular with the girls in high school, as much due to my family's name as to the confidence I'd exuded, and this had been a favorite nighttime spot when bringing them to the ranch. Add a blanket and a six-pack, and the setting was the perfect spot for romance. For hookups. For losing yourself in the scent of a woman.

But in all the years I'd brought other people here, I'd never seen someone who looked like they belonged the way Sadie did. She looked as if she'd sprouted from the water, taking form only to lure unsuspecting humans.

And she did just that. She lured me.

My feet, sliding along the slope in my inappropriate dress shoes, found their way through the boulders and the damp grass to where she sat. She'd seen me before I'd seen her, so her eyes were turned toward mine as I approached.

Wary and nervous, but somehow defiant all at the same time, her pointed chin was lifted, shoulders back, ready for a fight.

I wasn't sure what I'd do to her once I reached her. Would I kiss her until she forgot Puzo existed? Or strangle her until she gave up her secrets? Either way, I needed to keep her here on the ranch until I discovered the truth. Until I could ensure my family was safe.

I took a seat on the boulder next to hers, all the while convincing myself I wouldn't touch her. Wouldn't pull her to me just to see if she still tasted like honey and bourbon. She wasn't mine to taste. She was likely the enemy. But something inside me screamed in objection at that idea.

"Find what you wanted?" I demanded, careful to keep my emotions reined in.

"The night was peaceful until you showed up," she said, and I knew she didn't just mean right now on the rocks by the waterfall.

"What does he want with me?" I asked. I felt exhausted by all of it, but I didn't show it any more than my disappointment that she'd fallen in with my nemesis.

When I risked looking at her, the moonlight showed every expression on her face. Confusion had her brows drawn together, yet she still vibrated with life, glowing from within like a bioluminescent pixie.

She was magnificent. Stunningly beautiful. A dazzling display of pure energy. If I had even one ounce of artistry in me, I'd paint a picture of her here, just like this, and hang it over the mantel in the library. And even though she wasn't wearing a ball gown or diamonds, she'd easily outshine Great-grandma Beatrice, entrapping whoever saw her.

Chapter Eleven

Sadie

COWBOY CASANOVA
Performed by Carrie Underwood

Rafe's face was cast in shadows with the light of the moon shining behind him. I wondered, if I could see them better, if his eyes would be full of the icy disdain he was so good at or if they'd hold the glimpse of hurt and anger I'd caught before he'd schooled his expression earlier. Either way, it disturbed my peace. The intense stare. The emotions—or lack of them—he tossed my way.

He'd been good at disturbing my peace since the moment I'd met him. I'd finally recovered some of it after the confrontation at the house by sitting here, watching the stars twinkle, and listening to the sounds of the wild rustling around me. Now, my emotions were in shambles again, simply because he was sitting a boulder away.

My desire was muddled with uncertainty. I didn't understand why he thought I was working with Lorenzo to ruin him somehow, and I really didn't understand how, even knowing he thought the worst of me, my body still craved him. Still wanted those firm, commanding lips to give me the heady rush I'd felt in his penthouse. Wanted the release he'd promised and not delivered.

I could do nothing about my body's reaction to him, but I could try to change his mind about what was happening with me and my potential cousin.

"I have no idea what Lorenzo wants with you. I have no idea what's gone on to make you hate each other just like I had no idea you were related to the Harringtons. I'm here for personal reasons that have nothing to do with you."

He didn't respond. Not a sound or a scoff or even a heavy inhale, and yet I could tell he still doubted me. After all, if I *was* working with Lorenzo to destroy him, I'd hardly admit it.

"Look. I don't know what I've stumbled into, but that's all I've done—stumbled into a situation I know nothing about. If I'd known I'd see you again, I certainly wouldn't have come onto you in the bar or agreed to go with you to your penthouse. I was looking for one night of pleasure. That's it."

"I find it hard to believe," he said, his voice low and deep but not angry. It sounded tired instead, as if he'd just waged a battle, and even though he'd been declared the victor, he'd taken no pleasure or relief in winning it.

"I don't even understand how you're here," I told him. "You said it's your property, but your name is Marquess not Harrington, right? And after Sunday, I knew you had a daughter, but I didn't see her. I had no idea she was the girl I saw on the website with Lauren and Spencer. I thought she was their child."

"Fallon is mine." His tone brooked no argument, possessive in a way my body responded to all over again. I'd wanted to be his, even if only for one night. "It's a complicated, long story. The short of it, my brother and I both loved the same woman. He won in the end, but we got my daughter out of it, which was the real prize."

A love triangle, then. Brothers who'd battled over a woman. Romantic on the page and screen, painful to live with, especially if you were the loser. I couldn't imagine Rafe losing anything, let alone a woman. I obviously hadn't met Spencer before he died, but I couldn't imagine anyone choosing another man over the overflowing power and splendor of Rafe. I was having trouble controlling my emotions and attraction even after he'd been cruel. What would it be like if he'd come at me with love? With the sole purpose of winning me?

It would be nothing I'd be able to resist.

Dangerous. Alluring. Tempting.

Maybe it was good he seemed to despise me suddenly. Maybe this was the only way I'd survive being in the same house with him for a few days. I swallowed hard before forcing myself to focus on the basics, the simple tasks of understanding why he was here and what I could do to make him trust me. "Did you have separate fathers? Is that why your last names are different?"

"We had the same parents. Legally, our last name is Marquess-Harrington, thanks to our mom's desire to keep her surname. She was an artist at a commune near here, bent on taking the art world by storm and then leaving to travel the globe. But she fell in love with Dad and gave up all her dreams for him. Keeping her name was her way of retaining some piece of herself while losing others." The words were torn out of him, as if he couldn't believe he was telling me anything about himself. "But try writing an eighteen-letter, hyphenated last name on your papers in elementary school. It was ridiculous. Spence chose to use Harrington, and I did the opposite. At the time, I told myself it was because it had made Mom sad when he'd chosen Dad's name over hers."

There might have been many reasons she wasn't around anymore, a simple divorce being one of them, but the grief I heard in his voice was the kind that came from real loss. Hearing it in this commanding man who'd seemed so sure, so strong, left compassion burning in its wake.

My voice was gentle when I asked, "What was the real reason you chose her name?"

"Even then, I bucked at following in my big brother's footsteps."

I wasn't sure it was true. I thought the first reason he'd given me was more likely the real one.

Silence settled between us, allowing the rhythm of the night to take over. The water rushing and pounding down from the height. The chirp of the crickets. The whisper of the wind through the trees. I shivered. The combination of the mist from the waterfall dampening my skin and the breeze coasting over it chilled me.

After retreating from the library, I'd barely slipped back into my boots before leaving the house, determined to get air, to put distance between me and the emotions flooding the family. I hadn't grabbed a flannel or a sweatshirt to put on over my tank. I hadn't thought I'd need it with the night still warm and tomorrow's forecast being for more heat.

"Why were you talking to Lorenzo Puzo?" he asked, a determination in his tone that said he'd find out one way or another.

Adam had asked me not to tell the family about the jewelry yet, and I understood his reasoning for not getting anyone's hopes up. Although, the logic was muddied now with Rafe here, as he certainly had enough money to invest in the ranch if he wanted, so maybe it was simply all the unknowns that had me holding back some of the truth. Or maybe it was because I couldn't stand the idea of giving Rafe the satisfaction of seeing my family as thieves when it was exactly what he'd already expected. So, I told him part of the truth but not all of it.

"I was researching our family history. No one knew my great-grandmother's maiden name until I came across an old photograph of her that had Carolyn Puzo written on the back. I've been contacting any Puzo families I could find to see if they knew her."

Even though I couldn't see his expression in the shadows, I knew he was scrutinizing me to see how truthful I was being. I didn't flinch. I didn't look away. I just met his gaze with as steady of one as I could muster.

"You don't want to be tied to Lorenzo," he said with a certainty I didn't necessarily disagree with. But I still wanted to know about Carolyn. Why had she left and never mentioned any of them again? Was it simply because she hadn't agreed with their lifestyle? Or had they not approved of Harry McFlannigan, the son of Irish immigrants living in a tiny town in Tennessee, like Lorenzo had insinuated? Or was it because she was a thief?

"No matter how ugly, it's always best to know the truth,"

I said and meant it. No matter whether Carolyn had stolen the jewelry, or it had already been hers, or whatever else might have happened, knowing would help us to set it right.

"Careful what you wish for," he said darkly.

I didn't respond, couldn't argue with that statement. I shivered again, both the night air and the conversation getting to me. Add in Rafe and his constant bombardment on my senses, and it was all almost too much to keep up with. I rose, sliding down off the rock, and it brought me momentarily closer to him. The heat and sizzle of the attraction that wafted between us sparked stronger. A promised flame that had to be squelched.

"I don't normally believe in coincidences," I told him. "But that's all this is. I certainly had no idea you were tied to both Lorenzo and the Harringtons on Sunday night. You can believe that or not, but it's the truth."

He stepped off the boulder, and our toes touched. I was surprised to see he still had on his fancy dress shoes instead of something more appropriate for hiking through the woods.

"You're going to have blisters tomorrow," I said without thought.

He looked down, and a grunt of something that might have been acknowledgement drifted through him. The sound came from deep in his chest, a tantalizing lure that made me want to taste him. To see if I could make him rumble for all the reasons we'd planned the other night. To finally receive the satisfaction we'd both craved.

I stepped away and headed up the path the way I'd come instead. I heard him behind me, moving through the rocks and grass at the same pace as me, watching my every move. It kept the electricity drifting between us, a heady drug-like pull that left me craving more.

"How long are you staying?" he asked.

I briefly looked back over my shoulder. "The plan was to leave on Sunday after the wedding. You?"

"I'm here for the week."

I couldn't help the dart of something like hope that

whisked through me. Maybe we'd get to finish what we'd started in Vegas. Would I risk it for a chance at putting to rest this damn desire he'd stoked, even when there was just as much of a chance of him embedding himself permanently under my skin? It didn't matter, because if he'd all but tossed me out of his penthouse once his daughter had come home, he wasn't going to sleep with me when Fallon and his ex were under the same roof.

A possibility hit me like a brick. Maybe he'd come to reignite whatever he'd once lost with Lauren. With his brother gone, no one was here to stop them from being together, right? Except, the way they'd talked to each other in the library hadn't sounded like any kind of rekindling. It had sounded like loss and betrayal and disgust.

As we wound our way up along the smooth path at the cliff's edge next to the falls, Rafe let out a startled rumble. I turned just in time to see him slide toward the cliff in those fancy shoes. As he fought to keep from going over, pure panic had me grabbing at him and hauling him back onto the path.

Our bodies collided, and he wrapped his arm around my waist, still trying to right himself. Those sparks I'd been fighting burst through me, every nerve ending happily remembering and rejoicing in the strength of him. The feel of him. The yearning for him.

We were both panting, from the sudden adrenaline rush of the near accident as much as from our bodies tucked together. When I glanced up, his face was now on display in the moonlight. Dark eyes sparkled with shock and passion. We stayed there, frozen, for several heartbeats. Stuck as if by a force we couldn't see. Melded together.

I didn't believe in coincidences, but I had enough Irish in me—I'd been around Uncle Phil enough in the last days of his life—to completely believe in fate and gods and otherworldly beings playing mischief. Or acting as matchmaker. Maybe all of this was always supposed to happen.

Maybe I was supposed to end up right here with my body almost grafted to Rafe's.

Before I could even register he'd moved, Rafe's mouth crashed into mine. Liquid flames ran through me at the touch, like the burn of alcohol going down, spiking through every nerve. Golden ambrosia that sent my head spinning. After a second of pure shock, I returned the kiss. Pushing harder. Desperate and needy in a way I'd never been. He groaned, fisting my hair and steadying me as his lips took command. Demanding I yield. Demanding I give entrance. And when I opened for him, he invaded. Caressing and driving. Dancing and exploring.

Every sound, every sight, every feel of the night air disappeared until there was nothing left but Rafe. His body. His strength. The taste of him. Vibrant and addicting.

Something I'd hunger for over and over again.

Something that made me think the fates were right. We belonged. Our bodies and souls were meant to be together just like this.

But just as the thought hit me, he was gone. Nothing but space and the rush of the mountain air between us as the warmth of his body disappeared.

He stared at me, lips tight, expression dark.

"You're a damn siren. A temptress." The words were a growl, unforgiving and harsh.

My hand found my lips. They tingled from the force of his, warm and delightfully bruised.

I was grateful for the night sky and that, with the moon behind me, it would be my face that was now cast in shadows so he couldn't see my embarrassment. Humiliation at my ridiculous thoughts, and how easily I'd responded to his touch, and how he'd once again pushed me away as if I'd stolen the kiss from him.

"That's twice you've started something you didn't finish, Slick. Either do the job right or don't bother to do it at all." I whirled around and continued up the path at a much faster pace.

He kept up damn well for being in those stupid shoes, and we soon left the falls behind, the sound disappearing as the trees thinned and the fields around the house emerged. I sped up, almost jogging in my attempt to get away from him, to shut myself in my room and leave behind the fire burning in me. To forget the absolute *want* that had been replaced with humiliation.

Even if I wanted him, I couldn't have him. So imagining fates or wee folk having brought us together was just ridiculousness. We had more reasons to *not* be together than simply him not trusting me. Our lives would never line up. I lived in Tennessee, not in Vegas or California or even on the West Coast. I may be scrambling to find my place in this world, but that didn't mean I'd leave my home permanently in order to find it. I'd always want to keep the people I loved close. I wanted to leave a mark on my community, not run from it to follow a man.

So, whatever this was that burned between Rafe and me, it wasn't a forever after. It wasn't the gods sending me a sign. It wasn't even close to that. It was meaningless. It was nothing.

"Sadie," he called out to me as I reached the back door, and I ignored it. I swept into the mudroom that led into the laundry before racing into the sea of corridors running from the back to the front of the house. I'd almost reached the stairs before he grabbed me, hauling me to a stop. "Tennessee…"

I looked purposely from his face down to his hand with as much disdain as I could. "Let me go."

"Nothing good can come of us finishing what we started." Why did his words hurt even when I agreed with them? "But I won't deny wanting to." Astonishment drew my eyes back to his. When I didn't say anything, couldn't because I'd lost my voice, he continued in a controlled tone that took away the passion the words might have held. "We'll both be here for the week. Maybe it's what we both need. To finish what we started so we can leave it behind us."

"What—" My voice cracked, and I hated it because I didn't want to seem weak in front of him. "What are you suggesting?"

"A night. Maybe a few nights. And then you go back to Tennessee, and I go on with my life."

"You don't even trust me."

"I don't have to trust you to want you. I don't have to trust you to quench this thirst. You stay out of my life, and I'll stay out of yours, but we can at least walk away satisfied."

Would doing what he suggested, spending a night or two wrapped in his arms, be any different than the one-night stand I'd originally planned? We'd have sex, get the relief we both sought, and then I'd, hopefully, leave him and the ranch behind. Was I willing to take the risk I wouldn't be able to forget him?

"What about"—I waved my hand up the stairs—"the other people here?"

"I'm not staying in the house. There's a cabin down past the stables that used to belong to our horse trainer. I practically lived there as a kid." He clamped his lips together as if I'd drawn another truth from him, more revelations of his past, when I'd done nothing but ask a basic question.

He dropped his hand from my arm but didn't move away, and the heat of him seared through me unrelentingly. My heart rate increased, pulse pounding out a rhythm that was hard to ignore. My body was clearly screaming, *say yes*, but my brain was telling me to run before things got even more complicated. Before the fae played havoc with my life.

He was the one to move first. He left me at the base of the stairs and strode toward the front door where he picked up a rolling suitcase. He shot me one departing look as he said, "Think about it."

Then he was gone, leaving me spinning with turbulence. Head and heart and body all fighting to see who'd win.

Chapter Twelve

Rafe

UNDER THE WEIGHT
Performed by Bobby Bazini

What the hell had I just offered up? What had I gotten myself into?

My pulse was pounding as if I'd just stepped out of a boxing ring as I strode past the barns to the small, single-room cabin tucked behind them that had belonged to Levi, our horse trainer, for as long as I could remember. Like always, it was unlocked, welcoming me in a way that caused more memories to bleed.

The darkness inside was almost blinding after the bright moonlight, and I found the light switch using old muscle memory. A soft glow filled the room from an old, cloth-shaded lamp, revealing little of the cabin had changed in the years I'd been gone. Levi had passed away not long after my father had, and Spencer hadn't replaced him, saying he could do as good of a job breaking in the horses as the old man. It wasn't the truth. The only one who'd ever been as good with the horses as Levi was me, but Spencer likely couldn't have afforded to hire someone new. At the time, I'd thought it had been arrogance.

My forehead throbbed from my attempt at not feeling guilty over it.

A full-sized bed was shoved in one corner of the cabin, the frame made of simple pine logs that matched the two armchairs and side tables sitting in front of a small, river-rock fireplace. A small, two-seater table of cheap metal and green Formica was squeezed in front of a tiny, white refrigerator from the 1950s. The kitchenette had a chipped ceramic sink and a two-burner stovetop. The furniture was basic and worn, the wood floors scuffed from years of boots traveling over them, while an ugly, circular braided rug of mustard and camo green tried to tie the place together without success.

Levi hadn't cared. He'd rarely been in here. In fact, I'd probably spent more hours of my life in the cabin than he had. The barn and the horses had received the majority of his time, and back when the bunkhouse had been full of ranch hands, he'd eaten his meals with them in the mess hall, mostly using the kitchen to make coffee or pour himself a finger of whiskey.

After I'd stayed here for Spence's funeral, Lauren must have cleaned the place. It smelled of pine cleaner and bleach now instead of the dusty staleness that had greeted me after burying my brother. It was nowhere near the comfort and elegance I lived in at The Fortress with masterpieces on my walls, top-of-the-line linens welcoming me to bed, and furniture hand-selected by a very expensive interior designer. And yet, I felt a sense of home as I dropped my bag next to the beat-up dresser that had once held all of Levi's worldly possessions.

A hand-carved wooden frame sat atop the chest of drawers, holding a photo of Levi and me on either side of Firestarter. He'd already been old and weathered by then, his cowboy hat hiding a mostly bald head with a single ring of gray hair. His visible skin was a deep tan, the color of dirt, even though his feet were as white as cotton balls the few times I'd seen him without his boots. I was only fourteen in the picture—the same age as Fallon, I realized with a start—and yet, I'd thought I knew everything there was to know about breaking and training horses. My hair was a mop, the shape of my cowboy hat embedded into it, with my hat thrown to the ground. I was smiling so large you could almost see my tonsils, full of pride and joy because we'd finally gotten the saddle on the stallion. The giant roan had given us a run for our money. It had taken every trick and both our steady hands to finally break him. And even then, he'd been sneaky and independent. But he'd been a hell of a horse.

It had been twenty-one years since that picture was taken. Sometimes, it felt like I'd barely blinked since then, and in other ways, it felt like I'd lived an eternity. I'd certainly lived a completely different life than the one that teenaged boy had thought he'd have.

What would Levi think of what I'd built?

He'd been around for four years after I'd left, and two years after Dad had passed. He'd asked me repeatedly when I was going to get my head out of my ass and come home, and I'd told him I didn't have a home anymore.

Those words had wounded him far more than they'd ever wounded Dad.

Our father had invested his time and energy into his oldest son from the day my brother was born. Spencer was his legacy. He'd been just fine with me spending my days with Levi, learning a trade that was good for the Harrington name, but it had been Spencer he'd imparted his personal wisdom to. Maybe it was as much my fault as my dad's that we'd barely tolerated each other. I'd always been more focused on the horses than the entirety of what needed to be done to make the ranch successful. I hadn't cared about the cattle or the hay fields. On the other hand, maybe I'd had no interest in them simply because Dad had no interest in me. Was it the chicken or the egg that had come first? I'd never know.

I shifted my jaw side to side and pressed my fingers into the tightness at the joint, attempting to ease the clench sending spikes of pain into my temples. I wasn't the teenager from that photo anymore. Nor was I the stupid young man who'd knocked up Lauren with pride, thinking I could keep her. I wasn't even the angry, betrayed brother who'd stormed at Spence when he'd come back to the ranch from Vegas with a ring on the finger of the woman carrying my child.

I'd left all three of those versions of myself in my past. Buried them, just as I'd buried Dad and Levi.

But maybe you could never truly bury the versions of yourself that lived inside you. Maybe you had to meld them together rather than cast them out. Maybe fate was forcing me to do just that, face all my pieces so I could no longer lock them behind a door labeled *Warning—Enter at Your Own Risk*.

I stepped into the tiny bathroom. A stained white porcelain tub took up a good portion of the room with the shower curtain freshly replaced since I'd stayed here last. The pedestal sink was cracked, and the pull-handle toilet was barely functional. It could have been retro-cozy if it didn't look so abused.

I dropped my clothes and stepped into the shower, trying to rinse away the day. The memories. The loss and heartache that threatened to rip me to shreds. The desire that still thundered from being so close to Sadie Fucking Hatley.

I had to duck to fit under the showerhead.

The water was cold and smelled of rust and ill-use.

It smelled of the farm.

I turned the water off and stepped out with demons chasing me. I pulled on a pair of boxer briefs and then landed on my back on the bed with my feet hanging over the footboard. When I'd stayed here for the funeral, I'd had a good chuckle at the realization of how short the man I'd looked up to had to have been to sleep without complaint in the little bed. As a kid, I'd thought he was the size of a mountain, and he'd turned out to be just a hill—one that had shaped me, but still a hill.

My phone rang, and I groaned but rolled out of bed to dig it out of my suit jacket. Steele's number flashed along the screen.

"What?" I asked.

"The man following Sadie Hatley is Nero Lancaster. He has a long rap sheet of possible crimes but nothing that's stuck. Almost did some time for a protection racket in Eastside LA before he moved to Vegas in the early 2000s. Technically, he owns an investigative firm—not sure how he got his license with his past, but he did. I'll do more digging to see if Puzo is a client, but I doubt either of them have left behind a record of their business."

"Where is he now?"

Steele hesitated. "I'd have to tap into some resources you don't like me using to find that out."

Meaning we'd have to illegally find the GPS on his phone or on his car, if the man even had any of it turned on. If he worked for Puzo as a muscle-for-hire, he'd know how to hide his tracks. And regardless, Steele knew I wasn't in favor of bending the law.

"According to Adam, Puzo has land up here in Rivers," I told him. "He's been *helping* the local businesses. I want to know what that's about."

"Well. Damn. I'll see what I can dig up that's public record. One more thing. I couldn't find a flight for Sadie Hatley that left yesterday."

The warring parts of my body reacted at her name. "She's here. At the ranch."

It took him a beat to respond—and it took a lot to surprise Steele. "What? She's there? Why the hell would she be there?"

I explained what Lauren and Adam had told me about the dude ranch exchange of information, as well as what Sadie had told me about her great-grandmother and the Puzos.

"Do you believe any of it?" Steele clearly didn't.

I thought about Sadie's face in the moonlight as she'd told me she didn't believe in coincidences, but that was what this was. I thought of the way she tasted when I'd had my tongue tangled with hers. I thought of the feel of her body, and the way she'd all but run from me after I'd backed off, and the astonishment coasting her face when I'd suggested we spend a few nights twined together. She was either a hell of an actress, or she was telling me the truth. Or at least as much of it as she was willing to share at this time. She'd held something back. Her eyes had darted away before she'd told me about her great-grandmother.

"I do."

"You think she doesn't know the truth about Puzo?"

"I have no idea how much she knows about him. I do know that both times I suggested she was working for him, she was surprised and pissed."

"Your judgment isn't exactly clear when it comes to her."

It wasn't. I wouldn't deny it. I was entranced. Captivated. And I desperately wanted for her to be telling me the truth. I wanted her to be exactly who she said she was, so I could lose myself in her skin a few times without regret. So I could get the taste of her out of my system and go on with my life.

"What else did you find out about the Hatleys?" I asked.

"They seem to be exactly who and what they say they are. Long-standing ties to the Tennessee community they live in. They had an ugly confrontation with the Laredo cartel a little over a year ago. The oldest brother is married to a former NSA agent who helped bring the cartel down. The other brother is the local sheriff."

"So not the type to get in bed with Puzo."

"On the surface, no, but who knows what goes on behind the scenes. Maybe the Laredos were muscling in on their turf. If they are into something dirty, they've kept it small and local."

We let that set for a moment. "I may need some help with something else here, but I'm not ready to talk about it yet."

There'd been something about Adam that had set off my signals earlier. Something more than the resentment he'd tossed my way since we'd been kids. Maybe it was what Fallon had told me about him and Spence arguing the night my brother died, or how he'd tossed Spence's failure at me with glee. Or maybe I just wanted him to be involved so I didn't have to live with remorse that was starting to find a home inside me. I wasn't sure yet.

"You still planning on selling the place?" Steele asked.

My thoughts by the waterfall, of keeping the land whole and safe from developers, returned. Dad had seen it as a duty, keeping the ever-diminishing wild of California safe from the hordes that wanted nothing more than to tear her up and fill her with structures and people. I'd forgotten about it until today—or I'd let myself forget it.

"Unless this dude ranch idea can show me it's

salvageable," I said and despised how mere minutes back on the ranch had me questioning my plans.

My father had been good at carving uncertainty and doubts into me. He'd taken Spence's side in every argument, even when we'd all known Spence was wrong. Just like he'd taken my brother's side over mine when it had come to Lauren. From the moment he'd caught me dating her, he'd told me I was in the wrong. He'd said you didn't muscle in on your brother's girl, and I'd known he was right and hadn't cared. Truth was, my dad's disapproval had made me all the more determined to win her love.

As I hung up with Steele, I wished for a rare second glass of bourbon. The one I'd downed in Dad's old office had long since burned through me. My mind whirled with questions, memories of long-lost hopes, and unexpected grief until I finally fell into a fitful sleep where I dreamed of pixies.

They carried me off into the moonlight, spinning me wildly around the falls before dropping me from the clifftop. I landed in nettles that stung my entire body like a whip on bare flesh, and when I woke with a pounding chest in the dark, more memories I despised came with them. The one and only time my dad had used anything but a hand on me, and the way Mom had stepped between me and the horse whip. The way she'd grabbed it, and thrust it back at him, and told him if he ever touched me that way again, he'd lose everything he loved.

I bit my tongue that day, knowing it wasn't me he cared about losing.

♫ ♫ ♫

When I left Levi's cabin the next morning, I was dressed in jeans, a T-shirt, and scuffed cowboy boots I'd dug out from the back of my closet when I'd packed the day before. I couldn't remember the last time I'd worn them and wasn't even sure how I still owned them, but they would serve their purpose this week.

My head craved coffee, and my stomach was objecting to having missed dinner, so I was headed for the main house for food when I was frozen mid-stride by the view of Sadie Hatley sitting on the top rail of the nearest corral. Her face was sheltered by the brim of her black cowboy hat, body encased in jeans and a thin, cotton button-down in a shade of blue that would make those eyes even more vivid.

The sun practically shimmered around her. When I turned to look at what had brought a smile to her face, my heart grew a thousand times. Fallon stood on the back of her horse as it trotted around the ring. She was in jean shorts that barely covered her butt with a short-sleeved shirt knotted just below her chest. She wore bright-pink cowboy boots that matched the cowboy hat sitting on two long braids. Her smile was so large it could have touched the sky.

That grin, that happiness I rarely saw in her anymore, slammed into me, smoothing away the remnants of my sleepless night like a salve.

She spun a lasso above her head before sliding it down around her body and then jumping over it and landing cleanly on the horse's back. The buckskin quarter horse never broke stride, steady and strong as it made its way around the paddock with its mane, done in a flourish of braids and ribbons, blowing behind it. My daughter moved fluidly from the jump into a three-hundred-and-sixty-degree spin, all while continuing to dance with the lasso.

I finally unstuck my boots, striding over to lean on the rail next to Sadie. I felt rather than saw her look down at me. But when she inched away, it made me want to put my hands on her waist and drag her back so our skin was touching. Instead, I let her go—at least for now.

The only positive of my restless night had been the renewed determination it had left me with when it came to Sadie Hatley. I'd break her just like I'd broken dozens of mares before her. Not brutally. Not even to prove I could. But simply so I could capture every moan and gasp she'd offer up. So she'd be mine, even if it was only for the handful of days she was here. And in those moments, I knew I'd find the truth of her. Good, bad, or ugly.

Fallon drew her horse up into the center of the ring where

both she and the horse took a bow. Sadie clapped wildly, put two fingers in her mouth, and whistled. It took a whole hell of a lot of physical control to draw my gaze away from those pretty lips back to my daughter.

Sliding off her horse, Fallon walked over to us with a confident saunter that made me remember those conversations I wanted to have with her mom about dating—or rather, not dating. Her horse followed without even a command, devoted to my daughter. Did Fallon know I felt the same? Had I ever shown her that I would do just about anything to make her happy?

Anything but the one thing she wants the most, my devil taunted.

"That was incredible," Sadie told her. "How long have you been doing this?"

Fallon took off her hat and placed it on the post rail. "I don't know. Since I was maybe five?" She looked at me for confirmation, and I nodded.

I may not have been on the ranch, but I knew what went on with my daughter. I'd always made her my business. When Lauren had first told me Fallon was already doing tricks and wanted to take lessons with one of the instructors at the Western riding school, I hadn't been sure about it. Sending her off to do stunts on a horse felt like the opposite of protecting her. It felt like throwing her outside at night when you knew the wolves were coming.

"Have you ever gotten hurt?" Sadie asked.

"I broke my arm once, and I've had lots of cuts and bruises and strains, but you know what they say, 'No pain, no gain,'" Fallon said with a smile.

"Your mom said you want to put on shows for your guests," Sadie said. It wasn't really a question, but it encouraged Fallon to talk in a way I wasn't good at doing these days.

"My friend, Maisey, and I have a whole act worked out. And some of the other students at the Western riding school would be happy to perform. We can easily put on a show a couple of nights a week. I figured we could set up bleachers on the south side of the corral and maybe even sell popcorn and soda, that kind of thing. Maybe donate the profits to an equine rescue."

The hope on my daughter's face and the pride I felt at her thinking of a charity rather than lining her pocketbook was enough to almost split me in two. That had always been the Harrington way—you helped out your community. For Fallon, that meant the horses she loved as well as the people.

"We just have to convince old stingy here that we can actually make a go of it," Fallon said, elbowing my arm so it slid off the rail. What would it mean to the community if the ranch was running at full capacity again? If it drew people to the area? I bit my cheek, uncomfortable with the idea of the ranch digging itself into me again.

Sadie turned to me. "Did you ever perform like that?"

I raised a single, sarcastic brow.

When I didn't answer, Fallon did for me. "He did. You should see this picture of him that I have. He's wearing a white outfit with *sparkles*!"

Sadie's mouth fell open, and her eyes glistened with humor. It had me fighting back my own smile.

"I lost a bet with Spence," I explained. "Ended up in a *Saturday Night Fever* outfit—to which he added glitter, I might add—and then had to ride to the lake and back."

"Did he *make* you do the one-handed handstand on the horse's back also?" Fallon smirked. I reached out and tweaked a braid.

"That was so Suzanne Perk didn't get the idea I was more interested in her brother than her. I'd say she understood the message I sent."

"Dad!" she laughed, and for the first time since leaving the ranch fourteen years ago, I was glad I was there. Seeing her happy like this, enjoying herself…it was a gift. One I didn't want to lose.

But the reality was, even I might not be able to sustain the ranch for long at the rate it was losing money. Not without making Marquess Enterprises bleed too.

As if she'd read my mind, Fallon's smile faded.

"I gotta go rub Daisy down, make sure she gets a treat." She grabbed the horse's reins and took off toward the exit of the corral.

I watched her, and all the while, Sadie stared at me. When I finally turned my head to glance up at her, there was a look of something like awe on her face before she tucked it away.

I wanted it back. I wanted her to be in awe for more reasons than I could count and more than were healthy for either of us.

"You're good with her." The amazement in her voice bit at me.

"It's easy to be good with Fallon. She's always been an even-tempered and agreeable kid." Even with her gloomy, teen years torturing us right now, she'd never been rebellious, never argued for the sake of arguing—at least not until Spence had been ripped away from her.

"But she lived here, and you didn't?" Sadie said.

Curiosity rippled off her, as if she had a thousand questions to ask, and I realized that was the way she'd been since I'd first met her. Insatiable. I wondered if she was that way in every aspect of her life, and what it would take to try to quench her ravenous nature. A hint of panic spun through my chest because giving Sadie pieces of me, telling her my history, might not allow me to walk away without leaving a mark, and I hadn't let anyone brand me in years. But I also knew I'd have to give her something if I expected her to trust me with those secrets she was still hiding.

"You want answers, and so do I," I told her. "You come to my place tonight, and I might give you a few, but I'll expect some in return."

She caught her bottom lip in her teeth and glanced away. "With what you offered last night, I didn't think we'd be doing much talking."

"We'll get to that too."

Her skin flushed, turning a delightful pink I wanted to lay my hands on. Those bright bluebell eyes turned dark like the deepest parts of the lake in the sunshine.

I backed up enough to hold my hand out to her. "You have breakfast yet?"

She slipped one leg over the rail and then the other before taking my hand and jumping down. She pulled away as soon as both feet were on the ground, but her touch lingered on my skin.

"I tried to help, but Lauren shooed me out to watch Fallon." We headed toward the house, and she added on, "I think Lauren might work harder than anyone I've ever met. Harder than even my brother, and I didn't think I'd ever meet someone who worked harder than Ryder."

I didn't want to think about what Lauren was doing these days, so I didn't respond.

As if she hadn't noticed, Sadie kept on going, "I think she's taken on all of Spencer's chores in addition to her own. She doesn't have the money to hire anyone else, so she's trying to do it all. And grieving. And raising your daughter. I can't imagine."

I heard the judgment in her tone, and it took my good humor and sent it into the sky. She could be curious, and she could want to understand me and mine, but she didn't deserve to judge me. Lauren had made her bed, just as I'd made mine. We'd all had choices, even Spencer, and now we'd been left to live with the consequences.

Chapter Thirteen

Sadie

DEAD SET
Performed by Max McNown

The smiling, charming Rafe who'd watched his daughter and flirted with me had been almost more entrancing than the broody bar owner I'd first met. I regretted that mentioning Lauren and the work I saw her doing with no help—not from her brother or from her child's father—had closed him down like a book shutting, and yet I could read the cover. The tight muscles of his shoulders and hard line of his jaw made it very clear it wasn't my business. I might not know what had happened in order for Lauren to wind up married to his brother after having given birth to Rafe's child, but I could see it had left wounds behind. Ones that would be hard to heal if you had to face them every time you wanted to see your daughter.

For a brief moment, I'd thought maybe he'd try to win Lauren back, but he'd asked me twice now to come to his bed, and somehow, I doubted he'd do that here if he intended to woo Lauren back. And the tension between them yesterday had not shown any indication of easing. So I knew the hot and cold he'd sent my way didn't have anything to do with her. It had everything to do with seeing me with Lorenzo.

After going to my room last night, I'd tossed and turned rather than slept. The lingering need he'd ignited had never drifted away even though I'd tried, once again, to shake it on my own. It had been my rampant curiosity as much as the lust that had kept me awake. I'd tried to make sense of all the pieces of the story I'd garnered about Rafe, his daughter, Adam, and the ranch without much success. There was still too much of their history I hadn't been told. How Lorenzo fit was an even bigger unknown.

But it wasn't the mystery of their pasts that was the last thing I'd thought about before I'd fallen asleep. It was that feeling I'd had by the waterfall of fate, so when I did finally drift off, I dreamed of laughing wee folk. They pulled strings on me like a puppet, making me dance around Rafe in a bluebell-studded field, and I'd woken with the word *forever* rolling from my tongue in a forbidden whisper that had sent my heart racing.

Rafe walking up to the corral in jeans, cowboy boots, and a hat this morning had spiked my pulse all over again. He'd looked damned good, almost better than he'd looked in his handmade suit. It made me want to peel back his layers and understand what had turned the farm boy into a multi-million-dollar business man. It made me want to show up in the cabin he'd said he was staying at just to get answers.

We walked through the back door of the castle-like house after watching Fallon and left our boots and hats in the mudroom. I felt his gaze on me the entire time, trailing after me as I made my way down the hall to the enormous kitchen, but he didn't say a word. Knowing he was saving them all for tonight only made my blood pressure spike more.

The dark cabinets and older appliances in the kitchen screamed of a 1990s remodel, but it was large enough that, with some slight changes, it could be used as a restaurant kitchen. The addition Ryder had added on to our farmhouse had a large hall with oversized bench tables perfect for the family-style bowls of food we served, but the Harringtons' formal dining room, with its mahogany table and gilded mirrors, could easily accommodate a buffet that would meet their needs. Or perhaps they could use the old bunkhouse mess hall.

I was surprised to find Lauren had a full, hot breakfast on the table with scrambled eggs, bacon, grilled tomatoes, and avocado toast. No grits, but there were country potatoes instead, reminding me that we weren't in the South but rather in

California.

"You didn't need to do all this," Rafe grunted out. "Each of us could have found something on our own."

She hardly acknowledged him, stacking dishes she'd already used in a large dishwasher. "I wanted Sadie's opinion on the breakfast. Do your guests order off a menu, or do you serve buffet style?"

"All our meals are served family style. Large bowls and platters on long tables in the restaurant with multiple families at each one. But the guests can also order room service until about ten o'clock or so. We set up picnic lunches and sack lunches for those who will be out exploring during the day. We find most of the guests want the full experience though, and they like coming to the restaurant and feeling like they're part of the ranch."

Fallon and Adam joined us, and an awkward silence settled down while everyone ate. Adam had set a folder down on the table when he'd first entered, and he slid it toward Rafe. "Here's Spence's login information. Take a look through the accounts, and let me know what you have questions about. Should be fairly straightforward. I imagine your books for Marquess Enterprises are a lot more complicated."

Rafe didn't take the folder, but his gaze lingered on Adam's for a moment with something a lot like suspicion before he slid it behind his blank façade. Fallon watched the exchange with skepticism that mirrored her father's, but Lauren seemed oblivious to it. Everything about the silent conversations added more questions to the pile that had kept me up at night.

"I'll be out in the alfalfa fields this morning, baling," Lauren said, looking at Fallon. "I'll need you to take care of getting the horses fed and exercised."

"I already started before I came in," Fallon responded without even a blink.

When I was her age, I'd despised doing chores on the ranch. It had felt like it ate away at all my free time, and I'd been jealous of my friends who lived in town and got to play their way through their weekends and school holidays. Fallon didn't look like she cared, and I wondered just how much responsibility she'd been given now that Spence had died. How much had she picked up right along with her mother?

Adam didn't seem obligated to help either of them, and Rafe's jaw was stiff again, as if he was biting his tongue not to intercede.

"If you give me a list of things to do, I can help," I offered.

"Yesterday, we mostly talked about our weddings, and we have so little of your time, so I'd really rather you work through the details of your ranch's conversion with Adam," Lauren said.

"I can do both. I'll leave Adam all the information Ryder sent me with, and he can go through it while I work on some of the chores this morning. After lunch, I can answer any questions he has." When Lauren hesitated, I smiled at her and said, "Seriously, my family would tell you it's best to put me to work. Otherwise, I get up to all sorts of mischief. Idle hands and all that."

She looked hesitant but said, "If you could help Fallon, that would be great. Her instructor is coming this afternoon for her trick riding lessons, and I want to make sure she's done before then."

"Why aren't Kurt and Teddy doing the baling?" Rafe asked tersely.

Lauren flushed. "We had to let them go last year."

"They were here when I came for the funeral."

"They were just helping out because of what had happened, pitching in like our community always does," Lauren's voice got small and pained.

"So, how many people do you actually have left working on the ranch?" he demanded.

A tense silence filled the air until Fallon answered, "No one full-time."

"No one?" Rafe's voice held astonishment and a hint of frustration.

"It's cheaper and easier to bring them in for one-off jobs.

We'll have staff on hand to help out while we focus on the wedding, but we can't keep them year-round and pay all the employee benefits. Adam suggested the contract work last year, and it's worked out for us," Lauren explained.

"Has it," Rafe said, and you could hear in his tone that he didn't agree. "And how's that working out for Teddy and Kurt and the others? Do they even have health insurance now? How are their families getting by in between the jobs they do for you?"

Adam dropped his napkin. "Don't act like you care about us or any of them, Rafe. This community has done what it needed to do to keep everyone afloat. Kurt has a job in town bartending. Teddy works out at the national park."

Rafe ignored Adam and looked at Lauren. "So who's helping you bale today?"

"I don't need help. The machines do it all," Lauren said.

Rafe's gaze narrowed. "Cut the crap, Lauren. One person *can* do it all, but it's easier to have at least two working it."

She didn't say anything. Instead, she got up and started cleaning up the kitchen.

"Why aren't you helping?" Rafe addressed the question toward Adam. His cheeks flushed, and the hand that reached for his coffee cup actually shook.

"You know I'm allergic to alfalfa," he said. "I'm loaded up on meds as it is during harvest with the wind blowing pollen all over the place."

That explained his red eyes and runny nose, but I couldn't help but think his tone was a tad bit too defensive and whiny. It made me like the guy just a hair less. I understood allergies could be deadly, even something seemingly as simple as hay fever could cause a person's lungs to close. But to my ears, that wasn't what kept Adam away. He simply didn't like the work.

Farm labor was dirty and hard. You had to truly love the land and the life it provided you to continue to do it day after day, year after year. My dad and Ryder would never stop working the ranch. While I didn't mind lending a hand here and there, I certainly didn't want to do it as my job every single day.

Just like I wasn't sure I wanted to sling pints across a bar top every night. But I preferred spending my time at the bar more than cleaning rooms or stalls at the ranch.

Still, I did all of it whenever my family needed me. I'd never leave them short-handed.

I'd never leave Ryder alone baling hay. It was dangerous, even if it was doable.

I scraped my plate clean then rose to help Lauren clean up. In my family, if you cooked, you weren't allowed to cleanup.

In the strained silence that had settled in the room, Rafe's deep voice sounded like a gunshot. "Fine. I'll help."

Lauren whipped around to stare at him from the sink. "What? No." She shook her head. "Spence would hate that."

"Last I checked, Spence was dead and didn't have a say."

It wounded her. Fallon gasped. Even I felt like I should snap at him for being so harsh.

He didn't wait for anyone to say anything. He just stormed out of the kitchen.

"You know it isn't a good idea to have him here," Adam said dryly.

"Like I have a choice!" Lauren bit back.

When I looked across at Fallon, she was staring down at her plate as if she wanted to cry. No sight of the girl who'd danced on a horse's back just minutes ago with a vivacious energy all but beaming from her. This one looked as if she'd slowly withdrawn, making herself as small as possible.

The air in the kitchen had already been tense, and it grew now until it felt like it was an actual entity. As if suddenly realizing they had an outsider watching the exchange, Adam shot a smile my way. It was friendly and full of a charm I might have been taken in by if I hadn't witnessed everything else. "Sorry to let our family drama ruin your day, Sadie, but you can probably tell how important the information you've brought is to us." He wasn't just talking about the ranch's conversion but about the jewels.

I didn't know how to respond and wasn't sure I could

because my heart was in my throat. So, I simply nodded. Sympathy and compassion welled inside me for Fallon. For Rafe. For all of them caught in this limbo of pain and betrayal and loss.

Fallon brought her dishes over, set them in the dishwasher, and then left the kitchen as if she was a ghost floating on light feet. Neither Lauren nor Adam even acknowledged her as she disappeared down the hall. My sympathy disappeared in a surge of anger on the teen's behalf.

Even when things had been tight growing up, even when there'd been the threat of having to sell off the land lingering over our heads, my parents had never argued about it at our kitchen table. We'd always been a family at mealtimes—siblings razzing each other, and Mama and Daddy asking about our day. We'd had all of their attention. Their kids had always been their priority, even over the ranch, and we'd known it.

I finished helping Lauren clean because I felt like I had to after I'd started, but I made quick work of it. I ran upstairs and got all the documents Ryder had sent with me and left them in the office on Adam's desk before heading back out to the outbuildings.

I found Fallon cleaning water troughs. She'd exchanged her vibrant pink hat and boots for worn tan ones that look like they'd seen better days.

I dove in without asking, filling feedbags and mucking stalls.

"You shouldn't have to help," Fallon finally said. "You're our guest."

I leaned on the handle of the pitchfork I was using, tipped my hat back, and smiled at her. "The good thing about opening a dude ranch was finding some people actually *want* to experience the work firsthand. You're charging them to clean stalls for you."

Fallon's mouth dropped. "No one really signs up to do the work, do they?"

"Not a lot. And even less now that we've built a reputation for having plenty of first-rate outdoor experiences, but you'd be surprised."

We worked in silence for a few minutes before Fallon asked with an almost breathless hope, "Do you think it would work here? Do you really think we'd be able to keep the ranch if we made it a resort?"

I wanted to tell her yes, just because she seemed so desperate, but instead I told her the truth. "I don't know. It saved us, but every ranch has a different cost base, and I'd say things are a lot more expensive here in California than where we're at. It also means you might be able to charge more though. In truth, my brother worked all the numbers and figured out just what we could afford to invest in order to make it profitable. I just did some of the grunt work. And now, I'm pretty hands-off as I spend most of my time running the family bar."

Fallon snorted. "Is that how you met Dad? Because you're both in the bar business?"

"Is he? I mean, I know he owns The Fortress, but I guess I don't know much else about his business."

"You knew enough to be in the penthouse Sunday night. I saw you leave."

She was staring at me, and I met her gaze with my own, trying not to blush, wondering what I'd looked like storming out with my tail between my legs and fury trailing behind me.

"I didn't know you saw me."

"I wasn't sure it was you yesterday, and I didn't get why Dad was freaking out. But this morning, when I saw him next to you at the corral, it clicked. Did you have a fight before I got there?"

Definitely not fighting, but I willed myself not to blush. As I teased Gemma all the time, there was nothing wrong with sex, engaging in it, enjoying it. Nothing wrong with talking about it, but not with a teenager who wasn't mine.

"No. We'd just started to get to know each other, and when you showed up, he wanted you to be his focus." Her eyes went wide. "Then, there was a misunderstanding when he saw me the next day."

"Dad can be cold and hard at times, but I've never seen him as icy as he was with you when we got here, so I thought you'd fought. But then this morning…" She trailed off, and it was her turn to be embarrassed. Her cheeks, already flushed from working hard in a barn that was nearing eighty degrees, turned even more heated. "He seemed to like you."

"It's complicated," I told her.

"I've never seen Dad with anyone," she said with a careless shrug, turning back to her task. "I actually thought maybe his heart was made of stone."

That hit me solid in the gut. Not only the fact he'd never brought another woman around her but that she wasn't sure he could love at all. Feel anything. I'd been on the receiving end of multiple emotions with Rafe. Passion. Anger. Disappointment. Even charm and laughter.

"I can see he loves you," I said softly.

She looked up and then away. "Yeah. It's easy to pretend when you only see someone for a few days here and there."

"I don't think it's a pretense."

She shrugged. "If he really loved me, he'd do whatever he could to let me stay here. He wouldn't threaten to sell my home out from under my feet. What am I supposed to do with Daisy if I have to move to the Hurly house? Or worse, if I have to go live with him in Las Vegas?" She threw a hand toward the buckskin's stall. "He wants to sell all the horses. I can't lose her too…" her voice cracked, but she caught herself. Anger took over, pushing away the threat of tears. "And all my friends are here. Everything I love is right here in Rivers. The last thing I want is to go live in some cold penthouse in a casino and go to school with a thousand other kids whose parents work in Sin City."

I didn't miss the fact she'd said everything she loved was here, but that her dad didn't live in Rivers. And I felt sorry for Rafe all over again, for all of them, but especially this girl who'd been raised in the middle of some strange-ass dynamic that included an uncle as a father and a dad as a weekend-warrior parent.

It wasn't my place to fix any of it. I was here for a handful of days, and then I'd be gone, but I found myself wanting to. I wanted to leave them in better shape than I'd found them. Wanted to soothe and heal and somehow see them wind up as a family again.

I had the means in my hands of giving them some of what they needed to turn their lives around. I could hand over the jewels without telling the insurance company, or even my family, that I'd done it. If anyone ever asked about the costume jewelry again, I could just say I'd sent it off to Goodwill with the rest of Great-grandma Carolyn's movie props. Someone might be disappointed, but they'd never miss it. The money could help the Harringtons turn things around. It would give this girl what she said she wanted most. But I had this uneasy feeling that until I learned more, I shouldn't make any rash decisions. And the truth was, handing over the jewels wouldn't give Fallon what she really needed, which was to feel loved and wanted. She needed a place in the family that wasn't the crack breaking it apart but the one welding it together.

Chapter Fourteen

Rafe

THE COWBOY IN ME
Performed by Tim McGraw

Sweat dripped from my brows and ran down my back as I headed toward Levi's cabin. It had been a long time since I'd stood in the middle of the alfalfa fields, playing handmaiden to the tractor and baling equipment. Now, I had a sunburn from hours spent in the full July sun and blisters under the work gloves I'd borrowed, proving I'd done my part when Lauren *could* have handled the baling on her own and had done her best to remind me of that all day long. But Sadie's look, full of judgment, had gotten to me, and I wasn't sure what to make of it besides being irritated it had taken me away from the real business I'd needed to do today for my legitimate company.

To be fair, it hadn't just been Sadie's quiet condemnation that had landed me in the field. It had also been Adam's absolute refusal to take on any of the workload. He'd used his allergies as an excuse growing up too, but then we would come in from the field to find him lazing in an inner tube at the lake with the bluebells and yarrow in full bloom all around him. Once, when I'd complained about it, my dad had cuffed me on the back of the head and reminded me the Hurlys didn't own the land. If Adam's dad didn't want to make him work, that was on them. Dad was paying their father for his time as foreman, not the son.

More than once, I'd wanted to respond by telling my dad I didn't own the land either. Instead, I'd bitten my tongue, know ng if it had ever slipped out, I would have spent days in the grueling heat, baling hay by hand the way he'd had to do growing up instead of using the equipment. So, I'd simply done whatever job he'd assigned me as quickly as possible so I could return to Levi and the horses, who never made me feel like I'd somehow disappointed them just by breathing.

In the cabin, I showered and pulled on clean clothes before heading back toward the main house. We'd stopped for lunch midday, but I was still starving, so I wolfed down a sandwich, standing up in the cool of the kitchen, and then made my way to the office. The door in the bookshelf that led to the walk-in vault was open, and Fallon's story about Adam and the time he'd been spending there came slamming back into me.

Silently, I made my way over and looked inside. Adam was flipping through papers in an old file box, glasses slipping down his nose, brows drawn together in a frown. He was muttering to himself, but I couldn't quite catch what he was saying. Something about knowing it was there somewhere.

"What are you looking for?" I asked.

He jumped, dropping the box on the floor, and the paperwork scattered.

"Jesus Christ!" He put a hand to his heart as the other pushed his square frames back up his nose. "Don't sneak up on me like that."

He squatted down and started tossing items back into the box. I joined him, the musty scent of old paper wafting up from the yellowing files as I collected them.

"What is all this?"

"Nothing that shouldn't have been thrown out decades ago," he said too quickly, raising my hackles.

My hands landed on a black-and-white photograph of Great-grandma Beatrice. She was wearing an evening gown that would have been popular in the late thirties, satiny and shimmering. It was the same dress she was wearing in the painting over the mantel, and like in the portrait, diamonds that had put the family and the ranch on the map glittered over her body. A heavy necklace draped over her collarbone and dipped into the V of the neckline while matching layers of bracelets and chandelier earrings completed the set. A stunning tiara I'd never seen before sparkled from the depths of her dark hair.

"I remember your dad mentioning some old movie company stocks the family had inherited. I've never seen anything about them in the asset sheets or online accounts, and I wondered what had happened to them," Adam said in response to my question. "What do you got there?"

"Family picture." For some reason I couldn't explain, I didn't want his hands on it, so I tucked it into my pocket.

Once all the paperwork was shoved back into the box, in no particular order, he slid the lid on and shelved it. I scanned the other boxes. Some were labeled, some not, and I was reminded of how little I knew about the actual business of the ranch, and when I'd had the chance after Dad died, I'd only cared about getting my share of my inheritance.

"I took the stocks," I told him. "They were for a film studio called Ravaged Storm Productions. The family has owned them since the studio's inception. Taking them was part of the deal Spencer and I made."

Adam's expression turned grim. "Damn. I was hoping they'd be worth something, and we'd be able to sell them to fund the renovations." When I didn't reply, he tucked his hands in his pockets and rocked. "How much did you get for them?"

"Don't worry, Adam. I didn't rip my brother off. What I ended up with was far less than my due."

"And yet you're the primary reason the ranch is failing."

My gaze held his, and it was Adam who looked away. "Or maybe you and Spence have mismanaged it," I said just to see his reaction.

His mouth drew tight, and his eyes were cold when he said, "Don't lay your guilt at my feet. I've done my best with what we were left with."

And somehow, I didn't think he was just talking about the loan Spence had taken out. He brushed past me and stood at the door of the vault, waiting for me to leave. I walked out and straight to the desk where he had his laptop open with a stream of paperwork spread out next to it. Some were architectural designs, others were detailed spreadsheets, and one was on Hatley Ranch letterhead. When I read the initial paragraph, I realized it was the business plan the Hatleys had given the bank to obtain a loan for their renovation.

"How much do you think you'll need?" I asked. "And how long before it turns a profit?"

"The Hatleys were profitable in the first four years. They would have been in the black sooner, but I gather someone ran off with a chunk of their money. They had to pay it back anyway." I didn't miss the tone that said he knew what that was like and ignored the irritation that flared.

"Again. How much do you need, Adam?"

"A minimum of seven hundred thousand. A million would be better," he replied.

It wasn't as much as I'd expected, seeing as I'd just spent nearly nine hundred million getting The Fortress launched, but then again, we weren't talking about a five-star Vegas hotel and casino. Much to my annoyance, I found myself interested in the idea of what it would take to build an up-scale resort here in my hometown. My mind immediately went to work on upgrading the facilities, obtaining a liquor license, hiring a world-class chef, and assembling a team of outdoor guides.

I pushed a finger into my jaw, attempting to ease the tension that seemed to have taken permanent residence there this week.

I picked through the paperwork, landing on the architectural designs, noting the name on them was Ryder Hatley. He'd done the work himself. An all-around renaissance man. For some reason, it made me like him when I didn't even know him. "They had cabins built?"

"A dozen or so, and they converted an apartment over the barn. We have the old homestead, the bunkhouse, and Levi's cabin. Plus, there are a dozen rooms here in the main house we could use if we added bathrooms to them all. We'd actually have more space than they do even as it stands now."

I'd started to flip through the business plan Hatley had

outlined to the bank when Adam's hand came down on top of it. "She won't let you get involved." His voice was dark. "We don't want you here. Spencer leaving you in charge of the ranch's trust on Fallon's behalf was an oversight. He meant to change it to Lauren and me, but you know how he was with things like this. He put them off as long as he could."

The irritation I'd felt since finding him in the vault grew. "You don't have to tell me what my brother was like. He always put the ranch first. He knew what he was doing."

"People change. You weren't around to see it. The ranch was failing on his watch, and it was eating at him. He and Lauren were fighting daily. He was angry and cruel."

Not Spencer. He never would have been cruel to Lauren.

Except, he had been once before. He'd broken her heart when he'd left her behind to go to college and told her they shouldn't see each other for a while. But that was the one and only time I'd seen him hurt her. Even after he'd found out she was pregnant with my child, he'd only taken it out on me—a singular hit before he'd stormed away.

Adam reached across me to his laptop, closing the lid, but I caught a glimpse of an open email before he shut it, and my insides froze when I saw the Puzo name. The sinking feeling I'd had since arriving yesterday that Fallon was right about something being off with Adam morphed into real concern. Adam was somehow involved with Puzo. Did it have something to do with the ranch, or was he just the money man for the mob family? Would Adam have gone so far as to kill Spencer? I wasn't convinced yet that he would have, but I intended to find out.

"We can easily fix Spencer's oversight," Adam said. "All you have to do is sign over the control of the trust to us, and then you can go on your merry way like you've always wanted."

Before I'd shown up at the ranch, it would have been tempting, even if it would've given my daughter another reason to despise me. Now, she'd see it as another abandonment, especially with her concerns about Adam.

I wasn't sure why Spencer had trusted him when we'd both

been damn good at smelling liars and deceit growing up. It was how I'd ferreted out the money laundering at Puzo's club when I'd been working there. Back then, I hadn't understood the danger it put me in. Without thought, my hand went to my chest and the scar that remained. It ached, as if telling me something. As if telling me to watch my six all over again.

Instead of responding to Adam's dig, I tossed back, "What the hell are you doing getting mixed up with someone like Puzo?"

His eyes darted to the closed laptop as he pushed his glasses up again. "He's a smart businessman who's taken an active interest in the area. He sees the potential in not only our town but the ranch. He knows if we had something drawing people to the area, even more than just the slopes in the winter and hiking in the summer, the entire community would prosper."

"And he thinks the Harrington Ranch could be that draw?"

"Sure. Why not?"

Could it really be that simple? I'd told Sadie I didn't believe in coincidences, and it was true. Puzo had come to Rivers because of me and my family. But had he stayed because he'd seen something I'd been too blinded by hurt to see? "Puzo hates me with a passion you probably wouldn't understand, so I find it hard to believe his interest in the ranch is truly benevolent."

Adam scoffed. "Of course, what would I know? I'm just some stupid, small-town businessman, and you're some genius, world-savvy entrepreneur. You always did think your shit didn't stink."

I bit my cheek in an effort not to snap back. Instead, I sounded tired when I said, "You were never stupid."

He looked surprised I'd even given him that much.

Fallon walked into the office with her friend, Maisey. While I'd never met any of my daughter's friends in person until Spence's funeral, I'd heard about them and seen pictures of them. I made it a point to touch base with Fallon almost every day in some form, whether it was by text or a video or voice call. But seeing the way she'd clung to Maisey at the reception had made me realize how much of my daughter's life I'd missed experiencing because of my own damn stubbornness. Because of hurt I'd refused to let go of, and now it was too late. Too late for Spencer and me, at any rate.

The two girls were wearing yoga pants and tight tank tops that made me want to throw sweatshirts at them and tell them to cover up. The hair at their temples was sweaty and curling, and a sheen covered their faces from the workout with their trainer. I'd wanted to catch a part of it while I was here, and now I'd missed it because of the discussion with Adam.

Fallon's glance darted between me and her uncle as if trying to determine what I'd found out, and I just shook my head. Disappointment drifted over her face.

"Mom told me to order pizza for dinner. She wants me to find out what you both want," Fallon said. I grimaced. Knowing my dislike for pizza, ordering it was either Lauren's or Fallon's way of striking out at me.

"Meat lovers," Adam said without even glancing up from the Hatley document he was scanning. No please. No thank you. A grunted out, high-handed demand. It pissed me off. He acted like everything here belonged to him and was his due when, in truth, he only owned a one-acre parcel down the road. In actuality, he was nothing more than an employee. Interesting that he was the only full-time employee left when they could have contracted out his work much easier than some of the hard labor.

"Thank your mom for me, but I'll just find something here," I said.

"After we eat, Maisey and I want to take the boat out on the lake, but Mom won't let me without an adult. She says it's my consequence for taking the plane. I have to earn my solo rights back," Fallon said scathingly. While I knew for a fact Lauren wouldn't have let Fallon pilot the Cessna all alone, she likely had let our daughter behind the wheel of almost every other vehicle on the ranch. When I was her age, I'd driven nearly everything with a motor, but I'd never learned to fly the plane. Dad had reserved that privilege for Spencer.

When I didn't respond, Fallon rolled her eyes up to the ceiling and asked in a pained tone, "So, will you go with us?"

I hadn't even touched the long list of things I needed to do for Marquess Enterprises today, let alone looked through the ranch's accounts, but I'd also never spent time on the lake with my daughter. Never spent even one second playing with her here in the place she loved, and I suddenly wanted to give that moment to both of us.

"What's your mother doing?" I asked.

"Ironing all the linens for the wedding," Fallon said.

Lauren had spent hours in the seat of the tractor, baling alfalfa, gone straight out to check the cattle in the far field, and now, instead of showering and resting for the evening, she was starting an entirely different job. Sadie had been right. She was doing all of Spence's jobs on top of her own. As if reading my mind, Fallon shifted uncomfortably. "I asked if she wanted me to do it, and she told me she had it covered."

"Where's Sadie?" I asked.

"Helping Mom."

I didn't know why that pissed me off. Because I didn't want a woman I didn't trust ingratiating herself into my family? Because it should be Lauren's family helping? Or because I simply didn't want Sadie working her fingers to the bone in a place that had easily tossed me away and never looked back?

"We'll all go," I said.

Fallon snorted. "You'll never get Mom to come. She's either working or sleeping."

My chest burned because I heard in those words what she wasn't saying—her mother didn't make time for her. I hadn't made time for her either. I couldn't go back in time and change it, but I could at least give her something while I was here.

I left Adam and the desk and the questions behind, striding toward the door.

"We'll see what I can do about that. Where are they?"

Fallon looked shocked by my acquiescence. "The old housekeeper's quarters."

"Order the pizza," I said, heading toward the back and then stopping. "Are you getting it from Jack's?" When she nodded, I said, "Get me a meatball sub, no cheese."

"No cheese?" Maisey gasped as if it was a sin, and it made my lips quirk.

"Dad is such a weirdo. He'll only eat cheese if it isn't melted or mixed into other things. He says it's too slimy otherwise."

As I started toward the back hallway, memories of another girl gasping at my dislike of cheese, and both her and Spence trying to change my mind as we ordered food at Jack's, flashed before my eyes. Suzanne Perk had been shoved in one side of a dingy booth with me while Spence and Lauren had been on the other. I'd been only a year older than Fallon at the time, maybe a year before Spence had graduated. A year before he'd broken up with Lauren. Even then, I'd envied them. The ease with which they touched each other, sat together, talked together.

Looking back, I realized I hadn't wanted Lauren as much as I'd wanted what they had. And even when I'd been with her for a few short months, it hadn't been the same as it had ever been with them. But I'd held on tight to her, thinking I'd finally gotten what I'd always wanted, when really, I'd simply been her stand-in for Spence. And like always, to the people here, I'd ended up being a disappointment.

Just like I'd always be a poor stand-in for Spence in my daughter's eyes. But I was here now, and he wasn't, so I'd do my damnedest to not disappoint her more than I had to. I'd figure out how to be someone she could count on, even if I'd never be what she really wanted. Even if being that person meant making the hard decision of selling the ranch. I wasn't going to be sentimental about it. If it would never sustain itself, it had to go.

I stopped and looked back toward the entryway where Fallon and Maisey were still standing. "We'll take the food with us to the lake, so pack a cooler with drinks."

My daughter's face lit up, and that right there was enough to know I'd made the right decision—at least for tonight.

Chapter Fifteen

Sadie

THE FEELS
Performed by Maren Morris

After Fallon and I had finished with the horses, I'd helped her clean out the chicken house and fill the cattle troughs, then I'd come back to the house to shower. I'd changed into a long pair of shorts that hid my scars and a tank top before finding Adam in the office.

I'd answered as many questions for him as I could about the ranch, gotten some answers for him from Ryder, and then asked what he'd found out about the jewels. He'd said he hadn't had time to dig into anything more, which seemed off somehow. It felt strange that, at the moment they needed money the most, he'd put it off. But he'd promised he was going to spend the rest of the afternoon looking for anything he could find in the stacks of old paperwork.

When I'd asked where Lauren was at, he'd directed me to the old servant quarters at the back of the house beyond the kitchen. And when I'd found her hard at work once again, I'd offered to help. She'd shrugged and simply shown me how to fold the napkins she was ironing into roses that would be placed on each plate for the wedding on Saturday. We were never that fancy at Hatley Ranch. We used cloth, as it was more environmentally sound, but we just folded them into thirds and stuck them in wicker baskets on the tables. Down home. Picnic-like almost.

At first, I was quiet, concentrating on what I was doing,

but once I got the hang of it, I tried to start up another conversation, asking her more questions about the upcoming wedding. But for the first time, Lauren seemed reluctant to talk to me, answering in one or two words. It took me several minutes to realize her shortness had nothing to do with not wanting to talk to me and much more to do with whatever she'd taken—tranquilizers, pain pills, something.

The woman I'd seen for the first two days, the one who'd been constantly on the go, full of energy and ideas and passion for the ranch, had disappeared. Now she seemed utterly defeated. Her motions were slow and methodical, almost as if she was having to concentrate extra hard on setting the iron down in all the right places.

I felt Rafe before I even realized he'd found us. The intensity of his look vibrated through me as he leaned up against the doorframe. His wet hair glimmered. The warm strands which had already been a shade lighter than his beard, had been spun with hundreds of bronze-and-gold highlights after just a single afternoon in the sun. He'd changed into another pair of jeans and a gray T-shirt that stretched tight across corded muscles, but his feet were clad only in socks. It felt strangely intimate to see him this way. At home. Relaxed.

No. Scratch that.

He wasn't relaxed. He was full of wound-up energy. A cougar waiting to pounce.

He scanned me in the same way I'd scanned him, top to bottom and back. When our gaze finally met, his brow was raised, and I heard the unspoken question in my head, *Am I going to show up at his cabin tonight or not?* I rolled my eyes, and his lip twitched as if he found it amusing.

"Fallon says you want me to take her out on the boat," Rafe said, turning away from me to Lauren with his half-smile still in place.

She didn't even look up. "She was angry I wouldn't let her go on her own, but I told her she'd have to earn our trust back after flying the Cessna by herself."

Shock had the words gasping out of me. "She flew a plane

all alone?"

Lauren grimaced at my question, and Rafe's face turned into a scowl.

"It won't happen again," he snarled. "I locked the plane down in my hangar after she arrived in Vegas."

No wonder he'd been pissed the night she'd shown up. No wonder he'd tossed me from the suite. It had been more than just him not wanting his daughter to see me. He'd been reeling from the discovery that she'd flown a plane there. A plane! Holy crap.

Lauren hadn't stopped working once while we talked. She was like a robot. Iron one napkin, pass it off, iron a tablecloth, hang it on the rack so it wouldn't get creased, move on to the next one.

"Thanks for taking her," Lauren said, but it was listless. Tired.

He pulled himself straight and crossed over to us. He put his hand on Lauren's, stilling the movement of the iron. "We're all going. We'll take the food and a cooler and spend some time relaxing before the sun goes down."

She jerked away from him, stepping aside. "I'm tired. And I have a lot to do before I head to bed. I appreciate you taking her so she doesn't stay cooped up in the house one more night."

Rafe slowly took in her dazed expression and slow movements. He started to say something and then stopped, looking at me.

"You got a swimsuit?" he asked me.

I did, only because I hadn't thought I'd make it to the final round of the dart tournament, and I'd planned on spending some of my downtime at the pool. But now I wasn't sure I wanted to wear it. Not here. Not with Rafe's eyes on me. In Las Vegas, I wouldn't have cared who saw me in my bikini. I didn't know them and wouldn't see them again, and it was highly unlikely anyone would have asked me about my scars. But Rafe wouldn't miss them, and he'd remember I hadn't really answered him on Sunday night when he'd asked about them.

But I also realized Rafe was only asking me about my swimsuit as a polite way of getting me to leave so he could talk to Lauren in private. I finished the napkin I was folding, placed it on the pile, and then rose.

"I'll go change."

I stepped out of the room, but my feet stalled as I heard his voice, low and dark, asking, "What did you take? You said you were stopping."

"It was just a painkiller. I stepped off the tractor wrong after parking it and tweaked my back."

"Damn it, Lauren. It wasn't just an ibuprofen, was it? You can barely stand. You shouldn't be ironing. You'll burn yourself or the whole fucking house down."

"Stop swearing at me."

"Is this what it's been like since Spence died? You working yourself to the bone and barely breathing when you're not? Who's been looking after Fallon? Who's been making sure she's okay?"

"Not you!" she hissed back. "Don't you dare judge me when you could hardly wait to leave after the funeral. You haven't bothered to show up for over a decade. Not once since your dad died have you come to see how *we* were doing."

"*We*..." It was a snarl. "I was supposed to care how any of you were? You made your choice, Lauren. You chose Spencer."

"Oh, please. Like you didn't know I'd always choose him. We both got what we wanted out of it. We got Spencer's attention. He came running just like we knew he would."

"That might have been what you wanted, Lauren, but it wasn't what I wanted."

She scoffed.

I heard him move toward the door, and I set my feet in motion, not wanting to be caught spying. But I still heard his response.

"I truly thought I was in love with you. I didn't realize I was just a card in your hand until it was too late."

I didn't hear her response, but I wasn't sure I wanted to. It made me feel sorry all over again for them when neither of them would want my sympathy. Rafe wasn't a man to tolerate pity. And Lauren was proud, even though she was a pogo stick of emotions, bouncing between determined and dejected.

I did my best to forget the entire conversation as I ran upstairs and put my bikini on under my shorts and tank. I'd just come back down and reached the bottom step as the doorbell rang. Fallon screamed out she would get it, running in from the sitting room with cash in hand. I watched with a smile as she talked and flirted with the cute, teenage delivery guy until Rafe stalked past me to the door.

"Thanks for bringing it," he told the kid, grabbing the pizza boxes from him. "You can go now."

He shut the door in the kid's stunned face, and Fallon glowered. "Dad!"

"He's too old for you."

"He'll only be a junior."

"And you're fourteen and not dating. We've had this discussion."

She huffed, crossing her arms over her chest. The bikini top she had on with a pair of cutoff jean shorts left a lot of skin bared, and Rafe's face was a sea of disapproval.

"What the hell are you wearing?" he demanded.

She rolled her eyes. "A swimsuit."

"No."

She ignored him, twirling away and saying, "We've got the cooler packed in the back of the Jeep. Uncle Adam isn't coming. I'm assuming you couldn't convince Mom either, so it's just the four of us."

"Did you drive the Jeep?" he asked.

"Yes. Right up to the back door so Maisey and I could load it." His jaw clenched. "I'll drive the boat too. Spence always let me. We're leaving in five minutes."

She sounded nothing like the tortured teen I'd cleaned stalls with. This Fallon was completely grown-up and put together. The expression on Rafe's face said he didn't like it one little bit.

When I took the final step into the entry, his gaze shifted to me, taking me in from head to toe in that way that sent warmth spiraling through my chest into my stomach. I returned the slow look he'd given me, lingering over the pair of navy swim trunks he'd replaced his jeans with and the tan, muscular legs they revealed.

He had sneakers on his feet and a beach towel hung over one shoulder, and if I'd thought he'd appeared relaxed and casual before, this took it to another level, as if I was getting an intimate look into a Rafe very few people got to see. And just like seeing him in his cowboy boots this morning, I wanted more of it. More peeks behind the curtain he kept drawn tight around him.

He was the one to break our stare, waving a hand toward the hallway and saying, "I have a feeling she'd actually leave without us."

A soft laugh escaped me. "I'm pretty sure she doesn't want you to tag along at all."

I'd expected him to laugh in response, but instead, my comment seemed to strike at him, and we were quiet as we headed out the back.

Fallon had parked a battered Jeep from the seventies almost right up against the door. It had no top, just a black roll bar in a dented gray frame and black vinyl seats, worn and cracked from exposure and time. A cooler was shoved into the tiny space behind the back seat, and Fallon was behind the wheel. The friend who'd shown up for the trick riding lessons sat up front with her.

Rafe opened the driver's door and simply stared at his daughter. Several long seconds passed before Fallon threw her hands up. "Fine! You drive."

She unbuckled her seat belt and climbed into the back where her friend joined her, leaving the front passenger seat for me.

I'd barely climbed in when Rafe shoved the Jeep into gear and headed down the road, setting off a cloud of dust behind us.

He may not have been there for years, but you never would have known it from the speed and confidence with which he drove.

The sun had shifted west but would still batter the earth for a few more hours before it fell completely. It meant the heat of the day was clinging to the air as it whipped, heavy and warm, around me as we drove past the freshly baled alfalfa fields and untended pastures of wildflowers. As we crested a small rise, the lake was revealed, the white light of late afternoon sparkling and dancing off vivid blue waters.

We parked in a tiny gravel lot next to a grove of oak trees leading down to a pebbled beach where a wooden dock, stained and well maintained, sat next to a boat ramp. Four speedboats were tied to it, built for entertainment, screaming of skiing adventures and lazy days rather than fishing. County laws prohibited motorboats on the lake back home, and it was so small it really wouldn't have been good for skiing anyway, but this one stretched so far I couldn't see the end of it.

As Rafe climbed out of the Jeep, his brows were furrowed. "Who the hell do all these boats belong to?"

"Uncle Adam leases out dock space during the summer. This way, people don't have to drive all the way to the county park on the other side."

"And they have access to our property?" he snapped.

Fallon shrugged. "Just the gate code. Sometimes the owners rent out the old homestead for summer barbecues."

Rafe yanked the cooler from the back while the girls and I grabbed the food and our bags. We made our way down the dock to a dark blue and white speedboat that wasn't new but had obviously been well-maintained.

As we clambered in, Rafe untied it from the dock, threw the rope inside, and jumped in with an ease that spoke of years of doing it, just as his driving had. Fallon was already at the helm, and she didn't wait this time for her dad to dislodge her. Instead, she started the engine and tossed a defiant glance over her shoulder at him before setting off.

Every fiber in his being said he didn't like it, but Rafe took a seat at the back next to me. Fallon increased the pressure on the throttle, driving with an expertise that was almost as good as her father's had been in the car. It was loud where we sat by the motor, making talk impossible as we sped over the water, so I just let myself enjoy the ride.

The air was thick with the smells of summer, reminding me of inner tubes and jumping off the old dock in the center of the lake back home with my friends. Warm and beautiful memories I'd been lucky to create and sometimes missed with the responsibilities that had landed on me now with the bar being in my full control. Sometimes I felt two decades older than Fallon, when really only nine years separated us.

When Fallon finally stopped the boat at least a mile from shore, it felt like we were the only souls on the pristine waters.

"This is…" I shook my head. "It's really beautiful."

Fallon beamed at me, and even Rafe smiled.

While we ate, I asked the girls about the horses and what the training they did looked like. They were animated, talking about their coach and how she taught at the Western riding school but that she'd been a famous trick rider herself back in the day. She coached the girls privately because the school was more about rodeo riding than trick riding.

Fallon's face held the same excitement and confidence she'd had when showing me some of her act this morning. Her friend was quieter but seemed to smile more. Her soft brown hair and pale eyes were a contrast to Fallon's blond vivaciousness.

Rafe was silent while I chatted with the girls, his brows slightly furrowed as he listened.

When the teens had eaten more pizza than I could ever imagine putting away, they headed for the swim platform at the back, stripping out of their shorts and then flinging some pool noodles in a variety of bright colors into the lake.

"No comment about eating and swimming?" Fallon tossed out at her dad as she prepared to dive in.

"You get a cramp and start to drown, holler out, and I'll save you." He said it sardonically, as if he knew it wouldn't happen.

She dove off the back in a graceful move, and her friend followed suit. They grabbed the colorful toys and swam farther away from the boat before wrapping legs and arms around the noodles so they could float on their backs with their faces up to the sky.

I stacked the pizza boxes and the container Rafe's sandwich had come in, bundling the trash.

I knew he was watching me again, the burn on my neck only one of the many reasons, and when I turned back around, it was to find him lounging with his legs spread wide and his arms along the back of the seat.

"What?" I asked.

"You always like this?"

"Like what?"

"Stepping in to help. Doing more than any guest would ever do."

"I like to keep busy. Sitting still is hard for me."

He stood, reached behind him, and pulled off his T-shirt, throwing it on the seat with a careless ease. The sun was behind him, ringing him in a white halo that shadowed his face and made him seem more comic-book mirage than real. His stomach rippled with muscled grooves that drew my eyes downward to the delightful V just below his waist, but it was the jagged scar that ran up at an angle from his swim trunks and ended just below his heart that stole my breath.

He was scarred. Marked. Just like me.

He moved so his shadow swung over me, causing the halo that had surrounded him to blink away. I was finally able to read his expression and found it guarded, lids heavy. He'd locked away his emotions once more, leaving only a broody assessment behind.

I wanted to ask about the scar. I wanted to know what had happened and when and how he'd recovered from it. But I knew if I did, I'd be required to give him the same information back. And I didn't want to talk about the shooting. How we'd almost lost my niece, Mila, and how I'd almost not lived. How I hadn't protected her or me from being taken at gunpoint, but she'd been smart enough to hide once she'd been able to run away from our captor.

I swallowed hard, trying to slow my pulse, trying to inhale enough air so I didn't pass out.

"You're not going to ask?" His voice was low and guttural and held a hint of disbelief.

I shook my head.

"Because you don't want me to do the same."

It shouldn't have shocked me that he'd read my hesitation when he'd been good at reading me all along, but it still did. When I still didn't respond, he lifted a brow and turned away, stepping toward the swim platform. He glanced back over his shoulder. "Coming?"

I pulled off my tank top, and he watched every move, gaze lingering on my breasts barely contained in the bikini top. I'd never quite gotten my body back after my recovery, and I'd accepted it would never be what it had been, even with the workouts Gia had put me through. I wasn't embarrassed by it, but I also wasn't as ready to flaunt it as I used to be. The way Rafe's eyes heated, the way they took in every inch of my exposed skin, made me want to shed it all, bare myself and see what he would do with the entire offering.

"I'm just going to sit here and enjoy the view," I said, turning to look for the water bottle I'd been drinking from.

"I don't think so," he said. His tone had dropped another level. Darker. Sexier.

I turned back to him, raising a brow. "Excuse me?"

"Let's go, Tennessee. Time for you to cool off."

I laughed. "I'm not hot."

He moved so fast I wasn't prepared for it, snaking out an arm, hauling me to him, and then plunging us both over the side instead of the back. The water hit me like a bucket of ice. Cold and hard and staggering. Freezing my limbs. He never let me go, kicking upward until we broke the surface. I gasped for air and shoved hard against his chest, but his arm only banded tighter around me.

"I can't believe you did that," I sputtered.

The smile that took over his face caused my heart to stop again. It was wide and full, crinkling his eyes and showing off perfectly straight, white teeth and that sexy dimple.

"Loosen up, Sadie. Have some fun."

I snorted. "You're the one who doesn't know how to have fun. You're the one who stopped us when we were line dancing in your bar."

I struggled against his hold, but he just held on, fingertips digging into the flesh at my waist. "It's a piano bar. Not exactly the place for it. And I didn't like those two guys falling all over you."

"You were jealous?" Surprise rang through my voice. He pushed at the frown that creased my brows with a wet finger, sliding it along my forehead and down my cheek. His gaze landed on my lips, wet from the lake, and I found myself longing to taste him again. To have the contrast of the icy water and the heat of them against mine. I glanced in the direction of the teens, but they were hidden from us on the other side of the boat.

"You've had me in knots from the moment you walked into The Marquis Club," he acknowledged. I watched as his lips lowered, drifting close to my mouth before detouring to my ear where his breath coasted along the shell. "I'm going to enjoy working each of those knots out with you."

Every ounce of fight went out of me as I stared at him, dumbfounded by all his words. He let go and pushed me under the water again. When I resurfaced, he'd taken off, using his long arms to cut through the water, heading around the back of the boat toward his daughter.

It took me several long moments to gather myself together, and then I swam for the boat and the ladder at the back. My thin cotton shorts were clinging to me as I pulled myself up. I dragged them off and laid them out to dry before sitting and hanging my feet in the water, ignoring the white scars that marred my leg. Instead, I watched as Rafe tossed Fallon in the air, stole the noodles from the girls, and then swam away. The teens raced after him, trying to reclaim the pilfered toys as he batted them away with ease.

It was childlike horseplay that had Fallon and Maisey laughing and sputtering every time he dunked them. Rafe's deep laugh echoed over theirs, booming across the water. He was nothing like the domineering, growly man who'd sat across from me at the piano bar, and every time I saw another side of him, it landed another barb in my heart that would be impossible to remove when I left. It had already left me aching for all those things I'd just recently realized I wanted. A partner. Someone to cherish and who would cherish me back.

It didn't seem possible I could have any of it with Rafe.

But I could have this moment. A few purely joyful hours I might be able to follow up with a few delightfully sinful ones. So, I slid back into the water and started toward them as quietly as I could, trying to keep behind Rafe as the girls attempted and failed to sink him again. Neither of them gave me away as I approached with a finger to my lips. When I was close enough, the three of us launched ourselves at him, pushing and shoving until he finally went down.

He came up sputtering in false indignation, that wide grin stretched across his face, and we tried to push him back under. When he started tickling the teens, they released him immediately, swimming out of reach of those dangerous fingers. I was on my own this time as I tried to shove him down, and he simply caught my wrist and yanked me closer to him. His heated gaze found mine, and he lowered his voice so only I could hear, saying, "Payback is a bitch, Tennessee. I know just how to make you beg."

I believed him, and I didn't care.

I splashed water in his face with my free hand, pulled my knees in, and used my feet to kick off those muscular thighs. He gave chase, and the girls defended me with noodles and random attacks.

We spent a glorious hour playing in the water as the sun sank and the wind picked up.

We were all shivering, nearly frozen from the inside out, by the time we finally gave up and headed for the boat, but we had tired, delirious smiles on our faces. Our laughter echoed across the lake, winging along the wind. I couldn't remember the last time I'd felt this light. This happy. It was as if the wee folk I'd been thinking about since arriving here had filled the sky with their flutes and entranced us all. Except, I didn't feel like I was under a spell. I felt more like myself than I had in three years.

Chapter Sixteen

Rafe

THE WAY I WANNA
Performed by Max McNown

We were all smiling as I drove the boat back to the dock. Cold and tired but smiling. It was the kind of happiness you felt all the way to the bottom of your soul, and I couldn't remember the last time I'd felt that way. Maybe the time Fallon and I had learned to surf in Australia. Maybe longer than that.

The sun was sinking below the tree lines as we neared the cove. The shadows were long, and it was mostly on instinct and long-forgotten muscle memory that I traversed the waters and pulled up to the dock without incident.

Fallon jumped out and tied us off while Sadie gathered our trash, and I dealt with the ice chest. Climbing into the Jeep, we were all quiet in a sated, relaxed sort of way that lingered as the colors bled from the sky.

As we crested the hill, a cell phone tower came into view in the distance with the top lit up in warning for low-flying planes. I puzzled over it for a minute before I realized it was on Harrington land. It was on the far corner where the property butted up against the two-lane highway, hidden from the house but clear as day from the lakeside of the property.

"What the hell is that?" I asked.

Fallon leaned forward between the seats, glancing from me to what I was staring at.

"Another of Uncle Adam's ideas. We leased the land to the

cell phone company. The nice thing is, it means we have a great signal now, even on the lake."

"Jesus Christ," I grumbled. "It's a damn eyesore."

Fallon laughed. "Spence hated it. He said Grandpa Kade was probably turning over in his grave, but what needed to be done, needed to be done. It brings in a solid income every year. Money we can actually count on that isn't subject to changing prices of hay and cattle."

She sat back, and I had a hard time focusing on the road as the damn tower faded from sight in the rearview mirror.

I didn't know if I should applaud Adam for his ingenuity in looking at other revenue streams for the ranch, or if I wanted to strangle him for destroying the land and the peace that came with it. If Spence hadn't died, I wouldn't have known about any of it. Wouldn't have cared.

Now, something in my chest ached over all of it. The change. The loss.

I loathed how the land could still work itself into my bloodstream after years of trying to cleanse myself of anything and everything to do with it.

I parked the rig next to a handful of other vehicles the ranch owned, thinking about insurance and registration, and how much money was being forked out each year just to keep it stocked with the equipment needed to simply run the damn place.

Numbers ran amok in my brain, ways to improve the profit, ways to turn the ranch around. I had to fight to put it all aside just as I had earlier when I'd seen the Hatleys' plans laid out on Adam's desk. I needed to do something to stop the spiral before it got out of hand, before I found myself making promises to my daughter I wasn't sure I could keep.

My plans to get lost in a dark-haired dynamo would do more than just get the craving for her out of my system. It would shut off my brain for a few hours while I thought of nothing but discovering every inch of her, while I made her beg just like I'd promised when she'd ganged up on me with the girls.

I watched as Sadie strode toward the house with a

confidence I'd seen crumble for an instant on the boat when we'd been mulling over the scars the world had left on our bodies. I was hungry to experience more of both sides of her—the sassy strength and the open vulnerability.

I lifted the ice chest onto a shoulder, dumped it over outside the back door, and then stepped inside to find her and the teens in the hall. Fallon's face still held a happy smile when she said to Sadie, "We've got cookie dough ice cream. Would you like some?"

Another thing Fallon knew I couldn't stand. Who puts something like cookie dough in ice cream? It gave me the shivers just thinking about the mix of textures.

"Thanks, but I really think I want to shower off the lake and get some rest. It was a long day, and I told your mom I'd help her start setting up for the wedding tomorrow."

It felt wrong to be using Sadie as unpaid help. I wondered just how much she did back home between the ranch and the bar. Sometimes it was hard to remember she was twenty-three. She should barely be out of college, spending days learning a new career and nights out on the town with friends, flirting, dancing, living up those last few days of limited responsibility.

The demon in my head reminded me I'd never lived that way, especially not once I'd left the ranch.

"Do you want ice cream, Rafe?" Maisey asked with a shy smile so opposite of Fallon's whirlwind of energy.

"Fallon knows I won't eat that nasty excuse for ice cream," I said, softening the words with a wink.

Fallon snorted, and Maisey's grin grew. They started off down the hall, but then at the last minute, Fallon came running back. She threw her arms around me and hugged me tight, murmuring into my chest, "Thank you for tonight."

She smelled like the lake and sunscreen, and it filled my heart until I thought it might crack wide open. I hugged her back, kissing the top of her head. "Thanks for reminding me of all the things I loved about summers here."

She let me go and spun around, returning to her friend and nearly running for the kitchen.

My heart was in my throat as I turned and caught Sadie's eyes. They were watery, as if the scene with my daughter had affected her as much as it had me.

She looked away, rubbing a hand over her opposite arm and shifting on her feet.

She was nervous.

Of all the things I wanted from Sadie Hatley, nerves weren't one of them. I wanted the defiance and breathtaking passion I'd seen in her before. I needed the sexy taunt that had stirred my blood and had me offering something I never had to anyone—a trip to my penthouse. While the women I'd spent time with had seen the inside of a hotel suite, it had never been mine.

I closed the distance, entering her space and caging her against the wall. I twisted a lock of ebony silk in my fingers and tugged at it, not enough to hurt but to make a point. "We have unfinished business, Tennessee."

Heat flooded those vivid eyes. I could easily drown in them. And tonight, that was exactly what I wanted. Needed. A respite from thoughts that would only crack open more scars if I let them.

"I haven't decided if I'm interested in conducting business with you, Slick."

My chuckle annoyed her. She lifted her chin, and I grabbed it, thumb running along her lower lip. My other hand cupped her neck, dancing along the pulse there. I felt her inhale. Felt the way her body shivered. Damn, she was addicting.

"Yes, you have," I told her. "You just haven't decided why you like being told what to do."

A delightful blush covered her cheeks. I wasn't sure if it was embarrassment or desire or fury at my being right. Maybe it was a bit of all three.

She tried to pull her chin out of my hand, but I gripped it harder. "I'm heading to the cabin to shower off the lake. If you don't show up in twenty minutes, I'm coming back to remind you of what you started, and I'll charge an extra penalty for it."

The thrum of her heart sped up against my fingers, and my body grew tight.

"Maybe you'd like that too. The penalties as much as the begging." My voice had a low, savage growl to it, and her pupils dilated at the sound.

I stepped back, and cool air rushed between us. Her palm landed on her chest as if trying to slow the wild beat inside it.

"Twenty minutes, Sadie. Twenty damn minutes."

I didn't look back as I sauntered toward the door. I couldn't. If I did, I might end up taking that sweet mouth right here in the middle of the hall, and I wouldn't risk Fallon finding us that way. But I swore Sadie would be mine. I'd have her, taste every inch of her, and set her aside, leaving her in my past.

The devil inside laughed.

Hadn't I thought I'd put the ranch in my past? Hadn't I thought I'd cleansed myself of it? And one day here had proven it was still stuck inside me. What made me think I'd do any better with Sadie? When just the look and scent of her was enough to hook into skin and bone and soul?

I shoved those thoughts aside. I didn't have a choice but to try to burn through her and leave her in my wake. Otherwise, I might just go under the water for good.

♪ ♪ ♪

I washed off in the too-small shower and pulled on the jeans I'd worn earlier and a clean T-shirt. My small suitcase of clothes was dwindling since I hadn't expected to work on the ranch. But I'd need something more formal for the black-tie wedding on Saturday, in addition to more work clothes at the rate I was burning through them. I shot off a text to my personal assistant, asking him to pack a few more things and send them overnight.

A glance at my watch told me Sadie had five minutes to show up before I went and claimed her. But I wouldn't have to.

I poured two glasses of bourbon from the decanter I'd taken from the office bar and set them on the Formica table. The cut crystal seemed completely out of place in the ancient, worn décor of Levi's place. For the first time, I felt a hint of regret. Sadie deserved better than a deteriorated cabin with an iffy window A/C unit. She deserved thousand-count sheets, champagne, and stunning views that wouldn't ever be able to compete with the view I had of her.

I grimaced at the maudlin thoughts. All we really needed for what I intended tonight was a bed. Maybe a counter. Or a wall. The shower would never fit both of us, and the table would never hold up to the ideas that pummeled through me. The memory of her breasts, small and tight and smooth under my callused hands in the penthouse, was enough to send me right up to the edge. She was going to challenge my control, and I'd be only lying to myself if I said I didn't like it.

The knock on the door wasn't tentative at all. Once Sadie decided to do something, she went for it. The way she'd laid down her offer at the piano bar and the way she'd kissed me with everything she had, not holding back an ounce of herself, were both perfect examples.

I swung the door open and drank her in. She'd put on a lavender, halter-topped sundress with ruching at the side, showing a circle of exposed skin. It called to me, and I grazed the silky softness with a single finger. She shivered, and it had nothing to do with her damp hair flying around in the breeze.

I hauled her inside and slammed the door shut with my foot.

The color of the dress and the hint of warmth from the old lamp on the side table turned her eyes a periwinkle color, shooting memories through me of lying amongst the bluebells on a spring day. I'd stared at the white puffy clouds floating overhead, thinking there'd never be anything better than the ranch. But now I knew the truth. This was better. She was better.

It was enough to cause a hint of panic that I ignored.

"I like this dress on you," I said. My mouth lowered, skimming hers, and that breathy gasp I found so addicting escaped her once again. I wanted to drink it in more than I'd ever wanted my expensive bourbon. "I'll like taking it off you even more."

"Don't break it like you did my last one. That was a brand-new dress you ruined," she said.

"I'll buy you another one."

"I don't want you buying me anything. That wasn't the point." Her annoyance flashed as fast as the heat and, damn, I liked both. Liked that she wasn't reaching for my credit card like other woman in my past had at the mere hint of an offer.

"I'm missing your point," I said, moving to skim her temple with my lips and then the tantalizing softness below her ear.

She put a hand on my chest and pushed us apart. "The point was, don't destroy things that don't belong to you. Money isn't always the answer."

She stepped around me, leaving a pair of sandals at the door and heading for the table and the two glasses I'd poured. I watched as she picked one up with a trembling hand. She took a sip, then held the glass in front of her as if it could be some sort of barrier. She watched me with a guarded expression, full of those nerves I'd thought she was above, but maybe she'd had them that first night too, and I just hadn't been around her enough to recognize them like I did now.

I needed her settled. I needed her fully on board with what we were going to do to each other tonight. I wanted the woman from the elevator who'd stepped toward me with nothing but a dare between us. The one whose bare back had been up against my window with the nightlife of the Vegas Strip exposed behind her.

I stalked to the table, picked up the other glass, and took a sip as she eyed the cabin.

"You said the horse trainer used to live here?" she asked.

"Levi. He taught me everything I know about horses, breaking them, taming them, riding them." I hadn't meant it as an innuendo, but her eyes darkened, pupils widening.

"I get things are complicated with your family, but I'm surprised your business is so completely different from how you were raised. Didn't you want to stay? Didn't you miss it?" That restless energy had the questions spilling out of her one after the other.

I put my glass down and then took hers and set it on the table as well. I circled her wrist and tugged her gently toward me. "Tell me, Tennessee, where did these nerves come from? Where's the woman who bought me a drink and invited herself into my bed?"

She swallowed, tilting her head to look up at me. "It was easier when I didn't know you. It was just supposed to be one night. A few hours of good sex before I left Vegas behind."

I traced her jawline with my finger, and her breath caught, heart pounding so hard I could feel it in my rib cage.

"Good isn't the right word for what we're going to do, and you'll still be gone soon enough."

She stared at me for a moment. "But I'll see you tomorrow, and the next day, and the next. I can't—"

"Run away after I've exposed all your secret wants and desires," I said. I knew what she meant. I'd have to face her again in the morning. Worse, I'd have to decide what to do with this craving I had for her if it didn't disappear after a handful of nights spent together.

"I feel like… No one has ever been able to rip away my outer layers before, Rafe… I… You…" She swallowed, shaking her head. "I don't know if I hate that you discombobulate me or love it."

I fisted her hair with one hand, the other sliding to her waist as my mouth brushed against hers once more. Bourbon. Honey. Sadie. God, it was delicious. "You think too much, Tennessee. That's why you like the idea of me telling you what to do. It makes that big brain of yours come to a complete halt."

She tried to respond, but I didn't let her. I sank into her, tasting every corner, dragging out another gasp I got to swallow and make mine. The heat scorched me, dragged me into it like a fire that had jumped from the grate and burned like a raging inferno.

When I relinquished her lips, she moaned in objection,

trying to reclaim mine. Instead, I slid my mouth along the sensitive slope of her neck before biting the notch at the top of her collarbone. "You taste like campfires and honey and damnation."

Her hips slammed into mine, and when I looked up, her eyes had shifted into deep midnight skies. The kind where shooting stars left fiery trails behind.

I tugged at the bow of the halter top, and her entire dress came tumbling down, revealing those snowy slopes, those gorgeous ripe breasts I'd been unable to forget since Sunday, and a pair of lace underwear that made my mouth water. I dipped my head, taking a taut tip in my mouth while twisting the other between my fingers. I rejoiced in feasting on her, not a quick inhale that would soon fade, but a slow and languid savoring that required me to taste every inch.

Tongue and fingers danced in a sensual rhythm, determined to torment her the way she'd been tormenting me for days. I reveled in her every response. The way her hips shifted against mine, the way her breath became a desperate pant, and the way her nails dug into my neck.

When she yanked at my shirt, I stepped back enough to pull it over my head and send it sailing before returning to my worship of her smooth skin and pebbled tips. Her fingers skated over my shoulders, my back, my side. I knew when she found the scar, because she hesitated for a second.

We'd get there. I wanted to know what had happened to her. Wanted to know who to hunt down for wounding her. But first, I needed us to lose ourselves in each other. In this moment. In the way our skin felt sliding against each other.

I recaptured her mouth as I picked her up, and those long legs wrapped around my waist. My palms squeezed her soft curves, and she bit my lip, letting out another enchanting moan. She was a delightful mix of muscles and curves. Force and kindness. Fire and rain. I found myself ridiculously close to losing control simply from having her twined around me. I was already desperate to sink into her. To thrust inside and pound away until we both got relief. That wild need was too heady. Too fast. And I fought to regain my restraint by dropping her on the bed and putting distance between us.

"No," I said, my voice loaded with emotions.

Her lids were heavy and sexy but her voice was confused. "What?"

"I'm taking my time with you," I told her. "This isn't going to be over and done within minutes, Tennessee."

She sat up, hair tousled, lips red from my kisses.

"Lie down," I told her.

She hesitated. I leaned in to pinch a pebbled tip, and she gasped.

"Lie down, Sadie."

She pushed herself back onto the pillows, eyes following me as I sat next to her, trailing a finger down her unmarked thigh, over her knee, down her calf, and to the graceful arch of her slender foot. Delicate bones. Delicate toes. I started there. Kissing, licking, caressing my way up one side, worshiping each inch of skin until I reached the hot juncture between her legs. I let my breath coast over the delicate lace, and she quivered, drawing a wicked smile to my lips before I skipped over her center to her other leg.

When my fingers and tongue found the scars on her thigh, I spent an inordinate amount of time worshiping them, and her breathing turned even choppier, hands landing in my hair, tugging and caressing. I wanted to destroy whoever had put the scars on her. Marred her. Hurt her. I'd get the truth out of her. I'd get the truth, and then I'd make sure they never found happiness again.

First, I'd spend hours giving her the pleasure she deserved. But it would be done my way, on my terms, and I wouldn't rush it. I caught her wrists, pulled her hands away from me, and leaned up to latch them on the headboard. "These stay here," I told her.

I watched as she fought her natural instinct, resisting being told what to do, and when she finally gripped the frame on her own, I smiled.

"That's it, darlin'. Let go. Let me do all the thinking," I

told her.

"Don't push your luck, Slick," she tossed back.

I kissed her to shut her up, kissed her because I needed another taste of that honey and smoke before I continued my onslaught of her body. Greedy, she met me lick for lick, slide for slide, and I almost lost focus again. I loved every moment of it. Every desperate attempt to hold on to control and how she was capable of pushing me right up to that edge.

Chapter Seventeen

Sadie

TAKES TWO
Performed by Maren Morris

I watched through half-closed eyes as Rafe pulled his lips from mine and trailed them down my neck and chest before torturing my breasts again in the most delightful way. My body felt hot, needy, ready, and all I wanted was for him to sink into me. To give me release. To pull me up and over the edge I was already frantic to find. And yet, I also loved every second of the denial. The anticipation. The control he was insisting I give to him.

Because he was right. I didn't want to think. I didn't want my brain to spiral with what we were doing, and what would come after, or the hundred other things I should be doing with my night…my life…

I just wanted to exist in these long minutes where there was nothing but sensation.

Where only pure want and frenzied desire existed.

My hands tightened on the headboard as he continued to slide that sexy mouth over every inch of me. His beard gently scraped along my skin, sending waves of sensation over me, goosebumps bursting along every surface. My breath caught as he nipped at the curve of my belly button just as he pushed aside the single scrap of lace left on my body. A guttural moan, feral and raw, escaped us both at the same time as his fingers brushed over my core.

He'd just dragged the fabric aside, just landed a heated kiss on my center that had me gasping and arching up, when he froze. His hand pressed on my stomach, pushing me into the mattress, and for a second, I thought it was a new sensual demand. *Stay still.*

But his voice was anything but sexy. It was full of a tension that had nothing to do with carnal activities when he said, "Don't move."

The sound hit me next. Not from him but from the other side of the bed. An unmistakable rattle. An unmistakable slither and coiling sound that made my stomach sink as if I'd dived from the cliff above the lake back home when everyone knew it was foolish.

I fought every instinct I had that wanted to turn my head and look at it. Every flight instinct screaming at me to leap from the bed and put distance between me and the snake waiting there.

"It's pissed," Rafe said quietly. "At being here as much as at us being too close." Rafe moved ever so slowly away, and the speed of the rattle increased. I finally couldn't stop myself from turning to face the danger and saw the snake had its head pulled up and back, ready to strike.

Panic rushed through me. I'd felt this kind of wild fear once before. The time I'd had a gun shoved into my forehead, and I'd known I was going to die. Nothing in my body seemed to function correctly, as if everything was frozen while simultaneously working in overdrive. My naked skin suddenly seemed all sorts of wrong. I'd left myself completely exposed and horribly vulnerable.

"Let go of the headboard, Sadie." And when I started to bring my arms down, Rafe stopped me with a quick and quiet demand. "Don't move them. Just let go."

I did as I was told while trying to control the thunder of my heart.

The black-and-white stripes on the snake were different than the rattlers we had back home, but the sound coming from its tail left no doubt of what it was and what it could do to me.

Even knowing it was likely as scared as I was, that it was our reciprocal fear that would have it striking, the reptile still felt evil. Dark eyes watched every breath I took, the long tongue flicking in and out, almost mesmerizing.

Rafe took another slow step back, and my gaze darted to his. I was sure he saw the panic in mine, but he seemed calm, assessing the situation in order to come up with a plan. He was much more collected than me, but then again, it was easier for him to be cool-headed when there was plenty of distance between him and the angry creature. A rattler could leap at least half their body length during a strike, and Rafe was now well out of reach.

The vicious beat of my heart had me scrambling for a breath I was afraid to take, and my vision turned spotty. I fought desperately for a single inhale, trying to be ready for the moment Rafe said it was safe to move, knowing with a surety that stunned me that he would do everything he could to ensure I was unharmed. And that simple thought eased the pressure enough for me to breathe again.

Rafe stepped toward the middle of the footboard, and the snake's head twisted and turned, the smooth ripple of its body echoing Rafe's movements. He grabbed the edge of an old quilt slung over the footboard.

"I'm going to count," Rafe said, his voice a deep, low lull that had the rattler's tail shaking faster. "And on three, I'm going to toss the blanket over him, and you're going to roll out of bed."

His gaze met mine, making sure I'd heard him, making sure I understood. And I did, but I was too afraid to respond. Too afraid to even nod in the slightest. How was I going to get my frozen body to move?

"He'll strike the blanket, Sadie, because that's what will be coming at him. He won't even pay attention to you."

His voice was composed and sure, but I saw the way his jaw was locked, saw the anger and fear thundering through his dark depths.

"You're not getting bit by anything but me." It was a joke

as well as a promise. He was trying to relax me, trying to make sure I could move.

He lifted the blanket more, and the snake slithered again, the beady eyes no longer directed at me but still too close. He could still shift. Could still strike. *God, get a grip, Sadie*, I told myself. It wasn't like I hadn't faced a rattler before. I'd come across plenty back home, especially hiking. You just moved away from each other, and everyone was fine.

Rafe must have seen something in my face that showed the shift in me, the moment my fear faded into determination, because he started counting aloud. "One. Two. Three."

The quilt flew toward the snake, and I willed my body to rotate. I landed on all fours, knees and palms screaming in objection. The rattler's tail was beating a furious rhythm as it fought with the cover. I flung myself backward, crawling farther away from the bed.

Rafe scooped the snake up tangled in both the quilt he'd thrown and the plain blue comforter I'd been lying on. He strode toward the door, sliding his feet into a pair of shiny black dress shoes. He yanked the door, and it swung fully open, slamming into the wall and making the entire cabin shake and shimmy before he disappeared into the night.

I scrambled for my dress, pulling it on and tying it with shaky fingers. I slipped my feet into my sandals and followed him into the darkness.

I was too late to see which direction he'd gone.

I pulled my phone from the pocket on the dress, turned on the flashlight, and spun it around. The nearest building was one of the stables. The one with the paddock where Fallon had performed this morning. God, was it really only this morning?

"Rafe?" I called out.

Nothing.

An engine caught, and lights flashed. He was in the Jeep we'd driven to the lake. He headed away from me, gravel and dust kicking up behind him.

I went back into the cabin and straight to the glass of

bourbon he'd taken from me. I downed it in two large gulps and then poured myself another finger. The adrenaline crash left me shaking from head to toe, but the alcohol burned, coating my nerves. Instead of concentrating on what had almost happened, I focused on the alcohol, swirling it around in my mouth, tasting the layers and undertones.

By the time Rafe came back in, I was on my third glass, and my shaking had slowed. My mind was no longer seeing the rattler on repeat. But Rafe didn't look like he'd had time to calm down. His face was a dark glower.

"You kill it?" I asked.

He shook his head. "Not its fault. I shook it out in a rock outcropping rarely visited by any of us."

I was glad he hadn't. We did the same any time one neared our ranch. They were an important part of the food chain. They were needed to keep the rodents under control, but it didn't mean you kept them close enough to hurt you, a guest, or one of your animals.

He eyed the glass in my hand, crossed over to the table, and downed his before pouring himself a second glass as well. "How many have you had?"

"This is my third, but I think I'm entitled to one or two more."

He sat in the rickety chair across the table from me and ran a hand through his hair. "Fuck."

It tore a shaky laugh from me. "You can say that again."

His eyes never met mine, but I could still see his expression. Grim and dangerous and furious. "If you'd been struck…" His throat bobbed.

"I wasn't," I said, trying to reassure us both.

The alcohol had slowed my tremors, but watching Rafe lift his glass to his lips, I could see they'd found a home in him. He'd abandoned his calm with the snake, and the idea of this man, this large force of nature, trembling because of what had almost happened, tore into me. But just like seeing him play with his daughter, getting to witness this utterly human side of him felt like a rare gift. Something very few people would ever see—Rafe Marquess undone.

I set my glass down, rose, and went to him. When I sat on his lap, he finally met my gaze, and I was taken aback by the regret I saw swimming in those chocolate depths. One of his hands went to my waist, and the other set the glass down in order to cup my cheek.

"You got caught in the middle of something that was meant for me."

Shock winged through me. "What?"

"Don't be dense. No way a rattler just slithered its way into my cabin, wound its way up the bedpost, and tucked itself under my pillow."

The shaking that had pretty much disappeared from my body returned to match the tremble I felt in his. He was right. Someone had put the snake there. Someone had meant for it to strike Rafe. And what would have happened? Who would have heard him this far out? Would he have had time to get to a phone? To call for help?

"You need to leave," he said. It wasn't really a request. It was one of his mighty commands.

"Who would want to hurt you like this?" I asked, gripping his chin like he was fond of doing to mine.

His teeth ground together before he uttered, "There's a list."

My mind flashed immediately to Rafe and Lorenzo on Monday in his café. The barely leashed fury that had vibrated through him and the disgust he'd sent my way when he'd thought I was working for a man who may or may not be my cousin. Those thoughts were followed by the image of the long scar traversing his body.

I touched my forehead to his, bringing our mouths so close our breaths mingled, but it also forced him to meet my gaze straight on. "Is that how you got that scar? Someone hates you enough to try to kill you? Why?"

I could see the debate warring within him.

"I'll show you mine if you show me yours," he said in a deep, guttural voice that told me, more than anything, he had no desire to tell me what had happened.

But I wanted to gather yet another piece of him, another one he didn't share with many others, so I gave him my past in order to have a chance at receiving his. "My brother Maddox is our county sheriff, and the leader of the local motorcycle club wanted him under his thumb. Chainsaw tried to kidnap my niece to use her as leverage, and I just happened to get in the way."

Anger flashed over his face, and his hand tightened reflexively on my waist. I let his touch ground me enough to continue the story I despised telling. "I didn't even know he was at the ranch at first. One minute, Mila and I had parked and were getting out of the car, and the next, Chainsaw had my ponytail in his hand and a gun at my temple. He demanded Mila come to him or he'd hurt me. I slid my boot down his shin and used his loosened grip to kick him in the balls. When he let me go, I screamed at Mila to run. She headed for the creek, and I followed, but he was faster than both of us. He tackled me, shouting for my niece to come back or he'd kill me. I tried to give her time to keep running by fighting him off, but he was too strong. Too angry." My palms grew sweaty, feeling again the hopelessness and terror I'd felt then. I'd known I was going to die, but I'd just wanted to give my five-year-old niece a chance to live.

Rafe stroked my cheek. A gentle hand that almost undid me.

"Instead of running away…" Chills ran up my spine as I remember seeing Mila stopping, seeing her head back toward us. "While he was ranting about Mila's mom stealing his money, she came back, and just as he pulled the trigger, she launched herself at his arm." I inhaled sharply. "She's why I ended up with a hole in my leg instead of my heart."

Rafe's scowl grew. "She's okay?"

I nodded. "When he turned to go after her, I grabbed his ankle, and he fell. I was able to hold on long enough for her to get a good head start. I tried to get up, tried to go after them, but

I lost consciousness. Thankfully, my sister had found my car abandoned with all the doors open, my purse and phone on the ground, and had called Maddox. When he got to the ranch, he had his girlfriend, McKenna, with him. She's an emergency room doctor, and she worked on me while Maddox went after Mila and Chainsaw."

"Give me his real name, Tennessee, and I'll make sure he's destroyed if he ever happens to get out of prison."

His voice held a deadly promise. It sent a thrill up my spine I couldn't explain. More of those ancient Homo sapien instincts resurfacing—a woman attracted to a man beating his chest and fighting off anyone who threatens something that was his.

Except, I wasn't Rafe's.

"He's dead," I said, and my voice was shaky from the dozens of conflicting emotions slinging their way through me.

"Your brother shot him."

I nodded. "He didn't die at first. He made it to the hospital but not through surgery and recovery."

"Good." Not a hint of regret or remorse existed in that single syllable.

And then he kissed me, long and slow, with a bevy of emotions flying behind the flame and lust that normally flickered between us that had nothing to do with sex. I pulled back enough to whisper, "Good distraction, Slick." A hint of a smile lifted the corners of his lips, but it disappeared as I said, "But now it's your turn."

"I don't talk about it, Sadie. My family…" He shook his head. "They think it was a mugging gone bad." I tried to soothe him as he'd tried to do for me while reliving the worst day of my life. I ran my palm along the bristles of his clipped beard before resting my forehead against his once more. He inhaled, closing his eyelids briefly before opening them and saying, "I stumbled into some things when I first went to Las Vegas. I was working for Puzo and had no idea the mob still had a hand in almost every dark corner of the city. I thought it was ancient history."

My entire body stilled at Lorenzo's name, Gia's warning

coming back to me as Rafe's focus turned inward and backward in time. "I collected and turned over evidence against some of his men. Racketeering. Money laundering. Drugs. The district attorney was hoping they could get one of the men to flip on Puzo, but it didn't work out that way. They all went to prison with their lips sealed, much more afraid of him than anything that would happen to them behind bars. Two of them got ten years, and the leader of their crew got life.

"No one was supposed to know it was me who'd turned over the evidence, but in Vegas, you can find out just about anything you want for the right price. I was one of the secrets offered up, and it resulted in my being attacked in an alley by three people. The only reason I got out of it alive was because Jim Steele was running security for a casino nearby and saved my ass."

"It was Lorenzo?" I asked. It stabbed at me, knowing a part of my family might have struck out at Rafe. "He sent his men after you?"

"No one could prove it. They'd all been wearing masks and gloves. No fingerprints. No DNA. No camera catching them in the act," Rafe said. "But yes, everyone knew who'd done it."

"If it was him, why hasn't he come after you since then?" I asked and then paled when he looked behind me at the bed. "Have these sorts of things been happening all along?"

"No. At first, with the police watching, he backed off. It allowed me to hire Steele and get security measures in place. Then, I started building clubs, growing Marquess Enterprises, and the more I became a part of the Las Vegas community, the harder it was for him to come at me without revealing himself."

Our stories proved there was a lifetime of differences between Rafe and me, but somehow, revealing our darkest moments had narrowed the gap. We were no longer strangers merely having sex. When I kissed him this time, it wasn't in an offer of a momentary escape. It could never be that simple between us again. In giving each other these intimate pieces of ourselves, in sharing trauma that no one could truly understand until they'd had death standing at their door, we'd handed each other a piece of our souls. We'd staked a claim on one another that was much more than two bodies connecting with neurons and electrons flashing.

Those thoughts shook me to my core, and I pulled back to give myself a chance to recover from them.

"Is this why you've kept Fallon away from you?" I asked. "Because you're afraid she'll be a target?"

His nostrils flared as if I'd asked an off-limit question. "Yes and no. Like I've told you before, what happened with Spence and Lauren and me…it's complicated. But this added to it."

Those words brought back Fallon's face in the kitchen this morning when she'd all but made herself invisible and the things she'd told me in the barn about her dad not having a heart. She needed to see him like this, all but torn apart because of the complications his life had wrought on hers.

"She thinks it's because you don't want her," I said softly. "That no one has ever wanted her. She sees herself as a mistake that ruined your family."

He inhaled sharply, and his voice was almost a growl when he asked, "She told you this?"

I shook my head. "Not exactly, but I could read between the lines."

"Having her was never a mistake."

"You should tell her that."

He didn't respond, but we sat twined together, giving each other some comfort. The adrenaline had gone, and while the haze of lust that always burned like an endless flame between us was still there, it was now accompanied by something much fiercer.

I wondered if this was how my siblings felt while holding the person they loved. As if somehow, in a world filled with billions of people, you'd managed to find the one soul who could truly know you. See you. Love the *you* that existed at your core.

Except, this wasn't love with Rafe.

It couldn't be.

Sure, we'd formed a bond, a deep friendship and unearthly attraction, but just yesterday, he'd looked at me with disgust and mistrust. Love couldn't bloom in its place that quickly, could it? What would I do if it had? With no easy answer to those questions, I shoved all my thoughts into a closet in the far recesses of my brain and locked them away before they could take permanent hold.

Chapter Eighteen

Rafe

AIN'T NO LOVE IN OKLAHOMA
Performed by Luke Combs

Sitting with Sadie on my lap, twined in my arms, felt right and wrong and everything in between. She'd gotten her scars by defending her niece. The bravery of her actions, the self-sacrifice of it, turned me on almost as much as those stunning eyes flashing with desire. The fact she'd almost had her naked flesh attacked by a snake because of me tore into my veins with a brutality that left me nearly breathless.

Having someone come for me was one thing, but coming after people I cared about was entirely different. It wouldn't be tolerated. I would find and punish whomever it was just as I'd wanted to punish the person who'd shot her.

The person who hated me the most, who I knew wanted revenge, was Puzo, but I hadn't made my company into what it was without racking up a few more enemies along the way. I needed to talk to Steele and start making our way through that list, as well as find out if he'd found Puzo's thug or discovered more about Puzo's business in Rivers.

Except, tangled up with Sadie, having her arms around me, her warmth in my lap, and her compassion draped over me, I found it incredibly difficult to move. Holding her, I had a glimpse of something I'd never thought I'd have again—a relationship with a woman that was more than sexual release. Having that, having her for more than a few nights, was more than I'd earned or deserved.

But the truth was, I couldn't keep her, not even for the handful of days I'd originally suggested. Not when she might be collateral damage if whoever had placed the snake in my bed came for me again.

What could I do to prevent it? What could I do to stop the ache in my chest and loins? I'd never wanted to finish what we'd started as badly as I did now. The need to hear her gasp and moan and see her naked and shivering because I'd taken her over the edge was almost blinding in its intensity. And maybe it was just that, the strength of those emotions I always tried desperately to leash, that had me standing up and setting her aside.

I made my voice as cold and impassive as possible, saying, "I'll walk you back, and tomorrow, you should leave."

Anger and hurt flashed across her face. Good. Those emotions were sure to send her running.

Except, if she ran, what would Puzo do? I couldn't imagine he cared one iota about her potentially being a long-lost cousin. No. His interest was for another reason. Maybe it had grown because of my angry reaction to seeing them together. Simply seeing me lose my temper over her might have put her in his crosshairs.

Or maybe the snake had nothing to do with Puzo and everything to do with what had happened to Spence. Maybe this was Adam, and maybe Fallon really was right that my brother's death wasn't an accident. Then, I remembered the email on Adam's computer with the Puzo name, and my blood went cold. Perhaps Puzo really was responsible for all of it. *Fuck*. That just meant Sadie and everyone here was in more danger than I'd ever expected.

The idea my choices and my life might have bled into all of theirs set acid boiling in my stomach.

"I'm not leaving until Sunday," Sadie said, crossing her arms over her chest. "You're not my boss, Rafe. Don't confuse my letting you control our sexual encounters with you being able to control me. Even if what we just shared didn't mean something to me, I wouldn't leave. I told Lauren I'd help with the wedding, and I told Adam I'd answer all his questions, and I always meet my commitments."

Her words struck at all those tender spots inside me I was trying to bury.

After glaring at me for another few seconds, as if waiting for a response I couldn't give, she turned on her heel and headed out the door. She stormed out without even a glance to see what was in the dark waiting for her. My teeth ground together, and I had to jog to catch up to her.

"It's not just the snake, Tennessee. I have enough to watch over while I figure out what's going on here. I can't add you to the list," I told her.

"I don't need you watching over me! And what's that supposed to mean? What do you think is going on here?" she asked, coming to a halt and turning to face me.

I dragged a hand through my hair and bit the inside of my cheek. If I told her the truth, would it make her dig her heels in more, or would it be the final push to send her on her way?

Stalling, I looked up at the sky and almost expected thunderstorms to be brewing, thunder and lightning that would reflect the chaos inside me. Instead, I saw millions of stars stretched across a clear, inky expanse. It reminded me of just how inconsequential I was. That we all were. In a continually expanding universe, we were nothing. Dust motes floating through the air that could easily be swept away. Easily forgotten.

Like I'd tried to forget my brother and the ranch and the land that had first formed me.

If I'd brought this trouble to my family, I had to fix it.

"Fallon doesn't believe my brother's death was an accident."

In the moonlight, it was easy to see the shock on her expressive face. "You think he was murdered?"

I rubbed my hand along my beard, pushing into the tension at the apex of my jaw. Fallon was right. Spence would never have driven the tractor anywhere near the cliff where it went over. What would even have been the point of having the tractor up there? Above the river on a cliff that had been eroding for decades?

"Fallon does, and I promised her I'd look into it. Now that I've found out Puzo has been sniffing around town and that Adam knows him, it's something I have to consider. You being here—"

A scream lit up the night.

It was female and high-pitched and had come from the open windows of the main house.

Fallon!

I sped toward the front door, heart in hand, stomach sinking when I realized the door wasn't locked. It was probably never locked—just like Levi's cabin hadn't been. No damn protection.

I took the stairs two at a time with Sadie hot on my heels.

I wanted to thrust her away, lock her in a closet, keep her somewhere safe.

Fallon and Maisey had just stepped out of my daughter's room as I hit the landing. Their expressions startled and scared. My gaze dragged over them, looking for injuries and finding none.

"What happened?" I demanded.

Fallon shook her head, running toward her mom's room. "It wasn't us!"

I barely caught her before she opened the door. I shook her gently before sending her in Sadie and Maisey's direction. "Damn it, Fallon. Stay back. You have no idea what you're walking into."

I flung open the door of Spencer's room—my parents' old room—hitting the light switch and sending the dark shadows back into the corners of the eighteenth-century monolith of a bedroom.

Lauren was sitting in the middle of the four-poster bed, her eyes large but hazy with more than just sleep—the damn drugs she'd taken. Her hand was on her neck, her breathing rapid and wild.

"What's wrong?" I demanded.

"Someone was here... Someone..." She darted a look at a pillow tossed at the end of her bed.

Anger and fear took hold. Someone had been in the house! They'd all been alone. Unprotected. God. My daughter. Her friend. Sadie. Shit, how would I protect all of them?

Ignoring my command, Fallon pushed past me into the room. "Mom?"

I grabbed her arms, holding her back. Who knew if the intruder was still here. I had to clear the room. Clear the house. Ensure they were safe. I hauled her out of the room and handed her off to Sadie. "Take the girls to Fallon's room. Lock the door. I'll come and get you when I'm sure the house is clear."

"Dad! What happened? Is Mom okay?" Panic was in every syllable.

My voice softened slightly as I said, "She looks to be okay, Ducky, but I need you to go with Sadie. Let me handle this."

Sadie tightened her arm around Fallon's shoulders, drawing her down the hall. Our eyes met over my daughter's head. Concern and fear danced in the air between us, amplified by what had happened with the snake, amplified by the memories we'd shared of just what evil was capable of doing.

I waited until Sadie pulled both girls into Fallon's room and heard the lock click before I turned and strode back to Lauren's bedside.

"What happened?" I demanded.

"I-I couldn't breathe. I dreamed... I was drowning. I couldn't get enough air. I couldn't... As if I was Spence in the river where the tractor had fallen, pinning him in."

The tightness in my shoulders eased. *A bad dream*, I thought. *A damn nightmare. That's all.* She'd said someone was there, but it had only been a dream. I'd overreacted and scared everyone because of the dark memories that had haunted me tonight.

But then her next words sent a chill over my spine.

"When I w-woke up, someone was smothering me with the pillow." She glanced toward a stray pillow at the foot of the bed, far away from the pile that surrounded her. Tears streamed down her cheeks. "I struggled. I kicked… And then the pressure lifted, and when I tossed the pillow away, I saw a shadow heading out of my room."

Her gaze darted to the door I'd just entered and then back to me, wariness creeping over her.

"What the fuck? You think it was me?" I growled, taking a step back as if she'd hit me. I laughed darkly. "I was with Sadie, dealing with the aftermath of a rattlesnake placed in my bed, when we heard you scream."

Her alarm grew as she wiped at her face. "Wh-what? A rattler? In your bed?"

I couldn't deal with her questions. Not now. Not when whoever this was might still be in the house. "He left?" I asked. "Out your door? You're sure?"

She nodded.

"Lock the door behind me. I'm going to search the house."

As I turned to leave, it was to find Adam standing in the doorway. I hadn't heard him arrive, and it disturbed me that it could just as easily have been Lauren's attacker who'd snuck up behind us. He was dressed in perfectly unrumpled slacks and a button-down.

"What's going on? What's all the commotion about?" he asked.

"What the hell are you doing here at night?"

He straightened his glasses. "Not that I owe you an explanation, Rafe, but I've been staying in the main house since Spencer died. I didn't like the idea of my sister and my niece being here alone."

My eyes narrowed. "And it took you this long to respond to her scream? I was outside, and I got here faster."

"She screamed?" He glanced at Lauren with a frown. "Are you okay?"

"Where were you?" I growled.

He scoffed. "You really think I'd hurt my sister?" When he realized I did, anger kicked in. "Screw you and the horse you rode in on. I just got back from my girlfriend's house and was heading toward my room when I heard you making a ruckus and barking orders."

Every hair on the back of my neck was standing up. Lies. He was telling me lies.

But he loved Lauren. Growing up, they'd had a bond that hadn't been picked apart the way mine with Spencer had by our father. Adam had always looked out for his sister, enough to try and end me when he'd found out I'd gotten her pregnant.

I watched as he brushed past me now, striding over to Lauren who sat with her arms wrapped around her knees. He took her hand, asking quietly what had happened. She repeated her stuttered story to him while I watched the two of them. She leaned her head on his shoulder, and his brows furrowed in what seemed like genuine concern. Was it real?

I went to the attached bath, looked in the closet, and even ducked my head under the bed. When I saw no trace of anyone, I said, "We need to clear the house and then call the police and tell them someone was here."

"Come lock the door, Lauren," Adam said, helping her up. She wobbled, shaking like a leaf in a nightgown so thin it showed more than it hid. I averted my gaze as they came toward me. I stepped into the hall as Adam mumbled something to her. She shut the door behind us, and we both waited for the lock to turn.

"I'll start at the top and work my way down," Adam said.

The house wasn't as large as it looked. Not quite the English castle it had been modeled after, but it still had a slew of unused rooms. It took us longer than I liked to clear every cubbyhole, closet, and pantry where a person could hide. Many of the spots were ones Spence and I had found playing hide-and-seek as kids, not just with my brother, but with Adam and Lauren too. Adam had been impossible to find back then, gloating in his win simply because my brother and I should have known the house better than he ever could.

By the time I met Adam again on the second-floor landing, the past had a tight grip on me again, each room a pained reminder of the people now gone from my life. My parents. The grandparents I had no memories of but who'd shaped my father. The childhood I'd both loved and loathed.

"You find anything?" I asked.

He shook his head. "Nothing."

I dragged my phone from my back pocket, ready to call the police, wondering if the non-emergency number was still the same as it had been a decade and a half ago.

"If you're calling the sheriff, I'd suggest you wait," Adam said, pushing at his glasses again.

"Why the hell would I wait?" I demanded.

He took his glasses off and rubbed his eyes. "Do we even know if it really happened?" When my scowl grew, he sighed. "I hate thinking it. But there have been other incidents when she's been on sleeping pills and painkillers."

"Like what?"

"She cut herself with a knife while working in the kitchen and then swore someone else had done it."

"Maybe someone did."

Adam's mouth dropped open, shocked. If he was acting, he was better at it than he'd ever been at anything but hiding while growing up. "Fallon was there. She saw what happened. So, unless you think Fallon was the one to cut—"

"Don't you dare finish that sentence," I snarled.

"I'm just saying, I don't doubt Lauren had a nightmare or that she woke to a pillow on her face or near her face. But I can't trust she didn't hallucinate the rest."

"Well, I damn sure didn't hallucinate the rattlesnake in my bed tonight," I said, crossing my arms over my chest and glaring at him.

His brows went up, more dazed astonishment. But the hair on the back of my neck wouldn't lay down, warning me almost as much as the shake of the rattler's tail had. "A snake? In your bed?"

"Someone is terrorizing my family," I said. "Whoever it is needs to know that when I catch them, I will pull their lives apart atom by atom until there is nothing left."

I waited until his gaze met mine so I knew he'd received the message as intended.

"Don't act like I had anything to do with any of it," he snapped.

I stepped closer to him, forcing him to look up, and the simple fact that he had to do so irritated him. "If you did, if you're somehow tangled up in even a hint of this, I won't care if you're her brother or if your family has worked for ours for a century. I'll hang you myself."

"Are you threatening me? Do I need to get a restraining order?"

"It's not a threat, Adam. It's a goddamn promise."

I spun on my heel and headed for Fallon's room. The only thing Adam was right about was the fact that calling the cops was useless. If Lauren had been hallucinating, they'd never believe her, and with a hint of remorse, I realized I might not have either if I hadn't just had my own scare.

I knocked on Fallon's door and said, "It's me. Open up."

Sadie was the one to unlock the door. I pushed past her to see Fallon and Maisey, arm in arm, on my daughter's queen-sized bed. The little girl's room of pink and white that I'd once seen in photos had been redone. Now it was filled with rich cherrywoods and bold emeralds. Too grown up. A reminder of all I'd missed of the little girl who'd loved pink.

"It's okay," I told them. "No one is here."

"Was it just another bad dream?" Fallon asked, looking like she might cry.

"I don't know," I said honestly. "Adam said she's been hallucinating?"

Fallon pulled away from Maisey, darting a glance from her to me. That singular look told me she didn't want to discuss this in front of even her best friend.

I turned to Sadie. "Can you take Maisey and get us all

something to drink. Hot chocolate? Tea? Something soothing?"

"Sure," Sadie said. Maisey looked at Fallon for a moment, as if she was going to say something, but then just scrambled from the bed. At the door, Sadie shot me a look demanding answers. I wasn't sure I had them to give, but it seemed even more important that she leave, that she get the hell out of Rivers and not come back.

Once we were alone, I turned back to Fallon and watched her fiddle with the blanket. Nervous. Unsure. "What's been going on, Fallon?"

"It started when the cow shoved her into the fence last year. She broke a few ribs and pulled some muscles in her back. She had to take some strong pain meds to get through it, and then, after Spence…" She shrugged. "She couldn't sleep, Dad. She was like a zombie. So the doctor prescribed some sleeping pills. The nightmares and hallucinations seemed like a necessary trade-off if she got some rest and relief."

"How many times has something like this happened? Has she hurt you?"

She shook her head but then stopped. "Did Uncle Adam tell you about the time with the knife in the kitchen?"

I nodded.

"She thought I was someone else. A stranger. She never would have hurt me if she'd known it was me."

Acid burned up my throat. "She cut you?"

She shook her head. "No, she elbowed me out of the way, and I lost my balance. I fell and hit my head."

I rubbed my beard. Anger at Lauren welled inside me, self-loathing cresting like a giant wave for not being someone my daughter could trust with the truth, for not being someone she could rely on.

I softened my voice as much as possible so she wouldn't think I was upset with her. "You could have told me. I would have listened, Fallon. I should have known what was happening."

Tears ran down her face as she shook her head. "You

would have made me leave." The words were pained, and each syllable held a crack of agony that snapped in the air. "You would have had even less reason to keep the ranch if I wasn't here. And she needed me, Dad. She couldn't lose me and Spence at the same time. You said it yourself. She's barely surviving now."

My throat closed, and I had to fight back the tears that stung my eyes. It took me several long seconds to pull myself together enough to say, "I know it feels like you're an adult, Ducky. At your age, I would have sworn I knew everything important there was to know, but you aren't, and you shouldn't have to deal with adult problems and situations." She started to protest, but I cut her off, surprising her by joining her on the bed and pulling her into my arms. It took her a minute, but eventually, she relaxed, settling her head on my shoulder. "You're not alone, even if I made you feel that way. You're not Buffy, Fallon. I'd never let you fight a battle to save the entire fucking world by yourself. I'm sorrier than I've ever been for anything in my entire life that you thought you had to."

She sobbed. "I wanted to be able to handle it myself so I didn't cause anyone more trouble."

Sadie's words from earlier, about how my daughter thought it was her fault our family was broken, returned to me.

I kissed the top of her head and squeezed her tight. "Listen to me closely. No one thinks you're trouble. Not a single person. You were a gift we were lucky to receive. It was our job—Spence, your mom, and me—to protect you and to make sure you knew how much you were loved. I'm so damn sorry we failed you in that way. So sorry that our adult bullshit, our screwed-up relationships, landed on you and made you feel as if you were responsible for breaking us."

My emotions leaked out, making the words deep and guttural and raw.

"I'm the one who did the breaking, Fallon. Me. Not you. Not your mom. Not even Spence." The truth of it hit me hard. I was angry when I left the ranch, and I'd taken it out on Spence and Lauren when the person I was most angry with was myself.

I was the one who'd let down my family. I'd known Lauren really loved Spence, and I'd tried to make her mine anyway. In hindsight, leaving was probably still the best thing I could have done, because it had allowed them to love each other without always looking over their shoulder to see if I was watching and brooding and staining what they had with my own ugly emotions.

I'd achieved every damn success in my life out of spite, determined to prove to them that I didn't need them. That I could make more money, achieve more, have more success than any of them could ever imagine. And I'd done it—done it in spades—but I'd lost my daughter, my brother, and the ranch in the process.

"I've tried to keep it from falling apart, Dad. I really have."

"Again, it wasn't your job. It was the adults in your life who needed to shoulder that responsibility. Not you. I'm sorry you felt like you had to. But I'm here now, and you won't ever have to shoulder anything alone again. I promise you."

She sniffed and pulled away, giving me a watery smile. "Does that mean you'll let me keep the ranch?"

A strangled laugh escaped me because she was so smart and savvy and so like me that it made me ache. "I can't promise you that yet. But I will promise to look at where everything stands and what it would take to make it viable, even if it means turning it into some damn dude ranch. Can I ask you to promise me something back?"

She looked nervous but nodded.

"I want you to consider what your life might be like if you left the ranch someday." She started to shake her head and protest, but I cut her off. "You're too young not to explore all your options and all the possibilities this big world has for you. I don't want you to get trapped into this life and someday look back and resent it. I don't want you to regret never allowing yourself to have any other dreams simply because you thought you needed to make Spence and Lauren's dreams your own."

When she looked away and down, I knew I'd hit upon a portion of the truth. She didn't want this to fail because she didn't want Spencer's dreams to wither away.

"And if this is what I really want?" she asked.

God. Would I keep the dying dinosaur alive just so she could have what she wanted most? Wouldn't any good father give his child the moon if they asked for it?

"Let's both just promise to look into all the possibilities for now."

A knock on her door was followed by Maisey and Sadie walking in, each carrying two mugs. The smell of steamed milk and melted chocolate drifted through the room. I rose from the bed, letting Maisey take my spot. She distracted Fallon, telling her how Sadie had made the hot chocolate from scratch and how it tasted a million times better than anything from a package she'd ever had, even better than the one at the coffee shop downtown.

I recognized the constant chatter as Maisey's way of easing her friend's worry, and I appreciated the teen even more than I had before when I'd seen her as the counterbalance to Fallon's energy.

When I took a cup from Sadie, our hands brushed, and heat zipped along my nerve endings. When I met her gaze, I could practically see the hundred questions she had floating in her eyes.

Sadie and I drank our hot chocolate in near silence, listening to the girls instead. When it was clear everyone had calmed down, that the tears and fear had been taken over by talk of high school and boys, I felt it was time to leave before I lost my cool—this time over the idea of some hormonal teen putting the moves on my daughter.

"I'm going to sleep in the guest room across the hall tonight," I told Fallon. "I'll be right here if you need anything. There's no one in the house who shouldn't be, but I still would like it if you slept with your door locked for the next few nights. And we all need to make sure the house doors are kept locked at all times."

She nodded.

"I'm going to help Sadie clean up the kitchen first, but I'll be back up."

A knowing smirk lit Fallon's lips, and I realized again just how savvy my daughter was. She'd clearly read the energy that existed between Sadie and me. But what Fallon didn't know was that I was more determined than ever to send Sadie away as soon as possible. If I could, I'd ship Fallon off too. I'd get them as far away from me and the ranch as I could to ensure nothing touched them.

Somehow, I had the feeling it would be easier to send my daughter away than it would be to send the fiery fae who'd snuck into my life like a thistle works its way amongst the hay. And just like the weed, Sadie would be determined to stick. Reedy and strong, she'd be impossible to pluck out without taking some of my skin along with it.

Chapter Nineteen

Sadie

COWBOYS CRY TOO
Performed by Kelsea Ballerini with Noah Kahan

As we cleaned up the kitchen, Rafe's face was lined with worry, and his voice was low and gritty as he revealed what Adam and Fallon had told him about what had been happening with Lauren. He looked exhausted, weighed down by heavy burdens that came from protecting the people he loved. Though he didn't say it, I could tell he felt somehow responsible for all of it. Every failure. Every wound. Every danger. As if his not being at the ranch was the reason everything was crumbling.

I wanted to smooth his brow, ease the load, bring a smile to his face. I ached to touch him again, and not just because the air between us was still burning intensely with unsatisfied desire, but because I wanted to bring him a respite from his troubles. I wanted the bond we'd formed in Levi's cabin to strengthen until I was the one person this strong, commanding man let permanently into his heart and soul. I could see the possibility of it shimmering around us, but it was overshadowed by all the ways our lives would never work. Not the least of it was that we lived thousands of miles apart.

I'd stumbled into far more than I'd expected when I'd gotten on the plane heading for Vegas. I'd found a man my heart wanted to claim as its own but also more mysteries than had already traveled with me from Tennessee. And the simple truth was, I had an entire life I needed to return to and my own worries to handle. I couldn't see a route through the mire that led to something permanent between us.

It meant I would leave. That I would eventually get on a plane and go back to my real life and the future I'd started to envision that somehow seemed emptier than ever before. But it wouldn't be until I'd seen this week through and helped him…helped all of them…as much as I could.

Silence followed us as we retreated to the second-floor landing. We stared at each other for way too long, all those possibilities and wants and needs and trepidations building and twisting and turning in the air between us. I was the one to turn away with a quiet goodnight. As I started for the stairs and my room on the next floor, his voice, soft and raw, stopped me.

"Thank you. For everything you've done in the last few days." He rubbed his beard, a mannerism that would be a tell if he was playing poker with us. Unsure. Uncomfortable. "You have a natural goodness, a kindness, that practically shines out of you. I couldn't live with myself if something happened to that light—to you—just because you were trying to help us."

He trailed off, that exhaustion settling over him again, and the ache in my chest grew. His words were beautiful and strangely sweet coming from a man who was mostly gruff and demanding, but I also recognized what he was doing. Instead of ordering me to leave as he had earlier, he was imploring me to do so. And maybe it would have worked if I wasn't already so set on staying.

"I'm not leaving until Sunday, Rafe. They may look small, but my shoulders can handle a lot. It would be my honor if you'd let me carry some of your load this week. *I* won't be able to live with *myself* if I walk away without at least trying."

I didn't wait for him to respond, to argue his way with a logic I'd know was right. This wasn't about logic. This was about following your instincts, your heart, your conscience. These people needed someone, a third party not tied up in all the history and hurt, to help mediate. To fill in the cracks before the splintering glass tore the family apart for good.

I'd do my best to be that person, to help them find their footing amongst the waves that were trying to knock them over.

It wasn't my responsibility, but I wanted to do it as much for myself as for them, and I hadn't wanted anything for myself in a long time.

♫ ♫ ♫

Lauren was essentially out of commission the next day. I wasn't sure if it was the sleeping pills or the terror of believing someone had tried to kill her that had left her huddled and small in her bed. But she'd given Rafe her phone with the long list of things that needed to be done, not only for the upcoming wedding but regular ranch chores.

Over breakfast, both Maisey and I insisted on helping. The only person who didn't offer was Adam, and when Rafe asked him what his plans were for the day, he said, "Tera asked that I handle some business for her in town. I'll be back this evening."

Then, he left without even a hint of remorse. After the back door slammed, Rafe turned to Fallon and asked, "Who's Tera?"

"His girlfriend. We haven't even met her yet because she doesn't live in Rivers full time. But he's been seeing her for about a year."

While I was frustrated on behalf of his family at Adam's lack of involvement in the hard labor of the ranch, I was also annoyed he'd avoided talking to me about the jewelry yet again. I wasn't sure what it meant. Was he trying to find a way to keep the jewels without telling the insurance company, who'd reimbursed them for the loss? Did I even care? I *wanted* to hand the jewelry over to this broken and battered family who needed something good to happen in their lives.

But first, I needed to tell my family the entire story so they'd understand why I'd handed over hundreds of thousands of dollars to people I didn't know.

Except, I did know them.

I might have only been here for a handful of days, but I saw and recognized their struggles. Even the danger that had hovered around them last night was something my family had experienced. We'd battled both bankruptcy and evil cartels.

If Adam wasn't going to help me figure out if an insurance company had any claim to the jewels, I'd tell Rafe, and we'd figure it out ourselves. I wanted to believe we'd built enough of a friendship that he'd realize, even if it turned out to be true that my great-grandmother had stolen from his family, it had nothing to do with me.

I had to wait for us to be alone though, because I wouldn't mention the jewels in front of Fallon for the same reason Adam hadn't wanted to tell Lauren. I couldn't get her hopes up. The problem was, instead of dividing the long list of tasks up between the four of us and sending us in separate directions, Rafe insisted we all work together. He told the girls it was because four pairs of hands would get each task done faster, but the way his eyes lingered on all of us whenever we drifted too far away proved he was still worried after the incidents from last night.

After taking care of the morning feeding and cleaning of the horse stalls and paddocks, we headed into Rivers to the grocery store for the items Lauren wanted stocked in the old homestead and bunkhouse for the wedding party that would be arriving throughout the day and into Friday.

We were just heading for the registers when a large woman dressed in an outdated suit approached.

"As I live and breathe, is it really you, Rafe Marquess?" she asked, brushing a hand over salt-and-pepper hair pinned back from a face wrinkled from years of smiles.

"Mrs. Nattingly, aren't you just a vision?"

She swatted at him with a flush to her cheeks. "You always were a charmer, and it's Mayor Nattingly now, young man." She took in Fallon and Maisey and then me before turning back to him. "Are you back to stay, then?"

His jaw worked overtime for a moment before he replied. "Just helping out at the moment."

Fallon couldn't hide her disappointment, and it was mirrored on the mayor's face. "You've made a name for yourself, Rafe. We could use some of that spread around here. The ranch falling on hard times has bled into our community. It may have been wrong of us, but we've counted on the Harringtons for generations to help lift us up. Not just by employing our hardworking citizens, but for the support your family gave to our arts and local charities."

As tension settled between everyone, it was Maisey who spoke. "Mr. Puzo has been helping out, Mayor Nattingly."

A flash of disgust raced over Rafe's face. The mayor patted Maisey on the arm. "You're right, dear. Such a nice man." But the look she gave Rafe said otherwise, as if she seriously doubted the veracity of those words. "I can see you're busy, so I won't hold you up, but maybe you can spare a few minutes of time to come see me before you leave town?" She gave Rafe another meaningful look and then headed out.

The conversation added another heavy burden to Rafe's shoulders, and I wanted to defend him. To tell them to stop expecting one man to be everyone's savior. A man no one seemed to have missed until everything went to hell. But instead, I bit my tongue and did the one thing I could—offer my hands to help with the physical tasks that needed doing.

After hauling the folding chairs, runners, and arches out to the wedding ceremony location, we stopped to wolf down sandwiches before we were going to head back out to finish more of the regular chores of the ranch. Fallon and Maisey had left to take lunch up to her mom, and Rafe and I were cleaning the kitchen when my phone rang.

A glance told me it was Gia. She'd been texting me for nearly twenty-four hours, and I'd been putting her off. Last night, she'd threatened to tell Ryder what we were doing if I didn't bring her up to speed today.

I looked at Rafe and said, "I'm just going to—"

"Sadie, you don't owe me an explanation or your time. Go. Take your call," Rafe said.

I hit the call button and hurried out of the kitchen in search of a quiet place.

"Hey, Gia," I greeted.

"You've been avoiding me," she said.

"I've just been busy," I said as I made my way into the office and over to the windows.

"Meeting with people you shouldn't be seeing by yourself!" she hissed, and my stomach fell. "I warned you about Puzo!"

"How did you find out?"

"I told you I know people who are watching the Puzos. You were flagged in a photo with him in the café at The Fortress. You promised me you wouldn't meet up with him on your own. How could I ever look Ryder in the eye again if something happened to you, and I knew what you were up to?"

"I didn't promise. I just agreed with you that it wasn't necessarily a good idea."

"And was it?"

No. But she'd only worry more if I told her that. Plus, how could I possibly explain the strange way Lorenzo was connected to Rafe and the ranch now? How was it that our three families, all with possible connections to the jewels eighty years ago, were now entangled in these current events? It was strange and improbable. It whispered of laughing wee folk making mischief. But I doubted Gia would believe that either.

So instead, I told her the simplest thing I could. "He said there was a Carolyn in his family who went off to work in Hollywood and disappeared."

Gia inhaled. "So, we've found her. She was tied to them."

"It would seem so."

"The way she ended up in Willow Creek makes me think she was running from them." It was the same discussion we'd had when we'd first uncovered who and what the Las Vegas Puzos were all about.

"The Harringtons' manager confirmed that the family loaned jewels to a movie studio and that they were stolen. Do you think Great-grandma Carolyn took them in order to try to get away from her mobster family?"

It wouldn't make it right, but at least I'd understand why.

"Maybe, but then why stuff them in a trunk? If she'd taken

them for the cash, why didn't she ever sell them?" She was quiet for a second as we both considered what might have happened. "Maybe she kept them in case she ever had to run, or took them and then was afraid to sell them in case it led people to her?"

Or maybe she'd felt guilty but didn't know how to return them, and so she just shoved them in the trunk and hoped to forget all about it.

A deep voice on the other end of the line told me Ryder had found Gia. She covered the phone and said something that was lost in a silence I could imagine was Ryder kissing her. It was almost disgusting the way he couldn't keep his hands off her—disgusting in the sweetest sort of way. How had I not realized how much I wanted what they had for myself? A partner. A lover. Someone who knew all your secrets, and saw all your scars, and loved you anyway.

Rafe hadn't been turned off by my wounds. He'd been growly and protective over them instead. Those possibilities I'd seen shimmering around us last night reappeared, taunting me with hopes I couldn't imagine coming true. I didn't know how to take the glimmering mirage and turn it into the real love my siblings had with their spouses.

Instead of Gia coming back on the line, it was Ryder. "Sassypants, I'm sorry to end this call, but Gia and I have stuff to take care of."

"My God, Ryder, I'm all for having a good sex life, but do you ever leave the poor woman alone? She's already knocked up. Maybe you can let her have a chance to breathe."

He laughed, low and soft, and I could imagine that big smile of his easing over his face. It relaxed me just a hair. Even though there were thirteen years between us, I was actually closer to Ryder than either Gemma or Maddox. I'd always felt like I could give him all my truths, and he'd accept them without judgment.

"I wasn't talking about sex," Ryder said, the grin evident in his voice. "Gia has a doctor's appointment we need to get to. She seemed worried when I walked in. Everything okay out there with you? Nobody on the Harrington ranch is giving you a hard time, are they?"

"I'm fine." I swallowed over the lump in my throat.

He hesitated, as if he knew I wasn't being completely honest, but let it drop. "I've been thinking about this wedding business. A lot of folks around here hold theirs at the country club. Martin and Wendall have always been self-important pricks, who thought they were too good for Willow Creek after they built that damn golf course. I wouldn't feel so bad about stealing business from them."

I bristled. "I'm not talking about stealing business from anyone. This is about drawing clients to the area who wouldn't have come otherwise."

A clink of glass had me whirling around to find Adam had slipped into the office behind me and was fixing himself a drink at the alcohol cabinet. A chill traveled up my spine, not only at the stealth at which he'd entered the room but the look that was on his face. It was weirdly triumphant, as if I'd handed him a prize. I thought back over the call and couldn't figure out what he'd heard that would have made him feel that way.

"I gotta go," I said quickly.

"Fine. We can talk about it more when you get back," Ryder said.

"Sounds good. Give everyone my love."

"Will do."

After I hung up, I placed my phone in my pocket and crossed my arms over my chest. Adam held up the rocks glass. "Want one?"

I shook my head. "No. We have a lot of work still to do."

He raised a brow, a smirk on his face that felt off again. "Trying to pay penance for your ancestor's sins, Sadie? You'd have to work a hundred years to pay back the jewels."

"I'm not working anything off," I tossed back. I wasn't, was I? "I just don't like seeing people drowning and not offering them a hand."

His smirk disappeared into a glower. "Don't preach to me. You know nothing about these people, how things work, or just how much skin and bone my family has given to this ranch. All the things that were *stolen* from us." He let the word stolen drift between us for a beat and then added on, "I'm not offering up anything more than is required."

"So you let the full load land on your sister's shoulders when she clearly isn't in a mental place to handle it."

"She made her choice." He said it darkly, staring into the alcohol in his glass. When he looked up, his expression brought goosebumps back to my skin. It was menacing. Ominous. "We were supposed to leave the ranch together. After our dad and grandfather were killed in a wreck while hauling Harrington cattle through the mountains, we promised each other we'd get out as soon as we could. We were going to finally break the cycle that tied our family to the Harringtons, that had left us crawling for leftovers for a century. Then she got pregnant. Fell in *love*." He said it scathingly. "And I was left to break the cycle on my own."

Holy hell. He'd lost his dad and his grandfather while they'd been working for Rafe's family? Another shiver ran up my spine.

Rafe had said their family situation was complicated, and I'd thought he'd meant the love triangle between him and Spencer and Lauren, but this was so much more tangled and twisted.

My pulse raced as I watched him try to tuck away his anger and disgust behind the affable charm that had first greeted me. Did he hate the Harringtons enough to put a snake in Rafe's bed? To smother the sister he felt had abandoned him?

Could he have murdered Spencer?

My palms turned sweaty, and I had to fight my way past a flight instinct that was telling me to get far away from Adam. Instead, I poked and prodded, hoping he'd reveal something, anything. "And yet you're still here."

"I left," he said, and all the darkness seemed to wash away, leaving behind only a tired acceptance as he sank into the chair behind the desk. "I'd actually made a life for myself and enough money to stay away for good, but Lauren begged me to come back after Old Man Harrington died of a heart attack. Rafe had taken off, and Spence couldn't manage the books on his own. She promised me it would be different this time. Promised me a merger that had been too long in the making."

"But it wasn't true, was it? They never intended to give you any of it."

His head jerked up at my question, defiance and fire returning as he slammed his glass down, and for a moment, he looked like the snake last night. Ready to strike. A rattle waving in warning. "Spencer respected me, appreciated what I did, and even implemented most of my ideas. He'd planned on making me a partner, adding me to the trust, and removing Rafe, but he died before he could do it."

Even if my instincts weren't screaming at me, I wouldn't have believed anything he said. I was suddenly very glad I hadn't given him the jewels. That I hadn't brought them with me.

"Everything okay in here?" Adam and I both jumped at Rafe's voice coming from the doorway. His all-seeing eyes narrowed as he looked between me and Adam. We weren't anywhere near each other. A desk and a carpet stood between us, but there was an insidiousness that hung in the air, and I knew Rafe sensed it.

"Fine," I said, whirling around and heading for the door. "I was just seeing if Adam was going to join us in the stables."

Both men scoffed at the exact same time.

I had to talk to Rafe. About all of it. My family's part in it, as well as the bitterness Adam had shown. I'd spill my guts and hope it somehow helped rather than added more burdens to Rafe's shoulders.

Chapter Twenty

Rafe

RUNNING ON EMPTY
Performed by Max McNown

Sadie's body was practically vibrating with unease. A hint of fear. I'd loathed walking in on them together, but it hadn't been jealousy that had tripped through my veins. It was a renewed concern for her safety. Every moment she was here, every moment she interacted with the people who might be coming for me, who might have killed my brother, brought her closer to the danger.

"Did he hurt you? Threaten you?" I demanded as I followed her out into the hall.

She shook her head and then glanced back at the office before taking my hand and dragging me out the front door. With worry pouring from her, she told me what Adam said about his dad and his grandfather, and how he and Lauren had promised each other to leave the ranch.

Confusion and doubt bled through me. Lauren loved the ranch almost as much as she loved Spence—certainly more than she'd loved me. How could Adam have ever imagined she would leave? Even when she'd gone to the local junior college, she'd enrolled in agricultural management classes. She'd always envisioned a life that involved the ranch.

Had she lied to Adam? Or was Adam lying now?

"Spencer would never have given him any part of the ranch or the trust," I said with a certainty I didn't quite feel. What did

I know of my brother or the relationship he and Adam had built in my absence. Had I left my brother to be taken in by the wolves? Were he and Lauren somehow involved in all of this together?

My chest squeezed tight before I shook the thought away. Lauren loved Spence wholeheartedly. I told Fallon it was like losing a limb when she'd lost my brother, and that was the truth. They were one soul that I'd tried stupidly to divide.

But what role had Adam's bitterness and resentment played in both the ranch's demise and my brother's?

"I need to look through the ranch accounts and see what's been going on. He gave me Spence's logins and passwords, but I haven't had a chance to use them yet." I'd been kept busy since he'd given them to me—first with tasks on the ranch, and then with Sadie and a rattlesnake, and finally an attack on Lauren that may or may not have been real.

Had it all been one big distraction to keep me from looking at the books?

When I'd talked with Steele last night, the only new information he'd had on Puzo was that the man had definitely embedded himself into the finances of the town's businesses. He still couldn't find Nero Lancaster, and he'd tried both legal and not-so-legal methods of locating him.

"I can look at them with you tonight," Sadie offered.

The way she looked at me, the openness and caring in those blue eyes, almost undid me. Almost made me forget sending her away for her own good was the right and selfless thing to do, because I wanted that goodness and light to be mine. I wanted to drown myself in it. To give up the power and control I usually required and let the time with her wash away every sin, every failure, every last ounce of grief.

But taking those moments, keeping Sadie close, would mean putting her in the middle of all the ugly that still existed in my life. And what I'd told her last night was still true. I would be the reason that light was dimmed and blew out.

"I don't think—" I started just as she said, "Rafe, there's something else—" when we were both interrupted by Fallon.

"Waiting for us?" my daughter asked as she and Maisey came out of the house. I glanced from Sadie to my daughter and then back.

"Later," I said, and Sadie nodded.

"Is he whining about how much he hates the next chore on the list?" Fallon asked, looking at me with a smirk. "Or admitting he's afraid of the chickens?"

"I'm not afraid of those scrawny-assed creatures," I huffed. "And how would you even know any of that?"

"Spence told me. He said they used to chase you around the pen, and you'd squeal like a baby and run away."

Sadie laughed, Maisey hid her snort behind her hand, and the tension that had stiffened my shoulders eased ever so slightly.

"I bet he didn't tell you it was all his fault, did he?" I taunted, but my lips were twitching upward at the memory. "When I was little, he used to put grain in my pockets without me knowing, so when I walked into the coop, they all came at me like I was a delectable treat. Chickens are mean when they're hunting for food." I pulled my arm sideways, finding a set of scars on the back above my elbow. "I have the war wounds to prove it."

Sadie leaned in and looked, then she twisted around and pulled up her shirt to show us her lower back. "That's nothing, you big baby. See this?" There was a jagged white scar about two inches just above her waistband. "Chicken grabbed on and wouldn't let go. Ryder had to basically strangle it in order to get it off me."

I had to press my nails into my palms to prevent myself from reaching out and touching her, running a finger along the faded mark.

She put her shirt down and punched me gently in the shoulder. "And I'm still not afraid of them."

Fallon was smiling, large and wide and happy, and I had Sadie to thank for it. Even after what had passed between her and Adam in the office and the panic in her voice, she was able to bring an easiness to others. She wanted people to be happy.

She wanted good things for me and mine, and that had me falling even harder for the blue-eyed imp.

♫ ♫ ♫

After another long afternoon of chores, I ached in places I'd forgotten I had muscles, and my hands, once callused and rough, bore the marks of skin gone soft. I'd never considered myself out of shape, but two days of manual labor proved otherwise. I could only imagine the disgust my dad would have sent my way if he could see me now. Weak in body as he'd once thought I was weak in spirit.

Fallon and Maisey hadn't complained once all day, and it made me determined to do something extra nice for them. Maybe give them a vacation before school started. Wherever they wanted to go, I'd take them. Money may not be able to solve all the world's problems, not even all of mine or the ranch's, but it could give my daughter and her friend some happy memories after months of sadness.

And what about Sadie? the little devil in my head asked. We both knew I wanted to give her memories of me inside her, driving her up and over the edge multiple times. I wanted to embed myself into every molecule of her being until she'd never forget that I'd been there. That I'd taken what she gave and given back more.

That was where my mind was at—on Sadie and actually finishing what we'd started twice now—as we made our way back to the house with the tasks on our list finally done for the day. A dark Mercedes pulled into the gravel lot and parked next to my Jaguar.

My gaze narrowed, taking a step toward it, but Fallon halted me with a hand to my arm. "It's just part of the wedding party, but we need to make sure Mom has everyone's keys ready."

Maisey's shy voice saying, "Oh, hey, Mr. Puzo," caused my head to jerk up from Fallon to the man who'd emerged from the car.

All the tension, all the anger and frustration I'd been

feeling for days now, dropped back into my stomach like a lead balloon as I watched the one person I truly despised step toward us.

"What the hell are you doing here?" I growled, pushing Fallon behind me.

He was dressed in jeans and a polo shirt with dress shoes on his feet. He looked as completely out of place here as I had when I'd shown up on Tuesday.

"Dad, Mr. Puzo keeps some of his horses here, and he has his boat parked at the dock." Fallon tried to step around me, but I held her back.

She hadn't told me it was Puzo's name on those contracts. I would never have allowed it. Never. I stalked forward, eliminating the distance between me and my enemy. "Hell no. Get off my land."

Puzo raised a brow, lips quirking. "Last I checked, it wasn't yours." His eyes landed on Fallon in a way that made me want to shove him headfirst into a watering trough. "And I'm paid up through the end of the summer."

He tried to step around me, but I blocked him, keeping us toe to toe.

He smirked, and it took everything I had not to wipe it off his face. I didn't want this nasty excuse of a human on the ranch. Near my family. Near me. The old scar embedded in my chest seemed to throb at his nearness. A telltale sign that something was wrong.

"Fallon, go inside with Maisey and Sadie," I bit out. When I felt her hesitate, I risked taking my gaze off Puzo to glare at her. Daring her to defy me on this. Daring her to choose the wrong answer. She met my glare with one of her own for a long moment before stomping off toward the main doors with her friend following.

It didn't surprise me Sadie didn't go with them. Instead, she came to stand next to me with tension all but radiating through her body. Puzo didn't seem shocked to see her there, and it reminded me that I still hadn't told her about the thug he'd had following her. My lungs burned from all the decisions

I'd made in the last week that had ended up being the wrong ones.

"It's good to see you again, cousin." He watched me carefully as he stated their relationship, as if expecting her to have kept it from me. "Had I known you were looking to take in the mountains of California, I would have let you stay at my place."

"You have a house here?" Astonishment drew her brows together.

"A little vacation cabin up the road," he told her with a small smile before glancing at me with a sly cunning that sent savage hate spinning through me. "I visited Rivers a few years ago—a little trip to squelch my curiosity—and found I had a lot to offer the community. Lots of possibilities I couldn't resist. Bets with just the right odds."

His gaze journeyed in the direction my daughter had gone. Goddamn it, he knew my daughter. Had looked at her before. Been on the ranch and turned those slimy eyes upon her. I was going to kill Adam. Lauren. How dare they let him near her.

I leaned into his space more, muscles tense and ready for a fight, just as guilt hit me like a sledgehammer. None of them had known any better. They didn't know the knife wound in my chest had been because of him. I'd kept my life as separate from my family's as possible, and this was the consequence. While I'd been facing the other way, a monster had slunk onto the land.

"Bets are closed," I snarled. "Everything here is now off-limits."

He didn't back down. If anything, he pressed himself into my space as much as I'd entered his, daring me to take the first punch. I would win in a physical fight. It wouldn't be easy. It'd be ugly, and I'd come away with my fair share of bruises and breaks, but I would win.

"No one tells me what is and isn't off-limits." His voice was as cold as mine.

"Then let me be the first. My family, this land, and even the goddamn town is off-limits. I'll refund your money for any lease you've signed, and tomorrow, I'll haul your boat out of the water and your horse out of my barn and drop them off wherever you want. You will not step foot on Harrington land again. Am I clear?"

His shoulders relaxed instead of tightened at my words, the tension in his body being replaced by a patronizing smile, as if he was watching a toddler throw a tantrum. I had to clench my fists in order to hold myself back while I fought wildly to regain control of my anger.

"I rather like my things here, so even though we could break the contract giving me rights to the dock and the barn, I have no desire to do so." He spoke casually, as if it meant nothing to him, but there was a steely resolve underneath it. "Plus, my cousin Marielle is getting married here this weekend. You might remember she's like a sister to me. With her parents gone, I paid for the wedding. My money is lining those empty Harrington Ranch coffers. I believe you should be thanking me for helping hold it up a bit longer."

He took advantage of my stunned silence to step around me and head for the house.

If I'd had any doubts before about what was happening here, they were gone. Puzo was involved. I didn't know how or when he'd gotten his claws in here, and I had absolutely no proof he'd been responsible for the ranch's failure or my brother's death, but every fiber of my being told me he was. And it was my fault. I hadn't even thought to warn them to watch their backs. I wouldn't have dreamed of interfering in Spence's business and would have been nauseated at the idea of telling him even a piece of mine.

My pride and arrogance had allowed Puzo to weasel his way in with Adam and Spence by doling out advice and appearing to help, but the truth was, he wanted to make the ranch his. He wanted to take my heritage, my roots, and destroy them as he hadn't been able to destroy me. He'd spent time in the community, cozied up to the people in charge, and lined their pockets, probably so when he took over the land, no one would stop him from cutting it apart and parceling it out to developers who'd build on it—ruin it.

No wonder the mayor had looked worried earlier.

He said he'd a signed contract giving him the right to be there, and the law would be on his side, but I'd tear it apart. He may have a contract, but I'd find any and every loophole I could to free my family of the hooks he'd stuck into us. He'd completely lost his mind if he thought I'd stand by and let him destroy the ranch, destroy Lauren and Fallon, just to get to me.

I'd started to wonder what it would take to make the ranch a success again for my daughter, but as I strode into the house, the mission became clearer. Stronger. I wouldn't do it just for her. I'd make this ranch an icon of success simply to shove it in Puzo's face. The Harrington-Marquess name would be the benchmark every other resort of its kind hoped to replicate. I'd loosen his claws from my family, from this town and this community, and once they were all free, I'd use those vicious nails of his to slice through the heart of him. I'd end him.

Chapter Twenty-one

Rafe

MACBETH
Performed by Max McNown

Fallon had shown Puzo into the sitting room at the front of the house by the time Sadie and I walked in. I'd just taken a step toward them, fists clenched, ideas of tossing him out on his ass running through my head, when Sadie's hand on my arm stopped me in the entry.

"Rafe. I understand you're angry—"

"That's the least of what I am."

"He said he's here for his cousin's wedding, right?" My chest felt like it might implode it was drawn so tight. I gave a curt nod, and she continued, "You can't ruin her wedding by kicking them off the property. Think of all the planning she's done. The excitement. The people who are coming. No matter how much you despise him being here, she's done nothing to you. You can't ruin the best day of her life like that."

Oh, yes you can, my devil taunted.

I didn't reply. I couldn't. Instead, I followed my daughter and Puzo into the sitting room. It was full of florals and chintz and claw-footed furniture my great-grandparents had imported from Europe, as if dragging Old World elegance onto the ranch could somehow change the savagery of the land and make it more refined. But it could never hide the truth of this place. The wild was meant to thrive here.

Without even knowing it, I'd done the same thing at The

Fortress, attempting to bring grace and charm to a city that often reveled in addiction and sin. Attempting to show the entire world that *I* was more than a simple ranch hand with a knack for taming horses. But the me I'd forged, the life I'd created in Vegas, was as false as the façade of Mont Saint Michel I'd built to house my triumph.

Two days was all it took for this place to prove I'd never be able to cleanse it from my blood.

And I loathed it was Puzo who'd shown me the truth by trying to take it away.

"I'll just get Mom," Fallon said just as Lauren astonished those of us who'd seen her laid up in bed by walking into the room wearing a sundress littered with poppies. Her hair was up in a smooth ponytail, and she'd attempted to hide the shadows under her eyes with a layer of makeup. While it couldn't rid the sadness from them or the strain from her smile, it did leave her looking better than she had that morning.

"I didn't expect you until later this evening, Lorenzo," she said, greeting him with a cheek kiss that made me cringe.

"My plans opened up, and I thought I'd take the boat out on the lake," Puzo said with a smooth smile. As he stepped back, he ran his gaze over Lauren's figure in a way that sent the blood in my veins boiling again. Not in jealousy—I'd never want her that way again—but from a need to protect my family.

"Fallon, you and Maisey get cleaned up for dinner," I ordered.

My daughter's gaze darted between the adults in the room, but she didn't argue. She just rolled her eyes, grabbed Maisey's hand, and headed up the stairs. And while I liked that she was no longer in the same room as Puzo, I worried because I could no longer see her. Keeping her close all day had been a balm I'd needed after last night.

"I haven't heard from Marielle today," Lauren said. "I'm assuming everything is still set for her arrival tomorrow?"

"Everything is going according to plan." The sly smile returned, directed at me, and only Sadie linking her fingers with mine and holding me back stopped me from lunging for him.

"It's a beautiful location for a wedding. Marielle is lucky you were able to fit her in on such short notice."

"Just exactly how long have you been planning this wedding?" I demanded. Had it been after Spence had died? Before? What the hell did Puzo think he could do while he was here?

"Your welcoming committee could use an overhaul," he said instead of answering my question.

Lauren darted me a worried glance. "Let me get you the keys so you can get settled in."

She went to an antique writing desk I recognized as once being in the housekeeper's quarters. The cubbies were now labeled with gold numbers, and Lauren grabbed an envelope from one of them, handing it to Puzo. "It'll just be you and the groom's parents at the homestead. Nicky and his groomsmen are in the bunkhouse, and Marielle and her bridesmaids will be here. Do you need anyone to show you the way?"

"No, I've been here enough to know my way around." His lips curled upward again at the dark grunt that escaped my lips.

As soon as he stepped out of the room, Lauren hissed, "What is wrong with you?!"

Then, she hurried after him, and I followed on her heels. We'd just made it to the front door when Adam came hurrying in. "Lorenzo! I thought I heard your voice."

He extended his hand, and Puzo shook it, asking, "How's my favorite gambling partner?"

Disgust and disbelief punched me in the stomach. Adam was gambling with Puzo? Was that how he'd gotten his hands into the ranch? Because Adam owed him money? Adam had been all about chess as a kid. He'd despised cards simply because of what they'd cost his family. Since when had that changed?

"Can I offer you a drink? Maybe take you to dinner tonight?" Adam's affable charm was disorienting—a much shinier, more polished version of the Adam I'd grown up with or I'd witnessed this week. His wide-eyed honesty caused the hair on the back of my neck to stand up. It was all an act. But for whose benefit? Mine? Puzo's?

"Thank you, but I have other plans tonight. I'll have to come back another weekend."

It was another shot he sent in my direction. Another reminder he had his hooks into much more than the ranch and wasn't going to slink away at my say-so.

Adam and Lauren both gave him a warm goodbye that had me biting my cheek and tasting blood. The door had barely shut behind him when I said darkly, "You've let the goddamn devil in the door. Puzo's only goal here is to destroy all of you as a means of getting revenge on me."

Adam's charm dissipated in an instant. "Your ego is larger than ever, Rafe. As I told you before, Lorenzo has had nothing but good advice for us. He's the reason we got the cell tower contract and the reason we've got steady income coming in from the dock and the stables. Hell, he even sent hay sales our way."

"I doubt he did it out of the graciousness of his heart. How much do you owe him?" I demanded.

Adam's face paled ever so slightly. "Nothing. I don't owe him a damn thing."

I didn't believe him, and the way Lauren looked at him, I wondered if she knew he was lying too. But she turned to me and said, "I'm not sure why you hate Lorenzo, but Adam's right. He's been nothing but helpful. Spence wasn't always thrilled with how he handled business in town, but even he knew Lorenzo had stepped into the void we'd been forced to leave behind in the community. He's been good for all of us."

"Because it serves his purpose. But believe me, he'll take you for every penny he can and walk away laughing. And if you try to stop him, he'll have no qualms about wiping you out."

"You're overreacting," Lauren said.

"Am I?" Fear and fury fueled me. I yanked up my shirt, revealing the scars that slaked down the left side of my chest. "Is this an overreaction? Because this is how Lorenzo handles business with those he believes have crossed him."

Lauren's voice was barely above a stunned whisper when she said, "You told us you were mugged."

"I told you that in order to protect my family." But I hadn't. Instead, I'd ignored them and let him sneak right in the back door.

"I don't believe you." Adam's voice was contemptuous. "Lorenzo told me all about how you worked for him in Vegas and got involved with a bad crowd. How the FBI came after you, and you ratted out your supposed friends to save your own skin."

I pressed a knuckle into the knot in my jaw. "And of course you believed him."

"Why wouldn't I?" Adam glared. "He's given me no reason to doubt him."

And every reason to doubt you. The words were unspoken but hung in the air anyway. It bit at me in just the way he'd intended.

"I did gather evidence for the FBI, but it was on Puzo's criminal activities. He's involved in drugs, guns, money laundering. You name it, his family has done it."

"What?" Lauren demanded, her voice shaky and unsure. "Why isn't he in jail, then?"

"Because he lets the people below him do all the dirty work, and no one is willing to testify against him. People who do, end up dead."

"I don't believe you," Adam snarled. "Whatever your issue is with Lorenzo, it has nothing to do with us. You washed your hands of the ranch after you got your cut. We don't want or require your assistance. And we certainly don't need for you to cause a scene this weekend. Plenty of important people will be attending this wedding. People who can not only invest in the ranch's renovation, but who would be happy to sprinkle their money around by staying here and bringing other weddings to our doors. You want to do something for all of us now? Just leave."

He turned on his heel and strode down the hall.

Lauren put a shaky hand to her forehead, the fake bravado she'd put on in front of Puzo had disappeared.

As much as I loathed being the one to bring more anguish, more concerns to her life, I had to make her see the truth, if only to keep her and Fallon safe. So, I gentled my voice as much as I could and said, "If Adam owes Puzo money, it could explain what's happening."

Her eyes jerked up to mine. "Wh-what do you mean?"

"The rattler left in my bed, the person in your room last night, even the way the ranch is failing. They could all be warnings from Puzo."

She shook her head. "N-no. The ranch has been struggling ever since Spencer took the loan out to give you your money." Her face hardened. "Adam is right, Rafe. We don't need you getting involved now. You've done enough already."

She hurried after her brother, a wisp of the person she used to be. And for the first time, I wondered how long she'd been this way. Had she been fading away even before Spencer had died, or had his death truly triggered her slow dissolve?

Sadie was right. My hands were so completely and utterly tied. I had to let Puzo remain at the ranch this weekend, and it made me want to hit something until my knuckles were bloody and raw, until my outside matched the feeling inside my chest.

There is something *you can do*, the devil reminded me. And there was. I could look into the ranch's accounts. I could do what Spence had asked of me in that last voicemail. I could bury my pride once and for all and help my family.

The timing of Spence's call, as much as the location of his accident, should have made me question his death sooner. Maybe I'd been too shocked to process it, or maybe I'd just gotten so good at putting up walls between my brother and me that I hadn't wanted to let them down enough to see the truth. If Fallon hadn't flown the Cessna to Las Vegas, I wasn't sure I ever would have.

"Rafe…" Sadie's voice was low and pained. Filled with sympathy for me. Pity I hated and was the last thing I wanted from her.

"Don't," I bit out. My voice was gritty and harsh, but she didn't take offense. She just moved toward me, wrapping her arms around my waist. Her touch, her warmth, the genuine caring in her expression almost brought me to tears.

I blinked fiercely, tugging on a lock of hair that had escaped her clip, and then told her the simple truth. "I'd like to finish what we started, Tennessee, more than I think you could possibly understand. But even more than that, I want to know you're safe. I'd like you to get the hell out of here."

Her chin went up automatically, and that fierce determination to stay with me, to not walk away from the battle, was almost as much of a turn-on as her siren-like eyes. When was the last time someone had stuck by me simply because it was me? I couldn't remember. I wasn't sure it had ever happened.

If I asked her to take my daughter, to get them both as far away as possible from Puzo and Adam and whatever ugliness had draped itself over the land, I thought she just might. But could I stand to have them out of my sight either? To have them where I couldn't reach them?

It would be agony either way. To have them gone or to have them stay.

Wheels on the gravel drive outside had me moving away before she could respond. I opened the door and watched as a black SUV parked next to my Jaguar. The pressure in my chest eased ever so slightly when Jim Steele emerged from the driver's seat. The passenger door opened, and Steele's son, Parker, stepped out just as two wide-shouldered men got out of the back. Part of our security team, Noah and Barry traveled with me whenever Steele felt I needed extra coverage.

And goddamn did I need it now. Not for me, but for the people I needed to protect.

The pressure in my chest loosened even more. Not quite relief, but a feeling of being not quite so alone. With four men here to watch my back, watch my family's, I might just be able to breathe.

"Thank the fucking stars."

"Who are they?" Sadie asked.

"My security team." She glanced from them to me, and I saw the tension ease from her shoulders as well. "Can I ask you to do me a favor?"

"Anything," she said without hesitation.

"Can you stick by Fallon? Make sure she's safe while I get them up to speed?"

"Of course," she said. Then, she lowered her voice and said, "We still need to talk."

We did. But I had to get Steele and my men caught up on what was happening, see what cameras we could get up quickly, and figure out how long it would take to overhaul the mansion's antiquated alarm system no one had used in years. Then, I needed to peel back the layers on the ranch's accounts and find out what had shaken my brother enough to ask for my help.

"We will," I promised and meant it.

Instead of walking away as I expected, she glanced one more time at the men pulling bags and crates out of the SUV and then closed the distance between us. She cupped my face and brushed her lips against mine. The heat of her, the honeyed goodness, bled into me instantly, igniting the ever-waiting embers and sending a craving through me so strong it almost blocked out all the other bullshit.

And then, she was gone, leaving behind the smell of burnt ash in the air as if I'd been singed by a passing flame. Except, there was nothing passing about what I felt for her. I was hooked. By that mischievous smile and silky hair. By the mark of bravery on her skin. By the way she rolled up her sleeves and dug in to help without a hint of hesitation when she had zero reason to do so, other than to be kind. She'd seen me at my worst, angry and cold and selfish, and she still stood there looking like she wanted to devour me. As if she cared.

She moved farther away, walking backward so she could watch my expression as she said, "I've been turned on by you in more ways than I can count, but the way you love and protect the family who let you walk away without blinking…that's sexier than hell. That kiss was to remind you that our unfinished business is about more than just talking. Do you remember what you promised me? I think you said something about begging and loss of control? I'm not leaving here until I've gotten what you anted up. Neither of us is folding."

She winked and spun around, leaving me speechless.

Filled with a craving to not only finish unraveling her but to keep her.

Chapter Twenty-two

Sadie

TWO IS BETTER THAN ONE
Performed by Boys Like Girls with Taylor Swift

My heart was racing as I left Rafe in search of Fallon. It wasn't just the promises I'd made to him about our unfinished business that had my pulse hammering. It was the devastation I felt for him, and the anger I felt toward his family for the utter disregard and complete lack of compassion for what he'd been through with Lorenzo.

He'd been visibly relieved to see his security team show up, and for that I was grateful to them. I hoped they could ease some of his worries, and I would do what I could to lessen them as well. For now, that meant shadowing his daughter like he'd asked. The only thing I wouldn't do that he'd asked was leave. I wouldn't cut and run when he had so few people looking out for him.

When I finally found Fallon, she was with Lauren in the kitchen. I told them four of Rafe's men had shown up, and Lauren let out a sigh of pure frustration. "And where the hell am I supposed to put them when I've got an entire wedding party coming?"

"Other than Sadie, no one else is on the third floor," Fallon suggested, and Lauren tossed her an exasperated look.

"I haven't cleaned those rooms in months." She rubbed her forehead. "Fine. Go make up the beds, and I'll figure out a meal for a team of people I hadn't planned on feeding tonight."

If Rafe hadn't asked me to look after his daughter, if I hadn't still been irritated with Lauren for her treatment of him, I might have stayed to help her cook. Instead, I found I needed distance before I said things I couldn't take back and weren't my place to say, so I followed Fallon to a linen closet on the third floor.

We worked quietly down the row of rooms past mine, making beds and wiping down surfaces.

"Where's Maisey?" I asked.

"While all the so-called adults in my life were arguing, her mom picked her up for her lessons at the riding school. She'll be back on Saturday to help with the wedding. Mom pays us both to act as hostesses."

After we'd finished up the final room and headed toward the stairs, Fallon stopped, chewed worriedly at her cuticles, and then asked, "Why does Dad hate Mr. Puzo?"

I shifted, uncomfortable with being put on the spot and knowing Rafe would dislike it if I told his daughter things he didn't want her to know. "I think you need to ask him."

She sighed in disgust. "He won't tell me. He treats me like I'm five instead of fourteen. That's fine. I'll find the answers the same way I've always found things out in this house."

Worry crept through me. "And how's that?"

Fallon grinned at me. "I'm not giving *my* secrets away if you won't give me any of *yours*."

I almost snorted because it sounded so much like her father. Negotiating deals. Negotiating relationships. "I can't tell you anything about your dad and Lorenzo, Fallon. I'd be breaking his trust, and the little bit I've earned from him is on shaky ground as it is."

"You and Dad have a thing going."

Was that what it was? A *thing*? It felt enormous. It felt like a black hole sucking me into its vortex from which there would be no escape. I was a bit terrified by what I felt for Rafe. Because what I wanted with him was impossible.

When I didn't respond, Fallon said, "I like seeing him here.

Seeing him with you. He's a different person. More relaxed. Or at least he was until Mr. Puzo showed up. Is Mr. Puzo really your cousin?"

"Honestly, I don't know."

"How can you not know?"

I told her a bit about my great-grandmother. Not the jewelry part, but the other parts of it. "My family is just trying to trace our roots."

"My roots are really messed up," she said. "One side of my family stole from the other and then basically made them indentured servants. I think those bad seeds were what caused Mom and Spence to fight. Uncle Adam told me Spence promised to make it right after nearly a hundred years, but that he'd died before he could. He wants me to give him half the ranch when I take over." My surprised exhale had Fallon tilting her head toward me and saying, "I don't believe him. I told Dad that Uncle Adam was up to no good. He and Spence had a huge argument the night Spencer died."

"Where was your mom?"

Fallon looked away. "She hurt herself last year. A cow rammed her into a fence, and she'd been taking these hefty pain meds. They knocked her out cold." She stopped on the stairs, hand sliding up and down the dark, lacquered wood. "I couldn't wake her at first when they came to tell us about Spence…"

My heart fell into the pit of my stomach. She'd faced it alone? Goddamn it. No one should have to find out about losing someone they loved like that, let alone a kid.

"I called Uncle Adam, and he came over. He was still living at the Hurly house then, but he was here in just a few minutes."

"Who found Spence?" I asked quietly.

"Teddy. He's one of our part-time ranch hands. It was only five in the morning, but he was coming to help with baby bull castration." Fallon shuddered, and I wasn't sure if it was at the ugly job or if it was the way Spence had been found. "He'd been dead for hours they said." Fallon's voice cracked.

"I'm really, truly sorry you lost him." I knew the words were useless, but I still offered them as they were all I had to give her.

She bit her lip, as if holding back tears, and continued downstairs, heading for the kitchen. I hurried to keep up with her.

"I get why Dad wants to sell," she said. "It's all falling apart. It was falling apart before Spence died. They kept having to lower the size of the herd because they couldn't afford the staff to work them, but that meant we had even less profits. They were trying to shore it up with the other revenue, but it wasn't enough. We had a whole field of alfalfa destroyed last year, which meant we didn't have any to sell when we had to keep what was left for our animals. It just was one thing after another."

"Fallon." I pulled her to a stop with a gentle hand. "My family went through a really rough time too. We almost lost everything. I heard the discussions my parents had, but they never let me take that burden on as a kid. You shouldn't have it weighing on your shoulders either."

She looked back at me, and her expression was so grown-up, so knowledgeable, that it was scary. "It's my ranch, Sadie. I'm the last Harrington here. Dad is just the executor of the trust because he gave up his rights to it before I was born. I may be just a kid, but it's *mine*. Spence left it to me." Her voice was fierce with pride, and determination sparked in those eyes so like her dad's. "I should have a say in what happens to it and how we dig ourselves out of this hole."

I swallowed hard, wanting to shield her, and realized that was the last thing she wanted. She'd already faced some of the worst things alone and handled it with more strength than a lot of grown-ups would have. "You're right. You should have a say. Have you told your dad how you feel?"

"He keeps trying to box me into little-kid mode." Her frustration was clear.

"I don't think it's because he doesn't believe you can handle it. I think he wants you to hang on to every last moment of your childhood because once you become an adult and accept all your adult responsibilities, it never lets go. You have seventy, eighty, or even more years to be an adult, but you only have a handful to be young and free." It was why Ryder hadn't wanted me to take on the bar when Uncle Phil died. He'd wanted me to go off and play college girl for a few more years, to goof off and party and just live in the moment, but everything had changed once I'd almost died. I couldn't go back to being the freewheeling Sadie who threw darts and hooked up with boys.

Fallon's life had taken the same kind of hit when Spencer had died.

The teen tilted her head, considering what I'd said, but she never got a chance to respond as the back door slammed open, and Lauren hustled out of the mudroom with a handful of reusable grocery bags. "Oh good, you're done upstairs. I ran to the store to get something to feed Rafe's guests. Can you help grab the rest from the truck?" Lauren asked Fallon.

The teen simply nodded, hurrying out the back.

I followed with my heart wrung to pieces for her. The belief that this land was hers, that it was her legacy, had her working to the bone when all Rafe wanted was to free her from its weight. And unless they could find a compromise soon, it was going to leave a nasty scar on both of them.

♫ ♫ ♫

It was late, the house was quiet, and my body was exhausted, but I couldn't sleep. The talk Rafe and I needed to have and the promises we'd made had me pacing the room and watching the clock while my stomach fluttered.

When Fallon and I had taken dinner down to him and his team in the cabin, he'd told me not to wait up. He'd said he'd be caught up helping to install cameras and then digging into the ranch's accounts, and he'd see me in the morning.

But I couldn't settle. Not with so much still needing to be said. So, I propped my bedroom door open, hoping I'd be able to hear if and when he returned to the main house.

When my phone vibrated in my hand, it nearly had me jumping out of my skin. Seeing it was the bartender at McFlannigan's had a new worry rushing through.

"Hi, Ted. What's up?"

"Fire marshal fined us."

"Damn it," I swore as frustration and guilt hit me. "What happened?"

"Patti and I didn't realize we were over capacity. We knew we were busy. Grady and his band had a whole crew show up from UTK for Throwback Thursday, but I wasn't keeping count."

"Where was Bart?" Our part-time bouncer kept a counter going on our busiest nights.

"Called in sick. I thought we could handle it."

It wasn't his fault. He'd told me all along he didn't want to manage the bar. It was my job to find a fill-in for Bart or, at a minimum, keep track of our numbers. It was a harsh reminder I had responsibilities waiting for me. A real life that I'd been ignoring while I was playing detective, pretending to be Sadie-the-dart-champion again, and falling for a man who it would be impossible to build a life with. My stomach twisted.

"I'll be home on Sunday. I'll try to convince him to rip up the fine."

We spent another couple of minutes with him giving me an update before hanging up.

I paced some more, frustration brewing. I'd put aside my plans and my ideas for my community while here, letting these people sink into the void that had been slowly growing inside me. The roots they'd placed in my heart were all but set, vines twining around me in a way that would be painful to remove. But the truth was, none of these people were mine. I couldn't keep them. Worrying about them wasn't my place, just as their relationships weren't mine to fix.

I had a life to go back to before it crumbled too.

So why did this feel like reality…and the life I'd left behind feel fake?

It was nearing midnight when I heard the quiet hush of footsteps on the stairs and doors closing down the hall from me. Just because some of his men had come in didn't mean Rafe was back, but I couldn't stand waiting anymore. Couldn't stand making a circuit through the tiny room one more time.

If he wasn't back, I'd find something else to do to fill the time and shut off my brain. I made my way silently down to the room below me where Rafe had moved his things the night before. Light bled out from under the door, and I thought of knocking, but I didn't want to wake Fallon across the hall, so I simply turned the knob.

He was standing at the window, shirtless with a pair of sweats clinging to his lower body. His palm was on the glass, but he wasn't looking outside. His head was bent, shoulders leaning forward, as if he was carrying the weight of a hay bale on his shoulders.

The click of the door shutting behind me had his head jerking up. Dark eyes met mine, worry and pain dancing with lust as he slowly watched me step closer, and that same heady desire that roared through me whenever he was near rushed back in. It pooled in my stomach and made me forget everything I'd come to say. All I wanted was to get lost for a few hours in the sinful promises we'd taunted each other with, if only to give him a respite from the worries dragging him down.

"I know we need to talk, but I'm not good company tonight," he said. He picked up a glass of bourbon from the dresser next to him, tossed it back, and set it down empty.

"Let's be honest, Slick. You haven't exactly been burning up the air with your repartee at any time."

Only the slight raise of his brow showed that he'd enjoyed my little dig.

I moved forward again, and this time, I didn't stop until our bare feet were touching. Until the musky scent of him, soap and fields and bourbon, filled my lungs. "We do need to talk," I said. "But right now, I think you need something else more."

He watched as I slid my palms over the cuts and lines of his stomach, up over the dark hair sprinkled across his chest, along those strong, wide shoulders carrying the world. I pressed closer, sliding between his legs, brushing our hips together, and was rewarded with the hard length of him surging into my stomach. When I followed the path my hands had made with my lips, he inhaled sharply. A hiss of tortured pleasure.

"Sadie," he grunted, and I ignored the warning in his tone, flicking a tongue over a dark nipple. He fisted my hair, dragging my head back so his eyes, ablaze with need, scorched into mine. "Tennessee, I won't be gentle. I won't be kind. I have too much burning me up inside tonight."

"I don't want gentle or kind. I want you as you are now—raw and gritty and tormented. Let me ease it all for a few hours."

He stared for several long heartbeats, and then, his mouth slammed into mine. Just as he promised, it wasn't gentle or kind or tender. It was agony and flame and deliciously rough, causing my core to clench and my pulse to race.

Teeth grazed and hands bit into my skin, digging deep and anchoring me to him.

Our breathing was harsh and feverish.

His kisses and his touches were savage and all the more beautiful because of it.

I surrendered everything to him. Control. Heart. Hope. I gave, and he took, inhaling me. His head dipped, finding the pulse beating wildly in my neck, nipping and sucking at it before continuing farther downward, and when his mouth ran into the neckline of my tank, he simply tore it from my body. Heedless of my gasp, he latched on to a hard tip waiting for him.

I moaned, fingers tangling in those locks bronzed by the sun, trying to find enough air to keep from drowning. When his mouth moved away from that tormented nipple, I whimpered in protest, and I felt him smile against my chest before he slid over to the other breast and gave it the same attention he had its partner.

Then, I was up in his arms, and in two long strides, he had tossed me on the bed and dragged my pajama bottoms and underwear off my legs. He flung them away and then slowly, thoroughly, took in every single inch of me.

"God, you're beautiful." He said it as if it caused him pain. As if the mere sight of me hurt. He even closed his eyes to block me out, thick lashes resting against bronzed skin. His chest heaved as if he'd run miles. Finally, his lids opened to reveal a delectable inferno waging inside him. One I wanted to devour me.

"Rafe." His name was a tortured beg as my hand skimmed low over my stomach, seeking relief to the growing ache inside. He cursed under his breath, grabbed my wrists, and yanked them above my head as he landed on me, the delicious weight pressing me into the mattress.

I leaned up to take his mouth with mine, slanting to join them perfectly, and heat burst along our lips. A bonfire I wanted to flash and flare until I was nothing but ash. With one hand, he held my wrists captive while he pushed his chest up and away from me with the other.

"My way, Tennessee," he growled. "My way or we stop."

I wrapped my ankles around his calves, and the movement dragged his hard length right where I was aching for it to be. "Then, get to work, Slick."

His lips curled up for all of two seconds before he leaned in and bit my lower lip hard enough it brought as much pain as it did pleasure. "I want to use both my hands to worship your body, darling. Can I trust you to leave yours where they're at?" he asked.

"Why can't I touch you too?"

"I'll let you. Just not yet. My turn first," he said.

For a moment, defiance flickered, but then, because I ached with a desperation that felt fatal if it went unfulfilled, I simply nodded. There wasn't much I wouldn't have agreed to in that moment just to feel him on me. In me. Around me.

He slowly let go of my wrists, and when I knotted my fingers together and left them above my head, he smiled. A wicked, sinful smile that had lust spinning through my veins, pounding with the speed of a racehorse. And then he did just as he'd said he would. He worshipped every piece of me with hands and tongue and teeth until I was vibrating.

He'd said he wouldn't be gentle, and while his touch wasn't soft or slow, it wasn't cruel. Every stroke demanded a response. Every twirl, every brush, left a flaming trail behind it. I was writhing with want, the pressure and intensity inside my chest and loins growing second by second. My lungs felt like they'd stopped working, my heart was hammering against my rib cage, and my core felt like it was going to erupt.

It physically hurt. This torturous wanting. This absolute craving for release.

And when his fingers finally sank into me, it took nothing more than one single thrust before I was crying out.

He silenced the sound with his mouth as I rode out the waves on his palm.

When I opened my eyes, the cocky grin on his face about undid me all over again, sending another wave of release through me that he felt on his hand. His grin widened.

He rolled away, and I uttered a curse of objection.

I hadn't gotten my turn. I hadn't gotten to torment him.

He chuckled, a low, dark sound that rolled through me as strongly as his touch. "You have to stay quiet, Tennessee. Too many people around. Can you do that?"

"I'll do my best," I said with a hint of irritation making itself known.

But then, he dropped his sweats, and my annoyance disappeared. He'd called me beautiful, but he was utterly magnificent. Cut and grooved, corded muscles tensing and contracting gently with each movement of his body. I wanted to touch and bite and suck on every piece of him just like he'd done with me. When I started to drop my arms from over my head, he grunted out, "I didn't say you could move those yet."

My lips twitched, but I simply shifted to release the strain on my shoulders and waited.

He dug around in a bag and came back with a condom wrapper, and all I could do was stare, with a pounding heart and desperate desire creeping in again, as he slowly rolled it onto his impressive length. I swore my core shook when he landed between my legs again.

His mouth found mine in a punishing, breath-stealing kiss before he eased down my body one more time, tasting every inch all over again. Savoring me. When the coarse bristles of his beard landed on my thighs and his tongue flicked along my heat, I shuddered, hips arching. It was too much. Too much and not enough. I was going to shatter.

I couldn't stop my reaction, lowering my hands and tangling my fingers into his bronzed locks. He looked up at me, stopping all the delightful licks and swirls.

"Hands off, Tennessee," he growled.

"Please," I begged in a tone I'd never heard myself use before, husky and deep and full of all the want I had flowing through me. "Please don't stop, and please let me touch you."

His gaze darkened, flames burning, and his mouth found mine once more, tongue lashing out a swirling answer. I couldn't tell if it was punishment or acquiescence, but he didn't stop me from touching him this time. My fingers dug into wide shoulders, nails slid along his back, and my back arched, molding every curve to his.

His eyes closed, hiding those dark flames from me. His jaw clenched, and then, without warning, he was inside me. Full and hard and perfect. I barely had a chance to inhale before we were moving. The pace was sure and steady and controlled at first. Completely Rafe. But in mere seconds, the restraint disappeared, breaking into frantic, chaotic thrusts. And if I'd thought I was going to shatter before, if I'd thought I'd already gone over the edge with his fingers stroking me, the mountain he took me up this time threatened to ruin me.

"Now, Sadie. Damnit, now." The whispered demand, tangled with my name, sent me free-falling over the cliff, my body heeding his command, shivering and shaking and soaring.

He swallowed my cries before rolling us over so he was on his back, and I was on top. He fisted my hair, pulling my head back so he could look at me and said, "Your turn, beautiful. Take what you wanted. Make me yours."

I didn't hesitate. I straddled him, the shift of position

causing a pleasured moan to escape my lips I tried to bite back. And then, I did what he told me to do, taking what I wanted, moving fast in an instinctive rhythm, one he met with every slide and thrust of his hips as his eyes turned black and his fingers dug into my hips.

The pressure built again. I'd never gone up and over so many times. Never had anyone demand I hand over every last piece of myself to them. I'd always held back a few morsels of myself in my other encounters. A few bits that meant I wouldn't lose myself entirely. That I wouldn't crumble after the onslaught as I'd seen each of my siblings do at different times. But even knowing the truth, even knowing I was going to be permanently marked in a new, unrecoverable way by Rafe once I left on Sunday, I still gave him every single part of me, including those last tentative pieces.

I watched his face as the roar built inside us and all but lost my breath when I saw him hand over pieces of himself in return. He opened the door to his soul and let me sneak inside just as he dove over the edge. And I did the only thing I could, which was to follow him into the abyss one more time.

Chapter Twenty-three

Rafe

LOSING SLEEP
Performed by Chris Young

I didn't know what to think...to feel...as my arms banded around Sadie, pulling her tighter into my chest. The wild pounding of our hearts and the frantic breathing of our lungs made it impossible to grab hold of the restraint I normally craved. Instead of pushing her off and rolling away as I would have with any other woman, I buried my face in her neck and let her dark, silky strands surround me. I'd never lost myself like I had with her. Never given up those last few moments of control. My pleasure had always come in being the one to lead that final, frenzied drive. Instead, Sadie had taken it from me, ripped it out of my hold with her fevered plea and those damn blue siren eyes.

Liar, my devil screamed. *You happily handed over the reins. You liked giving her the power in those final thrusts. You liked letting go.*

Ever since she'd thrown out her dare to me in the bar, I'd tried to tell myself that once I had her, the craving I had for her would dissipate, even as my devil had laughed at me. And he'd been right once again, because we'd barely finished, and I was hungry to begin again.

The feel of her naked body draped over me, the smell of her, the taste of her on my tongue, only caused the yearning to beat more chaotically inside my chest. I didn't want anyone else to *ever* have her this way. What she'd given up in those last few moments, those pieces of her she'd handed over, needed to belong solely to me. But how the hell was I supposed to make that happen?

I finally moved, dragging a hand into her hair and tugging so she was forced to share those deep, blue pools with me. Instead of reading her emotions as I'd intended, I lost myself completely, found myself drowning in them. Every breath I took belonged to her.

I loathed it. And loved it.

From the moment I'd first seen her, I'd been captured by her beauty, but she was especially stunning like this, with her dark locks tousled, lips swollen from my kisses, and skin flushed from coming apart multiple times at my demand.

My body responded to that look, tightening and hardening beneath her.

I captured her mouth, and the heat of her burned through me like the very best bourbon. In one swift move, I picked her up and carried her to the dresser. Taking a step back, I dealt with the first condom and slid on another.

"You're ready to go again, Slick?" Wonder danced over her face.

In response, I stepped between her thighs and slid a thumb along her center. She gasped. It was sexy and beautiful and mine.

I swallowed it, mouth pummeling into hers, taking ownership, claiming her as much as she'd claimed me. I slid into her with a barely controlled thrust. As I bottomed out, pleasure rippled through me. The world grew hazy until there was nothing but the blaze burning between us and the honeyed taste and smell that was Sadie.

I'd told her I wouldn't be gentle, and I hadn't expected to be. The need in me, the anger and frustration spiraling through me when she'd walked into the room, had me expecting to be anything but. And yet now, watching the need crest over her face, I wanted every move to be a caress. Every thrust an adoring worship.

It was Sadie who took the mellow edge and turned it wild

and rough once more. She dug her heels into my ass, easing forward on the dresser until there was no space between us. Until our bodies seemed forged together. One entity engaged in a feral search for another release. This singular mating dance was all that mattered. The promised heaven the only call we could heed.

Her sweet moans and whimpers were quiet, and I suddenly hated we were in a house full of people, because I wanted to hear her scream. I wanted to hear the sound she would make when there was nothing but moonlight and bluebells and water rushing around us.

"Rafe... God... Rafe." It was a frantic plea.

I picked her up and moved so her back was up against the wall, so the force was full and intense as I slammed back into her. She went off like an untamed mare sensing freedom, a quiet, beautiful cry escaping her that sounded like chimes on the gates of heaven, and I followed her through the pearly expanse, my body and heart and soul all landing deep inside her.

Our chests heaved, our breathing labored, but when she pushed the lock of my hair that had fallen over my brow away, I saw her lips were tilted upward. A softness surrounded her I vowed to keep. Our lives weren't anywhere near suited, but I was good at problem-solving, and I'd figure out how to blend our worlds together. That forging I'd felt as we'd gone over the edge together would be the base of a beautiful future.

I kissed her, slow and deep, saying with my lips everything I couldn't quite find the words to verbalize yet.

She'd ripped away my anger and frustration, leaving behind nothing but goddamn tenderness. Caring. *Love*. Goddamn it, I loved her. It should be impossible to feel so much for someone in such a short span. And yet I did.

I slowly eased her to the floor, and our eyes met again, a mix of emotions swimming between us. I tucked her hair behind her ear, finger stroking her cheek. Then, I twined our hands and led her back to the bed.

I left her there to step into the bathroom and dealt with the condom, and when I came back, she'd picked up her torn tank top and was trying to figure out how to put it on.

I ripped it from her hand and threw it over my shoulder.

"Rafe—"

"No. I'm not done with you," I told her and dragged her onto the mattress with me. I landed on my back with her sprawled over my chest and our legs tangled.

She propped her chin on a hand, watching me as she said, "I'm happy you weren't all huff and bluster. You backed up those promises pretty damn well, Slick."

I tugged a single lock. "You rushed me, Tennessee. I wanted to take my time."

She laughed softly. "That wasn't you taking your time? I thought I was going to explode. I think I actually might have."

I felt the grin from the bottom of my stomach all the way to my lips.

She touched my mouth with a look of awe on her face. "You're stunning when you let go. When you let yourself feel."

My throat constricted.

She closed her eyes briefly before meeting my gaze again. "We said we'd talk."

I wasn't sure I wanted to now. Wasn't sure I wanted to know what additional hurdles lie between us, but ignoring the elephant in the room wouldn't do us any good either.

"You go first," I told her.

"When I first contacted your family, it wasn't about weddings and dude ranches." She inhaled a shaky breath, but she didn't stop. Once Sadie decided something, she went at it with everything, and that was how she treated this. As she slowly unwound the story about her great-grandmother, and the stolen Harrington jewels, and why Adam had asked her to keep it all quiet, the constriction in my throat grew to my chest and my heart, frustration boiling once more, but not at her.

"I swear, we didn't know they were real until recently. At first, I was going to use them as a down payment for a performing arts center I want to build in Willow Creek, but then

I realized I couldn't create a legacy on something that seemed a bit hinky. So, I started researching...and that led me here."

I could tell she was nervous, because she was talking fast and furious.

"You want to build a theater?" I asked, almost more stunned by that than the other things she'd revealed.

"Not just a theater. A center with spaces for art and music lessons as well as a stage. It might be silly. But I just really wanted to find a way to make our community better and maybe draw more visitors to the area." Her words were strong, but there was worry behind them, as if she was reaching for something too big. But all I could think was how much I admired her goals and how Spence and my dad would have liked her, would have liked her ideas about community and paying things forward.

When I'd stayed silent for too long, she shifted, looking away and trying to pull herself from my hold. I wasn't sure if it was because she was embarrassed by what she wanted or worried I was upset about the jewels, but I didn't let her go. I tightened my grip and held on.

"Wanting to do something for your community is never silly."

She stilled. "Are you angry about the jewels? You've barely started to trust me. I don't want this to get in the way of that."

"You're not responsible for what happened back then any more than I'm responsible for my great-grandfather winning the ranch in a hand of poker. The only person I'm upset with right now is Adam."

Relief coasted over her face, and I couldn't stop myself from stroking her cheek. The wild animal in me longed to forever have a hand on her, to never stop molding our skin together.

"Did you find anything in the ranch accounts?" she asked.

I shook my head. The cursory look I'd been able to give it after helping Steele with the cameras hadn't shown me anything. The expenses were high, but then again, the cost of running a business like the ranch required heavy expenditures. In the past, the diamond mines that had turned into granite mines had been enough to offset the expenses and leave a hefty profit, but those endeavors had stopped mid-century. In the last decade, Spence had slowly depleted nearly a century's worth of savings.

As much as I detested admitting it, Puzo *had* brought the ranch additional revenue. Boarding horses and renting slots at the dock were easy ways to make money off practically nothing. The cell tower was an eyesore, but it brought in a steady annual income just like Fallon had said. Even the wedding business Lauren had started brought in a small net income. But none of it was enough to keep the ranch afloat for more than another year or two.

But if Adam had done something underhanded to speed the ranch's demise, I hadn't caught it at first glance. In the morning, I'd hand over the chores and the protection of the women in my life to Steele and our team while I peeled back more layers of the numbers. I'd still worry about Sadie and Fallon, even with a team who was more qualified than I ever would be protecting them. But none of my men would let anger or past wounds interfere with the job of keeping them safe.

While I'd already failed to do just that with both of them.

"Puzo had you followed," I told her through gritted teeth.

Her mouth dropped open. "What?"

I explained how we'd seen Nero Lancaster leaving The Fortress at the same time as her and what we'd learned about him working for Puzo. "It was why I thought you were more involved than you are. I thought Nero was your muscle."

She forced herself up and away, sitting crisscross next to me with the sheet pulled up around her breasts. "Why would he have me followed? I didn't tell him about the jewels, and he basically dismissed me when we were at The Fortress."

"It might simply have been because of the way I reacted when I saw the two of you together." Putting her at the center of Puzo's scope was one more thing I regretted. "I should have told you as soon as I realized it."

As if hearing the remorse in my voice, she leaned in and stroked the scars Puzo's men had left on my chest. "It's not like you had my phone number. We hadn't planned on our one night turning into anything more, Slick."

She was right and wrong. That may have been our intention, but if Fallon hadn't shown up and we'd tangled ourselves together on Sunday as we'd planned, I knew now that it wouldn't have been enough. I would have wanted to see her again. I would have wanted more. Even without having seen her selflessness and generosity this week, that spell she'd woven around me the minute she'd walked into my club would have branded me.

"You seemed disgusted when you saw me with him in the café. I thought you hated me," she said softly. While there was no anger in the look she gave me, not even a trace of frustration that I might have put her in danger, I had plenty for both of us.

"What really irritated me," I said, "was the fact that I didn't hate you at all. That I wanted to drag you back to the penthouse and finish what we'd started. I couldn't understand it." I gripped the sheet she was still holding up and yanked it down so I could see her sweet curves. "Now, I hate that I wasted minutes we could have been together almost as much as the asshole who put these marks on you." I brushed gently along her scars, a loving caress.

A little breathy gasp left her mouth—one I wanted to claim all over again.

"I've never felt this way, Rafe," she said, brows furrowing. "I'm confused and scared on the one hand, and clearheaded and sure on the other."

I knew exactly what she meant. The certainty she was mine was an absolute truth. She'd stormed into my life right when I'd needed her. But even knowing I loved her, I wasn't sure how I could keep her. The future was cast in a foggy haze like an early spring morning mist settling over the fields. So, instead of trying to find my way through the unknown, I did what I could with this moment. I dragged her back to me, kissed her forehead, and said, "I know exactly what you mean, Tennessee. But we don't have to figure it out tonight. We've talked enough for now."

And I spent the next few hours showing her what I couldn't yet say, proving to her the only truth that mattered at the moment was the way we blended together.

♫ ♫ ♫

When I woke, the body I expected to have tucked up next to me was missing, and the shadowed gray light of the predawn hours filled the room. I was more pissed she wasn't there than I was at the morning having found us.

I sat up and discovered her sitting on the floor next to the bed with my computer in her lap.

A hint of trepidation flew through me—old wounds and old doubts about those I could and couldn't trust returning like the baggage it was—before it faded just as fast. Sadie didn't have a malicious bone in her body. I wasn't sure if she even hated the man who'd shot her.

I fisted her hair, dragging her head back against the bed so I could lock my gaze on hers.

"What are you doing?"

She smiled at me, and somewhere deep inside me, the last wall I hadn't even known I'd left standing between us crumbled down, vanquished with that singular, stunning look. She put her hand over mine and squeezed.

"I think I found something." Her voice was full of excitement.

I leaned over her shoulder, looking at the screen. "What?"

"When I woke up, I was thinking about how messed up Uncle Phil's accounts were after he died. At first, I couldn't make heads or tails out of them. All I knew was they didn't reconcile. Then, Mama told me Uncle Phil was dyslexic, which meant he reversed numbers a lot. It was a pain in the ass to straighten it all out, but we did it in the end."

My brows furrowed, and her smile widened at my obvious confusion, saying, "You said nothing in the accounts looked off when you took a quick glance at them. That was what happened with me too. It was only when I started lining up every invoice and every deposit that I found the differences, the inverse numbers scattered through them. If Uncle Phil had hired an accountant instead of insisting on doing it himself, it would never have been so screwed up—which made me wonder what an accountant who wanted to steal would do so it wasn't obvious? Wouldn't they just invert a few numbers here and there in places no one would notice?"

With my head full of her scent and that dazzling smile capturing me, it took an enormous effort to tear my gaze from her and turn to the screen.

"I didn't have access to all the invoices," she explained. "But looking at the ones I did find, I saw a few differences in what he said he paid compared to the actual amount due."

She scrolled down through a spreadsheet she'd created. The first few columns were entitled *bills* and had both the actual amount on the invoice and the amount paid side by side. Next to those columns were ones listing the invoices the ranch sent to clients and the amount received. I slid out of bed, planting my naked ass next to her T-shirt-clad one. It distracted me, seeing her in my shirt, but then I forced myself back to the screen in her lap. I pulled the computer onto my knees, swiping through the document.

It was a handful of bills and invoices, nothing compared to the full scope of the ranch's books, but even in that small amount, she'd found twenty thousand dollars of discrepancies.

Fury burned through me.

He was stealing from his sister. From his niece. From my brother.

On the heels of that thought came a much worse realization. What if this was what Spence and Adam had been arguing about? What if he'd confronted Adam about the embezzlement, and it was the reason my brother was dead? Because of goddamn money.

"Is Adam dyslexic?" Sadie asked, but I barely registered her voice through the guttural roar and pain consuming me.

I tossed the computer onto the bed and headed for the

dresser as red filled my vision, and anguish tore through my veins like an insidious poison, tainting every molecule. My body was rigid, muscles straining against skin and bones as I pulled on a pair of jeans and dragged a clean T-shirt over my head.

I threw open the door, and it hit the wall with a bang that echoed like a gunshot through the silent house. The stairs were cold as I took them two at a time, but they did nothing to cool the raging inferno inside me.

"Rafe!" Sadie called after me, but I didn't stop. I leaped over the last three steps and barreled down the hall to the butler's quarters where Adam had been staying.

Through the blood pounding in my ears, I heard her call my name again, heard her telling me to wait, that she wasn't one-hundred-percent sure, and that we needed to do more research.

I wouldn't wait. I wouldn't be in control or stay calm.

I would strangle him until the breath left his body. Until he admitted the truth.

I half expected the door to the butler's quarters to be locked, but when I spun the handle, it opened easily. The door flew into the wall with the same ferocity as mine had, shaking a shelf where dainty tea cups were on display.

The room was dark and quiet.

I flicked on the light and found a sitting room stuffed to the gills with Harrington heirlooms. The once plain and functional servant's furniture had been replaced with a collection of items from around the house, including priceless art, antique Victorian chairs, and an irreplaceable escritoire desk.

Motherfucking thief!

I stormed through the pieces of my family's history to the bedroom door and found it wasn't locked either. The bedroom was fitted with more things that belonged to my family, including a beautifully carved bed that had once been in my childhood bedroom. He wasn't even afraid of being caught with the items that didn't belong to him! Didn't even have the goddamn decency to hide them behind bolted doors.

My hope of dragging him from it, of slamming my fists into his flesh, evaporated at the sight of the neatly made bed. He'd either woken even earlier than us, or he hadn't slept there at all. Through my simmering, blood-thirsty rage, I remembered him talking about a girlfriend. Some mysterious person no one seemed to have met.

I spun around, heading back toward the hallway, and came face-to-face with a breathless, wild-eyed Sadie. My shirt hung down past her thighs, baring long legs I loved, and I immediately despised the idea of anyone, especially Adam, seeing her like this. But even that torturous thought didn't stop me. I was determined to find him and take him apart limb by limb, both physically and financially. There wouldn't be anything left of him.

As I brushed past her, she latched on to my arm and spun me to face her with a strength that caught me off guard.

"Rafe. You need to calm down before you do something you regret."

I gripped her shoulders and shook. "He killed Spence. He killed my brother because he found out Adam was stealing. He killed my brother for goddamn money."

She squeezed my arms with the same desperation. "You don't know that for sure, and if you go flying at him now, with only the handful of items we've found, before we have all the proof stacked up against him, he'll be able to pass it off as a mistake."

"What the hell are you talking about?" The sharply snapped question had us turning down the hall. Lauren was dressed for the day in jeans, a plaid shirt, and work boots, looking more like the woman I'd grown up with than ever before. But the shock on her face was new.

"Did you know he was stealing from us?" I demanded, letting Sadie go and heading for Lauren. She took two steps back. "Did you suspect Adam killed Spencer? Is that why you've been losing yourself in sleeping pills and painkillers?"

"What? What are you saying?" She shook her head

violently. "No. He wouldn't!"

"We've only found twenty thousand right now, Lauren. That's in just a handful of lines Sadie was able to explore. How much you want to bet I find more? Hundreds of thousands more. How much does he owe Puzo?"

Lauren turned a violent shade of red and moved toward me instead of away this time, slamming her hand into my chest. "Nothing. He doesn't gamble like that. Not after everything the Hurlys have lost because of it. He wouldn't steal from family. And he'd *never* hurt Spence! He couldn't."

But I knew he had. A thousand memories shifted through me like a kaleidoscope turning. Adam's anger whenever Spence or I got something he wanted and couldn't afford. His rage when his daddy and his granddaddy died in a crash while driving our cattle to auction. The way he'd pummeled me when he'd found out Lauren was carrying my child.

Instead of doing anything about Adam's rage, instead of addressing it head-on, I'd walked away from the ranch. I'd left the door open, practically inviting all the monsters in at the gate, and hadn't cared what had happened. I'd abandoned my family.

The violent fury turned inward, accompanied by a clawing, desperate anguish, a brutal sorrow that wove through every fiber of my being.

Everything my father had ever called me rang through my ears.

Selfish. Closed-minded. Arrogant.

A piece of my soul I'd thought long buried screamed in protest. Fought to toss off the blame. And instead, it landed with a bitter, unforgiving truth in the pit of my stomach.

I'd played right into the wedge my father had driven between me and my brother. I'd hammered it permanently into place by taking what I thought I was entitled to and brought the ranch to its knees. I'd left my family to suffer the consequences because that was what I had been trained to do. I'd been taught that only one person could win, and I'd been determined it would be me.

Chapter Twenty-four

Sadie

LOVE IS A COWBOY
Performed by Kelsea Ballerini

Something in Rafe's expression changed. Seconds ago, he'd been ready to murder Adam when he found him. Ready to pay back the crime he believed Adam had committed against his brother, and I'd been terrified that he would. Now, all that anger, all the hatred seemed to have been tossed inward, as if somehow everything that had happened was entirely his fault.

When I tried to grab his hand, when I tried to pull him to me, he shook it off.

Lauren missed none of it. Her eyes were clear and unmedicated this morning but also tormented.

"Where is he?" Rafe demanded, but his tone didn't have the wildness it had moments before. It was composed and all the scarier for it.

"He probably stayed with his girlfriend in town," Lauren said, lifting her chin. "Whatever you think you've found, Rafe, he'll be able to explain. Adam wouldn't steal from us. And he would never kill Spencer! He knew how much I loved him."

"He hated that you did," Rafe said, and if those words hit me in the chest, I couldn't imagine what they did to Lauren.

He turned on his heel, and Lauren and I hurried after him, shooting each other concerned glances. He flung open the front door of the house with the same ferocity he'd used on every other door since leaving his room.

He waved a hand at an empty slot next to the Jaguar. "He's driving the Mercedes I saw parked here this week?"

"Yes," Lauren responded.

"Expensive car," he said, raising a brow.

"He made money at his old job, Rafe! Lots of it. He didn't need ours."

"He would if he was losing it to Puzo."

"It's just a friendly poker game. Guy friends throwing twenty dollars in a pot! It's not like they're gambling with real money," Lauren insisted again. Then she repeated the same words she had before, as if she was trying to convince herself as much as Rafe. "Adam wouldn't gamble anything significant! Not after all we've been through."

"But he does." We all spun around at the quiet, sure voice and watched as Fallon approached from the direction of the stables. Like Lauren, she was already dressed for the day, even though the sun hadn't quite made it over the hills yet. "It isn't just a friendly game with a twenty-dollar buy-in, Mom, and he plays every time Mr. Puzo is in town. Maisey heard from Jordan, who heard her parents arguing about how much her dad had lost, that the buy-in for each game is ten thousand dollars. Uncle Adam has been playing with him for…what? Two years at least? How much do you think he's lost?"

Lauren paled, her knees started to give, and it was only Rafe's quick reflexes that ensured she didn't hit the ground.

"What are you saying, Fallon? What are you saying?" Lauren sobbed.

Fallon's eyes filled, and she couldn't look at her mom as she said, "I think he killed Spence."

"No! No! No!" Lauren shook her head violently.

"They fought that night, Mom! I told you they did!" Fallon's face turned red. She took her hat off and threw it as hard and as far as she could. It landed in the field on the other side of the road where white dandelion puffs waited to be blown into the river. "No one ever listens to me."

"We're listening now, Ducky. Talk to us." Rafe's voice was deep and raw and tormented.

Tears poured down Lauren's face, and I stepped up to take her from Rafe so he could go to his daughter. He shot me a grateful look and did just that, tucking his daughter to him and saying, "Tell us what you think happened."

"I heard them arguing. But by the time I'd gotten to a spot where I could hear them…" She looked at her dad, hesitating for a second before continuing, "I'd already missed some of the important bits. All I heard was Spence saying he was going to hire a forensic accountant and Adam laughing. He said Spence had been watching too much TV. That if there was anything wrong with the accounts, it was merely a small mistake, easily rectified.

"Spence asked him about the poker games with Mr. Puzo and how he was affording it. Uncle Adam said he was using his money from his finance days and that Spence was getting his underwear in a wad for no reason. He said he'd go through everything with Spence the next morning, including his personal accounts if Spence needed to see them. That calmed Spence down some, and he agreed they could go through everything in the morning."

Fallon looked up at them, anger and hurt and defiance written all over her face. "So why would he be on a tractor before the sun was even up? Going up to the cliff above the river when he always told me to stay clear of it? Why? No way anyone will ever convince me he went there on his own. That he wanted to be there." She shook her head. "No, he would have been in the office with his cowbell coffee cup in hand, waiting for Uncle Adam."

Silence settled down, and the sounds of the ranch drifted around us. A cow's low moo in the distance. The bang of a gate. Normally, they'd be soothing, but they only served to remind everyone of what was at stake and what had already been lost.

Lauren was shivering in my hold, and she was as pale as a ghost. Her lids were closed, and I thought for a moment she might just drift away completely. "I can't believe…" She shook her head, a tortured look of despair crossing her face as tension spun back and forth between all of us.

It took her several long, ragged breaths before she opened her eyes again, gaze falling on her daughter, defiant and brave. She took another sharp inhale, shoved a hand into her stomach, pushed away from me, and stepped tentatively toward Rafe and Fallon. "I don't want to believe Adam is involved in this." When Fallon's expression darkened, Lauren continued, "But if he was… God…" —she shook her head— "If he was involved in any of this, he'll pay. I swear it on my life."

Fallon's face crumbled, and Lauren closed the distance, wrapping her arms around both Rafe and her daughter. My heart ended up in my throat at the vision they made. Three beautiful but tortured humans clinging to each other as if, somehow, they could weather this new storm simply by holding on to one another.

I knew exactly what those moments felt like. I'd seen the way my brother had clung to McKenna and Mila after they'd almost lost my niece to Chainsaw's rage. I'd experienced it myself when my parents had hugged me after I'd come out of surgery. This handful of seconds altered the fabric of a family. A series of mere heartbeats that set a fork in the path, requiring you to choose which one to take.

A painful thought wrung through me, stealing my breath. What would have happened if I wasn't here? What path would Rafe take? If I hadn't tumbled into his life and bed, would he have found a way to be a family with them again? Would he have gone back to the woman he'd once cared enough about to conceive a child with?

But the thought of walking away, of letting go of what I'd found with Rafe when we'd been tangled together, of giving back the pieces of him he'd handed over like a precious gift, made me sick to my stomach. I wanted him to be mine forever.

Because I loved him.

I loved Rafe Marquess.

It was a ridiculous time to realize it. And worse, it didn't matter if I'd realized it now, tomorrow, or three days from now, because forever wasn't in the cards Rafe and I had been dealt.

On Sunday, I'd be leaving, and this alternate universe I'd stepped into would be left behind. By this time next week, I'd be back behind the bar, slinging pints along the lacquered surface to Willy and my brothers and the hundreds of other locals who made McFlannigan's a regular part of their week.

We'd both known what exactly we had to offer when we'd started it. Nothing more than a moment's respite. A moment of sweet memories and sinful pleasure. Rafe was needed here with his family. I was needed in Willow Creek with mine.

It felt like a lifetime had gone by in those few seconds that ticked by from when Lauren had wrapped Rafe and Fallon in her arms until she wiped her face on her sleeves and stepped back. My heart had been stolen, and I didn't know if I'd ever be able to reclaim it, or if I'd just go through life with another permanent scar.

"Let me call Adam and see if he's in town with Tera," Lauren said. "Let me see if he can explain any of this."

"I want to know where he is and when he'll be back, but I don't think you should tell him what we've found yet," Rafe said, glancing toward me. "Sadie was right. We need to find every single penny that's off so when we lay it out in front of him, he can't say it's a mistake. If we have enough evidence, maybe he'll also tell us the truth about Spence."

He'd tucked away all the rage and sadness he'd shown just moments ago, returning to the calm man who needed to be in control. I wondered what it cost him to do it. Had anyone ever told him it was okay to have all these intense emotions? Did he know it was okay to give them to the people who cared about you, so they could help you through the tough moments? I wanted to be that person for him, even if it was for just a few days.

Lauren swallowed hard, pushing her fingers into her eyes. "I really want to believe he had nothing to do with what happened to Spence…" she said, but her voice trailed away, uncertain.

An old beat-up truck crested the hill and headed toward the

house, dirt trailing behind it.

And just like Rafe had pulled himself together and tucked away his emotions, at the sight of the truck, Lauren did the same. She turned back into the confident rancher I'd first met. The woman with a business that she ran efficiently and thoroughly.

"That's Teddy," Lauren said, rubbing her chest. "He and the other contractors are going to help set up the marquee and the dance floor, and then they'll help out with the regular ranch chores so we have time to prepare for the wedding rehearsal and the dinner tonight."

"While I'm going through every single line in the ranch's financials, I'll have Steele reach out to some of his contacts and see if we can find out more about these poker matches. Mayor Nattingly wanted to talk to me about Puzo yesterday, so I'll place a call to her. I don't want any of you going anywhere by yourself today." Rafe glanced at each of us as if expecting an argument. "I want one of my men with you at all times. That includes you, Sadie. We don't know exactly what Adam did or didn't do, but believe me, he's capable of violence if he's pushed." He glanced over at the corral as if remembering something in his past before shaking it off. "And if Puzo is part of this, we know exactly what kind of evil he can shell out."

Lauren turned to Fallon, touching her elbow gently. "I've got breakfast started for everyone. Let's finish it up and get on with our day."

Fallon looked like she wanted to argue and storm, but instead, she scrambled over to retrieve her hat and then followed her mother into the house. After they'd disappeared inside, Rafe closed the distance and wrapped me in his arms.

"Thank you," he said quietly. "For finding what I couldn't see. For calming me down. For being someone we could count on."

We stood there for a moment, chests joined, heartbeats crashing into one another as the adrenaline rush of the last few minutes faded away and all that remained was the solace we found wrapped together.

"Do you know what I hate?" he asked. I lifted my chin and met his gaze. "Besides what he might have done to my brother and the ranch…" He inhaled sharply. "I hate that he ruined our morning and that I didn't get a chance to tell you just how much I liked seeing you in my clothes and having you in my bed last night. And I hate that I wasn't able to wake up with you beside me and spend another few minutes lost in each other."

My pulse leaped and danced, warmth pooling deep inside me. Even after the multitude of orgasms he'd given me, I still craved him with every fiber of my being. What would happen if I spent another few nights tangled with him? How much would I be willing to give up to keep him? To keep this? What was I willing to cost him?

I swallowed hard, panic rising that I couldn't quite shake, and when I went to pull away, he held on tighter. I let myself revel in the embrace for a moment longer, let myself breathe in the man I'd fallen in love with in a heady jump from an unseen cliff. Then, I let out a shaky breath, bringing us back to earth, to our reality and the day that laid before us. "Do you need my help with the accounts, or should I work with Lauren and Fallon?"

He ran a finger along my brow, and my body all but quivered at the simple touch. "Now that you've pointed me in the right direction, I think I can manage the rest. But you'd be doing me a huge favor if you'd look after Fallon. I trust my men to protect all of you, but she might need someone to talk to."

"I'm happy to be there for her in any way I can," I said.

He stared at me for a long moment before asking, "Do you know what I'm wondering, Tennessee? I'm wondering if you ever stop giving long enough to let someone return the favor?"

His words hit a sore spot deep inside. I'd had to accept help after being shot, and maybe having it forced on me was the reason I was so determined to stand on my own now, why I hadn't told my family more about the jewels or my plans for the performing arts center. But instead of saying any of that, I did what I thought we both needed. I lightened the mood, grinning up at him and saying, "I think I was on the receiving end of a lot of gifts last night. Two at least."

"Five."

I raised a brow playfully. "Was it five? I'm not sure I remember. Maybe I fell asleep. Or maybe you thought you anted up and didn't pay out."

He let out a savage growl before slanting his mouth over mine in a brutal kiss that turned tender in a heartbeat, just like the kiss he'd given me last night after he'd taken me up against the wall. It was beautiful and caring and full of emotions Rafe spent the majority of his life bottling up.

And then, his lips were gone, and he was grinning down at me wickedly with a look that promised sin and salvation just like he had on Sunday night. "You ready to back that little taunt with a wager, Tennessee? How long do you think you'll last before you beg for relief?"

"Maybe you'll be the one begging, Slick."

He chuckled, and joy filled me at my ability to give him that moment of lightness in a morning that had been hard and heavy. He slid a hand under my T-shirt and flicked a finger over a pebbled tip. I shivered at the touch, loving the electricity that zapped through me. Loving everything about him and what he did to me.

"What shall we wager, Sadie?" Just the way he lowered his voice into a dark promise had me panting. He pinched and caressed and then stepped away, allowing the cold morning air to hit me like a splash of icy lake water. "I'll just leave you to think about it, shall I?"

He waved a hand, indicating I should go in front of him into the house. I tried to slow the hammering of my heart as I forced my feet to move and then compelled my legs not to wobble as I passed him. But once we were inside, once we were alone outside the bedroom he'd insisted on walking me to, I pulled his borrowed shirt from my body, and tossed it at him.

"How about I leave you thinking about this." I waved a hand over my naked body and then closed the door in his face.

♫ ♫ ♫

The sexy taunts I'd left Rafe with disappeared in the shower as panic hit me all over again. I'd fallen in love with Rafe, and I didn't know what to do with that fact. Didn't know if there was anything I could do about it. The entire time I was getting ready, I tortured myself with what-ifs and buts and if onlys.

Then I broke down and called my sister.

"Sads?" she said, sleepy and slow. "What's wrong?"

God. Everything? Nothing? "I think I'm in love with someone I just met."

"What? Jesus. You scared me. Hold on a sec." I heard a murmur on her end, her voice mixed with the deeper one of her husband's. Rex was almost as possessive of my sister as my brothers were of their wives. I understood it now because I felt deeply possessive of Rafe. Not just him, but his daughter too. And even Lauren because she was important to them.

When Gemma came back on, she was a bit breathless. "Are you and Ryder trying to pull one over on me again? Or have you really fallen for someone?"

I spent the next few minutes telling her some of what had been happening, skipping over all the dangerous parts and the issue with the jewels as much as possible, and sticking to the truth of Rafe and the messed-up relationships around him. "I don't know if it's just the situation making me feel things that aren't real or what. I mean, I've known him less than a week—"

"We both know time doesn't always matter. I fell for Rex in mere hours. Look at how fast things went for Ryder and Gia. It happens, *especially* when you're in the middle of an intense situation. It doesn't mean it isn't real. Honestly, seeing how people react and who they are in those stressful moments really shows what they're made of. You can't hide."

"Rex walked away from you when the shit hit the fan," I reminded her, not to be cruel but to point out that not everything works out.

She laughed softly. "I know. He hurt me—terribly. But it worked out in the end because we never stopped loving each other. When you know, you know. The question really isn't about whether you love him or not but what you're going to do about it."

"That's my point. What can I do about it, Gemma? I own a business in Willow Creek. I have a family there I love and want to be around. He has a daughter who lives in California and a multinational company to run. I don't see how we can have a happy ending."

"Let me ask you this…do you think I love my family less just because I'm not in Willow Creek anymore?" I heard the hint of hurt in her voice.

"No. Of course not! You were following your dreams and moved to LA before you met Rex. We knew you had things to accomplish, even if you never let any of us read your damn script."

Gemma chuckled. "Wow, none of you will ever let me live that down." When I didn't say anything, her voice gentled. "What are *your* dreams? They used to be about darts and traveling the world. Then, you got shot, and you became this shadowy reflection of yourself." When I tried to deny it, she rode right over me. "You pretended you were the same, but we all saw it, Sassy. None of us cared that Uncle Phil left you the bar, but Ryder isn't the only one who worried you'd let it drag you into a life you'd never imagined for yourself."

I swallowed hard. That was the thing about having a family who knew and loved you almost better than you knew yourself. They saw when you were pretending. I sighed and let out the truth I'd held back the other day. "Winning the dart tournament felt hollow. Empty."

"I can understand that. Throwing darts is in your past. That's an old-Sadie dream. What do you want now?"

Rafe. The thought was there before I could even process it.

And while it was the truth—I did want him—I'd also never be happy *just* being someone's partner. I wanted to *do* something. *Be* something. I didn't want to live my life forever as the helper and sidekick.

Gemma was making world-acclaimed movies. Ryder had

saved the ranch and built it into a destination resort. Maddox saved lives every time he walked out the door wearing his sheriff's badge. I wanted Sadie Hatley to have done something big as well.

McFlannigan's had long been a staple in Willow Creek, and I cherished being given the responsibility of carrying that forward, but I also wanted to make my own mark on our community. A lasting one. It was why the performing arts center had become so important to me. It was something I could do for Great-grandma Carolyn, for myself, and our home.

But how could I factor Rafe and his daughter into that? What they were facing here and the work that needed to be done in order to save their ranch was going to take years. Would being at his side, being a part of that, being a part of *their* community, be enough to satisfy the needs inside me screaming to *do* something important for mine?

I wasn't sure.

The night he'd shown up at the waterfall in the moonlight, I'd thought the Irish fae our McFlannigan side of my family believed in had led me here to him. What happened when you ignored the signs the wee people presented you? Would I ever find something like this, the intensity of what I felt with Rafe, ever again?

I thought of the way Rafe looked at me, the way he'd given me pieces of himself I was sure he'd never given anyone. Wasn't that more important than anything else? That affection…that love…wasn't it a legacy all its own? If we walked away from each other, we would leave wounds more brutal, more lasting, than the ones evil men had carved into us with knives and guns. The emotional cuts would have a ripple effect. On his family. On mine.

And maybe that was all that mattered.

Maybe with love at stake, the only answer was to go all in.

Chapter Twenty-five

Rafe

TRYING
Performed by Jordan Davis

Growing up, I'd had two things I'd been good at—taming horses and taming numbers. It had been a strange dichotomy, but they were both things Spence had never excelled at, and I'd basked in that knowledge. My brother could tell you when a cow was going to give birth and the exact right day to plant seed, and he could fix just about anything mechanical with a few twists of tools, but math and horses had eluded him. Those had been all mine. It was easy to see, in hindsight, that if we'd combined our skills, it would have allowed the ranch to bloom.

But we hadn't been raised to see it that way. Our dad had pitted us against each other, insisting, in life, there was only one winner, and I'd taken that lesson with me when I'd left the ranch. It had helped me build Marquess Enterprises into the indisputable success it was today.

Now, as the tally of what had been stolen from the ranch grew, my guilt did along with it. My ego, my drive, my need to be better than my brother was as responsible for this as Spencer's blind trust of someone he'd considered family.

When Adam never responded to Lauren's message or returned to the ranch, Steele had sent Parker to go check out the Hurly house. He said it looked like no one had stepped inside it in weeks. Steele wanted to trace Adam's Mercedes, but I wasn't at the point of stepping across the lines of the law yet. I might not have to. If I could put enough evidence together, I could hand it over to the authorities, and they'd search for him legally.

Midday, Mayor Nattingly returned my call, and after a handful of niceties, I cut her short and flat-out asked her what was happening with Puzo. "At first, everyone was thrilled to have him here," she said. "He doled out advice, donated to schools and charities, and fundraised for local politicians. He embedded himself in the community, filling in the gaps the Harringtons used to fill but couldn't afford to do anymore."

"And then he turned the screws," I said.

"It was that damn poker game. No one who's lost their business to him will admit that's how it happened, and he's kept them as the face of the shop, but he's now a silent owner in many of our local businesses."

My family had let the community down, just like I'd let them down. We'd turned inward, focused on ourselves. Days ago, none of that would have mattered to me. Now, I couldn't stop thinking how to make it all right.

After Dad's funeral, Spence had tried to tell me Dad had been wrong. When I'd asked for my cut of the inheritance in cash, he'd asked me to take a walk with him before we decided. We'd ended up sitting up on the cliff, looking out over the valley, the river, and a hint of the lake as the sun had gone down.

When all that remained was a hint of peach blending into the midnight blue, he'd said, "There doesn't have to be just one winner in life, Rafe. Success, coming out ahead, doesn't have to be about first place or who has the most money." He'd waved his hand at the land that had become part of our family's blood. "It isn't even about who has control of all this. The real winner is the person who has someone who loves them and a place to call home."

I'd scoffed, told him I expected my inheritance to be handed over by the end of the month, and then I'd walked away. I'd left him and his tentative peace offering behind on the same damn cliff he'd gone over in the tractor.

A chill went up my spine.

But he'd been right. Because now I had success, and I'd

won in the eyes of most of the world, but I had a daughter I didn't really know, and I'd lost my brother before I could tell him I loved him again.

The sun shifting through the windows of the office drew me back from troubled thoughts of what I'd lost. I stared at the computer and papers strewn across the desk and knew I'd had all I could stomach of spreadsheets and stolen money. I needed to find the love Spencer had insisted made you a winner. The family and home I'd gifted my daughter but denied myself.

I texted Steele to find out where everyone was at, and he responded they were down at the waterfall for the wedding rehearsal. I made my way down to the spot where the three rivers joined, gaze automatically finding Sadie and Fallon as they sat in the back row of chairs covered in blue linen. Steele and Parker stood behind them while Lauren talked with Puzo and his cousin Marielle. They were watching a bridesmaid finish making her way down the yellow runner to the flower-covered arch at the end.

The sun filtered through the trees, sparkling off the diamonds and sapphires at Marielle's neck, and it reminded me of the picture of Grandma Beatrice that had fallen out of the box Adam had been looking through. What had he wanted with the boxes? He'd said he'd been looking for the movie studio shares, but they'd been easy enough to find in the paperwork today, so what had he really been searching for? What had he wanted with the stolen jewels? Had he just hoped to keep them for himself and add to the kitty of stolen money?

Lauren sent Puzo and Marielle down the aisle. He smiled as he walked her down to her groom, kissing her cheek and stepping aside. From here, Puzo looked charming and suave without a hint of the evil I knew existed behind those eyes. Was he involved in the theft with Adam? Had they plotted the ranch's demise together? Or was one unrelated to the other?

My gaze lingered on Sadie again, my body tightening at the memory of the taunt she'd tossed at me before shutting the bedroom door in my face. How had she come into my life at just this moment? A slice of goodness arriving just as my world crumbled, as I was faced with all my failures rather than my successes. It would be so easy to allow myself to get lost in her sweetness like I had last night. To use the love I felt for her to make her mine. But even if there wasn't danger hanging around me like a chain, would it be the right thing to do?

In trying to win her, would I cost her the family and home she already had?

As if feeling me watching her, she turned, eyes finding mine across the distance. She whispered something to Fallon before rising and hurrying over to me. "So what did you find?" she asked, curiosity and worry crossing her face at the same time.

Lauren sent a sharp look in our direction, and I took Sadie's hand, pulling her back up the path toward the house. All my worries, all my grief felt less with her fingers twined with mine, as if, somehow, I could find the real win my brother had said was more important than anything else.

When we were far enough away that the sound of the waterfall faded, I answered her question. "Three hundred thousand dollars that he's taken in the last five years alone. That's as far as I got today. I'm sure it's been carrying on since he took over managing the money after Dad died."

"With Uncle Phil, the money was still in the bank, as it was mostly just screwed up on his end. Have you checked?" she asked.

"It's not in the bank, but I also can't find any withdrawals that show he moved the money. It's just disappeared. The police might be able to find it if they get warrants for the accounts and the banks records."

"Do you think someone at the bank was helping him?"

"It's a local community savings and loan that's been around since the forties, so it's possible someone there was helping him. There's got to be an electronic trail somewhere, unless Adam was using Puzo's hackers. Then it might be impossible to find."

"You really think they're in it together, then?" When I didn't respond, she said, "I told you about Gia, Ryder's wife, right? She still has a lot of her NSA contacts, and one friend there is an exceptional hacker. I bet Rory could find the money trail for you."

As we crested the hill to the field behind the house, a loud crack echoed across the open expanse that had me jerking to a halt just as the air by my ear buzzed. Shock was followed quickly by fear as the dirt kicked up in front of us.

"Was that a—" I shoved her to the ground just as a second shot boomed.

A sharp burn cut through my tricep as I landed on top of her.

Goddamn it. God fucking damn it. We were under fire. In a fucking field! How the hell was I going to protect her?

I glanced over my shoulder as another shot rang out from the east tree line, spraying dirt all over us. Shit! We were sitting ducks here.

"Someone is shooting at us!" she cried out. Panic was in every syllable, and her body tried to rise. To run. I pushed her back.

"Stay down!"

I had to get us the hell out of here! I had to get her to safety.

Rage and fierce resolve filled in over the shock. She would not be hurt because of me!

My phone buzzed as a fourth bullet landed to our left. Jesus Christ.

I scanned the yard, mind racing as I tried to calculate the distance to the house. Standing would make us even easier targets, but there was no other option. If we could get to the corner of the house, we'd be out of his line of sight.

"On three, we're going to get up, stay as low as we can, and zigzag our way to the house."

"Zigzag!" Sadie's voice held the terror I felt zipping through my veins. "This isn't the movies!"

My lungs were screaming, heart slamming into my rib cage as I counted off. I'd barely shouted three before I grabbed her by her elbows, lifted her off the ground, and propelled her forward.

Another shot had me lunging over the top of her. We were too slow. She was too exposed. Pure terror clawed through me at the thought of her being hit, and I wrapped my arm around her waist, pulled her up into my arms, and ran full-out for the corner of the house.

Two more shots sent dirt and grass flying at our feet. I couldn't breathe. I couldn't get any air, but I would *not* drop her. As I careened around the corner, another bullet sent stucco splintering off the house, pelting my face.

As we plunged into the shadows, I shoved Sadie up against the wall to keep her out of sight. Shouts came from the hillside as another shot pierced the side of the house.

Steele was bellowing orders, and a new wave of panic almost swallowed me whole. Fallon! They couldn't leave Fallon and Lauren unprotected!

Steele, Barry, and Noah crested the hill, leaving them all exposed. Sweat poured down my back, and I pulled in a pained gasp of air in order to yell, "Stay down! Shooter to the east in the trees!"

The men split off, Steele and Barry heading in the direction of the goddamn gunfire! Risking themselves. Risking Fallon all alone. Shit.

The two men stayed low, using the bushes at the edge of the field as cover. Noah headed around the west side, heading for the stables where he'd be able to approach the house from a protected angle.

The shots had stopped. Fury mixed with the adrenaline pumping through my veins.

I couldn't get to my daughter from here without stepping out into the field and risking the shooting starting again. I had to trust Steele would find him, would protect me and mine like he'd been doing since saving me in that damn alley.

I clamped my hand on Sadie's arm and moved her along the side of the house, deeper into the shadows, farther away from the gunfire.

All the blind anger and violence I'd felt this morning toward Adam came flooding back. Was this him? Was this why we hadn't been able to find him all day?

I'd kill him. I'd kill whomever they were.

A sob from Sadie drew my gaze. Her eyes were wild, hair tangled in all directions, and dirt was scattered along her face, neck, and arms.

"Are you hurt?" I demanded just as I caught sight of scrapes on her hands. "You are. Goddamn it, I hurt you shoving you to the ground. I was trying to keep you safe, but I hurt you."

She was shaking her head, even as I brought her palms up to examine them. "I'm fine. God. I'm fine." Tears poured down dirty cheeks. She yanked her hand away from mine to reach for my face. "You're bleeding!"

I pulled her fingers away. "It's nothing," I insisted just as we both saw the blood trailing down over my elbow.

"Oh my God. You're hit!" Her face blanched, and her body convulsed. "We have to call 911."

Shit! I pulled up the shirt sleeve, but there was no hole, just a long, thin slice of cut skin. "It's nothing. Just a scrape. I'm okay."

"You were shot! Don't tell me you're okay!"

I pulled her into me, resting my chin on her head, and I felt every single tremble as if they were my own. My vision turned hazy as white rage stormed inside me. "I'm okay, Tennessee."

"That sound! That horrible sound!" She sobbed, putting her hands to her ears. "I've never been able to forget that sound."

The tortured pain in her words hit me like a hammer to an anvil, ricocheting through every molecule. They scoured and burned through me, causing more agony than the wound in my arm. She'd been shot while protecting her niece, and now she'd had to relive it. Because of me. Because of whatever bullshit had arrived at my door.

I wouldn't just kill them. I'd destroy them first for making her relive it.

My head jerked up as Noah slid through the gravel to join us in the shadows. He quickly assessed the situation, face grim as he spoke into his two-way mic. "Shit. Rafe's hit. I'm taking him inside and calling an ambulance."

"I don't need an ambulance. It's a shitty-ass scrape. Why the hell aren't you with my daughter and Lauren?!"

"Parker stayed with them and the wedding party. The shots weren't aimed at them, Rafe, but we had them take cover until they received the all-clear from us."

Noah's eyes fell to Sadie trembling in my arms, face tear-stained, and his expression darkened, matching the rage that was boiling inside me.

"I need to get you inside," he said. I gave him a curt nod, and he turned, leading the way with his gun as we skated along the side of the house toward the front door.

I kept Sadie next to the house, blocking her from the world. The more she shook, the more her tears fell, and the more my insides burned.

As we approached the front, Noah put his hand up, halting us. Dread ran up my spine as we neared the front. We'd be exposed again, but the shooter would have had to cross the river to get to us here. Noah scanned the yard and the trees and fields across from it and then said, "Let me go first."

My body was rigid, hating the idea of him or anyone on my team taking this risk for me.

He stepped out, easing toward the front door. When nothing happened, he waved us forward. I practically dragged Sadie with me as I raced toward the door, keeping her between Noah and me as I unlocked the door. I shoved her inside first before sliding in behind her, followed by Noah.

The chandelier in the entry hall was off, so the only light came from the office. It cast a beam along the marble floors, and I directed us into that warm triangle. Inside, I grabbed Sadie's arm again and sat her in a chair by the fireplace before storming over to the windows and yanking the curtains closed.

Fury burned through me when I turned and saw Sadie had her arms around her middle, still shaking. I went to the liquor cabinet, poured a glass of bourbon, and then squatted down in front of her. Bile and disgust roiled through me.

She'd just had to relive her worst day. Because of me. Disgust welled. I'd done this. I'd kept her here instead of sending her away after the rattler had been in my bed.

I'd known. I'd fucking known to send her home.

Selfish. I'd been so goddamn selfish.

"Drink this." She shook her head, pushing it back toward me. "Tennessee, drink the damn bourbon. It'll calm your nerves."

Her gaze landed on my cheek, her fingers slid over it, and I winced as pain followed the movement. "Your face." Her voice was as shaky as her body.

"It was just the siding that hit me," I told her, wiping the blood along my shoulder. "Drink."

When she took the glass, I left her, even though it tore a piece of my heart away to do so. I strode toward the bookshelf that hid the vault.

"What are you doing?" Concern bled through the terror in Sadie's voice.

"To get a rifle and go get my daughter."

"Steele gave me orders that we're to stay here in case the asshole circles back around," Noah said, and the calm in his voice only made the burning in my chest grow until I thought it might explode.

"I agree. You'll stay here with Sadie."

"Fallon and Lauren weren't the ones being shot at, Marquess," Noah insisted, and I shot him a glare. "If you head out, you'll make yourself a target again. You want to have Fallon next to you when he starts shooting this time?"

His words drove into me like a knife. The agonizing truth was I'd put them all at risk. Every single one of them could have been hit tonight. Goddamn it.

I closed my eyes and slammed my fist into the bookshelf. Decades older than me, the wood caved underneath the force, splintering and cracking.

"R-Rafe," Sadie's voice shook as she approached. "Noah's right. Whoever this is…they didn't shoot at the wedding party or Fallon. They shot at us. You and me."

"Me." The single syllable was a dark snarl.

She came closer, hand resting on my uninjured arm. "If you are the target, you can't leave right now. You're bleeding. Sit down. Let me get a first aid kit and clean you up before your daughter sees it."

The color was coming back to her cheeks, and with it, the defiance I so loved. It was the fire and brimstone that made her a force to be reckoned with.

I turned to Noah, acid burning up my esophagus as I said, "Go get my daughter and bring her to me." I was desperate to hold her, to ensure she was safe and unharmed, but they were both right. If I was the target, going after Fallon might only put her in more danger.

My stomach curled, and my vision spun along with it. I clamped my jaw, fisted my hands, and met Noah's hesitant expression with a fiery one. "I'm the one who pays your salary, Noah. Go get my daughter and bring her the fuck here."

At the deadly seriousness in my tone, he whirled around and left.

Sadie's shoulders eased ever so slightly, and she asked, "Where's your first aid kit kept?"

"Mudroom. Cupboard next to the washing machine."

I watched as she traveled out of the room and down the hall. I listened as she banged several doors before finding the right one and came back with the first aid box. She grabbed my hand and shoved me toward the chair she'd been in. The untouched bourbon sat on the side table. I picked it up and tossed it back as she set to work on the wounded arm.

It was nothing, a scrape, but it stung like hell when she poured the disinfectant over it. "I want to kill them. I want to cut off their balls and force them down their throat. For terrifying you. For making you relive that day. For bringing this terror to my daughter's life."

The thought of what could have happened to Sadie, to my child, to Lauren, if the shooter had decided to take aim when

I'd been standing down by the river, watching the wedding rehearsal, caught my breath and took it away. I felt the color drain from my face, felt the room spin again.

And then Sadie's hand was on my cheek, a soothing stroke that brought me back to her. "You going into shock, Slick? Wouldn't have expected a tough, macho guy like you to give in to a sissy feeling like shock."

I knew why she'd said it. To hit me in the ego and piss me off so I didn't let the adrenaline leaving get the best of me. She said it to keep me focused on her. But it wasn't shock that had a tremor running through me. It was agony at what could have happened to her just for being at my side.

In practically one motion, I grabbed her and hauled her onto my lap and planted my mouth on hers. Feeling the heat. Feeling the life. Feeling her instant response.

Her hands surrounded my neck, nails digging in. She leaned into the kiss, adding her own fire and strength to it. She bit my lower lip, and I growled, fisting her hair and slanting our mouths so I could deepen the kiss and slide my tongue inside those honeyed depths. She let me in, echoing every stroke with ones just as forceful, telling me as clear as if she'd said the words that she wasn't giving me control just now. That I'd have to let her guide this embrace as much as me.

And I did. Because we both needed it. We both needed to find some power after those terrible minutes of having none, when our lives could have disappeared with a single shot piercing mere skin and bone.

Slowly, the intensity eased into something softer, more tender. Gratitude for being alive. Relief that we were both there. I lifted my mouth from hers, grabbed her chin, and put enough space between us that I could meet her eyes.

"You're going home, Tennessee."

"On Sunday, Slick." Her chin jutted out in stubbornness.

"Tomorrow morning. Your ass is on my plane, and my pilot is taking you home."

"I'm not leaving you or Fallon," she said.

And the simple fact she'd included my daughter in that statement tore another hole through me larger and more lasting than the damn graze the bullet had caused. Larger and more lasting than any wound I'd ever earned.

Chapter Twenty-six

Sadie

LOVE I GOT LEFT
Performed by Max McKnown

He was an idiot if he thought I'd walk away when he was in danger. He didn't know anything about me or my Hatley blood if he thought I'd turn away from the person I loved when their life was on the line.

The shots fired at us had triggered a whole slew of ugly inside me. For several horrible seconds, I'd been right back in that moment at the ranch with my desperate fear for Mila squeezing my chest. Right back to watching blood pour from my thigh as my tiny niece ran for her life just as I'd lost consciousness.

It would be so easy to slip into the intense emotions of that day. The terror and agony of not being able to go after her. The relief at seeing Maddox. The panic of coming awake after surgery, and the doctors telling me I might never get full use of my leg back.

I wouldn't lie and say my hands weren't still shaking. That the memories and fear weren't still curling through my blood, but I refused to give in to it. Refused to let whomever this was coming for Rafe and his family send me cartwheeling back into the dark I'd been swimming against for nearly three years. I only wished, like I had that day with Mila, that I'd had a weapon to defend us. Some way of striking back as the bullets rained. A chance for a whisper of control in a situation where I'd had none.

His hand landed in my hair, drawing the strands around his finger, tugging so I was forced to meet his gaze again. "Sadie, I…" He swallowed hard, Adam's apple bobbing. "Damn it. I won't be the reason you get hurt…or worse. I'm so sorry this brought back those memories for you. That you had to experience any of it again."

The fact he was more upset about what this had triggered in me than being shot at snagged my heart and made it his more than it already was. I stroked his beard, hating the grief and remorse I saw in his eyes, the guilt and blame that would stick to him. I knew those feelings too. All too well.

"Some asshole shooting at you isn't your fault." When I saw he was going to argue, I shook my head and cut him off. "You want to do something for me, Rafe? Find out who it is and put them away."

His stare burrowed into me. I wanted to tell him I loved him. I wanted to tell him nothing was going to take me away, but my tongue locked to the roof of my mouth. Now wasn't the time. It would sound as ridiculous as it had when I'd talked to Gemma.

I eased off Rafe's lap and finished cleaning and wrapping his arm.

The entire time, his gaze was pinned to the office door, nearly coming out of his skin at every sound while he waited for his daughter. When Mila had run away from me that day, when she'd disappeared from sight, I'd been overcome with panic, unable to see how to protect her and knowing she was facing the danger alone because I'd failed. And even though Mila wasn't my child, I still loved her with all of me. I still knew the rage and guilt and terror he was feeling.

When the front door finally crashed open, he jerked to his feet, pushing me behind him just in case it wasn't his team and his family.

"Dad!" Fallon's voice echoed through the hall, and his shoulders dropped in relief.

She came sprinting into the office, eyes wild, braids bouncing behind her. She barreled into him, wrapping her arms around him and holding on tight. Her shoulders shook with sobs as she clung to him.

"I thought you were dead," her voice cracked. "I thought I'd lost you too!"

When I met Rafe's eyes over her head, his were filled with the same unshed tears as mine. He kissed her temple and held her tight. "I'm not going anywhere, Ducky. I'm here. You aren't going to lose me."

She stepped back and pummeled his chest with her fists. "You aren't bulletproof." When she saw the bandage on his arm, she gasped. "You're shot! Oh my God, why aren't you at the hospital?"

"It's just a graze," he insisted, pulling her back into his arms. "Sadie already took care of me."

Noah and Lauren came into the room, trailed by Lorenzo and Parker. The rest of the wedding party stood in the hallway beyond them in various stages of fear, anger, and dishevelment.

"What the fuck is going on?" Lorenzo demanded, back rigid, fury pouring from him.

"You tell me," Rafe growled, setting Fallon aside and stepping forward as if to protect us all from my cousin.

The terror of the gunshots was slowly easing away, but in its place, a new fear rose inside me. Had we escaped the gunshots only to let the wolf in the front door?

Lorenzo's eyes narrowed, and he didn't back away. Instead, he moved closer to Rafe. "You think this was me? That I'd ruin Marielle's wedding by taking a potshot at you that I could have taken any time I wanted when you were in Vegas?"

It was like watching two bucks go at it in the wild as they stood almost toe to toe. Feral and fierce and both equally determined to protect what was theirs.

What surprised me was that I believed Lorenzo. That even after everything Rafe had told me about being stabbed, I could believe him. But he was right. I couldn't see him hiring a gunman to take Rafe out in the middle of the wedding. Not when he'd treated his cousin with such love and affection all day.

"As far as I'm aware, nothing like this has happened at the ranch or in Rivers until you showed up, bringing your damn criminal activities with you," Rafe insisted.

Lorenzo scoffed, and the two men stared each other down, waiting to see who would make the first move. My heart thudded in my chest as the tension in the air grew, and I eased closer to Rafe, unsure what I would do but determined to somehow help.

From behind Lorenzo, Nicky stepped forward. "Puzo, what the hell is this?"

Lorenzo didn't break his glare with Rafe, and instead, it was Lauren who spoke, hurrying toward the wedding couple. "I'm so sorry this happened. So sorry your evening was ruined in this way. Everyone is safe here in the house, and if you could please just give us a moment to figure everything out, I promise we'll do everything we can to fix it." She waved a hand toward the sitting room across the hall. "Let's go in here, and I'll have drinks brought in while I arrange for the dinner to be moved from the marquee to our dining room."

"Lorenzo?" Marielle's voice was uncertain, her dark eyes sad, and her carefully arranged brown hair tousled and out of place.

My cousin finally looked away from Rafe to take in Marielle's worried expression. "Go with Lauren. I'll take care of this."

She hesitated but then let Lauren take her arm, leading her and the rest of the wedding party into the sitting room.

"I had nothing to do with this," Lorenzo insisted again. I was astonished when he was the one to back away, to put space between him and Rafe. But his next words proved he hadn't dropped the fight. "But *I* won't stand idly by while *my* family is in danger."

The insinuation Rafe had let this happen took the worry and fear inside me and layered it with my own rage. I stepped out from behind Rafe's broad shoulders, pointed a finger, and said, "If you think for even one second—"

"Someone tell me what the hell is going on!" Lauren demanded as she rushed back inside and shut the office doors behind her. Silence and tension flipped through the air, but no one said anything. She looked at Rafe and asked, "Did Jim and his men catch whomever this was?"

"He's still out there looking," Parker answered just as Rafe demanded, "Have you heard from Adam?"

Lauren paled. "He wouldn't do this… He wouldn't risk hurting me or Fallon…" But I could see the doubts filtering through her, and maybe her mind had gone to the same place mine had—to the person in her room with a pillow pressed to her face.

"If he killed Spence, why wouldn't he kill Dad?" Fallon said scathingly. "He wants all of you out of the way so he can get his hands on the ranch. He wanted me to sign over half of it. He would probably have offed me too."

Lauren inhaled sharply just as Rafe barked out, "What are you talking about?"

Fallon darted me a glance, as if amazed I'd kept quiet about what she'd told me. "He wanted me to sign over half the ranch to him once I turned eighteen. He kept saying Spencer had promised to right the wrongs of the past by giving him a share and that Spence had agreed it was as much Hurly land as it was Harrington."

Lauren shook her head. "It's what Adam wanted, hoped for, but Spencer never agreed to it. He was going to change the trust so Adam and I were executors, but he was never giving away the land."

Rafe's face was thunderous, and his head whipped back toward Lorenzo. "How much does he owe you?"

Lorenzo ran a hand through his hair, a tell showing just how much he'd also been rattled by tonight's events. "I never said he owed me money."

While I'd believed what he'd said about not being responsible for the gunman tonight, I didn't believe him now, and the fury in Rafe's face said he didn't either. "Have you been helping him steal from the ranch? Scurrying the money away to some offshore account?"

Lorenzo tugged at his suit jacket, regaining his control. His voice was calm, returning to that mocking condescension he'd used when he'd lobbed the insinuation about Rafe not protecting his family, as he said, "The only thing I did was try to help. Once I realized it was impossible, that Adam was still burning through more money than the ranch earned, it was easier to just wait for it all to crumble. I'd be able to buy the land for pennies on the dollar. It would have given me great pleasure to own what you'd tossed aside."

Rafe practically vibrated with barely contained animosity, and I fisted the back of his shirt, holding him back, because I knew if he lost control now, he'd despise himself later for it. He didn't want to give Lorenzo the power of his emotions any more than he wanted his daughter to see him react in violence.

Lauren and I shared a look, and she stepped in between Lorenzo and Rafe. "If you want your money back for the wedding, if you want to move it away from here, I'll understand. I'll do whatever I can to find a place nearby that can accommodate you tomorrow."

"My family wasn't the target tonight. If Marquess leaves, we'll all be fine," Lorenzo said casually as he straightened his suit lapels and pulled himself together even more.

"I'm not leaving my family with threats hanging over them," Rafe snarled.

"He's right, though, isn't he?" Lauren said. Her words struck me like a dart to the chest, and if they stung me, I knew they'd sliced into Rafe. "You've been the target."

"A man was in your room, smothering you!" Rafe shot back.

She paled. "I…that was just a nightmare. We don't know…"

But we all did.

Lorenzo pulled his phone from his pocket. "There's no need for us to leave. I'll send for my security team, and we'll have men all over the ranch protecting my family and our guests."

Rafe laughed. It was brutal and harsh. "You're crazy if you think I'm letting your men on my property. I can handle the extra security."

Lorenzo didn't even look in Rafe's direction as he raised a brow at Lauren and said, "If you want me to stay and not demand you give back every dime we've spent here, you'll let *my* men protect us."

"Lauren." Rafe's warning was gritty and deep, but she shot him a defiant look that matched the ones I'd seen from her daughter.

"No, Rafe. Spence may have left you in charge of the money and legal aspects of the ranch, but he left me in charge of the operations. You don't get a say in this. As far as I can tell, we need all the help we can get."

Rafe swore under his breath.

The office door opened, and Jim Steele and Barry came rushing in. Their faces were set and grim.

"Tell me you found him," Rafe demanded.

Steele shook his head, dropping a handful of shell casings he'd wrapped up in the bottom of his shirt on a side table. "We found where he'd holed up. He had a clear shot of the field and the back of the house." He waved at the shells. "I didn't have gloves, but I was careful, so we might get prints."

"He had a truck of some sort parked nearby that left tracks in the dirt and the grass. I'll get a mold kit, and we can trace the vehicle," Barry added.

Rafe dragged a hand over his beard. "Let's call the sheriff and see how he'd like to proceed."

Lorenzo made a noise of disgust. "Of course, running to the police is your answer."

Rafe's fists clenched, and his lips flattened, but he acted as if Lorenzo hadn't spoken. "We've had three attempts on our lives now, and from what I can tell, Adam has stolen—at a minimum—three hundred thousand dollars from the ranch in just the last five years." Lauren and Fallon both gasped. "The authorities need to be involved, and they need to reopen

Spence's case."

Lauren's hand went to her chest, rubbing, and she sank down into the nearest chair. Surprisingly, it was Fallon who tried to comfort her, leaning over the back of the chair to hug her. "It's not your fault, Mom. Uncle Adam was good at hiding things."

Lauren brushed a hand over Fallon's hair and then looked up at Rafe. "He's been angry many times over the years. It's not like I didn't know it. As kids, he wanted the two of us to leave and start new somewhere else. He hated that I stayed, but when he came back to help after your dad died, he seemed at peace with it. He even seemed happy here…"

She trailed off, looking into the empty fireplace, and all I could think was that Adam had probably been happy because he'd been stealing and plotting from the moment he'd returned to the ranch. If Fallon hadn't gone to her dad in Vegas, if Rafe hadn't shown up and rocked the boat simply by stepping onto the land, maybe he would have succeeded.

What would he do now that his plans had been interrupted? My vision swam with Chainsaw's face, ugly with fury as he'd waved his gun and ranted about what had been taken from him. Desperate men did desperate things. My mouth went dry, panic curling over my spine once more. What could I do to keep Rafe safe? To help protect all these people who'd worked their way into my soul in a matter of days?

Steele broke the quiet that had descended. "Let me go call the sheriff and see if I've gotten a hit on any of the alerts I set online for Adam."

Lauren watched him as he stepped out into the hall, and then she stood, shaking off the heartbreak and becoming that sure woman I'd first met again. I realized just how much Rafe and Lauren were alike in that way, hiding their emotions, tucking them away. And I wondered what their childhood here had been like that they'd both come away with the need to shield themselves so tightly.

"I need to get dinner served and reassure our guests that they're safe." She looked at Lorenzo. "I'd appreciate your help with the additional security and anything you can do to smooth things over with Marielle and Nicky."

The look of triumph Lorenzo sent Rafe took my panic and amplified it. But then he confused me by stopping at the door, gentling his voice, and saying, "Believe it or not, I've never condoned any illegal activity in any of my businesses. Not back when you worked at my club, and not now." Rafe snorted in disbelief. "Someday, you'll realize the enemies you have are all of your own making."

Then he left, striding away in that smooth way that made him appear like he wasn't moving at all and leaving anger and doubt singing the air behind him.

I could see his words had landed with Rafe, making him doubt what he'd always thought had happened. I was pretty sure that had been my cousin's point—to attack him in another way and tip Rafe over the edge when he was already tumbling.

I stepped toward him, wanting to reassure and comfort, but before I could go to him, Fallon had wrapped an arm around his waist and leaned her head into his uninjured arm.

He returned the hug and then said quietly but firmly, "Sadie, I want you to leave, and I'd like you to take Fallon with you."

"What?" Fallon said, jerking away from him as I shook my head.

"There's no reason for either of you to end up caught in the crossfire."

"I'm not leaving Mom! I'm not leaving my home!" Fallon stamped her foot.

Barry cleared his throat. "Steele already has more of our men on their way. Factor in Puzo's crew and the police, and I think just the number of bodies will deter whomever this is. If you stay out of sight, boss, there's no reason to think anyone else is going to get hurt."

Rafe glared at the man, and he wisely shut up.

I didn't agree with Barry. If Adam was the shooter, if he was the one who'd put the snake in Rafe's bed and tried to smother his own sister, then he wasn't thinking rationally. Another flash of Chainsaw's eyes, wild with desperation and fury, spun before me. But even if Adam came, even if it was him who'd shot at us tonight, he hadn't ever targeted Fallon or me. He'd targeted Rafe. And I wanted him to be safe more than anything. More than my own safety.

I took his hand and pressed it to my chest. "I'll go if you go."

"I'm not leaving."

I laughed, not because it was funny but because it was so entirely the man I'd come to love. "So, you'll send everyone you care about away, but you'll leave yourself wide open? Don't you think the people who love you want to see you protected as much as you want us to be?"

I swallowed hard after I'd let the words out. They weren't exactly me saying I loved him or that he loved me, but the meaning was there. The intent. The intensity of his gaze when it settled on mine rocketed through me like a shock wave.

"I *can't* leave, Tennessee." And I heard in his voice everything he wasn't saying. He was blaming himself for all of it. For leaving years ago and for not seeing what Adam was doing now. For the danger that had arrived on the ranch's doorstep. And he couldn't walk away again without trying to fix it.

"Then, we all stay," I told him, hoping to remind him that his daughter was part of that deal. I wanted him to leave and take her with him. To let the authorities handle the search for Adam or whoever it was who had shot at him.

Steele strode back into the room and said, "Sheriff is on his way."

Rafe cupped my cheek and said softly, "We have things to discuss, Tennessee. But not now. After."

I didn't know if he meant after the police had come and gone or after all this was over. But as I wasn't prepared yet to have the talk he wanted, wasn't sure I knew any more this evening how to meld our worlds together than I had this morning, I just nodded.

The one thing I was certain of was that I wanted to cherish every minute I had with him. I could have lost him tonight. He could have been killed as he'd shielded me from the shots, and knowing that made everything else in my life seem unimportant.

Chapter Twenty-seven

Rafe

FIX WHAT YOU DIDN'T BREAK
Performed by Nate Smith

The ranch had broken me open, taken the control I prided myself on and tossed it to the wind. I felt like the nineteen-year-old kid I'd once been, staring down my father's disappointment. Not because his girlfriend was pregnant but because of *who* the girlfriend was.

Dad had been clear—I'd let my family down.

And he hadn't lived to see the worst of it. To see just how I'd left the door wide open. To see how I'd all but welcomed the monsters in simply by turning my back on them.

I wanted to send everyone I cared about to the other side of the planet while I unraveled what was happening here and ended it. And yet, letting Sadie and Fallon leave my sight to help Lauren with the dinner was enough to turn my palms sweaty. The desperate need to keep them close and send them away was a dichotomy I couldn't fix.

Sadie's pretty little speech about the people who loved me wanting me as safe as I wanted them had scored through me. The idea of her loving me, standing up for me, standing beside me, had seared through the grief and remorse and fury. And then she'd all but slayed me with the new dare she'd laid down. *You stay, I stay.*

I could make her leave. I could forcibly remove them all. I could say things that would hurt her enough to make her run, but then what would I do when this was over? I'd have cut off my nose to spite my face. Because one thing was certain—I wanted a future with the dark-haired vixen who'd stolen my heart.

Steele sent Parker after Sadie and Fallon, and it gave the tension knotting every vein a miniscule amount of relief. He'd keep them inside. He'd keep them covered. The best thing I could do for them right now was exactly what Sadie had told me to do—find who this was and end it.

"We need to overhaul the house alarms right now," I told Steele. "What we have now sounds an alert at a couple of doors, and that's it. None of the windows are wired, and there are no cameras."

Steele nodded. "I know. But the kind of system you need takes coordination and time. I'll do my best to get it here and installed by Monday or Tuesday. Until then, I've got an entire squad of bodies on their way. You really going to let Puzo's men play a role here?"

I rubbed a hand over my head. "I'm not sure I have a choice." Something dark and ugly curled inside me as I asked, "Do you believe him? About not having a part in any of this? About not ever having condoned anything illegal?"

With a carefully placed dig, Puzo had caused me to doubt what I'd been absolutely certain was true. An ugly trepidation curled through me, leaving a sour taste in my mouth. I was missing something. Out of arrogance and pride, I might have made another colossal mistake.

"The evidence against Ike Puzo and his pals was ironclad, Rafe. Is it possible he was dealing drugs, running guns, and laundering money out of the club without Lorenzo knowing? Sure. Is it likely?" Steele hesitated before shaking his head. "I don't think so."

Noah stepped forward. "You know I grew up in Vegas, right?" We both gave him a curt nod. "The Puzo family has always played a huge role in that town, both the good and the bad sides of it. The urban legends that tell of what was done to people who went up against the Puzos, or even looked sideways at them, were gruesome enough we used them to scare each other as kids." I barely kept myself from rolling my eyes at him, and he waved his hand. "I get it. You've heard it all too. But have you heard the mumblings about trouble in Puzoland?"

"What kind of trouble?" I asked, crossing my arms over my chest.

"Like, not everyone in the family was happy when Old Man Puzo died and left his grandson in charge," Noah said. "Do you know Ike's twin sister? Theresa?"

I remembered her from my time in the club. She'd spent as much time there as her brother had. Dark-haired, athletic, and smart with a strong Italian nose, deep brows, and minimal curves. She'd flirted with me now and again, but I'd always steered clear, not only because I hadn't wanted to mess with my boss's family but because I'd heard rumors about the men she'd taken to her bed who'd gone missing.

That twinge returned, tightening my chest muscles and making it hard to breathe.

Barry walked in, leading the sheriff, and I had to leave the problem of Puzo behind. I spent the next few hours with him, reviewing what had happened since I'd arrived and trying not to react when he'd asked to speak to Sadie, Fallon, Lauren, and every single guest for verification.

It was nearing midnight by the time the house was quiet and Sheriff Wylee had left, taking Adam's computer with him. He left a deputy patrolling with Noah and promised to have a small crew on hand at the wedding the next day, but his staff was limited, and they had their normal patrol to handle too.

I poured two glasses of bourbon and handed one to Steele. "I can't seem to trust my gut, Jim. Tell me the truth. You think this is Adam, Puzo, or them working together?"

"I don't know Adam. He's an unknown to me. But whoever shot at you tonight either had really bad aim or missed on purpose."

"You think it was a warning rather than an actual attempt on my life?"

"The chances of you dying from the rattler were slim also.

You would have been able to call 911, and while the ranch is remote, it isn't out of range of the help you would have needed."

If it was Adam and he was issuing a warning to get the hell out of his life, he had to know this kind of challenge would only make me dig my heels in more, wouldn't he? Or maybe this was just like him luring me out with his rook and his bishop while he slid behind to try to take my queen when we'd played chess. He'd hated when I'd seen his strategy and evaded and defended my position. We'd ended in as many stalemates as we had with either of us winning.

"You find out who his girlfriend is?" I asked Steele.

He shook his head. "No, and I asked Sheriff Wylee if anyone in town knew, and he seemed shocked to find out Adam was seeing anyone at all."

I sat down, exhaustion finding its way into my bones. I'd been on alert for days now. Since Sadie Hatley had walked into my bar. And while I knew none of what was happening now was her fault, it had been the point at which my calm life had first spiraled out of my control. The adrenaline rush that had started my day, searching for Adam, and that returned during the shooting, had disappeared, leaving me numb. All I wanted to do was go upstairs, slide into bed with Sadie, and remind myself how to feel.

"I'm going to go check on the arrival time for our crew and dig some more into Adam's accounts. You still don't want me to track his Mercedes? His devices?"

Wylee had said they'd get a judge to issue a warrant, but it might take time. Would it matter if he did it or Steele? "See what you can find."

Steele's face all but lit up, and he strode out of the office without another word.

I leaned back in the chair and closed my eyes.

If Adam had done more than just steal from the estate, if he'd come at me and Lauren, it was because of years of jealousy and anger that had nothing to do with me. But had I done something to trigger it? His Grandpa Joe had been a bitter old man full of hate. I'd caught him staring at me like I was the devil incarnate more than once. Adam had loved the man, eaten up his stories like they were decadent candies.

There'd been some kind of talk about him and Great-grandma Beatrice being friends, hadn't there? Something about Hollywood and the parties Joe had gone to with her? I opened my eyes and stared at the portrait of my great-grandmother over the mantel, and my gaze landed on the diamonds all but dripping from her.

Adam had wanted them, but he'd also told Sadie he was looking into whether the family had been reimbursed for the stolen jewels by an insurance company. Is that what he'd been looking for in the boxes in the safe?

I swallowed the bourbon I'd poured for Steele that he hadn't touched and then forced myself up and into the safe.

It took me a minute to find the right box as most of them were unmarked. The first one I opened held files with neatly printed dates going back to the 1930s. I flipped through them quickly, noting some legal documents, old photos, and a handful of notebooks. I set it aside and opened several more before finding the one holding the mixed-up documents Adam and I had carelessly thrown back inside after he'd dropped it.

I took both boxes into the office and started sifting through them.

The exhaustion dragging at me as much as the alcohol I'd downed made the entire experience surreal. Like I'd stepped back in time. Old invoices. Contractor agreements for the build of the mansion. Payment to the armed guards who'd protected the mines after there'd been repeated incidents of people trying to sneak in and dig for diamonds themselves.

What caught my attention and had my hands slowing as I flipped through them were the black-and-white photographs taken at a ball held at the house when it was bright and new. Shots of the famous movie stars who'd been in attendance with Beatrice standing amongst them like she belonged.

I frowned, trying to remember more of the stories I'd heard, not from my dad but from my mom. Beatrice had been an actress who'd given up Hollywood to marry Great-grandpa

Alasdair, much like my mother had given up her dreams of her art for my dad. An image of Beatrice with Alasdair, elegant in evening wear, had more unease sifting through me. There'd been a large age gap between them, nothing strange for that time, and yet it was less than what existed between Sadie and me now. I didn't like the comparison of women who'd given up their lives for the men they'd married any more than the age difference.

At the bottom of the box Adam had been rifling through, I found a small leather journal elegantly embossed with Beatrice's maiden name. After opening it and reading the first entry, I realized it was her personal journal. It felt like an invasion of her privacy to read it, even though she'd long been gone, but her words drew me in.

Each entry was short and to the point, but they were mixed with vivid descriptions and random lines of poetry. I didn't know if they were Beatrice's own words or famous lines from poems I didn't recognize. She wrote about dancing with the new-to-Hollywood Clark Gable and the older, more famous Wallace Beery and about meeting Great-grandpa Alasdair at some movie premiere after-party. He'd already won the ranch by the time she'd met him, but they hadn't discovered the diamonds yet.

As I skimmed through pages of their whirlwind romance, engagement, and marriage, it hit chords that continued to resonate with me about my relationship with Sadie. The suddenness of it. The overwhelming feeling that it was right. Beatrice thinking fate had somehow led them to each other. But it also grew the worries I'd already had about what Sadie would have to give up if she became mine, because it was clear to see that, while Beatrice had started out ecstatic, she'd slowly started to miss her old life.

The excitement of the diamond discovery was overshadowed by Tommy Hurly's suicide and the loneliness that eked into the pages as Alasdair left her alone for days on end while dealing with the mine and the building of the mansion. Into that void, Joe Hurly had stepped. Seven years younger than her, she'd felt sympathy for him at first and then a common bond over the lives they were living that weren't what either of them wanted or expected. They'd formed a friendship.

But it wasn't until she and Alasdair fought over loaning the jewels to a friend at a small movie studio that things took a real dive sideways. She'd wanted him to go with her, for them to not only take the jewels to Hollywood personally but to spend a few weeks there. To take a vacation they hadn't had since their honeymoon. She wanted a chance to recover the love and friendship she'd felt like they'd lost. Alasdair refused. He couldn't leave the mine, not with the break-ins and sabotage that was happening almost daily.

And so, she'd gone without him, taking Joe so she wouldn't have to travel alone with the diamonds. Just seeing it in writing made the hair on the back of my neck stand up. Maybe it was simply what was happening now with Adam that had me reading between the lines and seeing it as something sinister, but I despised finding I was right when Beatrice's excited entries filled with talk of Hollywood parties disappeared altogether.

She wrote nothing for several weeks. And the first entry afterward was a tear-stained paragraph saying she was back at the ranch and that the jewels had been stolen. Beatrice felt responsible. She was anxious and depressed, although she didn't use those words, and her pen had all but sunk into the page, underlining the words heavily when she said Joe would never be allowed in the main house or near her ever again.

Had he taken the jewels and threatened her? Had he made moves on her? Or worse?

It sickened me. Worse, after discovering the returned jewelry were fakes, Alasdair accused Beatrice of cheating on him and planning the theft with Hurly. Even her newfound, violent disgust of Joe hadn't swayed him. When the small, up-and-coming movie studio had told Alasdair they hadn't insured the jewels, he'd demanded they find a way to compensate him. A handwritten letter from the president of the studio was tucked into Beatrice's diary. In exchange for keeping the theft quiet, Alasdair was given the fake jewels along with shares in the studio. The letter made it clear, if the real jewels were ever recovered, the Harringtons had full claim to them without owing anything back to the movie studio.

While I could imagine my fury if I'd been my great-grandfather, could imagine the doubts and hurt that would have accompanied the events, he'd still negotiated a decent deal out of it. While his shares of the studio had kept him just under majority ownership and he'd never had a say in what movies were made, he'd still gotten a significant cut of the profits. And holding on to the shares for over eighty years had allowed me to take advantage of the funds in building Marquess Enterprises.

I skimmed through the rest of the journal, the tension and sadness in the rest of the entries weighing on me. Beatrice only mentioned Joe Hurly once more after that. After months of being gone, he dropped off a wife and a son on the one-acre plot of land that belonged to the Hurlys and took off again, leaving them without any means of financial support. Beatrice took pity on them and brought the woman to work at the mansion. Whenever he did show back up at the ranch, Joe's wife told Beatrice he was drunk and often violent, rambling about LA and Las Vegas and those who'd done him wrong.

I closed the journal and leaned back in the chair with my eyes closed again. At some point, Joe had come home, because he'd worked for his son when Donnie had been my dad's foreman. The two men had both been ancient, crotchety, and crusty. Snapping at me and Spence. We'd avoided them as much as we could.

Donnie had been in his forties when he'd had Adam and Lauren. Their mom had been his second wife, but for the life of me, I couldn't remember ever hearing what had happened to the first. What I did remember was the way Adam had idolized both his father and his grandfather.

From the moment Alasdair Harrington had won the ranch, the Hurlys' luck had spiraled downward. Yes, it had mostly been because of their own bad decisions, but people had a way of shifting the blame to others. What might Adam have heard from Joe Hurly that had twisted the truth to fit his needs? What kind of poison had been spread through his veins, and what might Adam do to take back what he thought of as his family's lost inheritance? Would he steal? Kill Spence and me? What would I do if our situations had been reversed?

As it was, my jealousy for Spence had cost us both the lives we'd thought we'd have.

What had Adam hoped to find in these boxes that would have helped him? Nothing gave him rights to the land. If anything, it showed why there was even less of a reason for us to hand it over.

But he'd started digging in here after Sadie had told him about the jewels. Was he hoping to find the contract saying the jewels were ours if they were ever found? Maybe he'd simply wanted the diamonds for himself. Or maybe he'd hoped to prevent Lauren from finding out about them because he didn't want the ranch to be saved. Because he wanted to watch the Harringtons and the ranch be destroyed the way his family had been.

It didn't seem possible that, right at the crucial moment, Sadie had been brought into our lives, bringing the stolen jewels back with her. Was it that fate Beatrice had thought had brought her and Alasdair together? Had we all been cast under some spell only Sadie could break? Or would my taking her and keeping her bring the same heartache I'd read in Beatrice's journals?

All I knew was my time with her had not been nearly enough. I wanted to wake up to her impish smile and her passionate strength every single day.

I heard her calling my name, saying it in that same throaty, breathless way that she had while we'd been in the throes of passion. While she'd taken what I'd given and asked for more. I wanted to taste and lick and savor every inch of her all over again. Embed myself in her. Give her more of those pieces of myself I'd felt slipping away while staring into her bluebell eyes.

I woke to soft hands caressing my face, and I opened heavy lids to see Sadie leaning over me as if my thoughts and dreams of her had called her to me. The cut on my cheek protested, even though her touch was light, but I didn't stop her. I was happy to feel the pain. To feel anything. To feel her.

I dragged her onto my lap, slanted my mouth over hers, and feasted on her sweetness. She moaned, and I inhaled it, making it mine just like I wanted to make all of her.

But as I came fully awake, I found Beatrice's words clinging to me. The despair of those last few entries before she'd completely stopped writing. Loving my great-grandfather had cost her. I had to figure out a way to keep Sadie without her losing everything. I needed time to pull my shit together. To figure out what to do with Fallon and Lauren and the ranch. To find Adam and put an end to nearly a hundred years of family drama.

I broke the kiss, and Sadie protested, seeking my lips again. But I just rested my forehead against hers, wrapping my hand around her wrist so she couldn't continue caressing me. Her eyes narrowed, objecting without words that I'd called a halt to the embrace, and it made my lips twitch.

Damn, did I like riling her up, seeing the passion that burned when she was worked up. I yearned to have all that energy and defiance and strength under my control again, working her until she broke apart, until I could hand her some of it back and let her do whatever she wanted to me.

"Is there a reason you slept here instead of your room? I waited for you there," Sadie said, and the hurt and accusation in her tone hit me like a slap.

The idea she'd been in my bed, waiting for me, made me grow even harder beneath her. She felt my reaction, lips tilting upward. "You wouldn't be having this problem"—she palmed me through my jeans— "if you'd done the reasonable thing and come to bed."

"But then you wouldn't have slept," I grunted. My voice was raspy from lack of sleep as much as desire.

Her smile faded, and it was one more thing I hated in a growing pile. I wanted her always light and laughing. Sassy. Keeping me on my toes.

"It would have been less about sleep and more about the comfort we brought each other," she said. "It would have given us both a moment of forgetfulness."

In one swift movement that used all my waking strength, I set her on the desk and stepped between her legs. I lifted her chin and stared down at lips swollen from our kiss. With her black hair, blue eyes, and rosy lips, she was a Snow White remaking. Sweet but nowhere like the animated fairy tale. This woman was all badass Tomb Raider, holding men hostage and settling old debts. But both Snow White and Lara Croft had been wounded and betrayed. I had no intention of letting that happen to Sadie on my watch.

"We're not getting lost in any kind of forgetfulness, Tennessee. You're leaving today," I told her.

She pushed my hand away from her chin, fire brewing inside her. "We've already had this discussion. I'm not going unless you go with me, and there's nothing you can do to make me."

I laughed darkly. "You're wrong about that."

"Look, Slick, unless you can tell me you're leaving too, then I'm staying. Besides, I promised Lauren I'd help her with the wedding, and I don't go back on my word without a very good reason."

"Your word won't mean anything if you're dead." When she went to respond, I cut her off, playing the one card I hoped would win me the game. "I need you to do this for me. Not only because I don't want you anywhere near me when the shit hits the fan, but because I don't want my daughter near it either. If you take Fallon with you, I can concentrate on what I need to do here, because I'll know you're both safe. Right now, I can barely think clearly over the top of my worry for the two of you."

Her eyes filled with unexpected tears, and it tore into me but didn't lessen my resolve. "The fact you'd trust me with her, the thing that is most precious to you…" She shook her head. "It means more to me than you can know. But she doesn't want to leave you either."

"She's not the only thing that's precious to me, Sadie," I said, watching as her throat bobbed. "Fuck, I'm halfway in love with you." I inhaled sharply. "No, I'm all the way in love with you. More in love with you than I've ever been with anything or anyone in my life. But I can't offer you that love right now. I can't offer you a damn thing until I'm sure I don't have a target on my back that might hit you if it misses me."

Her legs encircled my hips, heels pressing into my ass and pulling me tighter into her core. She wound her hands around my neck, tugging my face closer to hers. "I've never loved a man, Rafe Marquess. Never. But when a Hatley gives their heart to someone, it's forever. I've done that. I've given you my heart. That also means, in typical Hatley fashion, I intend to face every damn thing while standing at your side. Both the good and the bad. You want to send Fallon away, fine. Send her off somewhere with half a dozen bodyguards protecting her, but do not ask me to walk away. It isn't in my DNA, Slick. Asking me to do that is like asking me to cut my soul out of my body and leave it behind. It would kill me."

Then, she crushed her lips to mine as if to stop me from arguing. Or maybe simply because she couldn't stop from following up those powerful and moving words with action that was the same. Strong. Emotional. Commanding I be the one to give in. The one to let go.

And I was surprised by my desire to do just that.

To give her whatever the hell she wanted.

Chapter Twenty-eight

Sadie

GOOD WOMAN
Performed by Maren Morris

My heart was leaping and pounding, a wild horse ready to escape the confines of the corral and run free over the hills. Rafe loved me. I'd felt it yesterday, and he'd insinuated it, but we hadn't said the words. To hear them, plain as day, was a heady drug. One I could easily get addicted to. I'd never get tired of hearing it. Feeling it. Wanting it. Wanting him.

I kissed him openly, no reservations, no holding back. I poured everything I was into it, feeling safe in handing him my heart. My soul. It didn't solve our problems. If anything, it added hurdles to whatever happened next, but it still felt right giving it to him.

One thing was certain. I wouldn't walk away from him when he had a gun pointed at him.

No way in hell.

I'd gone to Rafe's room last night and waited for him to come up, not only to give him comfort but in hopes of evading the memories that were trying to drag me back into the abyss from that day with Chainsaw. I'd fallen asleep trying to keep the good memories, the sweet ones of hands and mouths gliding on skin, at the forefront, but they'd still turned into terrifying ones of Rafe guiding me along a field as shots rang out, and we zigzagged to the house. His firm grip on my elbow had faded into pained memories of McKenna's fingers pushing into my wounds, trying to stop me from bleeding out.

When I woke with a start, heart hammering with fear and trepidation and loss, the bed had still been empty, even though the sky was turning gray outside the windows. And I might have hated that more than I'd hated anything else that had happened since I'd arrived.

Kissing him now, I tried to convey all of that—not only the love we'd declared but what he'd denied himself, and me, by not coming upstairs.

A throat clearing behind us had me pulling my lips from his. It hurt more than I'd ever thought it would to separate myself from another human being. I wanted to spend the day tucked up next to him, doing just this—kissing and touching and caressing. Soothing. Loving. But we couldn't have that. Not yet.

We turned to see Lauren hovering in the doorway of the office. I slipped off the desk, putting distance between Rafe and me. I wasn't embarrassed that she'd caught us kissing, but the entire situation felt awkward and confusing.

Rafe caught my fingers, as if sensing my sudden uncertainty, keeping me at his side.

"Have you been here all night?" Lauren asked, eyeing the papers Rafe had scattered all over the desk and some even on the floor.

"Yes," he said, picking up a small, antique journal. "Adam was going through these boxes, and I was trying to figure out what he was looking for."

Lauren's gaze darted down and away before they came back, her gaze hardening. "He texted me this morning."

Every fiber of my being went still and saw Rafe's spine stiffen. He practically vibrated with animosity as he spit out, "And?"

"He said I needed to trust him. That he'd explain it all soon, but that he was going away for a few days so he could right everything that had gone wrong." She rubbed her forehead, and I almost felt sorry for her because I could see she still wanted to believe her brother. Wouldn't I if the roles were switched? But then again, I couldn't imagine either of my brothers ever stealing from their home or shooting at people we loved.

"Did you tell him about the shooting? The theft?" Rafe demanded.

"I wasn't sure if I should, so I kept it vague. I told him I didn't understand everything that was happening, but that he needed to come home. Otherwise, people would assume he was guilty of stealing from the ranch and more."

"And how did he respond?"

"He didn't, and when I tried to call, it went straight to voicemail."

The front door slammed open, and we all jumped, turning toward the hall as feet pounded on the marble floors. Steele came storming into the office. His eyes narrowed at Lauren. "Did you tell them Adam texted you?"

She inhaled sharply. "You were tracing his calls?"

Steele ignored the question, turning back to Rafe. "He's in LA, near the airport. I left a message with Sheriff Wylee in hopes that he can coordinate with LAPD and have them send a SWAT unit to the hotel to bring him in for questioning."

"A SWAT team?! Is that necessary?" Lauren wrung her hands, looking from Steele's grim face to Rafe's equally dark one. "Please, I don't want to see him get hurt. We don't know what he has or hasn't done. If Spence's death wasn't an accident…" She shook her head, grief rippling over pale cheeks. "Until we have hard proof, I can't—I won't—believe it. Even if he's stolen money…it doesn't mean he did anything to Spencer. And he's still my brother. He's all I have left of my family."

"Well, I mean, you do have me," Fallon said dryly, coming into the office behind Steele.

Lauren twitched as if she'd been slapped. It was so heartbreaking. Every single moment with Fallon and her parents had torn at me.

"You know that's not what I meant, Fallon. You're the

most important person in the world to me. Adam is all I have left of my roots."

Fallon didn't look like she believed her, but as she passed her mother, I saw the love and anguish in Lauren's expression. She had a lot of work to do before she could earn back her daughter's trust, just as much as Rafe did. Fallon felt abandoned, and even as much as I loved Rafe, I couldn't blame her for those feelings.

Lauren swallowed hard and looked at Rafe. "Last night, I tried to understand why he would do this to me, to us. He idolized Grandpa, and they spent a lot of time together. Grandpa Joe was bitter about everything that had happened between our families. He'd been the one to find his father after he committed suicide, and he'd watched the Harringtons flourish while his family lost more and more. He grumbled a lot about it, even with me, but maybe it affected Adam more than I realized. If he did all of this… He just needs help. He needs deprogramming or whatever they call it when people are brainwashed."

Rafe's eyes were dark, and I was pretty damn sure he didn't agree. If Adam killed his brother, he wouldn't give Adam absolution. He'd be looking to send him away for life. But I also saw, just as I had last night, he felt somehow responsible for all of this, as if Adam's decisions had been his fault.

He looked at Steele. "I'll have the jet fueled. I can be in LA in just over an hour."

Lauren looked relieved. Her phone vibrated in her hand, and she looked down and then up. "Marielle is asking about breakfast." She rubbed her forehead. "Fallon, normally I'd have you go help out at the bunkhouse and old homestead, but I'd like you to stay inside as much as possible until the wedding. You'll help with the bride and bridesmaids, and I'll go down and deal with the groom and the families."

"Fine," Fallon said and turned on her heel and left.

Lauren watched her daughter leave, regret pouring from her. Then she turned back to Rafe, saying quietly, "Thank you. I know… I know if he's really done any of this, he doesn't deserve any of our grace, but I appreciate you doing this as a favor for me after all we've been through."

Then, she left, and I despised how she'd used the guilt Rafe felt against him. That she'd gotten him to do one more thing for them when, in my opinion, none of them had done anything for him. They'd watched him walk away and never demanded he come home. It made me want to do what I'd just told him I wouldn't do—break my promise to Lauren to help her today in order to go with him to LA. To make sure he didn't face one more thing alone, but also because the thought of him confronting Adam at the hotel made acid boil in my stomach.

Steele must have felt the same way, because he grumbled, "This isn't a good idea, Marquess. Let the authorities handle it."

"I agree," he responded, and the roiling in my stomach slowed. "I said I'd go to LA, but I didn't say I wasn't letting the police arrest him. I'm not angry enough, or dumb enough, to storm a hotel room if he's the one who shot at us yesterday. I didn't want to say it to Lauren, but what happens at the hotel today is on him. I just want to be there when the police question him. I want to be able to look him in the eye when I ask him about my brother."

I felt the relief that journeyed over Steele's face wash over me as well.

Rafe squeezed my hand. "I'd still prefer it if you and Fallon weren't here. If there's a chance this wasn't Adam…if it's Puzo…" he trailed off.

"If it's Puzo, he wants you, not Sadie or your daughter," Steele said. "You leaving the ranch gives him less of a reason to retaliate."

Rafe didn't look like he agreed or that he was happy about any of the choices before us, but then again, neither was I. The last thing I wanted was for us to be apart. I'd told him I was staying if he stayed and going if he was going, and I'd meant it. Reading my thoughts in that way he was good at, he ran a finger along my cheek.

"Jim's right. You're better off staying away from me until this is over."

"That's an argument we need to have when we've got

more time, Slick. We should be fine here," I told him, but even as I said it, the sound of gunshots flashed in my head, almost real enough to make me wince. I'd wished I'd had a gun, both last night and the day Chainsaw had taken Mila, and maybe having one now would help steady me. I glanced from Steele to Rafe. "Either of you have an extra handgun you can loan me?"

Rafe huffed out a laugh as if he'd expect nothing less from me, but Steele looked uneasy.

"A dartboard isn't the only target I can hit. I grew up shooting guns with my brothers. I have a steady hand and good aim. It would reassure me if I had something on me. Something I could use to protect myself and Fallon."

"We have twenty men arriving within the hour. Some of Puzo's men are already here. And Wylee's men will be here this afternoon. There'll be plenty of guns on site, and I have no desire for one itchy trigger finger to start a Hatfields-and-McCoys type of shootout," Steele said dryly.

Rafe ignored him. "I'll get you a gun, but Jim is staying here, so you won't need it." When the man started to protest, Rafe kept going. "I'll take Barry with me. I'd rather you be here with my family, keeping an eye on Puzo."

Silence bloomed while the two men argued with their eyes in a way that told me they were much more than employer and employee. I'd suspected it. I'd heard the affection in Rafe's voice every time he'd mentioned the man, but seeing it was a relief. At least there'd been one person on Rafe's side in a sea of people who'd just let him walk away.

"Let me catch Barry up and call Wylee again," Steele said, heading for the door. "I'll meet you at the car."

Rafe drew me toward the bookshelf he'd splintered the night before. "Let me show you the safe and give you the code in case you need something more. He pressed a rosette on the corner of the shelf's frame, and the entire unit opened to reveal a large vault door with a round, old-fashioned lock like in a bank. He told me the code as he spun the wheel and then pulled the thick metal door wide. Inside was a room made of solid cement and bricks. One wall was covered with metal shelves holding cardboard boxes while the one at the back was layered with glass cabinets holding an array of weapons.

"That's a lot of guns," I said. We had a handful on the ranch for necessity, but neither of my brothers hunted, and we didn't offer it as an excursion for our guests.

"When the diamonds were found," Rafe explained, "there was some trouble. It was the Great Depression, and people were sneaking onto the property, not only to get into the mines but to dig holes everywhere and anywhere, thinking they'd randomly find treasure. My great-grandfather had to increase the security, and it got pretty heated from what I understand. He ended up carrying a gun at all times."

I gravitated to a cabinet with the handguns and a tiny revolver that would almost fit in the palm of my hand. "What's this?"

"4.25mm Liliput. According to my dad, Great-grandpa Alasdair's brother brought it home from World War II. If the story is true, he took it from a German he caught trying to infiltrate the Allied lines. It's a straight shooter. Small enough for you to hide. Ammunition is pretty impossible to find these days, but last I remember, we had some bullets left." He pulled open several drawers before removing a decrepit box.

"I don't want to use an antique worth a fortune with only a handful of bullets left in existence. Give me something else," I told him.

"I don't give two shits if you use the gun and the ammo to protect yourself or my family, Tennessee. Take it, tuck it away, and use it if you need to. Just be careful. There's no safety."

I pocketed the bullets and carefully placed the empty gun in my pocket until I could find something to holster it with. When I turned around, Rafe was right behind me. His hands went to either side of me on the counter, caging me against the shelves.

The space between us was instantly charged, full of heat and electricity, zipping neurons flashing in the air with enough force I could almost see them.

"I hate that you're staying." Every syllable he uttered

sounded tortured.

I lifted my chin. "I hate that you're going, especially to see Adam, so I guess we're even."

Silence drifted between us. The I love yous we'd shared dangled out there again, tormenting and soothing at the same time. I lifted onto my toes and kissed him softly. Not with heat, not with passion, but with a gentle promise.

"Go," I whispered against his lips. "Hopefully, you'll be there and back before the wedding even starts this evening."

He ran a finger along my cheek. "It's extra incentive to come home as quickly as possible, because if I'm not here, all of Puzo's damn relatives and thugs are going to want to dance with you."

I snorted. "I'm the help, Rafe, not a guest."

"You're our guest," he grunted out. "And believe me, it wouldn't stop them from asking you to dance…or asking you for more."

"Jealous?"

"I already told you I was jealous of the two bozos you danced with at The Fortress. Now that I've had you to myself, the idea of any other man putting his hands on you makes me want to rip their fingers off one at a time."

A little thrill went up my spine, and heat pooled low in my stomach at the idea of Rafe going nuts because someone touched me. Wouldn't I feel the same if he was dancing with another person? If they held him tight? I'd want to rip them to shreds too.

"I'll make you a deal," I told him. He raised a brow as his finger continued to trail down my neck where it lingered on the curve of my collarbone. "You come back to me in one piece, and I promise you can have all my dances tonight."

"Just tonight?" he grumbled, leaning in, kissing the soft spot below my ear that made my knees weak.

"I can't promise you *all* my dances from here to forever."

"If you think I have any intention of watching while you dance with some other man after you told me you loved me, you can think again."

"Well, my brothers like to kick it up with me at times, and my father is a damn good line dancer. Are you saying I can't dance with them?" I almost laughed when I could see him considering just how much even that would bother him. "Can you even line dance, Slick? Cuz I'm not giving it up."

"I've got moves, Tennessee. Ones you haven't seen yet," he said. The heat of his breath coasted over my skin, making my entire being tremble with yearning for another kiss. Another touch. "We still have lots to figure out about each other, but one thing I can promise you is, if I'm in your life, you'll be saving all your dances for me. You'll *want* mine to be the only hands on you. The only body tucked up against yours."

"Hmm," I taunted, tapping my chin. "I'll have to wait and see if you can back up those words with the appropriate action."

His mouth was enticingly hot as it hovered near my lips. "We still had a wager we never finished, darling, about who would be begging first. How about I bet I can make you beg from just a dance? That you'll be pleading for relief even though there are people watching us. You'll want me to take you right there on the dance floor. I won't. Because no one else gets to see your face when you climax ever again, but I can promise, you'll want me to."

Just when I thought he was going to kiss me, to slant his delectable, torturous mouth over mine, he stepped back. I wanted him now, just as he'd said, not caring who was watching or that the safe door was wide open and anyone could walk by. I wanted him deep inside me. I wanted him whispering my name and demanding I give him every piece of me.

I swallowed hard, raised a brow, and put on my very best flirtatious smile. "You get back here safe and sound, Slick, and we'll see which of us ends the night begging."

Then, I ducked under his arm and sauntered out of the room with my hips swaying. I was rewarded by him swearing under his breath, and my smile grew.

It had been a raise I wasn't sure I had the cards to back up, because I was already trembling with need for him, but I'd do my best. I'd give him a run for his money and hope we could spend another night skin on skin before reality hit, and I had to do the one thing I didn't want to do anymore—get on a plane and fly away.

Chapter Twenty-nine

Sadie

UNIVERSE
Performed by Kelsea Ballerini

I didn't have much time to think about Rafe and me, or Rafe in LA confronting Adam, or what would happen after my plane left the next day, because the preparation for the wedding kept me going nonstop. The work was soothing, but it also made me wonder how Lauren had handled it without the extra pair of hands I provided. It wasn't until after the bride and groom had said their 'I dos' by the waterfall with the sun setting around them, and the party had moved to the tents up by the corrals, that I finally stopped to catch a breath.

The temperatures, that had remained pleasantly in the low eighties all day, drifted downward into the chilly territory as twilight settled over the land. A wind brushed over me as I stood at the edge of the dance floor, watching the bride and groom's first dance.

I looked down at my phone, hoping to hear Rafe had landed at the airport just outside of town. He'd texted me to say he was on his way over an hour ago. It had been another brief, concise, to-the-point text like all the ones he'd sent throughout the day, keeping me abreast of what was happening. If I hadn't heard the *I love you* he'd said that morning, the messages would have seemed cold and detached, but the simple fact he took the time to send them to me because he knew I'd be worried showed the depths of how much he cared.

Unfortunately, by the time the SWAT team had arrived at

the hotel by the airport, Adam had been gone. Rafe had spent the day with the LA police as they'd tried to find him, but he'd vanished from sight again.

"Is he on his way?" Lauren asked, stepping up next to me with a clipboard in her hand.

"He should be here any minute."

Lauren looked more put together, more beautiful tonight, than at any other time since I'd arrived. She wore a vivid magenta dress partnered with a pair of white cowboy boots that matched the ones Fallon was wearing. The teen and her friend were huddled on the other side of the dance floor, whispering and sending darted looks in Parker's direction.

He was not dressed for a wedding. Like all of Steele's security team, he was in black cargo pants and a black T-shirt with military boots on his feet. With his dark hair and gray eyes, he looked like he was made to blend into the shadows. If I'd been Fallon's age, I might have had a crush on him too.

The marquee was brimming with the security tonight, just like the ranch had been overflowing with the teams all day. While Rafe's men had been in black outfits like Parker, Lorenzo's had worn dark suits and sunglasses like some sort of Secret Service wannabes. The two groups had been hyperaware, eyes scanning the surroundings, bodies tight and ready to shift into action, but they'd given each other a wide berth.

Seeing all the highly trained men with guns hovering, I'd felt silly requesting my own weapon, but it had given me a piece of my control back the shooting the night before had stolen away. It also brought me some sort of strange comfort, simply knowing it was a part of Rafe's history that was touching my skin. This evening, I'd found a wide band that had allowed me to tuck the Liliput to my thigh under the lavender sundress I'd bought in Vegas—the same one I'd worn the night we'd found the rattler in Rafe's bed.

Lauren sighed as she watched her daughter. "She's going to have her heart broken if she keeps sending him googly eyes, but right now, she doesn't want to hear anything I have to say about Parker or anything else. She's furious at me for not seeing what she saw happening between Adam and Spence. I'm not sure she'll ever forgive me for how I abandoned her this year, and I'm not sure she should."

My heart cracked for all of them all over again, and even though I was frustrated with her for using Rafe's guilt against him and sending him on the hunt for Adam, I couldn't stop myself from trying to ease her concerns. "If it helps, I don't think you have to worry about her and Parker. She knows he's too old for her, and he certainly doesn't look at her in the same way."

"Sometimes, that only makes you try harder though. Don't you remember being a teenager and wanting someone so bad it felt like your insides were going to shred if you didn't have them?" she asked, turning from watching her daughter to me.

For the first time, I felt her truly assessing me. Not as the person who could help her with the ranch, or even as a guest, but as the person Rafe had been kissing.

"Honestly, no. I liked the boys I dated in high school, but it was all carefree teasing. None of the angst you read about or see in teen dramas. We were all just out to have fun most of the time. Didn't prevent me from getting into mischief that drove my parents and my brothers batty, but it was still mostly lighthearted."

"But what's happening between you and Rafe isn't lighthearted fun, right?" The hint of defensiveness in her tone took me by surprise. I was almost certain it had nothing to do with jealousy but an actual protectiveness for someone she cared about. Did she realize Rafe was as clueless as her daughter about how much she cared?

"I've never felt for anyone what I feel for Rafe. Is it crazy to think that everything that started all those decades ago with our families was supposed to happen just to lead me to him?"

Lauren smiled. It didn't happen often, and she was stunning when she did. In those moments, I could see how both Rafe and Spence would have fallen head over heels for her.

"I don't know what Rafe told you about what happened

between us…" She stopped, as if to see if I'd offer anything up, and I didn't. I knew some, but not enough, and I wanted to hear her side of the story. "The truth of the matter is, I loved them both. Spencer and I had a connection we couldn't deny. I never had to fall for him. We just loved each other from the get-go, so when he went off to college and broke up with me so we could see other people and make sure the love we felt wasn't just friendship, I was devastated. How could he ever think it wasn't? I went off the deep end a bit, but Rafe was there to catch me. And I didn't have to fall for him either because I'd always loved him too. If I'd had my choice, I would have kept them both."

I must have made some sort of noise at her shocking confession because she laughed softly. "I know. How forbidden of me to think it, right? But I would have been happy living here with the three of us together in some sort of polyamorous relationship. I didn't want to choose between them. But that would never have worked for Rafe or Spence. Their dad had fostered this stupid competition between them from the time Rafe was born. And worse, Kade always showed he was rooting for Spencer simply because he was the firstborn son. Or maybe it was because Rafe didn't fall into line and believe he was less just because he'd been born second. Either way, it hurt them both—deeply.

"Rafe wanted what Spence had, and Spence wanted what he perceived as Rafe's freedom to choose. They both envied each other. Spence never expected Rafe and me to hook up though, and when he found out I was pregnant with Rafe's child…" She shook her head, sadness in every syllable as she said, "I destroyed the tenuous bond they'd been able to forge even as their dad had tried to prevent it."

The music stopped and started, families filing onto the dance floor. The bride was now with my cousin, the groom with his mother. Maisey and Fallon joined the crowd, smiling and laughing and moving their bodies. I wanted to dance along with them. I wanted to let the rhythm wash away my worries. But while I hadn't exactly promised Rafe I wouldn't dance without him, after what he'd said in the safe, I didn't want any other body but his tucked up against me.

"What made you choose Spence instead of Rafe?" I asked.

"Spencer threw me in the car and started driving to Vegas." She laughed. "I mean, I could have said no. I'm not sure he would have let me, but he also wouldn't have forced me. I don't know if that makes any sense."

I thought of the way Rafe had taken control of everything between us and yet given me a way out at every step, and I nodded.

"I guess Spencer and I both knew we belonged here on the ranch and that our brothers needed something more. They needed the world to bow down before them," she said, and I heard the pain in her words as she thought about Adam.

"Your brother came home," I said.

"After Kade died, Spencer had a hard time keeping track of the money and accounting. Things were falling through the cracks, and Adam had lost a big account at the financial firm he'd worked for. He took a hit to his ego, and I told him to come home and regroup. I didn't think he'd stay, but he did, and he seemed happy here. We all seemed happy here."

Not all. Rafe hadn't been here. He'd been cut out, even if it had been by his own request. He'd created an entire empire and made a boatload of money, but from the very first moment we'd met, I sensed he'd been as lonely as I'd been. The fact that none of them had chosen him first, or insisted he come home, made me even more determined to show him someone would. That I would.

I swallowed hard, thinking about what that meant. Of the things—and people—I'd have to give up to do so. It hurt, but not as badly as it could have, because I'd have Rafe. Because I'd be doing it for the glimmering, shiny gift that was him and me—us.

As much as I despised asking her my next question, even thinking it, I still had to know the answer. So, I choked out, "Did you think you could have him back now? Rafe?"

Lauren looked startled by my question, and she was quick to shake her head, but there was a look on her face that said she was considering it. It made me want to unleash my claws and take aim. She was quiet for a long moment, watching Fallon and Maisey as they swung each other around, faces alight with happiness.

After too many seconds had passed for my tense heart, she finally said, "No. I lost Rafe when I chose Spence. He'd never give me a second chance with his heart. He doesn't give second chances easily. Besides, Fallon would despise me even more if I tried to make her dad mine. She loved them both too, completely and adoringly. She had two incredible dads, and while she had to share Spence with me, she's never had to share Rafe, and she likes it that way."

In giving up any chance with Rafe for her daughter, it was the first time since I'd arrived that I saw her doing something for Fallon instead of the other way around.

An alarm on her phone buzzed, and she looked down at it with a tired sigh. "Time for the cake cutting."

"Do you want help?" I asked.

She huffed out a half laugh. "You're good at that—helping. So much so people don't even realize everything you've done until after the fact. But I've noticed, Sadie. How you've made Rafe smile, and the way you've been there for Fallon. I saw how much of the load you took this week when you should have been our guest. Thank you. Thank you for all of it. But mostly for giving Rafe someone to love again. That's the best thing you've done all week."

And then she walked away before I could respond. I wasn't sure I could have anyway. My heart was in my throat. My stomach full of butterflies. I had no clue what my life would look like, how I'd spend my days while Rafe worked, but the most important thing was to wake up at his side and go to sleep tucked up against him. Love was what mattered. It was how I could make a difference in this world. I could be there for the one person who truly needed me.

The realization brought joy but also a fair amount of panic.

A body filled in Lauren's empty spot next to me, and I turned to see my cousin offering me a glass of champagne. I took it but didn't sip at it. After everything I'd learned about him from Gia and Rafe, I didn't trust him. Add in how he'd had me followed and all but threatened the man I loved, and it made it so I didn't even like him.

"Little cousin, I'm upset you've taken something from me I thought was mine."

My brows went up. What the hell was he talking about? The jewelry? I hadn't told him I had it, so how did he know?

"As far as I know, Lorenzo, I haven't claimed anything that was yours. If either of us has a reason to be upset, it's me, for multiple reasons, starting with how you had me followed."

That strange stillness that always surrounded him evaporated in a fairly loud chuckle. It wasn't the dark and broody one I loved from Rafe, and it wasn't the tense one Lorenzo had given me when we first met. It was almost light. "Marquess and Steele figured it out? Interesting."

He drank some of his champagne, waved at mine. "Lighten up, cousin, it's a wedding." When I still didn't drink, he turned serious. "He's poisoned you against me, I see. No one trusts anyone these days."

I scoffed. "Because you're the trusting sort?"

He shrugged. "You're right. I'm not."

After a beat, I asked, "So what is it you think I took?"

Puzo slowly waved a hand at the dance floor and the buildings beyond it. "I wanted the ranch, the entire community Rafe tossed aside without a second glance. Now, he won't walk away from it because you reminded him of what he had waiting for him."

"He'd kill you and himself before he'd let you have the ranch. That has nothing to do with me and everything to do with the two of you."

He pondered my words before saying, "Perhaps." After another few seconds, he added on, "He never believed me, but the reason my cousin's men could never turn on me like the feds hoped wasn't because they were terrified of what I'd do to them. It was simply because I hadn't been involved. I didn't know what Ike and Theresa were up to and would have put a stop to it if I'd found out.

"Since I took over the reins of the family business, I've done everything in my power to legitimize us. Ike's side of the family was pissed that our grandfather left me in control. They thought I was weak because I wouldn't do things the way our family before us had. Unfortunately, Rafe got in the middle of a war he didn't realize was being waged." I made a sound of disbelief, and he continued, "Don't get me wrong, I don't like Rafe's cocky ass, and I'd be happy to see him take a fall, but not at the risk of losing everything my family has built."

"I think he has a scar along his rib cage that proves otherwise," I said dryly.

"Yes," he said quietly, weighing every word before he spoke again. "An Italian family always gets revenge for crimes against their own."

Was he basically admitting he'd put a hit out on Rafe? I drew in a sharp breath, and Lorenzo heard it.

"You misunderstand. Ike may be in jail, but he has brothers and sisters. They're not here tonight because of our own disagreements, but plenty of my family hates Rafe Marquess for having put Ike behind bars. At the time, they demanded I get revenge, but I wanted nothing to do with murder. Instead, I came here, to Rivers, trying to understand the man who'd gone toe to toe with us. And I found things I'd never expected. Untarnished land. A community where the Marquess and Harrington names held respect not based on fear but based on years of good deeds. For the first time in my life, I was jealous of someone. I wanted what he'd had and tossed away.

"Our family has had lives in our hands that we crushed, businesses we decimated and then recreated. We have dirty city streets and dark alleys. Seeing what Rafe threw away made me determined to make it mine. What better way to get revenge for my family? I wanted the men in this town, the businesses, to look at me with gratitude and respect that was given because of the helping hand I'd extended rather than the slap I'd delivered. And I would have had it if you hadn't shown up."

Fallon and Maisey had made their way over to my side of

the dance floor, and with a darted glance in Lorenzo's direction, Fallon spun toward me and tugged on my hands. "Come dance with us, Sadie."

We all knew what she was doing, pulling me away from my cousin because of Rafe's hatred for him. If I hadn't promised my last dance, all my dances, to her father, I would have easily gone with her. Instead, I hesitated.

She pouted. "Come on, show us how it's done in Tennessee."

I laughed and then turned to hand my untouched champagne glass back to my cousin. "Thanks for trying to set the record straight. Still doesn't explain why you had me followed, and it still doesn't make me trust you, but"—I shrugged— "thanks for trying."

Then, I joined the two teens, and we shook our hips and raised our hands and celebrated like maybe only farm kids truly knew how to do. Because the work was done for the day, and it would start all over the next, but in these few minutes between night and morning, freedom and joy existed. A few hours untethered to endless tasks.

That was how I felt—untethered and in between. As if I had one foot out of my old life and one foot heading toward the new without it having arrived yet. I was in the great in-between place where demons lurked and lives could still be shifted.

I glanced in Lorenzo's direction, but he wasn't watching me. He was smiling at Marielle, who was slow dancing with Nicky, love drifting around them. I wasn't sure what to make of my cousin, of any of it, but Rafe's scars were very real and the Puzo family was the reason he had them. Just that was enough to ensure I stayed as far away from my cousin as I could.

Chapter Thirty

Rafe

I FOUND YOU
Performed by Nate Smith

By the time Barry and I had gotten to LA and made it to the LAPD headquarters, the SWAT team had gone into the hotel where Adam had been staying and come up empty. Frustration eked into every pore, not only because we'd missed him but because I'd left the people I loved behind for nothing.

I spent the rest of the morning and early afternoon pacing the halls of the police station while they sent officers scurrying in all directions, trying to locate him. Even though he'd been staying near the airport, Adam hadn't purchased an airline ticket in his name. He also hadn't bought a train ticket, bus fare, or rented a car, and yet his Mercedes had been left behind in the hotel parking lot.

The police assumed he'd somehow headed for the border. If he had the money he'd stolen from the ranch tucked into an anonymous offshore account, he could live for years in some non-extradition country. I was certain what he'd stolen in the last five years had only been the tip of the iceberg. If he started the moment he'd arrived back at the ranch, he likely had a million stashed away. And if he'd been smart and invested it rather than tossed it away in some ridiculous poker game with Puzo, he could have a much more sizeable amount waiting for him.

The only comfort I received from Adam's disappearance

was knowing he wouldn't be anywhere near Sadie or Fallon. Perhaps we were all safe.

Unless he'd hired someone to come after me.

Which brought me back to Puzo and his thug, Nero. Was that why Adam had been cozied up to Lorenzo? For his connections? For some sort of twisted revenge against the Harringtons? Or had he hoped to get even more money from a deal with Puzo?

All the unknowns meant I was still wound tight and anxious to get back to the two women who held my heart. Every instinct told me I was still missing something, and it frustrated me that I couldn't figure it out.

And that wasn't the only thing frustrating me. I'd spent half the day harder than a rock whenever I'd thought about Sadie and the way she'd thrown my taunt back at me before swaying out of the vault this morning.

I might not be able to solve the mystery of Adam or Puzo, but I had every intention of easing the tension Sadie had caused.

As soon as I stalked into the marquee, with its abundance of flowers, flickering candles, and elegantly clad guests, my eyes landed on the woman who'd tormented my thoughts all day. She was laughing and spinning around the dance floor with my daughter and Maisey. The way Sadie put her entire body into it, throwing her head back and exposing the long column of her neck, only increased my wild desire to claim her. I wanted to litter kisses along that smooth skin and suck on the pulse beating at the base, just as I had when she'd been tucked into my bed.

Movement on the other side of the dance floor brought Puzo into my line of sight. His focus was completely on Sadie too, and the intensity of his look triggered the savage beast inside me. Instead of stalking over to Sadie and pulling her into my arms as I'd intended, I crossed the floor to him.

"Keep your hands off," I snarled.

Puzo lifted a brow, and I loathed how I'd repeatedly given him my emotions this week. Worse, knowing how I felt about Sadie gave him one more thing to strike at me with and she could be hurt because of it.

"I'm more than happy to do so, if you'll tell her to do the same. If we wash our hands of each other, everyone can walk away friends," Puzo replied.

"What in the hell is that supposed to mean?"

"She's got the jewels, and that will have to be enough. She can't have any other piece of our pie."

I despised feeling confused as much as I detested my lack of control, but that was exactly what I was. How did Puzo know about the jewelry? Why did he even care about it? I couldn't see all the cards on the table in front of me, and rather than pretend I did, I gave him my honesty instead. "I'm not following you."

"The stolen jewels, Marquess. Keep up. She can keep those as her inheritance, but she won't get anything else. Carolyn Puzo forfeited it when she walked away from her family."

The only way he could know about the jewels was if Adam had shared it, or Puzo was watching us closer than I thought. Had Steele scanned the estate for listening devices? Cameras that didn't belong to us? The knots in my stomach grew more knots on top of them.

Puzo had collected his information on me and mine, piece by piece. He'd pushed a few of the pawns along the game board, just to make sure he had everything right where he wanted. What I didn't know was why the hell he thought Sadie was after his money.

"I'm afraid the stolen jewels don't belong to Sadie either. They belong to my family."

Puzo raised a brow and tugged on his tuxedo sleeve. "Actually, they don't. They were supposed to come to us as payment for gambling debts."

My gaze narrowed on him. "How do you figure that?"

"Your great-grandaddy owed the Puzo family thousands. He had two choices. He could either sell the ranch or sell the jewels to pay off his debt. In order to save face, we arranged for the jewelry to be stolen. Harrington worked the deal to loan them to the movie studio while we had fakes made. Carolyn was already working at the studio, so it was a slam dunk for her to swap them out, but then one of them double-crossed us."

"We're talking eighty years ago, Puzo. How can you even know all of this?"

"Italian families have long memories and the patience to exact retribution at just the right time. Harrington was supposed to get reimbursed from the insurance company, and our family would sell the jewels to pay off the debt. Any profit, if there was any, would be split between Harrington and my grandfather. No one expected Carolyn to betray her family. No one expected her to fall in love and run off. My grandfather wasn't even sure if it was Carolyn who'd betrayed him, or if your great-granddaddy double-crossed him, killed her, and dumped the body.

"I don't believe you," I hissed.

"Gambling runs in both sides of this family, doesn't it?" Puzo said, glancing to where Lauren was supervising the cake cutting. "After all, it's how the Harringtons ended up with this land to begin with, isn't it? Don't act like you're from some noble stock. Your family grabbed what it could, just like mine did."

The fury I felt at his attack on a family name that I'd long since tossed aside shocked me. And yet, he wasn't wrong— Alasdair had won the ranch on a gamble. But what he said also didn't line up with what I'd read in Beatrice's journal.

According to her, the movie studio hadn't had insurance, and Alasdair had been out hundreds of thousands of dollars when they'd been taken. There was no way he could have known the movie studio would offer up shares in the company as compensation, so he wouldn't have had the money to pay off any so-called gambling debts. Beatrice had said Alasdair had been furious about the swapped jewels. Her refusal to see Joe after they'd come back from Hollywood made me suspect this was much more about Joe's betrayal than my great-grandfather being dirty.

"You're lying," I said, turning to glare at him. "It wasn't my great-grandfather who owed your family money. It was Adam's. The entire thing was Joe Hurly's scheme, wasn't it? It backfired when he tried to pass off the fake gems to my great-grandfather, not realizing Alasdair would have them assessed before they even left the studio lot. Hurly likely thought he'd have days, weeks, maybe even years before anyone realized they'd been replaced."

Puzo's face darkened, and I knew I was right.

"But you couldn't have known Sadie had the jewelry when she showed up. Like you said, maybe Hurly was the one who'd double-crossed your family. So why would you care if the Hatleys claimed to be part of your family? What are you really worried about? Was there a clause in your grandfather's will that entitled her to a share of the family's wealth?"

Puzo didn't move, didn't react, but I heard a hint of anger in his voice. "As you said, it's been over eighty years. No court would give the Hatleys anything if they came sniffing."

"Maybe. Maybe not. So why would you be nervous, then? How big of a piece would they be entitled to? Half? A quarter? The way your business has been hemmed in with the FBI watching you, even ten percent might hurt."

Only the way he slowly straightened the boutonniere in his pocket proved I'd rattled him. "Carolyn couldn't claim her inheritance unless she came back and married the man my grandfather had picked for her, and she would've had to bring the stolen diamonds with her."

Italian families have long memories and the patience to exact retribution at just the right time.

"Did you know who I was when I first came to work for you?"

He gave me a look that said the question was stupid. "We do background checks on all our employees."

I'd stepped right into a nearly century-old vendetta at work and hadn't even known it. What else didn't I know? How could I protect the people I loved without all the information? "I bet some of those background checks aren't entirely legal. I bet they cross privacy lines all over the place. I bet you told Nero Lancaster to dig up all the dirty laundry he could on me when I first graced your doorstep. What were you hoping for? That the jewels would suddenly reappear, and you could somehow right an old family wrong?"

"Was I hoping to get the hundred thousand dollars owed to us, with eighty years of interest? Sure." Puzo glanced around the ranch. "But then I decided I'd rather have this instead."

He was trying to distract me by bringing up the ranch and the community he'd worked his way into inch by inch.

"Except, the Hurly family owed your family the money back then, not mine," I said, a calm settling in over me. "And you'd never be able to legally ask for it in a court of law."

"You're the one who insists it was Hurly who owed us the money, not me."

"If you've got proof it was Alasdair Harrington, cough it up, but you don't. I bet there isn't a single marker signed by a Harrington, but I bet you have quite a few signed by a Hurly. You never said yesterday exactly how much Adam owes you now." Puzo tried to move around me, but I cut off his escape. "What was the agreement you made with Adam? Bankrupt the ranch so it would allow you to buy it on the cheap? Every dollar he cut off the top of the purchase price by running it into the ground would be a dollar off his debt?"

When he shifted ever so slightly in discomfort, I knew I'd nailed it. Puzo wanted the ranch for whatever twisted reason he could come up with, maybe simply revenge on me and mine, and Adam wanted to burn it to the ground. Adam hated this place because it represented a century of Hurly family failures.

Some of those missing pieces had clicked into place with this conversation, but not all.

I smiled at Lorenzo—a dark smile full of promise—as I said, "Too bad you'll never get your hands on the ranch now. I've got more than enough money to keep it going from now until we're both dead and buried. Whatever it loses, I'll cover. Neither you nor Adam will ever get another slice of what belongs to my family. Italians aren't the only ones with long memories and a thirst for vengeance."

Adam's great-grandfather had lost the land in a poker match, and Adam had tried to grab it back, but he'd lost that gamble just like his great-granddaddy had. Puzo was right. Addiction ran in the family. Addiction and obsession.

Puzo glanced out at his family spilling through the tent, his profile stoic. When he finally twisted his head back to look me in the eye, the glimpse of exhaustion I caught was surprising. "I didn't need to motivate or help Adam with his plans. I just had to wait patiently enough for him to run the ranch into the ground so I could buy it on the cheap. Now that it isn't going to happen, Adam and I do have some outstanding business to take care of, and unlike my grandfather, I do have a contract in hand and a way to claim it in court."

"Adam's debt isn't mine or my family's," I seethed.

"Are you sure about that?" he said and then strolled away toward the crowd gathered around the cake table.

I took a moment to control the rage flowing through me at Puzo and Adam and decades of feuding family nastiness. Maybe my family hadn't earned the ranch in the most upright way, but we'd worked the land and grown it into what it was today. We'd put money into the community when we'd been flush. We'd done our best to pay some of it forward. Hell, the foundation my company ran gave millions each year.

But not to Rivers, the devil inside me taunted.

I'd distanced myself from the town as much as I had my family and the ranch. But I could change that. I could make some of it right again.

With the music stopped, my daughter, her friend, and Sadie had moved to watch the bride and groom as they sweetly fed each other cake. I glanced around, ensuring my detail was in place, and found Parker across the tent, his eyes glued on the three women.

I joined him, asking, "Everything's been quiet here?"

"Yep. But I think you might want to lock up your women before anyone gets the wrong idea." His voice was dark and broody as his gaze shot warnings to some of the guests who were sending appreciative looks at my daughter and the siren I'd fallen head over heels for.

After shooting some of my own bolts in those men's directions, I asked, "Where's your dad?"

"Hacking away at his computer. He thinks he might be able to find Adam when no one else can. He did say he's crossed some paths that show Puzo is searching for Adam too."

I shouldn't care what happened to Adam, especially if he'd killed Spence, and yet Lauren's plea from this morning still lingered in my soul. Her sad statement that they were the last of the Hurly family, just like Fallon was the last of the Harringtons, had hit somewhere deep inside me. Even before I'd left the ranch, I hadn't cared about our name the way my father had. Maybe it had been the way he'd pounded into me that Spence would be the one to carry on all the Harrington traditions that had forced me to choose my mother's name as much as it had been a child's defiant devotion to the one parent who'd loved him. Whatever the reason, I'd never considered before today what the weight of carrying both Dad's name *and* his expectations had been like for my brother—a weight that had been passed down to my daughter.

Fallon turned her head in our direction, and when she saw me, her face lit up. It was both a cut and a balm to my soul that she was actually smiling at me. She rarely looked at me with such joy anymore. The need to be right there next to both her and Sadie had my feet moving, but I stopped before I got too far, turning back to Parker. "When do you have to go back?"

"I report for duty on Friday."

My head and soul were torn on how to protect the women I loved, but getting them away from me and the ranch and the hate and retribution we both seemed to draw had to be the best thing to do until things settled down. "If I can convince Sadie to leave and take Fallon with her, would you escort them to Tennessee before heading to Virginia?"

"I can do whatever you need as long as I'm on base by oh-five-hundred on Friday."

"If this drags on longer than that, I can arrange for

someone else to take your place."

He gave me a curt nod, and I turned back to the two females who were calling to me with their smiles. From the moment I'd held her as a newborn, Fallon had taken ownership of a portion of my heart, and I'd never expected anyone else to own the other half. I thought the rest of it had become a dead muscle, and yet Sadie had brought it back to life.

I pulled Fallon into me with one arm and linked my fingers with Sadie's on the other side. "You both look beautiful tonight."

Fallon beamed at me, and it hit me right in the chest all over again.

The DJ kicked in a new song—slow and sensual—and the crowd around the cake table dissipated. Some slid back onto the dance floor while others grabbed dessert plates and headed for the tables. When Maisey dragged Fallon away to get cake, I turned to Sadie, wrapped her into my arms, and swayed us to the music right where we stood.

I ran my hand up her back, pushing her into me until I felt every soft curve pressed up against every inch of me. Until the rhythm of her heart echoed the beat of mine. A fluttering beat I wanted to capture and hold on to forever.

"You promised me all your dances from now on," I whispered in her ear. "And yet, I saw you dancing."

"You're remembering it wrong, Slick. I simply said you'd get my dances tonight, and look at that, we're dancing."

I swirled her out and around, and when I brought her back, I drew her even closer. Our hips shifted in perfect unison, as if we'd always been together, as if we'd spent a lifetime dancing with each other. We'd been that way in bed too, finding each other's rhythm instinctively. She might be a hell of a lot younger than me, but Sadie and I fit. I couldn't shake it. Didn't want to. I just had to figure out how to keep her and meet all my responsibilities, to which the ranch had now been permanently added.

I dipped her backward, kissed her lightly, and then swung her into my arms again, all while keeping the beat. I pressed my groin into her, and she let out a little breathy gasp.

"No one else should be able to touch you this way, Tennessee. I'm willing to negotiate. Line dancing with the men in your family is acceptable, but this, these moves with us tucked together, have to be mine and mine alone."

Her eyes turned the same deep shade of blue they'd been when I was deep inside her, and it took everything I had not to embarrass myself amongst the guests. I'd said she'd be begging me to take her on the dance floor, but now our roles were reversed. As much as I didn't like losing control, I'd found myself not only losing it repeatedly with her but willingly handing it over.

Sadie twined her fingers through the hair at my nape as she aligned herself into my every groove. She lifted onto her toes and kissed the corner of my mouth.

"How about if I promise you all my last dances?" she offered.

I shook my head. "Not good enough. All your last dances *and* all your slow dances."

She pretended to think about it.

"All my last dances and all my slow dances, unless planned and negotiated ahead of time."

I didn't let her see it, but inside, I was smiling. Instead, I grunted as if I'd barely agreed to her terms. But from this day forward, negotiating with her would be one of my favorite things.

Before I could answer her, before I could seal our deal with a full kiss that would leave us both breathless, my gaze settled on Noah cutting through the crowd toward me. His face was pale and unsettled. He was followed into the marquee by one of Puzo's men, who jogged around the outside of the dance floor to the back table where Puzo was talking to the bride and groom.

I turned so Sadie was behind me as Noah reached me. His words sent a chill through me. "Nero Lancaster has just stumbled up outside the tent. He's been brutally stabbed. I'm not sure he's going to make it."

Parker had joined me from the sidelines as Noah had approached, and I met his gaze. "Don't leave Sadie and Fallon alone for even a second. Not to piss. Not to fetch your dad. Not one second."

Parker nodded curtly, and Sadie called my name, but I just ignored her as I followed Noah outside. A small group of my team and Puzo's were gathered around the tailgate of a rig parked near the barn. The string of white lights Lauren had added to every building and every fence around the wedding marquee lit up the sky enough for me to recognize Nero lying in the truck bed. He looked like he'd been dragged through the brush. His clothes were torn and muddied, face and hands scratched.

But it was the long, jagged cut down his sternum and over his rib cage that set my pulse racing.

The matching wound on my chest threw me right back to the alley the night I'd gotten it. I could smell the trash covering the grimy pavement as my arms were twisted painfully behind me. I felt every punch as it landed in my stomach, my kidneys, my back. And I felt the tip of the knife as it broke through my sternum, slicing down toward my navel. I could even feel the blood oozing out of me with each heartbeat as I'd fallen to the ground.

I fisted my hands, nails biting into the palms, and pushed past the cloud of dark memories in order to ask, "Did someone call for an ambulance?"

One of Puzo's men responded with a curt yes. Another was in the truck, adding pressure to the wounds with the suit jacket he'd removed. Blood had already saturated it.

I looked at Noah. "Call the sheriff."

"The deputy on duty already did," he responded.

My ears rang. The slapping of feet on the asphalt of the alley tried to pull me under again. I'd thought this man had been responsible for the knife wound to my chest that night. And maybe he had been. Maybe this was someone getting retribution for his sins, or maybe I had misjudged everything. It wasn't just the blood and the memories that had me fighting back the bile that rose.

I swallowed hard and asked, "Where was he? And who found him?"

"He staggered his way into the parking lot from the direction of the waterfall," one of Puzo's men answered. "Bleeding all over the place and insisting on seeing Puzo."

"Let me through," Puzo ordered as he arrived. He brushed past me and climbed into the truck bed with Nero. The man's eyes were wild and violent as he grabbed Puzo's arm and yanked him closer.

His voice was choked with pain as he said one word, "Theresa."

Puzo jerked back, gaze darting into the darkness. "She was here?"

Nero barely nodded, and then passed out.

Fuck. Fuck. Fuck. Another person here seeking revenge. Another body bleeding out on our land. Anger and disgust rose and helped push back the nausea and the darkness of the past trying to drag me back into its seedy grip.

Sirens sounded down the lane, and Noah rushed away to lead the EMTs and the sheriff toward us.

As the medics moved in, trying to revive Nero, Puzo jumped out of the bed, and his gaze met mine. It wasn't the rage in his expression that caught me off guard…it was the fear. Lorenzo Puzo was afraid, and I'd never seen him that way before. It sent a chill up my spine.

When he stepped farther away from the truck, I joined him.

"What the hell is going on here, Puzo? What did you bring to my doorstep?"

"Not just me, Marquess. This was aimed at you as well." When I didn't say anything, Puzo went on, "Theresa wants revenge because you sent Ike away for life, and she wants my head on a platter so she can take over and run the business the way her side of the family has always wanted." He shook his head. "Two years ago, I called a temporary truce in the war that had only gotten worse since Ike went to jail. I brought her here so she could see what I'd done in Rivers."

"She's been here?" I swore quietly. Who else had been on my land who had it in for me? Who else had come here, putting my family at risk, when I'd been running the other way?

"I had her overseeing some of the business deals I'd made here in town. Clean, legal deals. I wanted her to see just what we could accomplish when we were on the right side of the law."

I scoffed, and my voice was full of scorn as I said, "By stealing them in poker games?"

He leveled me a look that said how much of a hypocrite I was for even saying it, and I despised that he was right. That my family had anything in common with the Puzos.

"Adam and Theresa struck up, shall we say, a friendship."

My stomach bottomed out all over again. Goddamnit. She was Adam's girlfriend. The one no one had known or met. She wasn't Tera. She was Theresa goddamn Puzo.

Had it been their hatred for me and my family that had drawn them together? Was she helping Adam even now? He'd said he'd been with her the night the rattler had been in my bed and the person had attempted to smother Lauren. He'd looked startled. Had it been his girlfriend doing the dirty work? Had they taken turns? The roiling acid in me grew another level. Pretty soon there'd be nothing left but burned stomach linings, ragged nerves, and holes that leaked.

"She's been escalating since January," Puzo said.

"What happened in January?"

"She tried to kill me by poisoning my coffee. That was when I cut her off from the family. Anyone who helped her was out." He waved toward the marquee. "If you'll notice, none of that side of the family showed up today for Marielle's wedding."

It had all gone down a month before Spence had been killed. Had Puzo cutting her off pushed her over the edge? Had she encouraged Adam to escalate his plans as well? Had Spencer found out about all of it and put himself in their high beams without even knowing it?

"You dragged my family into the middle of some mafia war?" I stepped closer, wanting to grab his lapels and shake him until his eyes rattled. "Not only that, you opened the door and led her right to me and mine without even a warning. No wonder she showed up here. Two for the price of one."

"Don't pin this on me. You put the target on your own back the day you called the feds on her and Ike, thinking it was me," Puzo snapped. "I told you I had nothing to do with it."

"But I didn't escort her inside the gates of my family's ranch and introduce her to Adam," I snarled. "I've never wanted my family tied up with what happened in Vegas. They didn't even know what really happened in that alley until this week."

A soft hand twined with mine, and I jerked in surprise, twisting to see Sadie had come up behind me. I glared toward the tent where Parker stood, holding Fallon back with an arm around her waist.

"You're not supposed to be out here. Go back inside," I demanded. Sadie did what she'd done since I'd first met her. She ignored my bark and tucked herself up against me.

"What's going on, Rafe?" But I didn't need to answer once she saw the body in the truck bed being worked on by the EMTs. The men Puzo and I had both hired to protect our families stood there, useless. Maybe having the additional bodies had slowed Theresa down, but it hadn't stopped her.

She'd still been able to strike. This time, it had been at her cousin, but would the next strike be at me? Had she been the one to shoot the rifle? Or had it been Adam?

My wound ached. Had it been Theresa that night in Vegas? I tried to reassemble the hazy image of the three people who'd attacked me. The two holding me had been wide shouldered and muscled. The person who'd wielded the knife had been tall and muscular as well, but it could have been an athletic woman. I'd done what every arrogant man before me had done—I'd assumed it had taken another male to bring me to my knees.

Panic wafted through me. The sea of bodies Puzo and I had hired no longer seemed nearly enough to protect our families. Adam and Theresa would just keep coming until they'd put us both in the ground. Was the simple truth that it really was Puzo and me who were putting our loved ones in danger? Was that what Puzo had really meant when he'd insinuated this was all on me last night?

Right before my eyes, the man seemed to be changing. I'd made him the villain of my story, and now every comment he'd ever made was trying to realign itself in my mind. The warnings he'd given me in the past carried so many different angles now. I'd never like the man. He'd never like me. But in some weird twist of fate, it appeared we were momentarily on the same side of the battle.

I didn't know what bothered me more. That my years of hate had been misdirected once again or that I might have to trust my enemy to get a resolution to this entire debacle.

My desire to send Sadie and Fallon away only grew.

But did I really believe Sadie would go on her own? She'd insist on standing next to me, just like she had all week. Just like she had right now, sneaking past Parker and coming out amongst the ugliness draped over the back of a truck bed.

What would it take to send her away?

Would it take me putting on hold whatever this was blooming between us? Would it take me telling her a lie? Would I have to tell her I didn't want or need her after I'd just demanded all her last dances from here until eternity?

I'd do whatever it took to make her go.

What. Ever. It. Took.

And then I'd beg her forgiveness after it was over. I'd lay down my heart and my life in any way she wanted. But right now, I needed her to be as far away from me as was humanly possible, and not even the other side of the country might be far enough.

Chapter Thirty-one

Sadie

SAY DON'T GO
Performed by Taylor Swift

I felt Rafe pulling farther and farther away with every second that passed. I stood next to him while the EMTs tried and failed to revive the man I learned was the same one who'd followed me to the ranch. I was there as Sheriff Wylee arrived and questioned Rafe and his men just as he had the night before. And I watched as Rafe told the truth and yet still held something back. Every question the sheriff sent Rafe's way, he answered curtly, keeping his responses brief and to the point.

My spine tingled as he and Lorenzo and their men all echoed the same damn responses in a polished and practiced way.

Rafe and Lorenzo had been in an intense discussion when I'd approached. What had they said that had somehow ended with them drawing some strange truce? Was it the same things Lorenzo had told me when he'd brought me a glass of champagne? Or was it something more?

The wedding party, disrupted by the sounds of the sirens, started to filter out of the marquee. When Marielle came out, she was in tears, and Lorenzo apologized profusely before the groom led her away, all the while glaring at my cousin. Already unsettled, Lorenzo's face turned nearly ashen as he watched Nero's body being taken away in a black bag.

Wylee had demanded the guest list, thinking anyone on it

could have been a suspect, before Lorenzo explained what Nero's last words had been. And when I heard that Adam's girlfriend was Theresa, I'd felt my legs go weak. Adam's hatred for Rafe took on a whole new meaning, fueled by not only the wrongs he felt the Harringtons had committed against the Hurlys, but now Theresa's personal vendetta against Rafe for sending her twin to prison.

In the dark, it was impossible to find and follow the blood trail Nero had left behind to the original crime scene, so Wylee had crime scene tape set up and said they'd be back at first light with more men and search dogs. Then, he followed Steele to Levi's cabin to go through the video taken by the cameras they'd set up.

When Lauren led Fallon and Maisey back to the main house with Parker trailing them, Rafe demanded I go with them, but I didn't. I waited at his side, hoping there would be a moment when he'd let the cold, commanding Rafe I'd first met slide away, and I'd see again the man who'd laughed at me, teased me, told me he loved me.

But even hours later, when the yard was empty, except for the crime scene tape and a sheriff deputy guarding it until morning, Rafe still hadn't let go of the wall he'd reassembled.

He'd closed every window and door, and I couldn't get past, no matter how hard I knocked.

Instead of stopping at his room in the main house, he all but dragged me up to my bedroom on the next floor. Once we were inside, I put my arms around him, pulled him close, and rested my head on his chest. I heard the discordant beat of his heart under my ear, loud, jagged, as if he was running a mile.

I almost knew what he was going to say before he did, not only because he hadn't put his arms around me in return but because I'd felt him drifting away over the last few hours.

"I'm asking you for another favor, Sadie. I want you to take Fallon with you tomorrow. Get her as far away from this as possible. I don't want her near me until we find Adam and Theresa. Once I'm sure I can protect her, I'll come and get her."

I lifted my head, resting my chin on his chest as I looked

up at him. "You'll come and get her and then try to vanquish me from your life."

His teeth slid over each other. The grinding sound should have been almost impossible to hear, but in the quiet of the room, it sounded like an alarm. The clanging ring of a gate slamming shut.

"What do you want me to say, Sadie? Our lives were always a million miles apart in more than just physical distance. This isn't going to work, and I won't be responsible for dragging you into my screwed-up life. If I had a choice, I'd separate myself from Fallon too, but she'll always be a target as my daughter. I have to keep her close to ensure she's protected, but I'll be damned if I *choose* to bring someone else into it. Not when it's easy enough to keep you out of it."

God, did that hurt—the idea of being easy enough to toss away. I knew he didn't really mean it. I knew he'd meant the I love you. But still, my heart throbbed.

"I see. And what if I don't agree? What if I see a million ways our lives are impossibly twined now? What if I know, deep in my heart, just as you do, that we're supposed to be together? That this is where I'm supposed to be?"

He scoffed. "I don't have the time or effort to spend on protecting someone other than Fallon. You don't belong here. You have a family and a business that needs you in Tennessee."

"I have a man I love who needs me more!"

His eyes barely flickered as he kept every emotion pushed behind the same wall I'd first encountered a week ago. "I don't *need* you. I may want you. May hunger for you. But I don't need you."

It was another slap to my face. A slap that stung more than if he'd actually hit me.

"You just told me you loved me! People who love each other need each other!"

"I was wrong," he said as coldly and cruelly as possible.

Even though I knew why he was doing it, even though I knew the words weren't true, they still wounded me. It tore me apart to do it, but I dragged my body from his, putting the physical distance between us he'd wanted for hours now.

I inhaled, trying to calm myself down, trying to calm him down. "Look, I understand why you're upset—"

"Upset doesn't even begin to describe what I'm feeling."

We'd done this dance before. It felt like everything we'd done was some big circle, repeating until we finally got it right. And this wasn't right.

"Okay, fine. You're furious. You want to kill someone with your own hands. But don't you get it? I feel the same damn way! I love you! I don't want you suffering like this, taking the blame for things outside your control. And I definitely don't want you sending me away because you think it's the only way to protect me."

"I'm not arguing with you about this. You're going. Whether you take Fallon or not, this is where it ends for us. Right here. Tonight."

I stepped closer and was surprised when he took a step back. It trapped him against the door, and I took advantage of it, putting my hands on either side of him, a mirror of how he'd trapped me this morning in the safe. "No."

His nostrils flared, gaze settling on my mouth for two beats, and his throat bobbed. When his hands settled on my waist, I thought maybe I'd won. That maybe I'd gotten through to him by just reminding him of the neurons flaring between us whenever we stood this close. Instead, he lifted me with ease and placed me aside, opening the door, and stepping out into the hallway. I followed him, but he placed a palm to my chest, shoving me back into the room.

"I know it's too much to ask after I've just told you we're done, but I need an answer. Will you take Fallon for a few days?" I wondered how I'd ever seen the cold reserve he'd had in the booth that first night as the real Rafe. Now, all I could see was the passionate man who came alive with a barely lit match. The man who was hiding behind the ice. All I needed to do was melt it in order to reach him.

But I also knew the Rafe in front of me wasn't just holding

that wall up because he was unwilling to bend. He needed that icy front so he wouldn't fall apart. So he could do the things he needed to do for his family. Fine, I'd let him have it for tonight. I'd let him hold it for the few days we were apart. But he had to come get his daughter, and when he did, I'd be ready. I'd have an entirely rational plan assembled on how and why we worked and all the reasons we belonged together.

He didn't know how determined I could be when I wanted something.

And I wanted him.

"Of course I'll take Fallon. She'll always be welcome with me."

"Thank you." It was guttural and torn, just as I knew his insides were at this moment. He shifted, removing the hand from my chest, briefly stroking my cheek with a finger before spinning on his heel and heading down the hall without another word.

I shut the door with a shaky hand. Emotions flooded me, threatening tears, but I didn't let them fall because they were unnecessary. We weren't done. We weren't over. He'd see. He may be accustomed to family letting him walk away, but he'd learn Hatleys didn't give up on the people they loved. He was mine. I was his. The rest of the noise buzzing around us was just that. White noise. Useless and irrelevant.

♫ ♫ ♫

It was Parker who knocked on my door the next morning just as I'd finished packing and not Rafe. When we made our way downstairs, Fallon and Lauren were hugging each other in the entryway. When I asked, they told me Rafe had already said goodbye to his daughter and then joined the sheriff's team following the trail of blood the dead man had left behind him.

I wasn't surprised, but it still stung. I wanted to send him a scathing text saying it was both cowardly and revealing that he'd avoided me. But I was saving up all my arguments for the big battle to come. The one that really mattered. The ever after I wasn't letting him walk away from.

Parker grabbed my bags before I could protest, heading out to the SUV where Noah waited behind the wheel. Fallon's face was all stubborn annoyance as she whirled away from her mother and followed him into the parking lot.

Lauren shocked me by holding me back and giving me a brief hug. "I know I said it last night, Sadie, but thank you." She wiped tears from her cheeks. "For opening our eyes and for bringing us back to life." Her gaze traveled over to her daughter, climbing into the back seat of the SUV. "It's strange how certain I am that she'll be safe with you. How I know you'll defend her with your life, just like Rafe or I would or Spence would have." She turned back to me. "In some ways, I think she'll be better off with you than she's been with me for the last year."

The tears that had pricked my eyes when Rafe left my room last night returned.

"She'll never be better off with me than with her parents," I said softly.

Lauren searched my face, as if unsure if I really meant my words, before saying, "You really believe that. It's one of the things I like about you. Your dogged positivity. You'll need it if you want to keep Rafe. He's going to try to push you away. Don't let him."

"He's already tried," I told her the truth.

"I sensed that this morning when he said goodbye to Fallon but refused to stick around to see you off. He thinks he's doing it for your own good. He thought leaving Fallon with Spence and me was for our own good too, and we let him. None of us tried to stop him. Not me or Spencer, and especially not their dad. We didn't show Rafe how much we loved and needed him because we were too caught up in our own baggage. By the time we realized our mistake, it was too late. He rebuffed any attempts Spence made over the years to bring him back in. He spent holidays alone rather than coming home. Don't let him do that again. I'm begging you."

The ache I'd felt for the entirety of this week for each of them returned at full wattage. But the sorrow I felt for the man

I loved exceeded anything I'd ever known. All I could do from here was promise he'd never spend a single holiday alone ever again.

♫ ♫ ♫

I'd never flown on a private plane, but I'd always imagined them draped in luxury, with soft leather couches, private bedrooms, and expensive linens. Rafe's plane seemed overly simple, lacking any of the flourishes that had been present in his suite at The Fortress. It had eight seats in two groups of four that faced each other over shared tables, a plain bathroom, and no bedroom in sight.

When I'd asked about it, Fallon said Rafe had wanted a plane that was small and fuel-efficient so the carbon footprint he left behind was as minimal as possible. And those words exposed another piece of Rafe I hadn't known—the man concerned about the environment.

As soon as we took off, Fallon put in her earbuds and lost herself in a show, and Parker pulled out a laptop, saying he had a paper to write. Before he could dive in, I leaned in and said as quietly as I could so I didn't disturb Fallon, "I didn't realize you were coming with us."

"It's just a precaution. No one thinks either of you will be in danger now that you've left the ranch."

"My brother is the county sheriff, my sister-in-law is ex-NSA and works for him now, and my eldest brother has had a whole host of security added to the ranch after some incidents over the last few years. Fallon will be safe with us." I wanted to believe that. I had to. Especially when Lauren's faith in me this morning had only raised the stakes.

Parker nodded. "Dad gave me the rundown on your situation."

I bit back my irritation at knowing they'd talked about me and my family behind my back, because I understood why they'd done it. Rafe's life had spun wildly out of hand, and he was looking for every way possible to reel it back in. If it made him feel better to send his friend's son with us, it was fine. Hell, if he wanted to send an entire Navy SEAL team, I'd take it.

"Have they heard anything more about Adam's and Theresa's whereabouts?" I asked.

"Dad finally uncovered one of Adam's bank accounts in Mexico early this morning. Someone pulled money from it at an ATM in Puerto Vallarta yesterday. They believe it was Adam, but there were no cameras to validate it. If Theresa is smart, she'll join him, and they'll head for a non-extradition country."

Something was eating at the back of my brain. Something that didn't fit with what he'd told me or what I'd learned. If Adam had so much money, why had he wanted Carolyn's jewelry? Had he simply wanted to keep it out of the ranch's coffer so it couldn't stop it from going belly up? Was that the real reason he hadn't wanted me to tell Lauren about it? He'd wanted his share of the ranch, according to Fallon, but had it been simply to sell it off to Lorenzo for much less than it was worth when it went bankrupt? Even failing, thousands of acres of land in California would have added a cushy number to his bottom line.

But it still bugged me that I didn't know the answers. It had me pulling at all the loose threads, trying to find which one would unravel it all. But we might never find it unless Adam was found, arrested, and tried.

Parker turned back to his laptop. In the silence that took over, I had nothing to do but ponder my life, Rafe's last words, and the uneasy feeling inside me that increased with each mile that grew between him and me. I wanted to be back with him. I wanted to start soothing the wounds Rafe hid better than I'd ever hidden the scars on my leg.

When the jet landed at a private airport an hour and a half from Willow Creek, I expected to find Mama waiting after I'd called her, but instead Ryder was in the arrivals lounge. My brother's dark-brown hair was ruffled from the cowboy hat he was spinning in his hand. The beard he'd kept since Gia had come into his life was neat, carefully sculpted, and his blue eyes that matched mine pierced me from across the small waiting room.

In his T-shirt with the Hatley Family Ranch logo, worn jeans, and scuffed boots, he looked exactly the rancher he was. His skin was tanned from years spent more outdoors than in, and his smile was large and real when he saw me.

"Sassypants," he said, pulling me into him for a hug that felt much more intense than it should have been for the handful of days I'd been gone.

When he let me go, I introduced him to Fallon and Parker. He shook both their hands. "Nice to meet you." Then he looked at me with a raised brow. "Is he coming too?"

"For a few days at least," I said.

As the four of us made our way to the exit, Ryder kept shooting me and Parker glances, and I suddenly realized my brother thought Parker was there for me. I almost snorted. I hadn't once thought of Parker as anything but a kid, but in truth, he and I were probably a lot closer in age than Rafe and me. Add in his muscled, good looks, and I could see why Ryder would think it. But all it did was make the nauseated feeling in my stomach grow.

There was only one man I wanted, and he'd done his best to temporarily push me away.

In the parking lot, Ryder led us to Gia's SUV, and I was glad he'd had the foresight to bring it instead of his work truck. When Fallon opened the back door, he stopped her. "Sorry, let me get the baby's car seat out of there. I didn't know there'd be three of you."

"You've got a car seat for the baby already?" The shocked disbelief in my voice had Ryder smiling.

"Planning ahead, Sads."

"You're having a baby?" Fallon asked, and Ryder's face morphed into a smile so large it could swallow the entire state.

"In November," he said as if it was tomorrow.

"Congratulations. After seeing and helping hundreds of baby horses and cows come into this world, I've decided I'm never having any," Fallon said with a shudder.

I bit my lip in an attempt not to laugh, because I knew she

was serious, but I also knew she had plenty of time to change her mind a million times over. Hell, I was nine years older than her and still had plenty of time to change mine too. I'd never given much thought to having kids, but the idea of making a baby with Rafe, of having his child…it had longing swirling through me.

It was something else I wasn't going to let him miss out on. A baby he got to help raise instead of one he kept at a distance for their own good.

Parker leaned his head back on the seat rest, closed his eyes, and seemed to fall asleep almost as soon as we left the parking lot. Fallon pulled out her earbuds once again and stared out the window as we left the airport and the larger city behind.

The roads quickly turned small and windy, drifting through the flat farmland, into the hills and valleys that I'd called home for twenty-three years.

Ryder's voice was barely a whisper when he finally spoke. Anger and concern leached into each syllable. "Why the fuck didn't you tell us you were shot at?"

My heart skipped a beat. "How did you hear about it?"

"Rafe Marquess called me this morning."

A million thoughts ran through my head, including how much I loved Rafe for wanting to look out for me and how furious I was for him telling my family what I'd chosen not to. I wasn't sure why he'd sent Fallon with me if he'd already assumed I couldn't protect her. It was why he'd sent Parker with us too. But then again, maybe he was right. Maybe I couldn't protect her. Maybe I'd end up sending her running to defend herself with her own smarts, just like I once had Mila.

The doubts and regrets I had seeped into me and caused my tone to be sharp when I responded. "He had no right to call you."

"What the hell happened while you were in California, Sadie?"

I rubbed my forehead. Where to start? I'd lied to my family and kept secrets. Sure, I'd done it because I was protecting them the same way Rafe was protecting me and Fallon by sending us away. But in the end, all it had done was keep us from sharing important things with the people we loved.

"Honestly, I should just tell everyone at the same time. Don't make me say it twice," I said, suddenly more tired than I could explain.

He rubbed a hand over his beard, jaw working in a way that reminded me so much of Rafe I almost wanted to cry. My brother and Rafe had a lot of similarities. They were both men who'd held the world and love at bay. Proud men who protected those they loved with a fierceness that was borderline controlling, but who also showered those same people with gifts and affection and laughter.

Except, Rafe might have forgotten how important laughter was. Even at his growly worst, Ryder had known how to laugh with his family. Rafe hadn't had that chance because he'd barred himself from their lives.

"You better text everyone to meet us at the ranch, then," Ryder said. "Because I won't wait much longer to find out what's been going on."

At least Ryder knew when to back down and let me have my way. Maybe it was because he'd known me longer than Rafe. The man I loved still hadn't learned I always did what I said I'd do, just like I always kept my promises. I'd promised him all my last dances, and I intended for him to have them. I wasn't letting him renege on the deal we'd negotiated any more than I was letting him take back the *I love you* he'd handed me.

Chapter Thirty-two

Rafe

LOVE ME BACK
Performed by Max McNown

As I leaned against the fence post and watched the horses engaging in an impromptu race down the field, exhaustion draped over me like a ghost clinging to my soul. We hadn't had time to exercise the horses today while chasing blood and crime. So I'd simply let them into the west field to romp as they liked. I wasn't even sure who'd cleaned their stalls and filled their feedbags. Maybe Lauren? All by herself without even Fallon to help her?

It couldn't be helped. Not until I rehired the ranch hands Spence and Adam had let go.

I'd spent my entire morning with the sheriff, following the trail of blood Nero had left behind to a spot beyond the covered bridge over the rivers. The best anyone could tell, he'd been stabbed right around the time the bride and groom had said 'I do.' The spot he'd been in had given him a good view of the ceremony.

According to Wylee, the coroner had said Nero had a large lump on his head where he'd been hit from behind. He had no defensive wounds that said he'd fought back while being sliced open. But then, how had he known it was Theresa who'd cut him?

I couldn't help the shiver that ran up my spine, thinking of his bloody chest. While what had happened wasn't exactly the same as what had happened to me, it meant she could have acted alone, without Adam, in order to do it. But my instincts were screaming that they were both involved.

With the bank account Steele had found in Mexico being accessed yesterday, everyone was searching for Adam south of the border, but no one knew where Theresa was. In truth, no one even knew if it had been her who'd attacked Nero, other than his last word being her name. She could have hired someone, or it could have been any of her other siblings acting on her orders.

Was she done and running like Adam? Was she going to hook up with him in a place where they could spend their days on a sandy beach, drinking margaritas and spending Adam's stolen hoard? Or was she more focused on getting actual physical vengeance? It was quite likely she was waiting to attack Puzo and me again before joining Adam. That was assuming they even really cared about each other and hadn't been partners in crime rather than in an actual relationship.

Nothing was certain but the determination I had to find them. Find them and end this so I could get my daughter back. So I might be able to find a way to make things right with Sadie.

She'd been pissed as hell last night, stubbornly refusing to accept that I was walking away, which made me love her even more. But her anger had at least given her something to focus on, and hell, maybe she'd find the answer to how we could possibly be together, how our love could turn into something permanent, before I did. Maybe by the time I went striding back to claim her, she'd have all the answers.

She'd called and texted several times today, asking for status updates, and asking how I was doing, but I'd ignored them. I'd responded via my daughter instead. Fallon had told me they'd arrived in Willow Creek and that she and Parker had been welcomed with open arms by the Hatleys. It had caused something close to envy to erupt inside me, shaking me to the core how much I wanted to be as accepted into Sadie's family as my daughter had been. A family who certainly wouldn't thank me for taking Sadie and moving her across the country, just so she could be next to me at all times.

Tormented by my own back-and-forth throughout the day,

I'd done my best to push it aside and spent the afternoon with Steele, sifting through any and all connections and leads we could find on Adam and Theresa before I'd dug into the Marquess Enterprises business I'd been putting off for nearly a week. My company was running like the well-oiled machine I'd built it into, but I knew how quickly things could go off the rails if you didn't keep a thumb on the pulse.

Look at what had happened to the ranch. It had slowly disintegrated without my tough-as-nails father running it. I couldn't blame Spence completely. He'd trusted Adam, and he'd added fuel to the fire, but the ranch had already been burning by that time.

From the time I'd left, I'd wanted it to burn.

I had to live with the guilt of knowing I had let it for the rest of my life.

Lauren found me with my forearms draped over the fence rail, watching not only the horses but the sky as it slowly turned various shades of rainbow sherbet. We didn't say anything at first. We just watched the shifting kaleidoscope that reminded me of Sadie and the strength of color burning through her cheeks as I brushed my fingers along her skin. She was sunsets and streaks of dawn and the bright light of midday all rolled together. There'd even been a hint of night in those blue eyes when I'd been deep inside her. She was everything I wanted. All my days and all my nights. My hope for a future.

"Do you remember the time the four of us hiked up to the top of the mountain and got caught between a mountain lion and her babies?" Lauren asked, breaking the silence.

I nodded, the long-buried memory coming back as if it was yesterday.

"Adam tried to run, and Spence threw him down on the ground and sat on him. I had to put my hand over his mouth to stop him from screaming," she continued, and I was right back in that moment, heart racing as I tried to figure out how to get us out of there without the cougar tearing us to pieces. "The three of us knew we couldn't make any sudden movements even though Adam's instinct to run was humming through all of us. Do you remember what you did?"

"What's your point?" I asked, not wanting to relive any of my childhood memories, good or bad. They were too damn painful because they'd always ended with me on the outside looking in.

I could feel her gaze locked on me, but I didn't turn to look at her. I just stared at the horses, galloping across the flower-strewn fields and realizing how damn much I'd missed it. How big of a hole leaving here had left in me. I'd tried to stuff it full by keeping myself busy and building a kingdom braced over an empty cavern. I should have known it would someday tumble into the void. But I wouldn't let any of it slide completely away this time, wouldn't let any of it disappear. I'd hold on to as many pieces of both worlds as I could.

"You put yourself between the cat and us, Rafe. You told us to pick up Adam and move slowly away. And we did. We let you stand guard, knowing if the mountain lion chose to attack, she'd strike you first. Knowing we'd likely be able to get away and get help, but you might not have survived."

"She just wanted her cubs," I said.

"You protected us, facing the danger alone. We did the same thing when you left the ranch behind. We let you go, knowing you thought you were doing the right thing for us and letting ourselves believe it. And here you are again, doing the same thing. Only, this time, I refuse to let you face it alone."

That jerked my gaze from the idyllic scene in front of me to her. Her face was set and stubborn. It reminded me of Sadie, a woman I thought fit into all the caverns and grooves of my soul in a way no one ever had, certainly not the woman standing before me now.

But I didn't deserve for Lauren to think the best of me, so I told her the worst truth I knew.

"He called me, Lauren. Spence called me the night he died, and I let it go to voicemail. And when I listened to it, I felt…glad he was struggling. Now, I keep thinking…if I'd called him back, if I'd shown up, maybe he wouldn't be dead," my voice cracked.

Her eyelids closed, pain raw and ragged crossing her face. "And if I hadn't been passed out on tranquilizers, maybe I could have saved him."

"How bad were you hurt?" I asked, trying to remember what Fallon had told me.

"Broke three ribs and pulled a few back muscles when a cow shoved me into a fence. I used the drugs to help me sleep, and then, when things started to go south, when Spence and I started fighting about whether we'd have to sell or not and what exactly we were going to do, I used them to escape." She sounded so sad, so lost, that it tore at me even when I didn't want it to. "When we got the knock on the door about Spence, it was Fallon who answered it. She couldn't wake me, Rafe. She had to get Adam…"

Tears poured down her face.

Chills went up my spine. Fury with her. Frustration for my daughter. Why hadn't Fallon told me she'd had to face finding out about Spence alone? But I knew. She'd told me. She'd been afraid I'd yank her from the ranch, and I would have. But I silently renewed the vow I'd made to Fallon the other night that she would never have to face these adult responsibilities alone again. I'd made mistake after mistake with those I loved most. But it stopped now. I'd fix it. There'd be no more errors.

You sent Sadie away. That was a huge mistake, my devil prompted.

I shook my head. No. It had been the right thing to do, hadn't it?

"Anyway," Lauren said, brushing at the tears, "if anyone failed them, it was me, not you. I was here, living it every day. I should have seen what Adam was doing. I should have known the toxic crap Grandpa had filled his ears with would come out eventually. But instead of stepping between the people I loved and the mountain lion, I let her take them while I ran."

"Lauren—"

"No. Don't try to smooth it over, Rafe. It's the truth. I have to live with it, and I promise I'm going to try to make it up to you and Fallon. You paid the price for both our sins for too long.

It's time I carried the weight."

"I pursued you," I told her.

"Takes two to tango. And as I remember it, I was the one who dared you to kiss me."

Our first date. I'd gone in for her lips and stalled at the last minute, my conscience screaming halt. Then she'd dared me, knowing I'd never say no to a dare.

"I loved you both, you know," she said softly. "Spence always had the lead by just a smidge, but I really did love you both. And even though I knew it was wrong for us to start dating, I was also a jealous teen who felt jilted. I wanted Spence to be jealous too, and I knew the best way to do so was by using the competition your father had flamed between the two of you.

"It's not okay I used you that way, but once you kissed me, I sort of forgot the reasons I should stop. You were damn good at what you did with women, even back then when you were just finding your groove."

I didn't know what to say to any of it. Her admission of loving me, or the fact she'd used the wedge our dad had shoved between Spence and me to her advantage—or disadvantage, depending on how you looked at it.

She gave me a weak smile. "I'd never admit it to Spence, but I think you were better at it than he was. The romancing… That thing you did with your tongue." She raised a brow, and I almost blushed. "If you were that good then, unpracticed and raw, I can't imagine how devastating you are now."

I finally found my voice, and it was with a hint of anger that I said, "Don't you dare flirt with me, Lauren."

She laughed. "Is that what you think I'm doing? Stupid, I'm trying to tell you not to lose the woman you sent packing. I've never in my life seen you look at anyone or anything like you look at her."

"How the hell do you think I look at her?"

"Like she's the only thing that can top this…" She waved her hand at the stunning colors flaming in front of us.

The truth of it settled hard inside me. Sadie did top this.

She topped anything I'd built for myself since leaving here too. I'd hand over my entire empire if it meant I could keep her.

"What's the deal with her and Lorenzo?" Lauren asked.

"As much as we can all figure, they're cousins." Her brows raised, and I rubbed a hand over my beard. "It gets worse. Her family… They have Great-grandma Beatrice's jewelry that was taken from the movie studio."

Lauren's eyes went wide. "What?"

I explained what I'd found out about the jewelry and what I'd put together from what Puzo had told me and Beatrice's journal.

Lauren tilted her head when I was done, asking, "So, you sent her away because you're holding her responsible for her great-grandmother's actions?" I shook my head. I wasn't. I didn't give a shit about what happened with our ancestors, but she didn't let me respond, just kept on going. "Wouldn't that be like me holding you responsible for your great-granddaddy winning the ranch from mine in a poker match?"

"Winning and stealing are two different things, but that isn't why I sent her away," I said. "And it won't stop me from trying to get her back. Whatever really happened eighty years ago wasn't her fault."

She nodded. "You're right. It's not her fault. Just like it isn't yours or mine. Somehow, Adam forgot that." She shrugged and was quiet for a few heartbeats before saying, "I told you he wanted me to leave with him after I graduated. When I was a kid, I used to agree because it was easier than fighting with him about it. I thought he'd eventually see the truth—I needed this place. It's embedded into every fiber of my being."

"You always belonged here," I said and meant it.

"I have, and our daughter does too. Once upon a time, you belonged here also, but I think, even if things hadn't gone down the way they had between the three of us, you would have outgrown this place. You needed to stretch your wings, fly away, and discover the world before you were ready to come back."

"I was forced to outgrow it."

Lauren blew out a frustrated breath. "We're right back to the same argument we've always had. What I did was wrong. Letting anything develop between us was wrong. I regret what I did to you. To both of you. Because I broke something beautiful. I broke a brotherhood that had survived the cracks your dad tried to place in it. But I also can't regret it because it gave us Fallon.

"She's fierce and protective in that way you always were. She's kind and generous just like Spence, and she has a bit of my sass and stubbornness. She's the perfect combination of all of us. She's the *best* of all of us, and she needs this place in a way you once did."

"I adjusted to not having it. She would too," I said, but I'd already made up my mind that she wouldn't have to. If Fallon wanted the ranch, she'd have it. Not just because I wanted to keep Puzo's grubby hands off it, but because I'd seen her here this week and realized if I took her from this place, it would leave an even bigger hole in her chest than the one I was still trying to fill in mine. Before I could tell her that, Lauren went on, making her case just as she'd tried to make Sadie's.

"Don't make her, Rafe. You look out at that sky and the horses, and I see you aching for it even now. Just like I see you aching for the woman you sent away. Don't make our daughter live without this when leaving it is still causing you to slowly bleed out. Don't punish our daughter for my tragic mistake."

"I'm not selling the ranch," I told her.

"You don't—what?"

"We're keeping it."

Relief bled across her face. "Thank you."

"You may not be thanking me once I start tearing it apart to make it better."

She laughed. "She's going to be so happy."

We let that settle between us, and for the first time since I'd left the ranch over fourteen years ago, I felt at ease in her presence. Lighter. We'd finally crossed the bridge to the other side, the one I'd refused to cross even when my family had tried to show me the way.

"Can I ask you something sort of personal?" When she nodded without hesitation, I asked, "Why didn't you have any more kids? Spencer was a good dad. I can imagine him with a whole brood."

Surprise shifted over her face. "Spence couldn't have kids. He was infertile."

The shock traveled through me. "What?"

She chuckled. "Yep. That cowboy had no fertile runners."

Guilt wafted in again as I realized my brother had faced that knowledge on his own, just like he'd faced his death. When had he found out? Had he wanted to talk to me about it? Anyone? He'd had Lauren, but sometimes you needed another guy to understand the full depth of what you felt about things like that.

After a moment, I said, "There are other ways to have kids."

That sobered her up. "We talked about adopting or IVF, but both are expensive, and money was tight. And truly, we were happy with it being the three of us."

It stung, knowing they'd been a family in more ways than I'd ever been one with my daughter. I couldn't change the past. I couldn't pick up Spencer's call, or be there for him when he'd found out he couldn't have kids of his own, or when he'd realized Adam was stealing from them, but I could be there for Lauren. And I absolutely would be there for my daughter.

Lauren was right. Fallon was the best of the three of us. Better than any of us. The ranch was in her blood. She needed it as I'd once needed it, and I couldn't and wouldn't take it from her. I didn't know what the hell that meant for Marquess Enterprises. Maybe nothing. Maybe it just meant I'd be pouring some of those profits into a dying business and making this my base instead of The Fortress in Vegas. As much as I traveled, would it really matter where I spent my days when I was on the West Coast?

But that also meant I wouldn't be able to be in Tennessee

with a certain dark-haired vixen. I didn't want Sadie to have to give up her family to be with me when I knew what walking away from mine had cost me. Even if we got past the current danger, even if Adam and Theresa were found and we put an end to the current attacks coming at me, I couldn't ask that of Sadie. She needed to stay right where she was at, doing the things she loved, being with the family she adored.

For the first time since Fallon had been born, I realized how much family and roots meant. I wouldn't tear Sadie from her soil and try to replant her somewhere else. It'd be like trying to take a breadfruit plant and make it grow in California. It would just wither and die. I wouldn't let that happen to her.

So maybe sending her away, making her think we were done, was really for the best.

My heart roared in objection.

My soul shouted into the cavern.

She belonged to me. She was mine as much as I was hers.

But sometimes that didn't mean anything in the real world. It only meant something in those moments caught between realities.

And reality always found its way back in.

Chapter Thirty-three

Sadie

HE CALLED ME BABY
Performed by Lee Ann Womack

"*Where are you going?*" *I turned* at the door to find Mila with her hands on her hips and a rainbow-colored stuffed unicorn shoved under each armpit. Her dark-blond waves were fastened into braids that were already askew even though Mama had barely tied them an hour ago. Her hazel eyes, the same color as Maddox's wife's, glimmered with mischief.

"Fallon and I are taking Parker to pick up the rental car," I told her, hand waving to the parking lot where both of them were waiting at the car.

In the four short days since we'd been back in Tennessee, Fallon and Parker had both embedded themselves into my family and the ranch. They'd stolen everyone's hearts by rolling up their sleeves and working just as hard as anyone else. It made me ache all over again because it wasn't *just* Fallon who I wanted welcomed into my family with open arms. I wanted her father to be accepted as well. I wanted our two families to be one.

"He's really leaving? Right now?" Mila asked, looking sad. Of all my family, it was my niece who'd fallen the hardest for the Naval Academy midshipman, and he'd done what everyone who ever met Mila had done—he'd fallen right under her spell. He'd played poker with her, using M&M's as chips, and patiently answered every one of her million questions about becoming a SEAL.

But true to his promise to Rafe, every time Fallon had left the house, Parker had been right there with her. He'd pitched in with the chores, gone riding with her, and taken long walks through the hills.

The time they'd spent together only increased the stars in Fallon's eyes so they glowed almost as brightly as my niece's. Parker saw it, and he'd done his damnedest to treat her as nothing more than a little sister. A friend. It made me think of Lauren's words about how hard you'd try to make the boy you liked look at you in the same way, but I was pretty sure Fallon saw the difference in their ages as an insurmountable hurdle at the moment.

I'd told Lauren the truth when I'd said I'd never had that strong of feelings for a guy before. But I had them for Rafe, and there was no way I was letting him walk away from me, regardless of our age difference and the miles that existed between our homes.

For now, I'd concentrate on doing the one thing Rafe had asked me to do—I'd look after his daughter. Even though, with Parker here, I hadn't had to do much—at least, not until today. With him leaving, I had to find a way to keep Fallon close while I continued to do the real job I'd ignored for nearly two weeks. Now, I had a pile of bills I needed to weed through, a fire marshal to make happy, and the next supply order to place.

That meant I couldn't drag Mila with me along with Fallon this morning.

"You just finished saying goodbye to Parker a few minutes ago, kiddo. You knew he was leaving," I told Mila.

I'd offered to drive him the hour and a half to the airport, but he'd refused. He said he'd feel better if Fallon and I stayed here, close to my brothers and our security until his replacement arrived. Ryder and Maddox had both been irritated Rafe was sending someone, but they'd let it slide. Maybe it was because they knew how it felt to have your loved ones under attack.

"But I may *never* see him again," my niece pouted, her voice taking on that loud, demanding tone we all were known for caving in to. She had us wrapped around her finger from the time Maddox had found her in a dirty hovel and brought her into our lives.

"What's going on?" Mama asked, hurrying down the stairs. Her dark hair, so like my own, swung about her face, and those blue eyes I'd also inherited flashed with concern.

"Nana! Parker is leaving *forever*. Auntie Sadie and Fallon get to take him to say goodbye, and I want to go too!" Her voice rose dramatically.

The concern on Mama's face turned into a wry smile. "Well, chick-a-dee, I believe you already got your way once today. Weren't you the one who convinced your daddy to take you and Addy to the lake?"

Mila spun her way over to my mother and tugged on the apron she had tied around her waist. "I can do both, Nana. I can call Daddy and tell him to pick us up later."

Just as the words left her mouth, Maddox's sheriff truck drove into the parking lot.

"Too late. Your daddy is already here," I said. Then, I squatted down in front of her, unable to handle the sad look that took over her face. I'd sworn, after we'd almost lost her because I hadn't been quick enough to save her, I'd give her whatever I could. "Fallon's going to be just as sad as you are that Parker is gone. How about, before I work my shift at the bar tonight, I take you and Fallon on a long sunset ride?"

Mila loved the horses almost as much as Fallon did, so she considered this carefully before sticking out her little finger. "Pinkie promise?"

I hooked her finger with mine. "Pinkie promise."

I tugged on a braid and then hurried out before my guilty conscience had me hauling her with me and messing up my brother's day. As I met Maddox on the porch, I said, "Warning. She's pouting."

He rolled his eyes to the heavens, took off his cowboy hat, swiped a hand through his dark-blond hair that matched Daddy's, and then set it back down. "Damn. What set her off this time?"

"She decided she needed to go with me to send Parker off *and* go swimming with Addy at the lake," I told him before noticing he was in his uniform instead of swim trunks and a T-shirt. "Are you not going to be able to take her? I can wait. She can come with us."

He shook his head. "McK and Gia are still going with the girls. I'm just swinging by to play taxi service while McK finishes her shift at the hospital. I got called in to handle some drama up at the West Gears' Nest. Nothing urgent, but it can't wait until tomorrow either."

"Okay. Well, be safe out there," I said, heading off the steps, and then turned back. "You haven't heard anything today, have you? About Adam or Theresa?"

My family hadn't been thrilled about any of the secrets I'd kept, but as always, they'd closed ranks around Fallon and me to keep us safe. The first night I'd been home, after Fallon had gone up to bed in Gemma's old room and Parker in Ryder's, we'd agreed we'd give the jewelry back to Rafe and the Harringtons. It meant I wouldn't have a large enough down payment to get the performing arts center started anytime soon, or at all, but the truth was, I was ready to give it up if I could have a life with Rafe. If the diamonds could help his family keep the ranch, I wanted that more than anything I'd wanted in a long time.

I just didn't know what it meant for me and my family. If I left to be with Rafe, would we have to sell McFlannigan's? We couldn't afford to pay a full-time manager to run the place. It was profitable, but just barely. In following my heart, would I have to give up more than just the dreams I'd started to form? Would I have to give up my family's century-old legacy as well?

None of my family would blame me. They'd want me to be with the man I loved, but I'd be lying if I said it didn't snag at my heart, if it didn't make me long to find a way to keep both.

"As far as anyone can tell, they've gone dark," Maddox said. "My best bet? Theresa has hooked up with him, and they're making their way down to South America using their stolen money."

It wasn't anything different than the last update I'd gotten from Rafe, but every time I asked, I hoped for a different answer. Just like I hoped every morning, the short, direct update I received via text from him would turn into something more. While the messages weren't unlike the factual, curt ones he'd sent the day he'd flown to LA, for some reason, they hurt more now. Maybe because, the day of the wedding, I'd known he was coming back to the ranch to claim my last dance, whereas now I knew he was trying to give them away.

Fallon heard from him more often, and she got actual calls. Ones where I heard her laugh and saw her smile at something he said, and it made my heart nearly give out. I wanted to hear his voice too. I wanted to tease and taunt and listen to it as it went dark and commanding and sexy.

I tried not to show how much it stung not to get an actual call, but Fallon saw it anyway. Just this morning, she'd told me not to give up on him. "Sometimes Dad needs a slap in the face to make him pay attention."

I'd laughed because she'd wanted me to, but I couldn't help the little shred of doubt that had started to creep into my thoughts. What if he never shook himself out of this? What if he really decided the only way to give me the life he thought I needed was to walk away?

As I hurried down the porch steps, I couldn't help but notice how Fallon and Parker leaned shoulder to shoulder up against the trunk of my silver Mustang GT. The sun peeked over the barn and cast them in a halo. His dark hair contrasted with her stunning blond waves as much as his gray eyes did her deep chocolate ones, and yet they seemed to fit.

I wondered if Rafe and Jim saw that the bond these two had forged wasn't going to be easily shaken. I'd seen the same deep and lasting relationship develop between Maddox and McKenna as they'd grown up together. I may have only been ten when McK had come to live with us, and I hadn't been able to put into words what I'd seen flashing between them. But just like everyone else, I'd known it was more than friendship, even when she'd left him behind for a while.

As I approached the car, Fallon looked away, brushing her

cheek to her shoulder as if hiding tears. It made that knot around my insides tighten and twist. Parker bumped her arm gently and then rose from his relaxed position. "Noah texted and said his flight was delayed. He might not be here till closer to midnight now."

"That's okay. We have security," I said, referring to the little addition that had been added on to the back of the barn that held not only a dozen computer screens watching over the ranch, our homes, and the bar, but also a person monitoring them around the clock. After Ryder and Gia's horrific ordeal had come so shortly on the heels of what had happened to Mila and me, Ryder had insisted our security be improved. One, or all of us, would be alerted if anything seemed off in even the slightest, and the entire staff had pictures of Adam and Theresa burned in their brains.

We all climbed into the Mustang and made the drive into Willow Creek in silence. It took mere minutes to get to the rental car office tucked into the back of the chain hotel at the edge of town, but the heaviness in the air made it feel longer. It wasn't just Fallon's sadness at Parker leaving. A buzz hung about us that felt almost expectant. A turning point was on its way.

I just didn't know if it was theirs or mine or all of ours.

Fallon and I waited outside until Parker reemerged with keys to a tiny sedan in hand. He tossed his canvas bag into the back seat, and she threw her arms around him, hugging him tight. He hesitated for a second before squeezing her back and then setting her carefully aside.

He tapped her on the nose and said, "You take care of yourself, Fallon," before turning and giving me a chin nod. "I hope I see you again soon, Sadie."

Then, he got in the car and drove away.

Fallon watched him until his car was out of sight, and I swore the ache in her heart mimicked my own. It hurt to watch the person you cared most about driving away.

"I need to stop by the bar this morning and pay some bills. Can I bribe you into coming with me by offering up a latte and one of Tillie's world-famous fritters?" I asked.

"I thought you didn't want me at the bar," she responded with a frown burrowing between eyes that looked just like Rafe's.

"Not at night. It can get pretty rowdy, and I promised your dad I'd keep you safe, not throw you to the wolves." I smiled. "No one will be there at eight in the morning but us."

She seemed to perk up a bit as we drove down the few blocks to the bar, taking in the restaurants and shops with interest. I parked in the back lot and headed for the rear door, stopping only when Fallon's feet stalled, looking at the apartment building across the street. The roof had fallen in in places, and the 'For Sale' sign was so old it was now hanging off its hinges.

It was an eyesore. Thinking about tearing it down and building something in its place had been what had given me the idea for the performing arts center. McKenna had lived some of her worst nightmares in that building. Replacing it with something good, something beautiful and uplifting would be a gift, not only for our community but for her.

When Fallon continued to stare, the hair on the back of my neck went up. "What's wrong?"

She shook her head and then started toward me. "Nothing. Just imagining ghosts."

I scoured the dying vegetation and boarded-up windows but saw no movement. Nothing out of the ordinary. "Let's go inside, and I'll beg Tillie to send someone over with our order."

I unlocked the back door, punched in the mile-long code Gia changed once a week, and then locked up behind us. As we made our way down the hall lined with green wallpaper, dark paneling, and dozens of frames with images of my McFlannigan ancestors, Fallon stopped to take in each one.

Some of the pictures showed our family in Ireland before they'd come to America, and others were the bar as it was being built. But the one that had gotten to me the most, ever since finding out the jewels were real, was the one of Great-grandma Carolyn holding Grandma Sarah in a white baptismal gown.

Great-grandpa Harry had his arms around them both, and he was beaming like a loon. Carolyn was more reserved, but her lips were turned upward at the corners. I wished I could ask her what had happened—whether she'd stolen the jewels on purpose, or if she'd run from her family without ever knowing the diamonds were in the trunk. It shouldn't matter either way, but it did to me. I wanted to think the best of her.

"How long has the bar been here?" Fallon asked as we made our way into the office.

"Opened its doors in 1912," I told her proudly.

As I placed a call to Tillie's, Fallon wandered around, taking everything in with those old-soul eyes of hers. The place didn't quite smell like Phil anymore, but it still held the scent of years of alcohol and sweat and old wood.

After I hung up, she turned and asked, "What can I do?"

I set my phone and bag down on the large desk with its claw feet that matched the pillars on the bar and headed out of the office into the bar itself. "Let's see how Ted left things last night."

The man was a good bartender, and he'd been here almost as long as Phil, but he'd told me repeatedly he didn't want to manage the bar. He said he was happy mixing drinks, offering an ear to those who needed it, and going home to his small house on a few acres of land where he kept emus that probably brought in more money than he made as a bartender.

Fallon took in the old vinyl booths that needed updating, the floor that needed rebuffing, and the huge carved expanse of polished mahogany that was the centerpiece of the bar. Carved in old-world style elegance, it had been much too fancy for Willow Creek in its inception, but it had aged well. It needed refinishing, and it was on my list of things to do with the money I'd been saving, but then I'd gotten sidetracked with diamonds and bigger dreams.

I did a quick check of the tubs in the small refrigerator behind the bar and asked, "How would you feel about cutting up lemons and limes while I pay bills?" I asked. "Or you could just play a little pool while you wait."

Fallon took in the pool table at the back shoved in by the small stage. "I actually don't know how to play pool, and I'd rather do something that helped."

"Okay, let me go into the kitchen and pull out what you need from the big fridge," I said just as a knock came from the back door. "Saved from work by fritters!"

And then I did the dumbest thing I'd ever done in my life. I opened the door without a second thought.

Chapter Thirty-four

Sadie

CAN'T HIDE LIGHT
Performed by Max McNown

The gun that pointed in my face had every ounce of breath leaving my body. Ugly memories rooted my feet to the ground as I stared at the woman and the weapon she pointed at me.

As my mouth went dry and my palms turned sweaty, I stared numbly at her dark-brown hair that had been colored a deep burgundy and cut into an extra-short pixie. Her tall, muscular frame was clad in a red tank, black leather pants, and low-heeled, knee-high boots.

I might have mistaken her for any of the shop owners on Main Street if I hadn't seen the look in her eyes. Rage and hate burned in them. A willingness to pull that trigger and end my life along with the life of the teen in my charge.

Goosebumps broke out over my body. I'd seen that look before. I'd seen it at the same time I'd faced another loaded weapon.

My throat tried to close, and blood rushed through my ears.

A millisecond too late, I tried to shove the door closed, but Theresa easily blocked it with a booted foot.

My first instinct was to scream at Fallon to run, to get the hell out via the front door, but I bit my tongue, hoping Theresa hadn't seen us come in together.

"Why are you here? What do you want?" I forced myself

to ask, hoping I sounded sure and unmoved rather than panicked and afraid.

"To start with, we'll take the diamonds. And then we'll see what else we can do to you that will torture Rafe Asshole Marquess when he finds you and knows he's the reason it happened."

"Hey, Sadie, is that an actual jukebox…" Fallon's voice drained away as she stepped into the hallway, and Theresa's gun shifted in her direction.

"Don't hurt her!" I cried out, leaping between them. "Please, there's no need. I'll give you the jewelry. We just have to wait for the bank to open," I told her, my voice shaking with the effort to stay calm.

"Nice try," a dark voice from behind Theresa said. Adam emerged from the sunlight outside into the darkened hallway. He had a baseball hat tucked over his hair that he'd bleached a hideous white, and he wore a fake mustache that was equally bad. "Too bad you already told me you kept them in the safe here at the bar."

He shut and locked the door behind him.

Sweat trailed down my back, and my lungs forgot to breathe as my brain screamed at me to move. To do something. Anything. But just like that day with Chainsaw, my feet felt like lead weights.

"Grab my niece," Adam told Theresa.

As she started past me, my body finally obeyed my mind's desperate plea, and I stuck out a foot, trying to trip her. She righted herself, and Adam lunged at me, swinging his fist. It collided with my cheek, and stars burst behind my eyes. I went reeling toward the wall, barely sticking my hands out to keep myself from slamming headfirst into it.

Fallon's flight instincts finally took over, and she turned to run, but Theresa was faster. She grabbed her by her braids and yanked Fallon backward, shoving the gun into her temple with a thud I could hear across the hall.

Adrenaline and fear mixed as dark memories tried to resurface and shut me down further.

I saw it all again. Chainsaw pointing his gun at me and then at Mila as an utter sense of uselessness sank into my veins, every molecule turning into solid rock until I could do nothing. I hadn't been able to keep my niece safe.

I fought back those frantic, hopeless thoughts and forced air into my lungs. "Please stop. Don't hurt her."

Adam stepped up behind me, twisting my arm so painfully I had to bite my lip to stop from crying out in agony. What had Gia said I should do when a larger opponent had me like this? Why couldn't I think of the answer? Why couldn't I react?

Theresa's eyes glinted as she watched the agony cross my face. She had Fallon in a clawlike grip, but it was Adam's hard words that made the fear inside me swell to a whole new level.

"You screwed everything up, Sadie. You. I had everything under control until you sent that damn letter about the diamonds. Then, Spence started asking questions, hoping and digging into things he'd let rest his entire life. I was forced to speed up the movement of my money, and it raised his goddamn alarms. You started us on this downward spiral. And then you had to drag Rafe into it, whoring and stealing from us and the Puzos, just like your great-grandmother. But we can end all of it today. Right every damn sin. Every damn curse."

Damn it, I had to do something. I had to move. I had to slap back before I lived through the same horror of what had happened three years ago with Mila. I'd be shot. Worse, Fallon might be shot.

Nausea rolled.

God... God... *Think, Sadie, think.*

As Adam shoved me toward the office, my gaze landed on the camera in the upper corner of the hall, and a brief, temporary sense of relief washed over me. The bar's outside cameras were tied to the same systems as the ones at the ranch. Someone would have seen Theresa and her gun. They'd have seen her with a man and known it was Adam, even if he'd tried to disguise himself.

I just had to give us time for the cavalry to arrive. For my brothers to show up.

I sounded as breathless and scared as I felt, voice wavering as I told them, "I don't have the jewelry here anymore. I moved it after I came back from California. You'll have to wait until the bank opens."

Adam's voice was dark and ominous when he said, "Liar. We can add liar to your list of sins."

I shook my head, and he hit me again, this time open-handed in a way that would leave the shape of his palm on my cheek and had me biting my tongue. My head spun. Spots drifted across my vision, and my stomach flipped once more. But I dug my nails into my palm, forcing myself not to pass out. I wouldn't lose consciousness again. Not like last time.

"I'm not lying," I insisted, the bitter taste of blood in my mouth.

"We'll see soon enough, won't we? Open the bar safe, and we'll go from there."

They hauled us both into the office. Fallon cried out as Theresa jerked her arm back farther behind her and forced her toward the desk. Every protective instinct in me screamed.

"Stop. You don't need to hurt her," I said shakily. "You can have the jewels. You just have to wait for the bank to open."

Theresa just laughed, yanking harder on Fallon's arm, and the fear turned to rage inside me. At Theresa. At Adam. At myself. I had to do something to stop this. To save Rafe's daughter. I'd promised him. And I'd promised myself I'd never let someone I loved be hurt while I simply watched ever again.

Adam thrust me farther into the room with so much force I ended up on my hands and knees. My entire body quaked. When I tried to stand back up, he kicked me in the stomach, and I landed on my ass as pain ratcheted through me.

"Please, Uncle A-Adam. Don't hurt her," Fallon begged, and I whipped my head around to see she was crying. Slow, scared tears she fought but couldn't be stemmed. More hatred welled at them for making her experience this and the nightmares it would leave behind, even if she got out of it somehow whole. "Why are you even doing this?"

He didn't answer her. He was having a hard time even

looking at her, and I thought I might be able to use that. Maybe he actually did care about her. How could anyone have watched her strength and resilience for years and not? I'd known her a little over a week and was stunned by her bravery and courage.

Theresa was the one who filled in Adam's silence. "It's simple revenge. It's been a long time coming for the Hurly family, in my opinion. I, on the other hand... At least I attempted to avenge my brother after your dad turned him in to the feds. He'd be dead if that asshole Steele hadn't intervened. But I have plenty of time to get him back too. After we take the jewels, after we deal with the two of you, I'll make my way down the list, one by one."

An uncontrollable fury built inside me as they talked. I absolutely would not let them hurt Fallon. Not another hair on her head. And I wouldn't let them hurt Rafe again either. Or Jim Steele or any of the good people who'd held the man I loved up at his lowest moments.

"Look," I said quietly, "you want the jewels? You can have them. I just want you to let Fallon go. Let her walk out this door right now, and I'll call the bank manager and have him open early."

Adam snorted. "And give her a chance to call Daddy and have him send one of his men to save the day? Not going to happen."

The one thing Adam didn't know, hadn't planned on, was that the Hatley family would come running way before Fallon had a chance to call anyone.

As if he'd read my mind, Adam looked down at me with a smug grin. "And don't think your gun-toting family is going to come either. Theresa turned off the cameras here at the bar as soon as we saw you arrive."

"You were across the street." It wasn't a question. The fact I hadn't trusted Fallon's instincts or mine only caused the nausea to return. Goddamn, I'd let them come this close when I could have taken her and run. We could have gone to the sheriff's station. To my brother and Gia. Anywhere but stay here, when our intuition had been warning us to bolt.

"After we have the diamonds, I'll never stay in a shithole like that again," Theresa said.

"If you hadn't spent the money I'd saved offshore, we wouldn't need the goddamn jewels," Adam growled. "And if we decided we wanted them, we could have hired someone to retrieve them."

"I had to protect my brother while he was in jail! And what kind of man sends someone else to get his revenge, anyway? I'll get great pleasure out of drawing blood for every sin against my family," she snarled. "More and more, I find myself thinking you aren't anywhere near the man I thought you were. Maybe that was why you needed my help finishing off Spencer, and why you missed when you shot at Rafe."

The derision in her voice had Adam's spine stiffening.

"Fuck you!" Adam growled, kicking the chair in front of the desk and sending it flying against the wall. "I told you! We're cursed! We've been cursed from the moment Great-grandpa Tommy hung himself instead of taking back what was his!"

Fallon's gaze met mine. Her cheeks were still wet from tears, but her look turned steely and grim at hearing the careless way Theresa had talked about ending Spencer's life. Anger flooded her face, replacing the fear.

I needed to hold on to the anger spinning through me as well. I needed it to fuel me. I needed it to shove aside the dread and regret and the terror blooming at the thought of never seeing my family again. Never seeing Rafe. He'd never forgive me for costing him the one thing in his life he held precious.

"The only way to end a curse that deep is to spill the blood of those who took what was yours," Theresa said, pointing the gun at Fallon's head again. "Let's start here."

My heart stopped, and it was with a harsh, croaked voice that I threw out, "You're forgetting Fallon is a Hurly too."

"And maybe she could have been saved. Maybe if her mother hadn't spread her legs for both the Harrington brothers, she would have been worth something, but instead, she gave herself to the enemy. And this little piece of trash chose the wrong side when she went running to Daddy to tattle on Adam."

"Shut the hell up, Theresa!" Adam growled.

"You don't get to tell me what to do. I don't put up with any of that macho, He-Man shit," Theresa said, turning to me with a smirk. "That's why your great-grandma took off, you know."

It took me several seconds to realize Theresa had switched gears and was talking about Carolyn. "She didn't want to marry the man her daddy had picked out for her. Didn't want any part of the family business. So she hightailed it out of Hollywood, taking the jewelry she'd helped steal with her. She walked away from her inheritance because she was too afraid they'd drag her home by her hair and force her to marry the pig they had all but lined up at the altar, waiting for her. Her inheritance is why Lorenzo has been foaming at the mouth since you walked into Vegas, asking about her. He's afraid you'll take him to court and get her piece of the pie."

I couldn't help the shock that sprang from her revelation. I'd put myself and my family in the bull's-eye because they didn't understand we'd never want a piece of anything they had. They didn't know what it meant to be part of a family that had more honor in our little pinkies than they did in their entire beings. "We'd never take it. We wouldn't touch a cent of Puzo money."

She laughed coldly. "Go right ahead and tell yourself that, sweetheart. But I bet you'd do just about anything to save the family ranch. This bar…" She waved her hand around the room and then landed the gun on Fallon's temple once more. "I bet you'd do anything to save her."

"Get your hands off her!" I shoved myself to my feet and stepped forward, but Adam caught me, twisting my wrist and making my eyes water.

"Open the safe," he said, voice dark and threatening. "Give me the diamonds, and we'll leave Fallon alone."

"Don't you dare speak for me," Theresa spat out.

He glanced over to where Theresa had shoved Fallon into the chair behind the desk.

I scanned the office, cataloging the contents, wondering what the hell I could use as a weapon, wishing once again I had a goddamn gun. Instead, I had a pocket knife that was miles away in a desk drawer and knives in the kitchen that might as well be as far away as the ranch. My gaze landed on the screwdriver sitting on the desk that I'd used to fix the roller wheel on the desk chair.

"The diamonds can't get my brother out of jail, but maybe I'll take a piece of Rafe's daughter for every year my brother was sentenced to serve." Theresa cocked the gun that was pressed into Fallon's temple, and my breath evaporated.

My gaze caught Fallon's, and I shot a glance to the screwdriver sitting on the edge of the desk in front of her. She looked down and saw it before her gaze flew to Adam as he squeezed my wrist until I gasped with pain.

"Stop procrastinating, Sadie, and open the goddamn safe." A part of me thought maybe he was rushing me in order to stop his partner from hurting Fallon.

I nodded just as a shuffle drew our attention back to the desk. Fallon had misunderstood me, and she'd gone for my phone sitting next to my bag. Theresa smacked her with the butt of the gun, and it sent the rolling chair into the wall. Fallon cried out, and my hands fisted.

The bile in my stomach ate up my esophagus, making my voice crack as I said, "I need the rolling alarm code as well as my fingerprint to open the safe. The number is in my text messages."

Adam stalked over to my phone and came back to me, shoving it into my face to unlock it. He swiped through the messages, found the text with the passcode, and then pocketed it before drawing out a small gun. It took me several seconds to recognize it as the Liliput I'd had back at the ranch. More chills ran up my spine as I realized he had to have been there after I'd left it behind on Sunday.

Adam saw my gaze fixated on the weapon, and he laughed, dark and scathing. "Rafe doesn't know his childhood home as well as I do. Everyone was scrambling, looking for us in the hills and down in Mexico, when we were right there inside the house the entire time."

"You know about the secret passages!" Fallon blurted.

My mind blanked. God…he'd been at the ranch this whole time? There were secret passages there that Fallon had known about? He could have done anything to Rafe and Lauren! Jesus. Were they even okay? When was the last time Fallon had talked to them? I couldn't pull the answer, and it made my legs wobble and my heart scream.

"You weren't in Mexico," I said, shaking my head.

"Easy enough to pay someone to take some cash out for you. Now quit stalling," Adam said, pointing his gun at me. "Open the safe."

I forced my feet to move, and I'd just opened the outer door of the cabinet where the safe was hidden when he closed the distance between us. He shoved the gun into my neck, pressed himself into me so I felt him everywhere, and whispered in my ear, "Don't try to outsmart me, Sadie. Theresa was wrong about one thing. Hurlys know how to get vengeance. We just don't splash it around like the Puzos. Tommy got a piece of it from Beatrice, Lauren got her hands on the ranch, and I'll savor what I get from you. Theresa has been a tool, and her usefulness has drawn to a close. Give me the jewels, I'll leave Fallon here unharmed, and you and I can take a ride."

I fought the tremor of disgust that wound through me.

"What the fuck are you two whispering about?" Theresa demanded, whirling her gun away from Fallon and taking a step toward us.

From the corner of my eye, I saw Fallon's hand snake the screwdriver from the desk while Theresa was turned away. The smart girl had used the phone as a distraction in order to give her time to get the tool. Now, I just had to be as smart and brave as she was—as my little, tiny niece had once been.

"Just a promise," Adam told Theresa, catching my eye. "A promise of payback."

I placed my finger on the safe's scanner, and Adam leaned over me to type in the code. When we heard the lock disengage, he shoved me aside.

My heart pounded against my rib cage with a bruising viciousness as I slowly eased away from him, trying to get closer to Fallon and the desk.

"Stop moving!" Theresa groused, pointing the gun at me as she asked, "Are they there?"

He pulled out the velvet bag with the jewelry in it, smiling large and wide when he looked inside and saw the jewelry. He draped the string around his wrist as he shot me a look of hateful promise. "You know what happens to liars, Sadie? Extra punishment."

He turned back to the safe and grabbed the deposit bag I'd shoved in there last night when I'd been too tired to drop it at the bank. With most people using a card nowadays, I didn't have to make the run so often, but it had built up while I'd been gone, and the bag was full.

"Looks like Sadie has given us an extra present." He flung the bag at Theresa. As she lifted a hand to catch it, the other one with the gun drifted downward, and Adam used the distraction to shoot her in the chest with the Liliput.

A deep mahogany spread across the vivid red of her tank. Shock stretched over her face, followed by rage. The money bag fell to the floor, the pistol in her hand lowered, and Fallon stabbed her arm with the screwdriver. Theresa screamed in fury, but the gun tumbled to the floor. I lunged for it, but a second shot from Adam's weapon had me freezing before I could reach it.

"Don't anyone move another muscle," he said in a deadly calm.

Theresa put her hands to her chest, trying to staunch the blood. Her voice was sharp and brittle with pain and anger as she stumbled toward Adam. "You shitbag, two-timing—"

She fell to her knees, eyes blazing, as she took two last gasping breaths and then landed on the floor at my feet.

Chapter Thirty-five

Rafe

THE MAN I WANT TO BE
Performed by Chris Young

Four days had passed since I'd sent Sadie and Fallon away. Four days and we were no closer to finding Adam and Theresa. No closer to ending the danger that hovered around me and mine. I loathed the useless feeling it left me with. The simple knowledge I couldn't control what happened to us made the rage I felt at the missing couple eat away at my insides.

I needed this to be over and behind us, not only for our safety but so I could put things right with Sadie. So I could convince her I'd found a way to blend our worlds without her having to give up any of her dreams.

I wouldn't let Sadie end up like my mother or my great-grandmother, feeling trapped and alone after having given up everything for the man they loved. As I reread Beatrice's journal over the last few nights, it wasn't her sadness that I'd felt, it had been my mom's.

I remembered my parents' arguments, her wanting them to take a trip to Florence or Paris or London so she could see and feel and learn from the great artists she admired, and Dad's ever-consistent response that it wasn't the right time. The young calves needed castrating. The fields needed seeding. The fire line around the buildings needed clearing. Something had always prevented them from going.

I didn't understand why Mom hadn't just flipped him off

and gone without him, just as Beatrice could have returned to Hollywood and made a career for herself without Alasdair. So why hadn't they? The answer was simple. They'd fallen in love with unyielding men who'd taken them for granted, who'd thought less of the dreams of the women they loved than they had of themselves and the ranch.

When the cancer had come for Mom the second time, I was almost sure she'd simply given up the fight because her life had felt so empty.

I wouldn't let the same thing happen to Sadie. To us. I absolutely refused to repeat the cycle of my ancestors.

So, in the dark of the night, I made my decisions and formed my plans. A way to keep Sadie and to ensure she had what she wanted. But I was smart enough to realize I needed to wait until we were face-to-face to explain it to her. If I tried to do it over the phone, she'd simply say no. She'd dig those stubborn heels of hers in and offer herself up as some sort of sacrifice without letting me do the same in return.

Which was why I denied us the relief and pleasure of talking on the phone. Part of it was to ensure she had time to really think about what she was getting into with me. To give her a chance to back out before she committed herself to a man over a decade older than her. A smaller part of it was a way of hedging my bets, hoping my absence would make her desperate enough to accept the deal when I laid it at her feet. But the biggest reason was because if I heard her voice, the siren who'd stolen my heart would be able to convince me that she didn't need the dreams she'd give up.

So instead, I concentrated on putting my plans in place, kicking them off so she'd have less reason to back down when she realized I'd already spent the money to get the ball rolling. I had the resources to make both my daughter's dreams and Sadie's come to life, and I couldn't think of a better way of spending it.

So, while I felt useless and out of control with Adam and Theresa on the loose, I dug into the plans I had to give the two women I loved more than my own breath everything they deserved and more.

I started by hiring back most of the workers Spencer had laid off. With the ranch hands managing the day-to-day chores, it left Lauren free to develop a detailed plan for the ranch's conversion with me.

I invited two companies to work up bids for the renovations we decided to make to the main house, converting it fully into a hotel, while we built a two-bedroom, two-and-a-half bath home on the hill for Lauren and Fallon that would give them privacy away from the resort activities. I had human resources post jobs for a live-in housekeeper and two assistants who would stay in the old servant quarters, and I talked to the head chef at The Fortress, compiling a list of his peers who might enjoy taking on the challenge of the five-star resort I was going to build in the middle of Nowhere, California.

And after Lauren left my side each day, I researched the feasibility of creating the theater in Willow Creek that Sadie had wanted. She likely had designs in mind already, and I'd honor those, but I hired a firm to look at similar performing arts centers around the country, not only for architectural and technical ideas but ideas on how they were run. A lot of similar centers in small towns were losing money, but there were successful case studies amongst the failures. I was confident, between the two of us, we'd make Sadie's one of the winning ones.

A little over a week ago, I'd been strolling through The Fortress, satisfied at what I'd created but at a loss to what came next. The routine had already been getting to me. I'd been ready for the next adventure. Now, I'd found it. And it had nothing to do with bringing my visions to life but in bringing Sadie's and Fallon's dreams to fruition.

If I could convince Sadie of it, we'd split our time between Rivers and Willow Creek. We'd stick close to both our families, to the people who truly mattered. I'd still have to travel, keeping a finger on the pulse of Marquess Enterprises and all the businesses underneath it, but I could also afford to hire a chief executive officer to run it.

I could devote myself to the women I loved.

I could find my way back to the land and the horses I'd

once thought I'd never leave.

And I'd make sure I was always there to be Sadie's last dance partner.

I could have it all.

I just had to find Adam and Theresa and make sure they were incapable of hurting me and mine ever again.

I turned away from the window in the office, glancing down at the expensive suit I wore for the meetings I had scheduled today. The suit felt tighter than usual, more restricting after days spent in jeans and T-shirts. But I'd wanted the businessmen showing up today to see the multi-million-dollar entrepreneur I'd become rather than the cowboy they'd watched grow up.

I wanted them to take me seriously, starting with the architect who was coming to give me his bid for the renovations to the main house. I opened the tube with the original floorplans of the mansion I'd ordered from the city planning office. I pulled them out, rolling them along the desk and anchoring the corners with office supplies. We weren't adding on to the house but were converting existing space to maximize it. As the vault was hardly used for anything more than storage these days, I thought we might be able to create a cozy, secret speakeasy bar out of it with a few high-top cocktail tables.

My finger skimmed across the plans to the office and the safe. I leaned down, squinting at some slanted lines that made no sense. My heart seemed to stop for several seconds before my finger ran along the drawing for the side wall, realization dawning at what I was seeing. Hidden goddamn passageways. They were so narrow a man could hardly fit inside them. They ran through several rooms downstairs, behind the butler's quarters, and to a stairwell running up to a secret room in the attic.

I'd lived here for twenty years and never known they existed.

It instantly brought back memories of playing hide-and-seek as a kid with Spence, Lauren, and Adam, and the way we'd never found him. The way he'd been like a ghost, disappearing and reappearing with a smug look on his face, all the while keeping his secrets.

Anger swarmed through me. That he'd known my home better than me. That he'd used the advantage to play parlor tricks.

A chill washed over my spine, thinking of the man who'd tried to smother Lauren. How Adam had appeared in her room out of nowhere. The hidden passage went right by her bedroom.

Shit. Was he still here? Were we searching for him in Mexico when he was still in the house?

I picked up my phone and dialed Steele. "I need you here. Now."

When he came running into the office, I put a hand to my lips and then silently pointed to what I'd found on the plans. His face turned grim, and we headed into the vault.

Steele pulled his gun from his holster, and I grabbed one from the wall. The Liliput was missing. I'd thought Sadie had put it back before she left, but maybe it was still in the room upstairs.

Between Steele and I, we found the switch behind the shelves that swung open the door to the first passageway. Well oiled, it didn't make a sound, and I cursed myself all over again.

We made our way, floor by floor, through the narrow halls with our phone lights casting dark shadows along the walls. The passages weren't dusty. No spiderwebs existed. They'd been used frequently and recently.

As quietly as we could, we cleared the spaces and ended in the hidden room in the attic. A brass bed with mussed sheets and a pile of recently used dishes proved someone had been here in the last few days. A simple, plain desk was strewn with computer cords along with a host of other electronics. Seeing them, Steele cursed.

"What?" I demanded.

"These are cloning devices for phones. If he's used them on Lauren's and Fallon's phones, he could be following everything we're doing."

How could I have been so careless? Why hadn't I demanded they use burner phones?

"Damn it, Steele."

We left the secret room through a door that led into the attic space I'd known well as a child, playing amongst the leftovers of the Harringtons' past. As we headed down the stairs, Steele said, "Give me your phone. I'll make sure it's clean, and I'll find Lauren and scan hers as well."

As he headed out of the house, I went back into the office. While I waited for him to return, fury built inside me. I stared at the plans with disgust, knowing my father had kept the secret of the passages for his benefit. Or maybe to see if we'd ever find them on our own. By doing so, he'd allowed the spider to spin its web, just like I'd allowed the monster in the gate.

When Steele walked in with a glower on his face, my heart sank.

"He was monitoring us?" I growled.

"Not you," he said, placing my phone on top of the floorplans. "But Lauren. Which means he was probably monitoring Fallon's phone as well. You'll need to tell Sadie to get her a burner phone."

"Fuck."

"But it was actually good news."

"How the hell do you figure?"

"I was able to use the link he established to backdoor him. I'm waiting for it to ping his location now."

I stilled, hope flaring. "You've got him."

"Not yet. But as soon as he sends a text or makes a call, I will."

It was good news, but I hated that I couldn't text my daughter to warn her. I couldn't even be sure he hadn't cloned Sadie's while she'd been here, so I'd have to contact one of her brothers and get them a message that way. She wouldn't like it any more than she'd like that I'd told Ryder about what had been happening here. Her text message to me once she'd found out had been scathing, but I'd done it for a good reason. I'd do it all over again if it meant keeping her safe.

I had to believe she'd forgive me for all of it once I told her my plans. Once I touched her again. She'd forget anything and everything but what we could be when we were together.

Steele's phone vibrated in his hand, and as soon as he glanced down at it, a look of triumph took over his face. "We've got him!" The glee disappeared just as fast as it had arrived. "Shit!" The hope that had soared inside my chest crashed as he looked up at me with pure panic and said, "He's in Willow Creek."

For a moment, I didn't believe I'd heard him right. The world went hazy, black swimming in front of me. Dread settled like a dead weight in my gut.

I reached for my phone, hitting Sadie's number with a hand that shook. It rang twice and then went to voicemail. Even knowing Adam could be monitoring it, I called Fallon. It went straight to voicemail as well.

The dread spread through my veins like a poison.

Why the hell would Adam go there?

Why would he have followed Fallon and Sadie?

Simply to get back at me?

Then it hit me. The goddamn diamonds. But why would he go after them now? If he had access to the money he'd stolen, he didn't need the cash. Being seen in Willow Creek, risking being arrested, seemed like a stupid play, and nothing he'd done so far had seemed stupid.

The only thing I could think was that he owed Puzo more than the man had admitted to me. What had Puzo said? He had a contract in hand that wouldn't be easily put aside. But if Adam ran, if he wasn't able to be found by the U.S. government or Puzo, he'd never have to pay back the debt.

Steele's voice asking something about flights jerked me back to the room and the need to get to Fallon and Sadie. I'd left the goddamn jet in Tennessee so Parker could take it to Annapolis, and now I was stuck without a means to get to them quickly.

I thumbed my way through my contacts, landing on Maddox Hatley's number.

"Hatley," the man grunted out. Relief swarmed through me, but it was followed by a hive of bees stinging at what I had to tell him, how I'd led danger right to their door.

"This is Rafe Marquess. Adam is in Willow Creek, and neither Sadie nor Fallon is picking up their phone."

Hatley swore before saying, "Sadie told my daughter they were going to go riding later. Maybe they went now. There's no signal in the hills. I'm forty minutes away, dealing with another issue, but I'll call the deputy I left in town and send him out to the ranch. Then I'll call Ryder. He'll know where to find them."

I hung up, not even bothering with niceties, and dialed Ryder Hatley.

"You got premonition skills or something?" Ryder grunted out.

Chills swarmed up my back and over my neck. "Where are they?" I demanded.

"At the bar. The cameras there went dead about ten minutes ago. I'm on my way now."

"Adam's phone just pinged in Willow Creek."

I heard the screech of tires and a roar of engines as Ryder cussed under his breath. "Call my brother. I need both hands to navigate."

"I already did. He said he's out of town, but he's sending someone to the ranch."

"You can call him back and have him send someone to the bar, but I'll be there in less than five minutes, and I will handle it." Ryder sounded absolutely sure of himself. Confident. Angry.

Relying on someone else to look after the people I loved left a bitter taste in my mouth. My voice was pained and gritty when I said, "If he's harmed even one hair on either of them—"

"I'll kill him myself," Ryder hissed. "After everything my sister has been through… Goddamn it!" I heard tires squeal again. "I'll call you when I'm at the bar."

He hung up, and I headed for Steele, who was waiting at the office door.

"According to the crew at the hangar where the Cessna was kept, there's nothing there that can get us across the country quickly, but there's a private jet in Bakersfield. It's the closest thing I could find."

We were ninety minutes away. Too damn far. Even then, it would take at least another five hours to get to Tennessee once we were in the air. And once we landed, it was another hour and a half to Willow Creek. I was an entire day away from them. How the hell had I let this happen? I'd never let it happen again.

"What's wrong?" Lauren's voice stopped me as we made it halfway out the front door.

I swallowed, closed my eyes, and said, "Adam's in Willow Creek."

Her face paled, and she ran at me. "You're going there now? I'm coming with you."

She didn't give me a chance to respond, just shoved past me and headed toward the Jaguar where Steele was waiting, hand out. "Give me the keys," he said as Lauren climbed into the non-existent back seat.

"Not a chance. I grew up racing on these roads. I know the quickest way to get us there." We eyed each other for a long moment. "Either get in or don't, but I'm driving."

I shoved past him and slammed my way into the driver's seat as he made his way to the passenger's side. I'd already shoved the car into gear and hit the accelerator as the door shut behind him. The gravel kicked up behind us as I sped down the road. I'd shave as much time as I could off the trip to the airport. If nothing else, it would keep me from losing my mind while I waited for a call back from one of the Hatleys.

I could only hope, could only pray to every higher power that existed, that it would be Sadie Hatley's number that lit up my phone.

Chapter Thirty-six

Sadie

LAYING LOW
Performed by Danielle Bradbery

Adam waved the gun in my direction, and it took everything I had in me not to flinch. The old wound in my leg ached as if it was new and fresh.

"Tie Fallon up. Gag her. I can't have her calling for help before we've gotten out of town."

"Uncle Adam, please," Fallon said.

"Sit back down," he ordered his niece, and my heart plummeted as the gun rotated in her direction. Then, rage so strong it nearly blinded me surged in my chest.

I'd kill him before he could hurt her.

Fallon pulled the rolling chair closer to the desk and sank down in it.

When I still hadn't moved, Adam grabbed the wrist he'd already hurt and squeezed until I winced. "I promised you I wouldn't hurt her. Don't make me. Go tie her up."

"I don't have anything to tie her up with," I said through gritted teeth, hoping to calm him down, hoping to somehow get the gun he was waving around away from him before he purposefully or accidentally used it on one or both of us. With no safety, the weapon was built to go off fast and easy, and I wondered if he even knew it.

His gaze narrowed on me in disbelief. "This is a damn bar.

You have duct tape or rope or something."

This time, when the gun landed on Fallon, it was firm and resolute. I barely stopped myself from lunging at him. The only thing that halted me was my fear the revolver would go off as we struggled, and she'd be hurt anyway.

As his finger landed on the trigger, I all but shouted, "I'll find something!"

I hurried behind the desk, opening drawers as he watched my every move. For two seconds, he looked down at his phone in order to dial someone, and my hand closed around the pocketknife next to the duct tape. In the blink of an eye, his eyes were on me again as he said to whoever had answered, "We'll be ready in an hour. Two passengers."

I grabbed the duct tape as I slipped the pocketknife up the sleeve of my flannel shirt. With my back to Adam, I faced Fallon and saw her gaze slide to the sleeve where I'd hidden the knife. I was so proud of her. For keeping it together. For paying attention. She was so much braver and smarter and stronger than I'd ever been at her age. More than I was now.

"I'm sorry," I said with every ounce of regret I felt. My fingers shook as I tore a piece of tape from the roll. My life felt like it was on repeat. Mila had jumped on Chainsaw and saved my life. Fallon had stabbed Theresa with a screwdriver before she could shoot her. The two girls were better at saving themselves and me than I could ever be at saving them. I'd completely failed at the one thing Rafe had asked me to do.

"He-he killed her. He didn't even hesitate. He'll kill us both if you d-don't do what he asks." Fallon was shaking so hard I could barely keep her hand on the arm of the chair.

"Stop talking!" Adam yelled. "You're right, Fallon. I did kill her, but she was planning on doing me in first. As soon as she had the diamonds in reach, she was going to get rid of all of us and use the money to fuel her feud with Lorenzo. So don't feel sorry for her. She gutted that guy Nero. Had me hold him while she did it. She bragged how she'd done the same to your dad. How she was going to do it all over again and make sure he died this time. I saved you by shooting her."

As he talked, I taped Fallon's wrists to the chair, trying to keep them loose, but Adam came closer and noticed.

He aimed the gun at me again. "Don't pull that shit, Sadie. Wrap them tight. Do her legs too, and then tape that mouth of hers shut. She likes to talk. Likes to rat people out when she doesn't even know what's really happening."

"She can't escape if she's tied to the chair, Adam, and no one is around to hear her," I insisted.

He swung his fist and clocked me in the cheek again. It was the exact same place he'd hit before, and pain radiated through the bone. I stumbled back, hitting my lower back and side on the desk with enough force it had me gasping.

"Don't argue with me. Just do as you're told."

"Please, Uncle Adam. Please don't hurt her." Fallon was crying again, tears streaming down her cheeks, and my heart tore in half. The expression on her face had returned to the wild fear instead of the anger that had been there moments ago.

He yanked the tape from my hand, juggling the gun as he ripped off a piece, and I used the cover from the noise it made to flick open the pocketknife. As he slapped the tape over Fallon's mouth, his hand with the gun drifted near me, and I dragged the blade over his arm with a strength that surprised us both.

He screamed, dropping the gun. It clattered beneath the wheels of Fallon's chair, and I dove for it. He kicked me in the ribs, sending me sprawling to the floor. The knife went flying from my fingers, sliding between Adam's feet and disappearing under the desk.

Adam cradled his wounded arm and bent to retrieve the gun, but Fallon kicked out at him, hitting him in the thigh. He lost his balance, tried to use the corner of the desk to stop himself, and ended up stumbling over my legs and falling on top of them. The momentum thrust Fallon backward until the chair collided with the wall.

Our eyes caught. Fear. Anger. Desperation.

I remembered seeing those emotions in Mila's eyes that day too.

I had to save Fallon. Had to save myself. Had to stop him.

With his weight on my legs, I was trapped, but I stretched my arm out, using every ounce of power I had to reach for the gun. Adam shifted, swearing, still cradling his torn flesh, trying to right himself, and the weight had my finger slipping off the grip. I bucked, my knee colliding with his wounded arm and causing him to scream again.

Hope filled me when my hand closed around the weapon.

I raised it shakily, shoving it toward his face and snarling, "Get off me!"

He used his good elbow to slam into my stomach, and even as I groaned and gasped for breath, I pulled the trigger. His body jerked backward, blood spreading along the shoulder of his white button-down.

"You bitch! You fucking bitch!" he wailed.

With one more kick, I was free of him.

The door of the office slammed open, and the sound of a rifle cocking filled the air, followed by my brother's voice, dark and furious, saying, "Get away from them, asshole."

Ryder eased across the room, blue eyes zapping with lightning, cowboy hat tipped back, lips stretched tight. His gaze darted from me, to Fallon, to Theresa's dead body, and finally back to Adam who'd scrambled to rest against the wall, cradling his wounds.

"You're bleeding," Ryder growled, eyeing the blood that coated my arms and clothes. "You're fucking bleeding."

He stepped toward Adam, aiming the rifle at his chest, and I was barely able to stop him from pulling the trigger. "It's not my blood, Ryder. It's his."

My brother grunted, a wolflike noise that warned of an attack, and then yanked me to him. For two seconds, I let myself lean into my brother's comfort. Let myself wallow in the knowledge I was alive. That Fallon was alive. Tears swarmed, but I held them back as sirens filled the air.

My entire body was trembling as I handed Ryder the pistol and dragged myself away from his comfort. After finding the knife I'd dropped, I fell to my knees in front of Fallon to cut her free.

Boots pounded in the hallway, and a voice shouted, "Sheriff's Department, put your weapons down," just before Deputy Walker eased into the room with his gun drawn.

It took Walker mere seconds to assess the situation, glaring at the sight of Ryder with two guns pointed at Adam and a dead woman.

"Goddamn it, Hatley, did you have to shoot them? Do you know how much paperwork I'm going to have to fill out now!"

"I didn't shoot anyone," Ryder said. "That was all Sadie."

Once Fallon was free, I pulled her to me, wrapping both arms around her trembling shoulders, burying my face in her hair as she clung to me. We were alive! Nightmares might haunt us for years, but we were alive.

Walker spoke into his two-way, asking for an ambulance, and I heard Maddox's voice demanding a sitrep. Ryder's phone started jangling, and then my ringtone went off in whatever pocket Adam had slid it into after using it for the code on the safe.

"He's got my phone," I told Ryder.

With the deputy's gun aimed at him, Adam didn't even move as Ryder searched his pockets, pulled my phone from the depths, and then ripped the bag with the jewelry in it off his wrist. Adam hissed in pain as Ryder glared down at him. "You're lucky you're not dead, asshole. You're lucky my sister has more goodness in her left hand than you do in your entire goddamn body. If she hadn't stopped me, you'd be on your way to hell. Just remember that when you're sitting in a prison cell, cooking up more vengeance and hate. You owe her your damn life."

Ryder stepped back just as his phone went off again, and he whipped it out. "I'm with them now." He assessed us both, slowing as he took in my face that was screaming and the ugly bruise already forming on Fallon's temple, and his jaw tightened. "They're alive. Some bruises. But they're whole."

I heard the dark voice on the other end and knew it was

Rafe just from the tone. My heart soared and broke at the same time. He'd sent me away, and I hadn't had time to come up with a plan on how to keep him. Now, he'd arrive to take his daughter and vanish from my life. It made the tears fall harder. It made me squeeze the teen in my arms just a bit more.

Ryder waved his phone toward me. I shook my head. I couldn't talk to Rafe yet. Not when I'd almost failed him. Not when Fallon had saved us more than I had. Not when I knew it was over between him and me.

"Let Fallon talk to him," I said softly.

Fallon's head whipped up. When she saw the phone extended, she reached out and took it. "Dad!" Her tears came harder on hearing his voice, and I just held on as she cried and talked through her sobs. "We're okay. We're okay. Sadie saved us."

It wasn't true. We both knew it wasn't true. She'd saved us.

Fallon paused, listening to her dad. "I love you too. I love you so much. Okay." More pauses. "Mom? Oh God, Mom... Uncle Adam... No. No. He's alive... He's alive. They're taking him to the hospital and then to jail. He killed Theresa. He just shot her, point-blank, as if it was nothing."

I tried to move away, to give her space to talk to her parents, but Fallon only gripped me harder with her free hand, so I stilled and then pulled her into me once more.

My gaze met my brother's over her head and saw them assessing me closely. I knew what he was waiting for. He was waiting for me to break. To fall. To stumble. But I didn't feel anything anymore except exhaustion. The short spat of tears had dried up. The fear was gone. Regret was somewhere in there, but I wasn't sure where. I was so damn drained and numb.

"Okay. Okay," Fallon said. "I'll see you soon. I'm okay. I'm with Sadie. She saved me. I'm okay. I love you."

Fallon hung up and handed the phone back to Ryder. He pocketed it and then wrapped both of us in his arms. I clung to him and let the void of nothing swamp me.

L J Evans

♪ ♪ ♪

Maddox and McKenna met us at the hospital. While they talked to me, I tried to follow what they were saying, but everything felt hazy and scattered. I felt like I was outside myself, watching an old-fashioned movie reel where part of the film had been destroyed. In and out. Glimpses of action. Glimpses of words.

When my brother strode off to arrest Adam before he went into surgery and arrange for a twenty-four-hour guard, I insisted McKenna examine Fallon. The teen was sitting with me on the ER bed, arm still wrapped around my waist with her head on my shoulder.

"I just have a bump," Fallon said, even though her skin was raw from where the tape had been pulled off her wrists. "Sadie took the brunt of it."

"Does she have a concussion?" I asked, and I had to focus extra hard on McK's mouth to ensure I heard the answer as I fought off the flickering film.

"No. Her eyes are clear." She turned back to the teen. "It's going to hurt for a few days, Fallon. And if the headache gets worse, you need to let us know immediately."

Fallon grabbed my hand and squeezed. "You have to check out Sadie. He hit her several times. And kicked her too."

My sister-in-law's thick brows furrowed as she took in the cheek I could feel swelling, and she swung her light in my eyes. For a moment, everything disappeared. It was almost a relief. Then, she pressed her hands in places that made me wince, frowning when I hissed at the pressure she placed on my ribs and my wrist.

"I think you're just bruised, but I don't want to take any chances that you have internal bleeding. You need an X-ray and an ultrasound, at a minimum, and I'll need a blood and urine sample. Let me go order the tests."

I'd do whatever they needed me to do in order to get out of the hospital, to escape before the memories of the smells and sounds ripped back my numbness and made me feel the fear I'd had the last time I'd stayed here.

While McKenna went out to the nurses' station, Fallon dropped her head to my shoulder again, whispering, "Thank you. Thank you for saving me."

The world in front of me flashed again. White. Black. I hadn't saved her. She'd saved herself.

Before I could respond, McKenna was back. She handed ice packs to both of us and gave Fallon some pain pills, apologizing that I couldn't have any yet until they were sure I didn't have any internal bleeding.

I didn't think I had anything seriously wrong with my body. I hurt. I could feel every place his hands and feet had touched me, could even feel the heat of his breath on my ear. But it was my emotions I was wondering about. Where had they gone? I didn't feel sad or mad or happy or relieved. I didn't feel anything. But then again, I wasn't sure I wanted to.

Mama and Daddy showed up, bursting into the room and surrounding us both with love. Fallon burst into tears, just like she had when she'd heard her father's voice. And for a moment, I clung to my dad before backing away as the room swam.

When I came back from radiology, Maddox was there, talking through what had happened with Fallon. I tried to follow what she was saying, but I still couldn't track all the words. After he'd finished getting her statement, he had our parents take her to the cafeteria. Once they'd left, he pulled me to him and hugged me for several long seconds before dragging a chair up next to the bed, making me sit back down and asking me to take him through what had happened.

I tried to tell him, tried to go through it in chronological order, the way I knew he needed for his paperwork, but I just couldn't seem to pull it all together. It was fading away so fast, blending in with what had happened with Chainsaw and Mila. I couldn't separate the two events, and I knew I had told him the wrong thing several times, told him things about that day at the creek instead of today at the bar.

He squeezed my hands and told me he'd give me a minute to gather my thoughts while he talked to McKenna.

He stepped out beyond the curtain, but the two of them were close enough that I heard her quiet response to his worried question. "It's the shock, Maddox. She's in shock. You'll likely get a clearer story from her tomorrow than today."

He came back and draped an arm over my shoulder. "I'm going to head over to the bar and make sure the crime scene techs have everything they need."

Oh damn…the bar…Jesus. I hadn't even thought about it. "Can you call Ted? Tell him not to come in? I'm sure the gossip has already spread like wildfire, but I want to make sure he doesn't make the trip into town when he doesn't need to."

"I'll handle it while I'm there."

He kissed me on the top of my head and headed for the door. He looked back and said, "Hey, Sassypants?"

I nodded.

"Good job giving the assholes hell."

But I hadn't, had I?

I wasn't even sure what had happened. What was real. What was the past. What I had wanted to do versus what had really occurred.

McKenna had already gotten Fallon's discharge papers ready by the time my parents and the teen came back from the cafeteria, but she wanted me to stay longer, at least until all the tests came back and she'd been able to monitor me for any nausea, dizziness, or signs of internal injuries. But what I wanted to do was leave, to get the hell out of the hospital with its beeping machines and smell of antiseptic that reminded me too much of being stuck here for weeks, fighting to feel my leg, to walk.

Hours had gone by, the sun drifting through its peak and into the afternoon shadows, before I finally called a halt to it. Fallon was asleep on the bed next to me, and McK was shining the light in my eyes for what felt like the millionth time. I grabbed her hand and said quietly, "I just want to take Fallon home, McK. I don't want to be here anymore. It reminds me too much of what happened before."

While it was true that what had happened with Chainsaw and Mila was still mixing with what had happened today, I'd mostly said it to get her to agree to let me go.

She stared at me for a long time and then nodded. She gave my parents a long list of things to watch out for with both Fallon and me and then, finally, allowed us to leave.

When we pulled up to the ranch, it felt like it had been a week instead of the better part of the day since we'd left to take Parker to the rental car office.

Mama tried to fuss over us, and when I headed for the stairs, she followed on my heels. I sent her back to Fallon, saying I just needed to shower. Maddox had taken my clothes at the hospital, but I still had splotches of Adam's blood on me. I needed to be free of it. Free of the body I could still feel weighing me down with my legs trapped.

How could I still feel everything physically when my insides were dead, as absent of feeling as some of the nerves in my leg from the bullet hole that had scored me?

As I showered, those flashes of three years ago continued to mix with today. I relived coming awake in the creek to find Maddox and McKenna bent over me. The desperate fear for Mila. The terror rolling off Fallon as I'd taped her to a goddamn chair.

I shoved my wet hair into a clip, strands already slipping out of it before I'd left the bathroom. My phone light went off, and I realized I had a message. For one brief moment, hope slid into my dead heart, thinking it might be Rafe. But when I swiped it open, it was to see Maddox had left me a message.

"Hey, Sassy, the crime scene techs are done. Ryder told me the cameras were down, but it must have just been the outside feed they hacked, because I was able to pull video from the internal cameras. Everything on them corroborates Fallon's statement. The entire case against Adam is going to be pretty cut and dry. I've pulled in a bunch of favors I had coming, and you should have the bar back tomorrow. Ryder and I are going to swing by in the morning to clean up. Ted and Patti can cover the shifts tomorrow. After that, we'll all pitch in until you're ready to come back. I just wanted you to know where it was at so you didn't worry. Give me a call when you get a chance tonight. I love you."

I should have felt something. Relieved at his worry and love. Glad he'd handled things for me with such care. But I didn't feel anything. All I knew was that I needed to be away from here almost as much as I'd needed to be out of the hospital. I needed to clean up the mess I'd made. I needed out of the house before everyone in my family showed up with their sad eyes and sympathy.

I couldn't handle it. Not again. God, I'd despised the pity so damn much the first time around. The pity and the worry and the shame. Ah, yes... there was an emotion finally. My cold, shutdown soul had finally come up with some deserving ones— shame and regret.

I pulled a pair of jeans from my dresser, but when I tried to drag them on, I found a whole set of bruises blooming along my hip and back from hitting the desk and the floor. I was certain they weren't from any internal bleeding, but if I mentioned them to anyone, they'd send me back to the hospital. So, I ignored them, tossing the jeans aside and pulling on a loose, high-waisted skirt. I topped it with a blue McFlannigan's tank before sliding into a pair of old cowboy boots I used for the sloppiest of work. They'd easily handle the clean-up at the bar.

As I went down the stairs, my old injury caused my leg to drag. Pushing it to function correctly took effort and slowed me down. Normally, it pissed me off, but instead, now I just felt resigned. It was misbehaving, not only because I was exhausted but because I was reliving that day at the creek, reliving every moment from when it had first been damaged.

Maybe I would always be damaged from now on.

Maybe I'd never feel anything but shame and regret ever again.

When I finally made it into the living room, it was to find Fallon asleep on the couch. She looked so young. So beautiful. But the crystal-clear bruise on her temple sent another stab of remorse through me. She'd been wounded on my watch.

Soft voices in the kitchen drew me and revealed my parents, holding each other and whispering. Mama pulled away from Daddy when she saw me.

"I fixed you a plate," she said, nodding toward the warming tray.

"Thank you, but I'm not hungry," I said.

Mama frowned. "You need to eat. Your body needs it."

I ignored her and headed for the door, snagging Daddy's truck keys from the hook there. My bag and my car were at the bar, but I'd risk driving without a license to get out of here.

"Where do you think you're going?" she demanded.

"Maddox said I could clean up at the bar," I told her.

"Sadie-girl, don't you dare leave this house." My dad's voice was strong but quiet. His blue eyes, never as vivid as Mama's and fading more as he aged, turned cloudy.

"I can't sit here, Daddy. I just can't… It won't stop," I said, pointing to my head and the flashes of the two awful days on repeat. "I need to fill it with something else."

Tears hovered in Mama's eyes, and I turned away, because if she started crying, I didn't know what I'd do. I needed the numbness that had surrounded me. I wanted it. I had to keep it for as long as my body and brain would give it to me. I'd love to keep it forever.

"Rafe will be here soon," I said. "You'll need all the rooms upstairs for him and Lauren and Jim Steele, so I'll stay at Uncle Phil's tonight."

Then, I turned and hurried out the door. Mama followed, hot on my heels. She stopped me on the porch steps with a gentle hand. When I turned, she rested her palm tenderly on my bruised cheek. My left eye was black already, a little swollen, and blurry, but I had another good eye. Just like I had two good hands and one and a half good legs that would let me do what needed to be done at the bar tonight.

"You love him," Mama said softly. It was the last thing I'd expected her to say and had me jerking away. It wasn't just my thoughts I was running from. I was running from Rafe, and I knew it. I couldn't handle the guilt of looking at him, knowing I hadn't done the one thing he'd asked me to do, any more than I could handle his goodbye. I couldn't handle anything else coming at me today.

I just stared at her, not denying or acknowledging it. Just thinking about how I felt for him might crack past my numbness, and that I couldn't afford. Not yet. Not tonight.

"You love Rafe, and you love his daughter," she said with a surety that settled somewhere in my heart.

I swallowed, pushing back the wave of hurt and longing threatening to swarm over my self-imposed defenses. "I'll just say I could have loved him. We had a moment when our lives crossed, brushing alongside each other's, but then we flew on past, going in different directions."

"So, make a U-turn and go back," Mama said.

I stared at her for several long seconds. Was it that simple? Just flip right around and head back to that moment when we'd been pressed up next to each other, admitting we loved each other? Go back to the stop sign where I'd promised him all my last dances?

When I didn't respond, she just hugged me to her and whispered, "At least think about it."

And then she let me go, knowing it was what I needed, knowing I had to keep myself busy or I'd go mad, thinking of all the things I'd done wrong, and the things I'd done right, and what I couldn't change.

Chapter Thirty-seven

Rafe

UNDER MY SKIN
Performed by Nate Smith

I'd made it to the airport in Bakersfield in record time, only to have the flight delayed due to a car accident holding the pilot up. We sat on the tarmac for way too long while anger and nerves practically crawled through my skin. When we did finally get off the ground, the flight was an agony of wasted time. I needed my arms around my daughter. Around Sadie. Goddamn it, they'd faced a gun. Been bruised and battered. And I'd been thousands of damn miles away.

"This isn't your fault," Lauren said as I paced the aisle.

But wasn't it? I'd sent them away, thinking I was keeping them safe. Why hadn't I realized Adam would follow them across the country to get his hands on the jewels? To get back at me by using them?

"She's right, Rafe. This isn't your fault. We all thought he'd done a runner." Steele's voice held a bit of anger in it, and I narrowed my gaze on him. "You did the right thing. We all thought if he came back for anyone, it would be you at the ranch. No one expected them to show up in Willow Creek. Not even Puzo thought that. Otherwise, he would have sent his men in that direction, and I know for a fact he didn't."

None of his words could ease one ounce of the anger and guilt I felt.

After landing in Tennessee, we had nearly a two-hour

drive from the private airport to Willow Creek that continued my hell. When we finally pulled into the driveway of the Hatley ranch, it had been more than twelve hours since Sadie and my daughter had faced the very worst.

The wrought-iron gate with its bucking bronco and the Hatley name opened to a paved drive lined with fully grown elms. The trees broke away to reveal a light-blue farmhouse with white trim, a slate-gray tiled roof, and a wraparound porch. The road led around the house to the rear, where a large addition jutted out from the back of it. On a pair of golden oak doors etched with stained glass, another wrought-iron sign hung. This one read *Sweet Willow Restaurant* in curving, vine-like letters.

If I hadn't shown up on Sadie's doorstep under such horrible circumstances, I would have been able to appreciate the charm more. Our family's ranch was a neat and tidy, old-English estate, whereas this was warmth and Southern grace.

The parking lot was nearly full, but Steele found a spot at the back near a barn even bigger than ours, painted a light blue that matched the house. A large metal H hung from below the pitched roof in the same font as the words on the gate.

As we emerged from the car, the back door of the farmhouse opened, and a man in his fifties, with dark-blond hair streaked with gray, made his way out to greet us. He introduced himself as Sadie's father, Brandon. His gaze rested on me for long enough that I wondered how much his daughter had told him about us. But there was no heat in his expression. No anger or judgment, even though it was my family who'd brought evil to their doorstep.

He led us inside, and Fallon launched herself at me. I caught her, the scent I'd come to associate with her wafting over me—innocence and sunshine. Except, now it was tainted with antiseptic. I squeezed her tight. Every ounce of love I felt, every ounce of gratitude that she was safe, poured into the embrace. Then, Lauren pushed herself in, and I hugged them both, silently promising myself and them that they'd never have to face these kinds of challenges without me again.

When we finally pulled apart and I could get a good look at Fallon, my teeth ground together viciously. She had a large bruise at her temple, her face was pale, and she had shadows under her eyes. But those brown depths were full of fire. And that finally eased some of the tightness that had gripped my heart ever since I'd talked to Ryder, and he'd told me the camera at the bar had gone dark.

As Lauren held on to our daughter, my gaze searched the warm farmhouse kitchen, noting immediately what was missing. The *person* who was missing. The woman I needed to hold to me so the remaining pressure on my heart could lift.

No one mentioned her. No one even said her name as Fallon introduced us to Eva Hatley. The woman insisted we sit down at the long oak table scarred by years of family dinners and plied us with food and drink I couldn't swallow. She fussed over us in a way that spoke of that hearth and home the ranch exuded from the moment you drove up.

I wasn't sure we'd ever had that kind of love drifting over us at the Harrington Ranch. Even before Mom had died, she'd been more the flighty, artistic type than the bread-baking, cuddling type. She'd loved Spence and me and never once held back saying it, but it always felt like we were watching a butterfly dance from flower to flower as she drifted through our lives.

And Dad had never been emotional. Hard. Determined. I wasn't sure he'd said he loved us ever. He'd needed Spence, been disappointed in me, and he'd loved the land. When I saw my parents together, I didn't know how they'd ever fallen for each other.

Eva and Brandon Hatley were the complete opposite. Affectionate, with love all but pouring from them. He was constantly touching her. Little skims of hands, assurances, and soft looks. She did the same in return. Their love boomed through the room like a sonic wave, vibrating through anyone it crossed. Sadie would have been showered with it growing up.

Doubts filled me. I wondered if the coldness and distance I'd learned from my dad and then cloaked myself with after I'd left the ranch would leak onto Sadie if I tied her to me. Would she look at me as Mom had once looked at Dad? As if she'd lost something she thought she'd been given? Would her words sound like the ones of Great-grandma Beatrice's in her journal. An agony of loneliness?

No. I refused to believe that. I'd shower her with even more goddamn love than her parents had. I'd wrap her in it so it was the only thing she ever felt.

"Where's Sadie?" I demanded, knowing it sounded aggressive and not even sure I cared. I needed to know where the hell she was, needed proof she, like Fallon, had only minor injuries that would heal if the emotional ones didn't hang on too tight.

Eva darted a look at Brandon, who dragged a hand over the scruff on his chiseled cheeks.

"She went to the bar," Eva said with a sigh.

"She's working?" I barked. "Why the hell is she working?"

Eva's eyes settled on me with the same assessing gaze her husband had given me outside but taking it deeper, going beyond all my walls to the truth beneath. It was as if, like her daughter, she had a bit of siren or fae in her, allowing her to read my thoughts and emotions and intentions before I even knew them. Finally, she said, "I imagine you've come to know my daughter pretty well in the last week, Rafe. You tell me why she's working."

She would have been unable to sit still. Her mind would have been full of emotions, the scene from the bar on repeat in her head. She would have needed to dive in. To help. And she'd have blamed herself for what happened. I'd asked her to protect my daughter, and she'd think she had failed. Just as I'd thought I'd failed. We were both right and wrong at the same time.

I turned to Steele. "Give me the car keys."

He didn't even hesitate. He just dug them out of his pocket and tossed them. I caught them one-handed and rose from the table. I tugged on Fallon's braid. "You okay here for a bit, Ducky?"

She gave me that cheeky smile I adored—the one I had been afraid might not show up again for a while after what she'd been through today. "I'm good with the Hatleys and Mom and Jim. But she thinks you're letting her go, Dad. I don't know what you said to her before we left California, but she's been eating herself up with it. Don't be a dick. Make sure she knows you love her."

"Fallon," Lauren warned, but it was with laughter in her voice.

When I looked around the room, I saw the same in the other adults' faces. But the laughter in the Hatleys' gazes also included a warning that screamed, *Don't mess with our daughter*.

I was halfway down the porch steps when Eva caught up with me. She handed me a velvet, drawstring bag. "These are the jewels my grandmother had that seem to belong to you."

I took them, swallowing. "Thank you."

"There's also a ring in there that belonged to Carolyn. I'm pretty sure it wasn't part of your set. The stones are too different, but it was made in the same era. It's been through a lot, that ring. It was given to people who lived the best and the worst days after receiving it, and it was taken from our family for a while. It found its way home though. I'd like you to have it. I'd like you to give it to Sadie when you make her yours."

My throat clogged. "She's already mine, Mrs. Hatley. I'm sorry about that. I'm sorry it might mean I take her away for months at a time because I can't stand the thought of spending even one more minute without her at my side."

To my surprise, she smiled, large and bright. "All I've ever wanted for my children was for them to have the love I've been lucky enough to find with Brandon. If they have that, everything else that happens in life is just icing on the cake or rotten eggs, both easily thrown out. If you have a love that sticks, it'll get you through anything. You give that to Sadie, you stick, and I'll be one happy mama. Just like the ring, Sadie will always be able to find her way home when we need her or when she needs us. I'm counting on you to make sure she doesn't need us very often."

She shocked me again by hugging me and then stepped back.

"Maddox said the crime scene was cleared, and Sadie went

to clean it up. Her bartender, Ted, called Brandon a while ago and told us half the town showed up to help. Everyone's trying to make her feel like nothing bad ever happened there, right down to the normal band showing up to play. That's Willow Creek for you."

She was trying to make me feel better in knowing Sadie wasn't alone. That she hadn't had to deal with the blood and memories on her own, but it didn't work. It only made me feel worse I hadn't been there to pitch in like she'd pitched in last week for me…for my family.

Eva squeezed my arm. "She wasn't planning on spending the night here at the ranch. That's not unusual as, more nights than not, she sleeps at my family's old house in town so she doesn't have to drive out here after closing the bar." She waited a bit and then winked and said, "I don't expect we'll see either of you tonight."

It took me a second for the realization of what she'd said to sink in, and then I couldn't help the huff of laughter that escaped me—the first laugh in going on fourteen hours.

"Don't disappoint me by showing back up." Eva's smile widened, and I realized how much Sadie looked like her, right down to the mischievous fire in her eyes.

After she whirled around and returned to the house with the same vibrant energy as her daughter, I stared down at the velvet bag in my hand. Inside were the jewels that had left our home eighty years ago and started a feud that had taken decades to resolve. They'd nearly cost my daughter and the woman I loved their lives and almost cost me mine. But like the ring Eva talked about, the jewels had found their way home, and they'd brought Sadie to me. I'd said it before, thought it before, but maybe that had truly been their purpose all along. Maybe the fates had been pulling strings back when Alasdair laid down his royal flush and snagged the ranch from Tommy Hurly to begin with.

I found there was power and hope in that notion.

Sadie was mine. I was hers.

Now, I just had to prove it to her.

The map on my phone led me back through the windy hills studded with ranches, past the exit to a lake, and past the Willow Creek sign declaring it was the home of football heroes, rock stars, and ranchers. I hadn't noticed the town when we'd driven through it on our way to the Hatleys. My eyes had been focused on my phone and the directions leading us to my daughter and Sadie. But the lantern-shaped lampposts casting a warm glow over the cobblestones and the brick shops held a quaint vibe that reminded me a whole helluva lot like the town I'd grown up in.

The GPS directed me past the stores to the edge of town where McFlannigan's sat on a corner. Every parking space on both sides of the street was taken, and I could hear music streaming from it even with the car windows up. I turned down a side street only to find the parking lot in the back was as full as the front. I bit my cheek as the desperate need to see her, hold her, kiss her, grew to a boiling point.

I finally found a spot down past a dilapidated apartment building and jogged toward the front of the bar in heavy, magnolia-scented air. The McFlannigan's sign glowed warm against the brick-and-stone front, and for a brief second, I hesitated. Would I have the right words to convince Sadie to forgive me? To convince her I'd made a plan for our future because I'd always known we belonged together? To reassure her I'd never again let her go? I'd rip my heart out and hand it over to her before I left her again. Before I left this town without her with me.

Would that be enough when she deserved so much more?

When I finally opened the door, I was immediately hit with sounds and scents I knew well. Chatter eased by alcohol. The clink of glasses. The smell of fried food from the bar's kitchen. Music. Country music that had never been my go-to, even in my youth, but had hovered around me ever since I'd watched an imp with bluebell-colored eyes dance in my bar.

I scanned the faces for Sadie and came up empty. My jaw clenched, worry coasting through me. I made my way to the bar, shrugged off my suit jacket, and hung it over the back of the stool. I sat down at the shiny, lacquered bar, tapping my fingers along the surface as I continued to search the crowd for the one person I'd come for.

"What can I get ya?" the bartender asked. He looked as old as the bar, with white hair, a mustache that could have easily graced a wanted poster from the 1800s, and skin that looked like crinkled leather. What had Eva said his name was? Tom? Tim? Ted.

"Bourbon. Neat. The most expensive you have."

Sadie had liked my bourbon. What did she serve here? Would it be the cheap, Tennessee knockoff I didn't consider actual alcohol?

Ted didn't take offense at the attitude dripping from my words. He didn't look like he got upset about anything. I wasn't even sure he was real.

While I waited, I took in the dust-covered décor, the cracked vinyl booths, and the floors that needed refinishing. They didn't deserve Sadie any more than I did. She was too bright. Too big. Too beautiful for them, but I doubted she'd see it that way.

More likely, she'd think I didn't deserve to be sitting on her worn leather stool.

Maybe I didn't. Maybe I didn't deserve to have her accept my apology, to have me go down on one knee and beg her to come away with me. But what I deserved and what I got hadn't been the same thing for a long time. I wasn't giving her up now that I'd found her. Not when I had a plan to give her everything she wanted and more.

I must have made a noise, grunted to myself or something, because the bartender raised an eyebrow as he set down my drink. I ignored him and picked up the glass, twirling it in the dim light. I was startled to see he'd served it to me in Baccarat crystal, and when I took a sip, I was astonished again to taste one of my favorite brands instead of the cheap stuff.

It made me take a closer look at my surroundings. All the decanters on the shelves were crystal. The bar back was a delight of stained glass, beveled mirrors, aged wood, and carved pillars. The lighting needed improvement, leaving the place broody and ominous instead of rich and luxurious, but that was an easy fix. The crown molding and decorative detail needed refinishing just like the sticky bar top, but if I squinted, I could see how it had all been elegant in its day. Expensive and old. And I knew old. The Harringtons had done their best to surround themselves in it, hadn't they?

The sound system had been blaring when I'd walked in, and now a band took the stage. I groaned internally as live country music winged through the room. The male artist dove right in, crowing about relationships gone bad, dead dogs, his grandfather's truck, and a broken heart.

I couldn't handle the idea I'd broken Sadie's heart, even temporarily. Just as I couldn't handle the idea of Sadie stomping her boots to music just like this with burly men joining her. Men just like the ones she'd been teaching to line dance in my piano bar. Determination hardened inside me. She'd promised me all her last dances, and I'd be damned if she went back on it. I'd be damned if she gave them to anyone else.

I pulled out my wallet, put five crisp hundred dollar bills out on the bar, and said, "I'll pay another five if you can get the band to stop."

The bartender's smile stretched wide. He glanced at the money, squinted at my face, and then threw the towel he was using over his shoulder before slipping out from behind the bar to join the lead singer on stage. The scruffy kid didn't look happy when he glanced my way, but he took the money and stormed off.

"Sorry, folks. Our nightly entertainment has been put on hold for now," Ted said into the mic.

Groans and moans echoed through the packed house.

All I could think was how blessed the silence was. It gave me a moment to think. To plan. To come up with a really good line Sadie wouldn't be able to say no to.

"What the hell happened to the music?" the smooth, sexy voice I'd heard in my dreams filled the bar, and my insides clenched. My dick hardened. My heart beat increased by a thousand-fold.

I knew what she'd look like before I even turned around.

Her eyes would be flashing warning signs. Her artfully shaped brows would be drawn together. And that utterly kissable mouth would be pulled down at the corners. It was the way she'd looked at me multiple times in the week we'd spent together.

But the way she'd looked spread out on my bed, the way she'd looked with the moonlight feasting on her just as I did…that was the reason I was sitting at a sticky bar, thinking about all the ways I could convince her to give me another chance. I'd spend thousands of dollars here, on a venture that made absolutely no goddamn sense, on anything she wanted, if she'd only forgive me for bringing pain and heartache and death to her door. If only she'd say yes to being mine forever.

Chapter Thirty-eight

Sadie

I'M GONNA LOVE YOU
Performed by Cody Johnson and Carrie Underwood

I'd shown up at the bar, expecting it to be empty, expecting to be able to use my muscles to quiet the thoughts in my head. Instead, I'd found Ted, Patti, and Tillie, along with several other Main Street business owners, already at work, setting things to right. It had ripped at my numbness, gratitude and love for an entire town attempting to slip past it.

When more people kept showing up, some to gossip and some for our normal Thursday-night specials, and every single one of them rolled up their sleeves to help, I'd had to duck into the bathroom to pull myself together. My blessed numbness had been threatened, but I caught it and pulled it back. Instead, I concentrated on ways I could pay them back. I wished I had something to give the community more than just a place to drink beer and catch up on the latest gossip.

When I'd gone back out and seen that the office and bar were sparkly clean, I'd sent Ted up front to start handing out glasses of beer and bourbon and turned my attention to the delivery that had arrived while I'd been at the hospital. I was just taking a stack of empty boxes out to the trash when the music cut off in the middle of the song Grady had been singing. I tossed the cardboard into the dumpster, but when I came back in, and the bar was still silent, worry shoved past the numbness.

I burst out of the hallway, demanding to know what was going on, but I knew the answer before Ted's gaze drifted in his direction.

Because I felt him. Felt every single fiber of his being vibrating toward me.

Rafe Marquess sat at my bar with a glass of my bourbon in his hand and the heat of his stare scorching me. Marking me. Reminding me of what it felt like to be taken by him. To be made his.

The numbness that the kindness of our town had threatened to break through tore back further until it felt like I might just lose it altogether. Until it might leave me falling apart with too many emotions instead of too few.

When Rafe rose and started toward me, he looked like a mountain lion stalking his prey, and I didn't know what he'd do when he caught me. Would he punish me for failing him and his daughter or devour me with kisses? Either way, he had something planned for me, and I wasn't sure I'd survive it. Wasn't even sure I wanted to if it meant he'd walk out of this town when he was through with goodbye on his lips.

"Did you do this?" I demanded with a wave toward the empty stage and was awed to find my voice sounded sure and steady when I was really shaking from head to toe.

"Don't get your panties in a wad, Tennessee." Rafe tossed my own words from that first night at the piano bar back at me as he crossed the room to me. "I needed silence to think. To find a way to put everything back to rights."

My foolish heart slammed hard against my rib cage with a wave of unexpected hope I tried to shove back into the box it had escaped.

Eyes watched us with the same anticipation of a new season of their favorite reality show. The town would have more to gossip about tomorrow morning at Tillie's than just the blood that had been cleaned from my office.

When Rafe was close enough to make out my face in the darkness of the bar, he let out a guttural sound of protest, and rage filled those chocolate depths.

"Goddamn him," he hissed, fingers gently stroking my bruised, swollen cheek. His voice turned dark and deadly. "I'll kill him for marking you. For touching my daughter."

"Life in prison will be worse than death for him. An apt punishment."

Next thing I knew, he'd hauled me to his chest and wrapped his arms around me. He held me so tight I thought I'd be wedged permanently to him. For two seconds, I savored his warmth, the smell of him, the zapping energy that burst into life whenever we touched.

But when he said, "Thank you for saving my daughter's life," and every syllable was loaded with deep gratitude, I froze.

Gratitude was the last thing I deserved. "She saved herself. I was just there to watch," I told him, fighting the horrible feelings of ineptitude and regret that tried to drag me under.

Rafe leaned back, searching my face, my eyes, my soul. "She told me what happened, Sadie. She told me how you kept your cool, how you kept putting yourself between her and danger, and how you pulled the trigger when it counted most. I want to strangle you for risking yourself and kiss you for doing so in order to protect Fallon."

Every word he spoke held a volume of tortured emotions I recognized. He blamed himself. Which was ridiculous…wasn't it? But then again, was his guilt any more ridiculous than mine? Could either of us really have done something different to change what had happened?

The last vestiges of the numbness that had tried to protect me splintered and disappeared, leaving behind a raw spot that burned from the inside out. I'd spent three years kicking myself for what I saw as my failures with Mila, and I would have added years more to it after the failure of today. But maybe holding on to it was just keeping me from fully healing. Maybe the damage that was clinging to my soul had nothing to do with Chainsaw or Adam. Maybe I'd done this to myself because I wasn't willing to forgive myself for simply being human.

My lungs seized, my heart stopped, and the world tilted as emotions flowed over and around me like a pint being filled. It was going to foam over any second if I didn't tip it right, if I didn't shut off the tap at just the exact moment. I'd lose control.

Lose it all.

I needed air. Space. I struggled against Rafe's arms, but he only held on tighter.

"Don't run," he demanded. "Scream. Yell. Throw my idiotic behavior in my face. But don't run."

"I can't… I need to breathe," I said, pushing against his chest.

He dropped his mouth close to my ear, lowering his voice so the rest of the room couldn't hear him as he said, "I'm not letting you go, Tennessee. You're mine. Did you forget so quickly what that means? I'll happily remind you. Happily show you right here and right now in a way that will make the faces of the town gossips blush."

Those words, his tone, sent molten heat through my veins, pooling low in my stomach. Feelings I thought I'd never have again, not after he'd sent me away. Not after I'd failed to protect his daughter and reminded myself of how much failing hurt. I'd almost convinced myself he'd been right to say goodbye. I'd been prepared for it, been prepared for him to sweep in, take Fallon, and disappear from my life.

But now, tucked up next to him, everything I'd wanted when I'd left California came flooding in behind the guilt and hurt, but it brought fear as well. It was different than what I'd felt facing Adam and Theresa. This was fear of the lonely, empty hole that would reside in my heart if he sent me away again. Feeling it, feeling that hollowness on the edges of my peripheral, reminded me I was angry with him for having shoved me out of his life with such ease.

I glared up at him and shoved a finger into his chest. "You told me it was over. You forced me out of your life. If anyone has forgotten the words we said, the things we did, it's you."

"How else could I get you to go?" He shook his head, remorse drifting through those brown depths. "I was wrong. I thought sending you both away was the best way to protect you. But nothing will ever be right when we're not together. I left you wide open, practically dared them to come after you. From the moment you boarded the plane, I was trying to find a way to apologize, to earn your trust back, to prove I'd never be an idiot again. You belong at my side. I belong at yours. End of story."

Every muscle in my body went lax, love crashing through me at the sweetness of his words. It soothed the regret and failure and hurt that had burned through me. He loved me. I loved him. Was that enough to overcome everything else? "You ignored me for four days. Never once called me or picked up when I called you."

Instead of sounding sure and angry, it came out sounding like a pout, even to my own ears, and he smirked. Those goddamn gorgeous lips tilted up in that way that made my heart skip beats and my insides ache in a beautiful instead of ugly way.

"I did. Because I knew if I heard your voice, I'd come running after you. But I'm man enough to admit when I was wrong. Damn wrong. I love you, and you love me. Your mama said everything else is just icing on the cake or rotten eggs, and she's right. This…" His arms tightened around me, and his lips brushed my forehead. "Us… It's all that matters."

Finally, I fully gave in, surrounding him with my arms and fisting the dress shirt that fit the Rafe I knew just as much as the T-shirt and jeans he'd worn at the ranch did. Rafe had so many sides, so many facets, it was like looking at a diamond and never knowing which side sparkled more, but they all came together to form the stunning whole that was him.

The warmth of his embrace allowed me to finally let the kaleidoscope of events from today that had merged with that awful time by the creek break away until I could see it clearly. Fallon had saved herself and me, but I'd stepped up and done the same. Like years ago, I'd gotten Mila away from Chainsaw, just as much as she'd saved me. Maybe that was what loving someone was all about. Not one person taking more responsibility than the other, but sharing it, protecting each other.

That was what Rafe had tried to do by sending me away. He'd loved me enough to let me go.

I'd take him back, take his apology, and try to push away his guilt at doing so because I loved him enough to want him free of those dark emotions. But it took too long for those images and thoughts to work through me, and he took my nonresponse as hesitancy.

He lowered his voice into a soft, sensual dare. "Ante up, Sadie. Play the game. I'm all in. I'll put everything I own, everything I have, in the pot. Great-grandpa Alasdair won the ranch by keeping his hand and raising the stakes, but I'll easily fold, easily give you everything I have as long as you promise to keep all of it. As long as you keep me."

I stood on my toes, shoved my hands in his hair, and dragged his mouth to mine.

Thunder roared through my ears. My heart exploded. I was back where I belonged, blended with him in that place where the world faded away and there was just him and me and the white haze of love and lust. For two seconds, he let me control the kiss, let me make my mark on him, and then he was in the lead again. He slanted his mouth to take me in deeper and dove inside with a tongue that demanded acquiescence as he took back possession of my soul.

Whistles flew around us. And through them, from next to his new partner, Willy shouted, "Thatta way to do it, Sadie!"

I laughed against Rafe's lips. He drew back, sparks flying in his eyes as he said, "I hear you have a house here in town."

"Yep, we can actually walk there from here." I grabbed his hand and dragged him toward the hall as I hollered over my shoulder, "Bar's closed, Ted. Send everyone home. I have other business to take care of."

Ted's laughter joined that of everyone else's in the bar. The parking lot was full, and I was turning down easy money, but I didn't care. None of it mattered. Only Rafe. His mouth. His hands. The "I love you" he'd given me. The forever his words insinuated. The us I wanted more than anything else in my life.

♫ ♫ ♫

I came awake with sunshine glimmering behind my closed lids and fingers slowly skimming my hip. When I opened my eyes, it was to see Rafe glaring down at the line his hand was making.

"Rafe?" My voice was clogged with emotions that only grew when he looked up, and I saw tears threatening to spill over his dark lashes.

"I'm sorry. So goddamn sorry. You're marked. Your face. The leg you fought so hard to heal…" He choked on the rest of his words.

When we'd landed in bed last night, we hadn't bothered with the lights. He hadn't seen the bruising on my body as we'd lost ourselves to each other in the dark. We'd devoured each other sloppily and hungrily with no control on either side. Only instinct had reigned. Savage and raw and utterly human. Driving need focused on only one thing—claiming each other. When he'd driven into me, it had been with more whispered promises in my ear. When I'd welcomed him home, it had been with words of love.

The pain in my body from the bruising in my ribs and back and hip had been nothing. It was worth it to claim him. That pain guided us past years of heartache and loss and remorse to the love we'd earned, so when I'd finally cried out, trembling and gasping for air, it had been only from the pleasure of having ridden up and over the summit with him inside me.

But now, in the morning light, every dark bruise on my hip and back from slamming into the desk and floor, every kick I'd taken to my ribs, and every hit to my face was on display. My body hurt, but not as much as it hurt to see him torturing himself all over again.

I cupped his face, adding my own strokes to the ones he'd continued to gently coast over my wounded body.

"It's nothing permanent, Slick. The bruises will be gone in a handful of days. But this…" I leaned up and kissed him softly. "Us… We'll still be here. And you were right. That's all that matters."

"You'll never face anything like this again. Never. And

certainly not without me fighting at your side." The vow wound its way into my heart almost as much as the *I love you* he'd sent my way the night before.

"I'd thought I'd have a logical plan to present to you by the time you came to pick up Fallon on all the ways our lives worked rather than how they didn't—" He cut me off with a finger to my mouth.

"We both have families and businesses that need us," he said calmly, as if he wasn't at all worried. "We'll simply divide our time between Willow Creek and Rivers. But we do it together, Tennessee. You and me. Side by side."

"Just like that? You'll snap your fingers, and it'll just happen like you say."

He huffed out a chuckle I was relieved to hear after the anger and heartache of moments before. "Sadie, I have more money than I could spend in multiple lifetimes. I have a plane we can use to fly back and forth as often as we like. The carbon footprint it'll leave behind won't be pretty, but we'll figure out a way to offset it. Hell, I'll plant a tree for every mile we travel if I have to. The point is, we can easily come and go. I'll have to be at the ranch quite a bit while we've got the renovations going, and I want to ensure Lauren has the support she needs during the transition. But after, we'll spend more time here, finalizing plans for the performing arts center."

My heart stopped for several long beats before it pounded into action again. "What?"

"I've already hired a firm to do a feasibility study, and depending on your designs, I've got an architect in mind."

I shook my head. "No. That's a beautiful idea, Rafe, but even if I had the money, I don't need it. I thought it was the only way to leave a positive mark behind, a legacy with Carolyn's name tied to it. But now, I've realized that leaving behind love, leaving behind people who will know what and who I was, is much more important than a building or a business or even a bank account stuffed to the gills."

"It's taken me these last two weeks to realize Marquess Enterprises was never really my dream either. It emerged from pure stubborn assholeness. I wanted to prove to my dead father and my brother that I didn't need them or the ranch to achieve success. I wanted to rub it in their faces. But now that my brother's gone, I realize I couldn't give two shits about rubbing it in his face. I only wished I'd spent more time with him. I won't make that mistake again with the people I love. I'll hire a chief executive officer to keep the business going but only so it allows me the money and means to do what I really want, which is to spend time with you and Fallon, making your dreams a reality."

I cupped his cheeks, meeting his gaze with a steady one, and asked quietly, "Who's going to make sure your dreams come true?"

"You are my dream, Tennessee. Home and family. That's all I want."

I closed my eyes, the words hitting so deep inside me that I knew they'd be there forever, twined into my veins, lodged into my soul.

"I love you." I said it softly, a promise in each syllable.

"I won't let it go, won't let you go, ever again," he said.

I nodded and then rolled him over on his back, straddled him, and set out to prove just what those words meant to me.

♫ ♫ ♫

When my eyelids fluttered open the second time, Rafe's fingers were on me again, but this time, he was dancing something cold and smooth along the exposed skin. When he saw I was awake, he ran the object over the swell of my breast, up my neck, and coasted it over my lips. It took me several long heartbeats to realize it was a ring, and not just any ring, but my great-grandmother's ring. The one Mama had given to Ryder, who'd offered it to his ex before she'd disappeared with it and their child. The ring had been returned to us because of Gia, and I was confused as to how and why Rafe had it now.

I tugged at his hand. "Where did you get this?"

"Your mama."

I frowned.

"She said the ring found its way home after many trials and tribulations—or something like that. All I really heard was that she wanted it to be yours when I made you mine."

"She did?" My breath caught. She'd seen my love for Rafe, but she would never have given him the ring if she hadn't seen he loved me back. What exactly had happened when he'd gone to the ranch? I suddenly wished I'd been there. Seen it. Heard what they'd talked about that had made Mama so sure this, the love blooming in the room between Rafe and me, was true and real.

"Marry me, Tennessee. Make a few Hatley-Marquess-Harringtons with me who will have to choose which name to go by once they're old enough to do so. Spend the rest of our days wandering hills and valleys, listening to waterfalls as the moon sets and the sun rises. Give me all your todays and tomorrows, and I'll give you mine."

I leaned in and kissed him, softly, embedding my love for him into every press of our lips. "I like the sound of that an awful lot, Slick."

That full, wide grin with the dimple appeared on his face as he lifted my hand and slid the ring onto my finger where it fit almost perfectly. I swore I heard the gleeful laughter of the wee folk and, over it, the sigh of the wind and the moon and the sun as they whispered that everything had finally and truly been set right.

Rafe's lips skimmed mine, almost sweetly, before pushing me on my back and hovering over me with a gleam in his eye full of as much mischief as passion. "You like the sound of it enough to start making one right now?" When my brows creased in confusion, he smiled. "Let's make a baby, Sadie. Right now. Today. Let's make one so we know we started our family the same day we started our new lives."

I laughed. "I don't think that's quite how it works, Rafe. You can't just decide it'll happen today, even if we did try."

He leaned in, warm breath coating my ear and making me shiver delightfully as he whispered, "Wanna make a bet?"

The Last Dance You Saved

♫ ♫ ♫

You can't see me, but I'm dancing with wee-folk glee at how Sadie and Rafe's happily ever after came together. I hope you are too, but if you didn't get enough of them, you can catch a glimpse of what happens when they're in the midst of opening the performing arts center, and Sadie's water breaks in the ***BONUS EPILOGUE***. It's FREE with a newsletter subscription. Plus, inside it, you'll also get a **sneak peek at the spin-off standalone book Fallon and Parker demanded** I write.

THE LAST DANCE YOU SAVED BONUS EPILOGUE

Free with newsletter subscription

And if you still need more single-dad, small-town, romantic-suspense stories, and you've read all the Hatleys, why don't you check out ***AFTER ALL THE WRECKAGE***. Keep reading right here, right now to catch the first few chapters.

After All the Wreckage Sample
Chapter One
Rory

AM I ALRIGHT
Performed by Aly & AJ

If panic attacks could have babies, I'd be having quintuplets. The thought landed in my chest as I pulled my royal blue Honda Rebel into a tiny spot on the street outside my dad's office. It was the last place

I wanted to be for more reasons than I could count. Some of those reasons were petty, full of old grudges and teenage hurts, and some were deadly serious.

The deadly part was why I'd swallowed my pride enough to come.

I slammed my foot on the kickstand and swung my leg over the seat before standing in my thick-soled Harley-Davidson boots and pulling off my helmet. I dragged the hair tie from my ponytail, slung it around my wrist, and ran a hand through the dark brown strands.

When I turned toward the small but expensive building that held Bishop Investigations & Security, my reflection caught in the two stories of glittering glass. I cringed, knowing neither my bike nor my appearance would help my cause today. My black jacket was naturally distressed with spiderweb cracks along the leather, and the hole in my black jeans was from a tussle with a cheater I'd been following rather than any designer styling. They'd be the first of many things my father would pick at today. A few more additions to the long list of my mistakes. But two could play at that game. After all, I had a list of his that I could recite too.

I shoved my shoulders back and strode through the doors. The inside of his office was professional and cold. Decked out in steel and gray leather, the lobby was elegantly arranged to impress Dad's clients. As if the surroundings screaming wealth proved he could get the job done rather than the fact he had a good interior designer. But the truth was, as much as it irked me to admit it, Dad always got the job done. Whether the client liked what he found was an entirely different story—one I knew firsthand.

My eyes drifted to my wrist and the black-and-blue fingerprints that had turned darker throughout the day. I tugged the cuff of my jacket down, clamping it against my palm with my fingers. If Dad saw the marks, any chance of asking him for the favor I'd come for would be lost. And I needed him to come through. For the first time in almost a decade, I actually needed my father.

I hated it.

At the desk, the latest receptionist in a long string of Georgetown grad students sat waiting. Each of them used their time with his company to launch a litany of justice and law enforcement careers. His name on their résumé was an exclusive D.C. insider's gold star that opened doors. Too bad I'd never been offered a chance to earn one. Maybe he'd known I would have rather been boiled in acid than sit at that clear glass desk answering his phones.

"Rory," Chanel greeted me with a snip to her tone. Her gym-toned legs below the hem of a gray pencil skirt crossed as she swiveled toward me, purple Prada pumps dangling from her feet. They were the only sign of color in the stark space. She fit into Dad's image perfectly whereas I looked like I'd been dragged in from the biker bar on the edge of Cherry Bay—the town I called home after leaving D.C. a few months ago.

"Dad in?" I asked her, trying to keep my voice light and even.

Her gaze flitted over me briefly, barely withholding her judgment, but I could hear it anyway. The silent *How on earth is this Sutton Bishop's daughter?* Because the only thing I'd inherited from the blond-haired dynamo in a suit who was my father was the cleft in my chin. He was tall with a square face and wide shoulders, whereas I was almost all Mom with honey-toned Italian skin and a lithe, short frame. Dad's green eyes screamed their color even over a distance while the tiny bit of jade that flashed in my brown ones was only visible if you were close enough to kiss me.

Not that I'd been kissed lately. It had been so long, my lips and vagina thought I'd abandoned them.

"He has twenty minutes before he has to leave for lunch on the Hill," Chanel said primly.

It was exactly what I'd hoped for. Dad spent more time wining and dining D.C. bigwigs these days than he did investigating. Although, maybe that wasn't much different from when Mom had been his partner. Back then, he'd brought the business in and she'd executed it... or I did. Right up until the divorce split them down the middle and me along with it.

As I headed for the stairs, I tossed a jab over my shoulder. "Dad has dining with sleazy politicians down to a science. They should give him the oil prospector of the year award."

"First, not all politicians are sleazy. Second, you're one to judge. How's it going swimming with the cheaters?"

My foot stalled on the first step, and when I looked back, her eyes were narrowed. I almost laughed at her quick retort, but then I wondered if her defense of Dad came from a sense of loyalty that went much deeper than an employee-employer relationship. I wondered if Dad had tucked this receptionist into his bed a time or two… or more.

It made me want to heave up the cold mac and cheese I'd called breakfast.

I didn't respond, turning back around to take the stairs at double time.

His office door was open, the low hum of his voice audible if not the actual words. He didn't have an assistant guarding the entrance. He didn't believe in having one. The fewer eyes and hands on sensitive information, the better in his opinion. And if for some reason the nearly perfect Sutton Bishop did need help, the highly paid receptionist downstairs would be tasked with it.

Dad had his chair turned toward the enormous windows looking out at the dome of the Capitol Building. I knocked, and he swung around to take me in. His eyes narrowed ever so slightly before a tight smile appeared on his lips.

"I'll have to call you back," he said into the phone, pausing to listen to the response. "I'm telling you, you're worrying over nothing, Roland. I'll see you tonight."

He hung up and watched as I moved to stand next to the pair of straight-backed chairs in front of his steel desk. The chairs weren't designed for comfort. Dad didn't want people to dally in his office any more than he wanted them lingering in his personal life.

Handsome and brimming with charisma, my father could have been a politician as easily as he'd become a private investigator. He could charm his way into just about anywhere… and anyone. It was a skill Mom said I'd inherited from him, and sometimes, I wasn't sure if it was a compliment or not.

"I'd love to say it's nice to finally see my daughter again, but I'm confident you didn't drive into D.C. on that asinine bike just to visit dear old Dad," he said dryly with a pointed look at the helmet under my arm.

I tossed it on the chair as he came around the desk to draw me into a one-armed hug. A catch and release he'd once shown me how to do while fishing. The nonchalance pricked at old wounds I couldn't afford to let show.

A wisp of pine from his cologne combined with a hint of smoke from his occasional cigar wafted over me. I was dismayed by the temptation to hold on to him longer, to use his strength to buoy me up. To once again be the little girl he'd beamed at when she'd handed him the proof of a certain congressman sleeping with a prostitute. Proof that had cost the man his reelection and his wife.

I gritted my teeth and stepped farther away. If I allowed myself to drop my shield even briefly, the weight I was carrying might slip off and I'd never be able to pick it up again. I wasn't even twenty-three yet, but I had both lives and a business resting solely on my shoulders.

As he leaned up against his desk, he scanned my outfit, his look lingering on the fresh cut and red skin visible through the hole in my jeans. I grabbed the cuff of my jacket extra tight, ensuring it stayed firmly in place.

"To what do I really owe the pleasure?" he asked.

I regretted the cold mac and cheese all over again.

Now that I was here, I didn't really want to make my request. I took a few seconds to run through the numbers in our bank accounts once more. Then, the image of Mom lying in the bed at the long-term care facility settled cruelly in my chest. Her skin was paler than ever before, and her eyes were always shut as a feeding tube, a host of cords, and beeping machines kept her alive. I forced back an unexpected rush of tears. I couldn't afford them any more than I could afford the damn hug to undo me. Tears never solved anything—the saying should have been monogrammed on our Bishop family crest.

"I need a loan," I told him.

I knew better than to ask for money straight up. Dad believed in earning what you got. Struggle built character. It was the one and only thing my parents had agreed upon after the divorce.

Dad crossed his arms over his chest. "How much and what's it for?"

If I said I needed it to cover the added expense of Mom's new facility in Cherry Bay, he'd object. He'd made it very clear he disagreed with keeping her on life support after the doctors had recommended shutting it off and the insurance had stopped paying because of it. But if I said I needed cash to cover Marlow & Co. bills, he definitely wouldn't give it to me. He'd be happy if the business Mom had created after divorcing him disappeared. One less competitor.

After my mistake in high school—getting suspended and almost expelled for stunning a drug dealer in the boys' bathroom—he and Mom had pretty much switched sides. Once he'd seen me as an integral part of their business, now all he saw were my errors.

Because neither of the real reasons I needed the money would sway him, I gave him the fake one I'd come up with on the commute into D.C. "I want to get my master's."

I tried to keep my face impassive through the partial lie. I'd once planned on going to grad school before applying to the FBI, but these days those ideas seemed like Neverland dreams, and I was out of pixie dust. After missing the spring semester because of Mom's accident, I'd transferred from Georgetown to Bonnin University in Cherry Bay where I was weeks away from squeaking out a bachelor's degree. Even though it was less expensive, I'd still had to take out a loan as every penny from the sale of Mom's D.C. condo had gone toward keeping her breathing.

Dad's eyes narrowed as if he was attempting to read me. My face remained stony, but I made the mistake of shifting ever so slightly on one foot, and he caught the small movement.

"You've applied and been accepted to grad school? Where?"

He wasn't buying it. Why had I humiliated myself like this when I'd already known it was a futile effort? Mom's face flashed in my head again, and those fricking tears I never let out threatened once more. I grabbed my helmet and headed for the door before I further humiliated myself.

"Never mind. Forget I was even here," I said.

"I didn't say I wouldn't give you the money. I just want to know the truth."

Gripping the chin guard of my helmet with one hand, I waved at him with the other. "Why does it matter? Your daughter needs a loan. I'm not asking for a handout. I'm not asking for anything I won't pay back. You set the terms, and I'll meet them."

The second he strode toward me with anger flashing in his eyes, I realized my mistake.

He grabbed my arm, demanding, "Who hurt you?"

"It isn't important." It was embarrassing was what it was. A stupid wardrobe malfunction that had let the cheating bastard lay a hand on me.

"Damn it, Rory-girl! How many times do I have to repeat myself? You aren't cut out for this business. You're going to end up dead just like your mother."

"Mom isn't dead!" I growled back, pushing him away from me and taking a step into the hall.

He sighed, the sound full of frustration and sadness. "She is, Rory. Even if, by some miracle, she comes out of it, she'll be a shell of a person. She won't ever be Hallie again."

"Just because you've given up hope doesn't mean Nan or I have," I hissed. "And Mom didn't die because some asshole cheater came after her. She crashed into the Potomac."

I stomped toward the stairs.

"Because someone messed with her car's computer."

As his words sank in, my feet stalled. My heartbeat sped up, doing triple time, as I whirled around to face him. "What?"

He rubbed his forehead. The regret and exasperation on his face were a clear message he'd let something slip he'd never intended for me to hear. I'd repeatedly asked the detective in charge of Mom's accident for the cause, and Muloney had told me they'd never know for sure. There hadn't been another vehicle involved. She'd just gone over the edge and into the river. A submerged tree had pierced the right side of her head, and she'd drowned before the rescue people got to her. They'd resuscitated her, but she'd never woken up. She'd gripped my hand a few times, her lids had fluttered open and closed, but she'd never really been cognizant.

And now it had been eleven months… Eleven months I'd survived without her. But it felt like twenty years. An eternity in which I'd lived in some alternate version of what had once been my life.

"Who told you that?" My words were garbled as pain and fury roared through me. He didn't respond, and it only goaded me further. "I can't believe you! You told Muloney to cut me out? You're not her next of kin. You don't get to make any decisions about her. You lost that right when you divorced her. Like it or not, I'm the one who's responsible for her now."

"Except you want my money to keep her alive."

"That's not what it's for."

"Isn't it?" he demanded, brow rising again. "I know you've gone through the tiny profit you got out of the condo, Rory. I know you've had to change facilities more than once. This bullshit idea about a master's degree? You and I both know it isn't what the money is for."

God, there were times I hated how good he was at his job. He really knew everything. He always had. It was why clients flocked from all over the Northeast to his doors.

"Keep your damn money. I'll do this alone, just like Mom and I have done everything else for the past ten years, and I'll figure out why someone wanted her dead while I'm at it."

"I don't want to lose my daughter *and* my wife."

"Ex-wife. Your latest girlfriend would hate to hear you call her that."

He blew out an exasperated breath. "You're not cut out for this, Rory," he repeated. "It's my fault you started down this path. I can admit I was wrong. I never should have asked you to do any of the things I did, and Hallie should never have let you coerce her into picking up where I left off.

"Jesus, look at you." He gestured toward me. "You're battered and bruised, racing around town on that deathtrap, for what? An idea that you can be some real-life Veronica Mars? Real detective work isn't anything like that goddamn show."

Each syllable was a hit to my already bruised psyche. Scars and scabs hidden deep in my soul started to bleed. Veronica had saved me. And ever since Mom's accident, my life had taken on an even more decidedly Veronica-like vibe. She'd stayed to help her dad after he'd gotten sick just like I was helping Mom. She'd gone back to running the family PI business, and I'd done the same. The clients and money I brought in weren't nearly enough, though. I was doling out more each month than I was bringing in, and Nan didn't have any extra cash to offer. She was barely getting by on Pop's widow's pension.

I swallowed hard, striking back the only way I could with words I wasn't sure were true but would hit home anyway. "At least Keith Mars loved his daughter. Fake show. Real love. The complete opposite of this." I waved a finger between us and then turned on my heel and headed down the stairs.

He followed me to the railing, calling after me. "Rory, don't leave like this."

I didn't respond.

"You know there are a lot of companies who would give someone with your computer skills a hiring bonus. If you're looking for money and don't want it on my terms, at least consider it. You need to leave this business behind and concentrate on what you *are* good at."

Chanel was pretending not to watch the show as I stormed past her desk, but I saw the smirk, and it only fueled the rage inside me. I wished I could slam the door to the building, but all it did was swing back and forth.

As I stalked over to my bike, the realization that Dad might be right caused bile to hit my throat. Maybe I did need to get some eight-to-five desk job in some corporate office peddling my computer skills. Not because a buckle had gotten caught in a trellis and the cheater had pulled me from it by my wrist, but because a job in a corporate office would pay a helluva lot more than my handful of clients.

But then Dad's slipped admission came back. Someone had messed with Mom's car! Someone had done this to her on purpose. There was no way in hell I'd let that go. I'd borrow money from Tall Paul, the biggest loan shark I knew, before I'd just walk away.

Just like Veronica Mars had once said, this was where I belonged. In the fight. It was who I was. And I could guarantee whoever had done this would regret it.

As I pulled on my helmet and merged into the heavy traffic of D.C. at lunchtime, I wondered how much Dad had paid Baloney-Muloney to keep the truth from me. Was Dad investigating it on his own or was he leaving it to the tiny force that made up Cherry Bay's police department?

If Dad had any information, I'd find out. I had a backdoor into his network that he was clueless to. I'd find out what he knew, and if it was nothing, there were other doors I'd start banging on—or hacking into.

Dad was right about one thing. I'd die before I let anyone get away with this.

Chapter Two
Gage

BROKEN
Performed by The Guess Who

I tapped my fingers along the edge of the Pathfinder's steering wheel, trying to push down the impatience I felt sitting at the back of the car line in front of Cherry Bay's only middle school. I had a long list of things to get done at the bar, which meant I barely had time to manage picking Monte up and getting back to the apartment before opening.

The car in front of me inched forward, and I did the same thing as I scanned the sea of tweens sidling down the sidewalk past the car. No copper-topped waves in sight. Had Monte worn a baseball cap today? I couldn't remember. My younger brother did more often than not. He hated his red hair. Hated the curls more. Hated that kids teased him about being Orphan Annie's twin brother. How the hell they even knew who she was beat me. I'd had to look it up.

"Bubba, I have to pee," a tiny voice from the back seat whispered.

Shit. I glanced in the rearview mirror, meeting Ivy's gaze. My sister's pale blue eyes were just like our mother's, but at the moment, they were wide and desperate. A look I wasn't sure I'd ever seen in Demi's. I'd seen fanciful, whimsical, and even clouded, but never desperate. More often than not, Demi's were strangely serene, even in the face of my anger.

Ivy wiggled in her seat, and panic filled my veins. I definitely didn't have time for a bathroom accident. Didn't have time to clean the car seat, the car, or tame the shamed tears that would flow. It wasn't her fault. What three-and-a-half-year-old hadn't had an accident or two?

"Hold tight, Ives," I ground out.

I flipped on my blinker, zipped out in front of a car in a way that earned me a loud honk, then cut off another car before it could block the driveway of the school's parking lot. After sideswiping the orange cone set up to keep people out, I pulled up along the sidewalk near the flagpole in front of the nondescript square building.

I was in the red zone, but I didn't care as I jumped from the driver's seat and jogged around to help Ivy unbuckle even as she protested. Holding her tightly to my chest, I ran toward the bathrooms outside the gym—smelly spaces I knew well from when I'd attended the school a lifetime ago.

I skidded to a halt outside the boys' and girls' restrooms, debating which to use.

"I don't know if I can hold it," Ivy's small voice squeaked out.

Her alarm raced through me. I rushed into the boys' room. When I didn't see anyone standing at the urinals, I sent a silent thanks to the universe. Two stalls were empty. I'd barely set her on her feet before Ivy was jumping up onto the seat. I winced, trying not to think about what was on the toilet. It wasn't like middle school boys were known for their hygiene. But the look of pure gratitude on her face eased the chokehold that had taken over my chest.

Her ponytail was askew. Little wisps of curls had escaped, surrounding her elf-like face dusted with a light sheen of freckles. If there was anything in my life that could make me feel like a failure, it was her damn hair. How did other parents do it? Every time I picked Ivy up from preschool, all the other girls seemed to have their hair still perfectly assembled—neat and tidy—while Ivy's seemed to come loose the moment I put it up.

How was I, at twenty-seven, even in a position to be thinking of a little girl's hair and where the nearest bathroom was? My life was so far from where I'd imagined it would be that there were days the simple weight of it was like an anvil sitting on my shoulders. I was living the wrong life. With that thought came the spike of anger and frustration that usually followed it. Fucking life. Fucking Demi.

Once Ivy was done, she leaped off the seat, and her face burst into a smile so bright it felt like heaven was shining a beam right down on us. It took every thought I'd just had about living the wrong life and all the rage, and zapped it away. She was worth it. She and Monte both.

"All better?" I asked.

She nodded, slipping her tiny fingers into mine, and we made our way out to the sinks where we both washed our hands. With our damp palms joined, we made our way back to the SUV as Ivy tried to skip. She looked like some malfunctioning robot, but it made my lips twitch upward for the first time all afternoon.

I was definitely going to be late now. But I had help at the bar. River would be there, and he'd pick up the slack by unloading the delivery. Audrey would handle the setup inside, and between the two of them, they'd shoulder the tasks I hadn't been able to get to. It would be fine. It always was.

When I got back to our gray Pathfinder, I lifted Ivy into the back seat and watched as she struggled to buckle up. She was extremely proud of being able to do it herself and would get frustrated if I tried to help. It took her five times as long as it would have if I'd done it, but it all came down to that old saying about teaching someone to fish... No one ever mentioned how much patience and energy it took the teacher to do so.

I hopped into the driver's seat and moved to a spot that had opened up near the school's front office. I left the car idling, pulled my phone from my pocket, and shot Monte a text.

> *ME: Ivy had to use the bathroom. We're parked in the lot.*

A couple minutes went by, and the number of kids wandering past dwindled. The vehicles in the car line beyond the sidewalk started to fade. Still no sign of my brother. He knew the timing was tight from pickup to the bar opening, so he usually did his best to get out quickly. I flipped my phone over to see there was no response.

ME: Hey? Did you have practice today?

I had his basketball schedule taped to the refrigerator, logged into the calendar on my phone, and burned into my brain. But that was the other thing I'd found out the hard way—nothing was predictable with kids.

The principal meandered down from the head of the car line, picked up the cones in the driveway, and set them aside. Three kids tagged along behind him, backpacks weighing them down, phones in hand, and walking while texting in the way teens did despite the warnings that it could be dangerous.

An inkling of something that wasn't quite fear but close hit me in the chest.

Nothing is wrong. Everything is okay.

It was a mantra I lived by these days.

Except last night Monte hadn't slept, and neither had I because of it. His eyes had been shadowed this morning, a sense of despair clinging to him as he'd shoveled in the eggs and toast that his growing body demanded.

"What's the point of even having the visions, Gage?" he'd asked. "I'm useless to stop whatever they show me. Nothing I can do. Nothing you can do. We've both tried."

What if he'd gone on his own to D.C.? That singular thought caused more alarm than any kind of pee accident could.

While waiting for his response, I shoved my hand through the pitch-black of my thick waves. I looked nothing like my brother and sister. They were all Demi—strawberry-blond strands with pale eyes and soft white skin that showed off their freckles. I was Dad from my dark hair, gray eyes, and square chin down to my skin that always carried a hint of tan year-round.

As the minutes ticked away, my anxiety grew. I stabbed out another desperate message.

ME: Please tell me you didn't go to D.C. I'm at the school. Ivy is about two seconds from melting down.

It wasn't Ivy who was having the meltdown. It was me. But Monte would do just about anything for our little sister. When she'd first been born, he used to crawl into bed with me for comfort whenever she was crying, even when it was just a normal *I'm hungry* type of cry.

My phone buzzed with a reply from Monte, and relief washed through me.

> *MONTE: I went home with India, remember? I'm spending the weekend with her to work on our science project.*

My relief was quickly replaced with guilt. Had he told me and I hadn't paid attention? I'd been so focused on his vision, sleeplessness, and growing restlessness that I might have missed him telling me.

> *ME: Are you sure that's a good idea with everything happening?*

> *MONTE: It'll keep my mind off it for a while.*

In my gut, I knew the truth. He was doing this for me as much as himself. He didn't want me hovering over him, worrying. But it was my job to protect him, not the other way around.

I put the SUV in gear and backed out of the spot, heading toward the bar.

The asphalt roads at the edge of town quickly turned into cobblestone streets in the town center. The first village in Cherry Bay had been founded in the late 1700s, but the college that had been built on the bluff overlooking the Potomac in the 1940s was what had put us on the map. It drew students and academics from around the globe.

I hooked a right at the alley between two stone buildings that would have been perfectly at home in a medieval English village and headed into the small parking lot at the back. The Prince Darian Tavern had been in my family for over two hundred years. It had first been a post inn, and now it was a bar and restaurant with a two-bedroom apartment and extra storage space above.

While Dad had leased out the restaurant several decades ago, the tavern had been run by a Palmer since its inception. Between the renovation loans I hadn't known he'd taken out and the pandemic closing us down, we'd been almost wiped out financially. After Dad had died, I'd had to sell the house, and we'd moved into the apartment that he used to rent to college students. We were squished together in a space crowded with furniture that didn't fit, but I refused to get rid of those last pieces of our family history. Selling the Victorian we'd grown up in had been painful enough.

I parked the Pathfinder and waited with gritted teeth while Ivy fumbled with her buckle. My gaze journeyed to the next parking lot over, and my heart skipped a beat at the sight of a dark-haired woman. I could practically feel the energy vibrating from Rory Bishop as she headed toward the doors of the Cherry Bay Police Department. The aura of brave confidence was the same as it had been when she'd been fifteen. A self-assurance that mimicked the fictional heroine she'd worshipped back in the day.

Lithe and edgy in all black, I was hypnotized by the way she moved. Unable to draw my eyes away from her.

How long had it been since I'd seen her? How many miles, years, and traumas had filled the space between us?

I was just about to call her name when Ivy jumped out of the car and landed on my foot. It turned any sound that would have emerged from me into a deep grunt, and I had to catch my sister as she wobbled and balance myself at the same time. When I looked back over to the station, Rory was gone, and something a bit like sadness filled me.

Which was ridiculous. I didn't even know Rory anymore. I'd barely known her as a teen.

I pushed aside any thoughts of her, stepped around the wrought iron staircase leading to our apartment, and headed for the rear entrance of the bar with Ivy's hand in mine. A delivery truck had its door rolled up, and as I'd expected, River was already unloading it on his own.

His wide shoulders flexed as he hefted a case of vodka onto his shoulder. His height and build along with his shaved head, pierced nose, and plethora of tattoos intimidated most people. They had no clue his aura radiated nothing but kindness when all they saw was a scary giant.

River had been working for my dad since he'd been in college himself, and decades later, he was still here. Although I was pretty sure that had more to do with not abandoning me and my siblings than because he needed the job. Not when his art was in high demand around the country.

"Sorry we're late," I offered before looking down at my sister. "Go into the office and get a snack from the snack drawer and your coloring books from the shelf. I'll be in after I help River."

"Can I have a chocolate cwinkle?" she asked, eyes wide, knowing I normally didn't let her have sweets this close to dinner. But with my nerves feeling frayed after the scare I'd just had at the school, I didn't feel like arguing with her.

"Yes, but only one," I said, narrowing my eyes at her.

She grinned and then took off down the hall, her messed-up hairdo bouncing around her.

"Hey, Squirt! Don't I even get a hello?" River grunted after her.

She waved her stuffed otter without ever looking back as she hollered, "Hi, Uncle Wivuh!" her R's lisping into W's.

"I expect a hug later."

I grabbed another case off the back of the truck, hauling it to the storage room above the bar. The dark interior stairs were small and groaned with age, but they were smooth and stained to perfection. Everything in the building might be old, but it wasn't shabby. Dad had made sure of it, and I'd picked up where he'd left off.

While River and I unloaded in silence, my thoughts kept drifting back to the brown-haired dynamo I'd seen next door. A piece of me longed to go back in time to when I'd known her. When I'd had nothing to worry about but internships and college tuition. To a time when I'd been adored by a girl who I'd known would take the world by storm and set some guy's heart on fire.

Last I'd heard, she was at Georgetown, but I vaguely recalled some mumblings late last year about her mom being in a car accident. I hadn't paid much attention to the talk because Rory and her mom hadn't lived in Cherry Bay for almost a decade. Plus, I'd been hip-deep in another of Monte's visions and finalizing the paperwork on Ivy's and Monte's adoptions. I'd barely been able to breathe at the time, let alone think of a young girl from my past.

But now I couldn't shake the image of her.

Why was she in town? Was she visiting her friend Shay, whose family owned the Tea Spot across the street? Or was she visiting her grandmother? Regardless of why she was there, I didn't have any more time now to let my thoughts dwell on her than I had a year ago.

I signed the receipt from the delivery and walked toward the tavern's office. I pushed open the antique wooden door with its beveled glass to find Ivy at a claw-foot table that had been there probably since the tavern had first opened. She was on her knees in a burgundy brocade armchair, draped in a mosaic of color from the stained-glass window that made her seem like one of the paintings of our ancestors hanging on the walls in their gilded frames.

When I got up close to her, the mirage broke, and a chuckle rumbled through my chest. She was covered in chocolate from forehead to chin. It never failed to surprise me how quickly and absolutely she could become a mess when eating. She'd need a full body scrub before dinner.

Which reminded me, I needed to call our babysitter and beg her to come over. I'd expected Monte to be home to watch Ivy, which only reconfirmed I hadn't known my brother would be at India's. Unease settled in my chest once again—a worry I couldn't shake. I was an Olympic champion at worrying these days.

I pulled my laptop from the old captain's desk on the other side of the room and brought it over to the table. I kissed the top of Ivy's head as I set it down in front of her. "Give me a few minutes, Ives, then I'll take you upstairs for dinner. Do you want to watch something while you wait?"

She nodded. "Scooby-Doo?"

Her addiction to the cartoon made me smile. "Sure."

I loaded the streaming service, started an episode, and then looked at her chocolate-covered face and hands. "Don't touch the computer. And wash your hands when you're done with the cookie."

She nodded absently, already watching Scooby and the gang as they scurried over the screen in the opening song. I stepped away, watching her with regret curling through me. She was loved and cared for, but she didn't have a normal childhood. Then again, none of us had been allowed one. Not with Demi in and out. Not with the abilities she'd branded us with.

But we had each other, and that was all that really mattered.

Keep reading *AFTER ALL THE WRECKAGE*
FREE in Kindle Unlimited
https://geni.us/AATWLJE

Wondering what happens with Fallon and Parker? You'll get to read their fake relationship, second chance HEA this August! It's going to burn up the pages with heat and suspense. Keep on top of what's happening with their book by checking out my newsletter:

Acknowledgements

I'm so very grateful for every single person who has helped me on this book journey. If you're reading these words, you *are* one of those people. I wouldn't be an author if people like you didn't decide to read the stories I crafted, so THANK YOU!

In addition to my lovely readers, I need to acknowledge these people:

My husband, who never ever lets me give up on myself, even when the battles seem endless. Your sacrifice, your strength, your laughter is what gets me through the dark, guiding me home.

Our child, Evyn, owner of Evans Editing, who remains my harshest and kindest critic. Thank you for helping me create my stories and driving me to be a better human. Love you, kiddo.

My parents, sister, and in-laws who listen to me gripe about publishing and then cheer me on as if I'm the greatest writer on earth. Thank you for making me feel loved and valid every single day.

Michelle Fewer, who patiently reads, uplifts, and plots without judgment and so much grace. Thank you for giving me your time, energy, and love.

Jenn at Jenn Lockwood Editing Services, Karen Hrdlicka, and Stephanie Feissner who have been on this journey with me since nearly the beginning and continue to have faith in me no matter how ridiculous my mistakes become. Your edits and proofs are always the perfect polish that my words need.

The entire group of beautiful humans in LJ's Music & Stories who love and support me. I can't say enough how deeply grateful I am for each and every one of you.

The host of bloggers who have shared my stories, become dear friends, and continue to make me feel like a rock star every day, especially Kassie at _chronicles_of_a_bookworm and Lindsey at romance_book_affair who go over and above to share my stories almost every single day. Thank you, thank you, thank you!

To my beautiful author friends, including Stephanie Rose, Erika Kelly, Kathryn Nolan, Lucy Score, Hannah Blake, Maria Luis, Annie Dyer, Alexandra Hale, Kelly Collins, Aly Stiles, and AM Johnson, thank you for proving to me over and over that my worth doesn't come from numbers, and for pushing me to enjoy the chaos and beauty of the book world.

All my ARC readers, who have become sweet friends and true supporters, thank you for knowing just what to say to scare away my writer insecurities.

Leisa C., Rachel R., and Stephanie F. Thank you beyond words for being the biggest cheerleaders, partners, and friends I could ever hope to have on this wild ride called life.

I love you all!

About the Author

Award-winning author, LJ Evans, lives in Northern California with her husband, child, and the three terrors called cats. She's written compulsively since she was a little girl, often getting derailed from what she should be doing by a song lyric that sends her scrambling to jot a scene down.

A former first-grade teacher, she now spends her days deep in the pages of romance and mystery with a bit of the otherworldly thrown in. Her favorite characters are those who live resiliently, stubbornly and triumphantly, getting through this wild ride called life with hope, love, and found families guiding the way.

Her novels have won multiple industry awards, including ***CHARMING AND THE CHERRY BLOSSOM*** which was Writer's Digest's Self-Published E-book Romance of the Year.

For more information about LJ, check out any of these sites:

www.ljevansbooks.com

Facebook Group: LJ's Music & Stories

LJ Evans on Amazon, Bookbub, and Goodreads

@ljevansbooks on Facebook, Instagram, TikTok, and Pinterest

Books by LJ

Standalone

After All the Wreckage — Rory & Gage

A single-dad, small-town, romantic suspense

He's a broody bar owner raising his siblings. She's a scrappy PI who's loved him since she was a teenager. When his brother disappears, she forces aside years of family secrets to help him.

Charming and the Cherry Blossom — Elle & Hudson

A small-town, he-falls-first, contemporary romance

Today was a fairy tale…I inherited a fortune from a dad I never knew, and a thoroughly charming guy asked me out. But like all fairy tales, mine has a dark side...and my happily ever after may disappear with the truth.

Title TBD — Fallon & Parker — Coming Soon

A single-dad, fake-relationship, romantic suspense

Second chances, childhood crushes turned into adult passion, and a mystery that will keep you on your toes.

The Hatley Family Standalones

The Last One You Loved — Maddox & McKenna

A single-dad, grumpy-sheriff, romantic suspense

He's a small-town sheriff with a secret that can unravel their worlds. She's an ER resident running from a costly mistake. Coming home will only mean heartache…unless they let forgiveness heal them both.

The Last Promise You Made — Ryder & Gia

A single-dad, grumpy-cowboy, romantic suspense

He's a grumpy rancher who swore off all relationships. She's a spitfire undercover agent who brings danger to his life. Desire is an inconvenience. Falling in love is absolutely out of the question…

The Last Dance You Saved — Sadie & Rafe

A single-dad, grumpy-cowboy, romantic suspense

Sadie's world is disrupted by a grumpy cowboy who thought he'd left the ranch and relationships behind for good. When danger finds them and he tries to send her away, she proves that with love at stake, she's willing to risk it all.

Perfectly Fine — Gemma & Rex

A fish-out-of-water, celebrity romance

He's a charming, A-list actor at the top of his game. She's a determined, small-town screenwriter hoping for a deal. They form an unexpected connection until heartbreak ruins their future. Available on Amazon and also FREE with newsletter subscription.

Matherton Family Standalones

Lost in the Moonlight — Lincoln & Willow

A grumpy-sunshine, small-town, romantic suspense

My new neighbor is all too enticing, but I have one job—to stay hidden—and the media's fascination with Lincoln can destroy my safe haven. So why can't I stay away?

LITD — Katerina & Axel — Coming Soon

A growly-bodyguard, single-dad, romantic suspense

LITH — Juliette's HEA — Coming Soon

A single-dad, tormented-musician, romantic suspense

The Anchor Novels

Guarded Dreams — Eli & Ava

A grumpy-sunshine, forced-proximity, military romance

He's a grumpy Coast Guard focused on a life of service. She's a feisty musician searching for stardom. Nothing about them fits, and yet attraction burns when fate lands them in the same house for the summer.

Forged by Sacrifice — Mac & Georgie

A roommates-to-lovers, second-chance, military romance

He's a driven military man zeroed in on a new goal. She's a struggling law student running from her family's mistakes. Nothing about them fits until a kiss threatens their roommate status and their plans along with it.

Avenged by Love — Truck & Jersey

A fake-marriage, forced-proximity, military romance

When a broody military man and a quiet bookstore clerk share a house, more than attraction flares. Watching her suffer in silence has him extending her the only help he can—a marriage of convenience to give her the insurance she needs.

Damaged Desires — Dani & Nash

A frenemy, bodyguard, military romance

Reeling from losing his team, a growly Navy SEAL battles an attraction for his best friend's fiery sister, until a stalker puts her in his sights. Now he'll do anything to protect her, even take her to the one place he swore he'd never go—home.

Branded by a Song — Brady & Tristan

A single-mom, small-town, rock-star romance

He's a country rock legend searching for inspiration. She's a Navy SEAL's widow determined to honor his memory. Neither believes the attraction tugging at them can lead to more until her grandmother's will twines their futures.

Tripped by Love – Cassidy & Marco

A bodyguard, single-mom, small-town romance

She's a busy single mom with a restaurant to run, and he's her brother's bodyguard with a checkered past. They're just friends until a little white lie changes everything.

The Anchor Novels: The Military Bros Box Set

The 1st three books + an exclusive novella

Guarded Dreams, Forged by Sacrifice, and *Avenged by Love* plus the novella, *The Hurricane*! Heartfelt military romance with love, sacrifice, and found families. The perfect book-boyfriend binge read.

The Anchor Suspense Novels

Unmasked Dreams — Violet & Dawson

A friends-to-lovers, forced-proximity romantic suspense

As teens, they had a sizzling attraction they denied. Years later, they're stuck in the same house and discover nothing has changed—except the lab she's built in the garage and the secrets he's keeping. When she stumbles into his covert op, Dawson breaks old promises to keep her safe. But once he's touched her, will he be able to let her go?

Crossed by the Stars — Jada & Dax

A frenemies-to-lovers, forced-proximity romantic suspense

Family secrets meant Dax and Jada's teenage romance was an impossibility. A decade later, the scars still prevent them from acknowledging their tantalizing chemistry. But when a shadow creeps out of Jada's past, it's Dax who shows up to protect her. And suddenly, it's hard to remember exactly why they don't belong.

Disguised as Love — Cruz & Raisa

An enemies-to-lovers, forced-proximity romantic suspense

Cruz Malone is determined to bring down the Leskov clan for good. If he has to arrest—or bed—the sexy blonde scientist of the family to make it happen, so be it. But there's no way Raisa is just going to sit back and let the infuriating agent dismantle her world…or her heart.

The Painted Daisies

Interconnected series with an all-female rock band, their alpha heroes, and suspense that will leave you breathless. Each story has its own HEA.

Swan River — *The Painted Daisies* Prequel

A rock-star, small-town, romantic suspense cliffhanger

The Painted Daisies are more than a band, they're a beloved family. With their star on the rise, life seems perfect until darkness strikes. When the group's trouble points to the band members' various secrets, it'll take strength and perseverance to unravel the mystery. Available on Amazon and also FREE with newsletter subscription.

Sweet Memory — Paisley & Jonas

An opposing-worlds, friends-to-lovers romance

The world's sweetest rock star falls for a troubled music producer whose past comes back to haunt them.

Green Jewel — Fiadh & Asher

An enemies-to-lovers, single-dad romance

Snowed in with the enemy is the perfect time to prove he was behind her friend's murder. She'll just have to ignore her body's reaction to him to do it.

Cherry Brandy — Leya & Holden

A forced-proximity, bodyguard romance

Being on the run with only one bed is no excuse to touch her…until touching is the only choice.

Blue Marguerite — Adria & Ronan

A celebrity, second-chance, frenemy romance

She vowed to never forgive him! But when he offers answers her family desperately seeks and protects her from the latest threat to the band, her resolve starts to crumble.

Royal Haze — Nikki & D'Angelo

A bodyguard, on-the-run romance with a morally gray hero

He was ready to torture, steal, and kill to defend the world he believed in. What he wasn't prepared for…was her.

My Life as an Album Series

My Life as a Country Album — Cam's Story

A boy-next-door, small-town romance

A first-love heartbreaker. What happens when you've pined your whole life for the football hero next door, and he finally, finally notices you? You vow to love him forever until fate comes calling and threatens to take it all away.

My Life as a Pop Album — Mia & Derek

A rock-star, road-trip romance

Bookworm Mia attempts to put behind years of guilt by taking a chance on a once-in-a-lifetime, road-trip adventure with a soulful musician. But what will happen to the heart Derek steals when their time together is over?

My Life as a Rock Album — Seth & PJ

A second-chance, antihero romance

Trash artist Seth Carmen knows he deserves to be alone. But when he finds and loses the love of his life, he still can't help sending her love letters to try and win her back. Can he prove to her they can make broken beautiful?

My Life as a Mixtape — Lonnie & Wynn

A single-dad, small-town, rock-star romance

Lonnie's always seen relationships as a burden instead of a gift, and picking up the pieces his sister leaves behind is just one of the reasons. When Wynn offers him friendship and help in caring for his young niece, he never expects love to bloom or the second chance at life they're all given.

My Life as a Holiday Album – 2nd Generation

A small-town romance

Come home for the holidays with this heartwarming, full-length standalone full of hidden secrets, true love, and the real meaning of family. Perfect for lovers of *Love Actually* and Hallmark movies, this steamy story intertwines the lives of six couples as they find their way to their happily ever afters with the help of family and friends.

My Life as an Album Series Box Set

The 1st four Album series stories plus an exclusive novella

In *This Life with Cam*, Blake Abbott writes to Cam about what it was like to grow up in the shadow of her relationship with Jake and just when he first fell for the little girl with the popsicle-stained lips. Can he prove to Cam that she isn't broken?

Free Stories

Get these novellas, flash fiction stories, + bonus epilogues for
FREE with a newsletter subscription at:
https://www.ljevansbooks.com/freeljbooks

Perfectly Fine — A fish-out-of-water, celebrity romance

He's a charming, A-list actor at the top of his game. She's a determined, small-town screenwriter hoping for a deal. They form an unexpected connection until heartbreak ruins their future. Also available on Amazon.

Swan River — A rock star, small-town, romantic suspense *prequel*

The Painted Daisies are more than a band, they're a beloved family. With their star on the rise, life seems perfect until darkness strikes. When the group's trouble points to the band members' various secrets, it'll take strength and perseverance to unravel the mystery. Also available on Amazon.

Rumor — A small-town, rock-star romance

There's only one thing rock star Chase Legend needs to ring in the new year, and that's to know what Reyna Rossi tastes like. After ten years, there's no way he's letting her escape the night without their souls touching. Reyna has other plans. After all, she doesn't need the entire town wagging their tongues about her any more than they already do.

Love Ain't — A friends-to-lovers, cowboy romance

Reese knows her best friend and rodeo king, Dalton Abbott, is never going to fall in love, get married, and have kids. He's left so many broken hearts behind that there's gotta be a museum full of them somewhere. So when he gives her a look from under the brim of his hat, promising both jagged relief and pain, she knows better than to give in.

The Long Con — A sexy, antihero romance

Adler is after one thing: the next big payday. Then, Brielle sways into his world with her own game in play, and those aquamarine-colored eyes almost make him forget his number-one rule. But she'll learn—love isn't a con he's interested in.

The Light Princess — An old-fashioned fairy tale

A princess who glows with a magical light, a kingdom at war, and a kiss that changes the world. This is an extended version of the fairy tale twined through the pages of *Charming and the Cherry Blossom*.

Made in United States
Cleveland, OH
09 April 2025